the

UNCROSSING

the UNCROSSING

MELISSA EASTLAKE

Entangled Publishing, LLC
2614 South Timberline Road
Suite 109
Fort Collins, CO 80525
Visit our website at www.entangledpublishing.com.

Entangled Teen is an imprint of Entangled Publishing, LLC.

Edited by Kate Brauning
Cover design by Fiona Jayde
Cover art from Period Images and iStock

Manufactured in the United States of America

First Edition November 2017

Chapter One

The world spun tighter on its axis when the Kovrovs came to visit. It took a lot of work to put on the necessary show—cleaning the house, planning the meal. Luke lingered in his room to avoid the chores and steel himself.

Luke had two ties draped around his neck, the plain black one he usually wore and a shiny red one his dad had given him that was supposed to look more mature. It did, probably, but in a costumey way Luke couldn't settle into. He'd been sitting through lunches with the Kovrovs for his entire life, but this was the first time Alexei Kovrov's request had been, *We have some business with your young man.*

It was time to step up, but the red tie felt more like dress-up than work clothes. He went with a third option, a skinny blue one, looping it into a loose knot under his unbuttoned collar.

His mother knocked on the door, one quick rap, as she opened it. Helene Melnyk was not a tall woman, but she carried herself like one, and she could peer down her nose at Luke even though he stood six inches above her. She was dressed for lunch, too, in a burgundy dress that shone against her dark-brown skin, and when she surveyed him, she was Queen Mom.

Luke pointed to the tie she had probably come to remind him to wear. She shook her head and reached for him, buttoning his collar underneath the knot and yanking it tighter around his neck.

Luke pretended to gag, and she laughed. "There you go." She patted the tie over his chest. "Look at you. We wouldn't be in this mess if you hadn't gone and grown up so fast."

He covered her hand. "What can I help with?"

"Go take the counter, will you? Camille's helping with the borscht."

Luke hid his smile. "Yes, ma'am." He ducked through the living room, where they'd moved the furniture around to add leaves to the dining table and his sister glared balefully over a bowlful of beet soup, and loped downstairs to the store.

Almost everyone who came to visit the back room of the Melnyk family's shop on East 149th Street thought they were crossed, straining against a curse or hex or binding, and almost no one was. Anyone in Luke's family could tell who was only sad or lonely, confused or broken, unlucky or poor, but Luke could feel a real crossing before it entered the room.

The front of Helene's Thrift and Sundry was a thrift shop, mostly clothes and hats. Luke hit the lights and flipped the sign on the door to OPEN. Somehow, though, the street knew this was a Kovrov day and not real life—the store stayed empty as Luke sat behind the counter, flipping back and forth between apps that couldn't hold his attention.

He worked his tie loose and popped the button open again, while he sat alone. The Kovrovs had *some business* with him. It was Alexei's style to be mysterious about everything, innocuous or not. There was no guessing what he'd meant.

Camille popped downstairs as the time ticked past one and the Kovrovs were due. She was stressed. Luke could tell because her fountain of curls was larger than usual, pieces spiraling free where she'd been pulling at them.

Luke mashed at his own head to make sure everything was in place. His sister was his mirror—the two of them were the only Ukrainian-Creoles they knew, and they had identical square jaws and narrow eyes, identical brown skin, and identical masses of hair that tended to give them away.

Luke's was all right, though. Camille must have had a more stressful morning. She was neat in her best white dress for lunch, but she presented her magenta fingertips furiously. "Borscht!"

"I owe you," Luke said.

She dropped her elbows to the counter, glance slipping out the windows. "What do you think he wants with you?" The question yanked at Luke's gut, but he shrugged.

"Probably to uncross something. I *am* the best." He smiled his big, charming grin, though Camille was about the only person it didn't work on.

She rolled her eyes. "I hope not. There'll be no living with you."

Luke's grin relaxed, truer. "It would be weirder if they wanted you."

She raised her eyebrows but nodded. When Luke and Camille had been born with their twin eyes and twin hair, they'd also been given twin gifts: she had a knack for crossing nasty curses, while Luke could uncross just about anything. She studied kitchen hoodoo like quarterbacks studied tape—not only to understand, but because there was a competition to win.

Luke couldn't hurt anybody, though. All he could do was *un*hurt people. The Kovrovs couldn't want anything too bad from him.

The more he thought that, the less true it felt.

Camille straightened, smoothing down her skirt, as an angel-white Bentley Flying Spur rolled up to the curb. "Here we go."

Villains always made an entrance, so Alexei's was flawless. His driver opened his door, and he whipped his aviators off his face as he stepped out, a tall man in a pinstripe gray suit. He wore his brown hair long, brushing his shoulders, and had large downturned eyes. The effect was poetically sad, like he was the hero of a tragedy, but he bestowed a wicked smile on the Melnyk twins as he entered.

He looked ready for paparazzi—he did catch them sometimes, as a socialite and real-estate mogul. Luke followed him on the blogs—who knew if it was true, but last night he'd read that Alexei had dumped the man he was seeing, a Broadway actor he'd started dating after having an affair with a woman in the same show. Seedier papers sometimes called him The Godfather, but he was also Luke and Camille's actual godfather.

Alexei greeted them with kisses on each cheek, like a European, even though everyone knew he was from Brooklyn. "Good afternoon! Any tales from the neighborhood?" He pointed his chin at the door to the back room, not the street. "I do love your stories. I don't know anyone else who has their own witch doctor."

Luke stiffened. He didn't belong to anyone but himself. When he didn't answer fast enough, Camille said, "Tell him about the pigeon lady."

Luke nodded. "She was crossed. Somebody had put a bunch of pigeon feathers in a mojo bag. Everywhere she went, they were bothering her. Even walking over to her place, I got whacked by a few of them."

"Gross!" said another voice, and Luke jumped. An outfit by the door shifted and resolved into Jeremy Kovrov, who'd been hanging back.

"Indeed," Alexei said.

Jeremy was a Kovrov cousin or something, but as he

sidled up to Alexei, it was hard to believe they were even the same species. Jeremy's head bobbed at Alexei's shoulder, his fair hair shaggy along his forehead and collar. And Alexei had never entered a room hanging silently on its edges.

Sometime during the past six months, Jeremy had grown up like everyone else—he looked like those where-are-they-now photos of child actors, all stretched out as they'd grown. He wore a bright pink T-shirt, and half his left arm was covered with rubber and metal bands, thread friendship bracelets in every bright color, and a clunky black watch.

Jeremy tagged along with Alexei to lunches, an apprentice to the family business. It was hard to name what the Kovrovs did—protection, cooperation, extortion—connecting magical suppliers and consumers across New York. If today was about a job for Luke, it was probably good news, a summer flush with cash. But the Melnyks owed debts to the Kovrovs, too, and sometimes these meetings left Luke's parents scrambling to cover the bills.

And while they struggled, Jeremy was being groomed for some Kovrov dukedom. Luke plastered on a charming smile. "What's up, Kovrov?"

"Not much, how are you?"

Luke glanced at Camille. "We're good. Ready to pound some borscht."

"Mm, borscht," Jeremy said brightly.

That was all anyone could be expected to squeeze out of that subject, but Alexei kept quiet, studying Luke sharp and cool. When Luke caught his eye, his face changed like a switch had flipped, the soft-focus light coming back on.

"Our cue?" Alexei offered an elbow to Camille, and Luke closed up the store as the others went upstairs. Before he followed, he paused in the dark room to give himself a pep talk: He was powerful, and the Kovrovs were allies. Whatever challenge Alexei had set, Luke would handle it.

Chapter Two

Jeremy tried to grab a seat at the corner of the Melnyks' table, but Alexei dragged him to the center, hissing, "Stop hiding."

He wasn't trying to hide. He had waved! But no one had seen him, and this wasn't the place to argue. He sat at Alexei's right hand and let them ignore him from there.

Only Alexei and Yuri Melnyk, the twins' dad, did much talking. Jeremy listened and tried to learn, but it was all stuff about the good old days and people he had never met and which cool bars had been turned into juice shops.

Usually, Jeremy came to business lunches because there was some way for him to be useful, babysitting or doing magic tricks. He didn't have a task today. Alexei had called this lunch a treat, but it was more like a test.

Jeremy knew—from Instagram, not from their acquaintance—that Camille Melnyk was deft and creative with makeup. She painted her eyes and lips in a whole rainbow of colors every day and dressed in outfits pieced together from the front room of her family's store. Today, she wore a neat white dress with a high collar and full skirt, and, to Jeremy's eye, no makeup at all. It might have been funny, how obviously her mother had picked out the clothes, but the Melnyks' politeness was too painfully stiff.

Yuri had a tie on, tight around his neck, and Helene wore a full-skirted dress. Jeremy hadn't thought this through. He had on trim dark jeans and his favorite pink T-shirt and shouldn't have felt so slobby.

On cue—the first lag in the conversation after they'd started eating—Jeremy said his line. "Thank you so much for lunch, Yuri. Everything is delicious."

Yuri nodded. "Of course."

Alexei nodded, too. Confidence inspired, Jeremy ad-libbed another: "I think you make the best dumplings in the city. These are so good."

Yuri chuckled gently. "I'm glad you like them. There's more if you want."

Jeremy did want them. He ate dumplings like they were rolling toward him on a conveyer belt until Alexei elbowed him under the table. The one other time anyone under twenty spoke was when Luke got a text or something, his phone buzzing. He pulled it out, saying, "My bad, I'll put this on silent," but he looked at it for too long to only be doing that, and a few minutes later he excused himself.

When he came back, phone hidden, his mother tried to glare at him, but he wouldn't make eye contact with her. It was miserable, this show they put on for Alexei, even though he ignored the whole thing. Alexei wouldn't care who was texting during lunch, and if it was some kind of personal drama, he'd love to hear about it.

Luke's text was probably more interesting than this small talk. Luke always seemed busy and independent for a teenager, very...was glamorous the word? Mature. Intense. Like the rest of his family, he wore formal clothes, but he carried them nicely. The top button of his white shirt was undone, a V of skin peeking under the knot of his tie.

What Instagram had taught Jeremy about Luke: He liked cats, purple Gatorade, and street art. He liked his parents' cooking better than restaurants, unless it was okra or beets, and he worked a lot but he enjoyed it. He liked math and science better than English and history, which Jeremy could hardly even imagine.

Also, one of his friends posted weekly Thursday thirst traps of models and celebrities, all across the gender spectrum, but Luke only ever commented on the pictures of guys. Once, the friend had posted a picture of a wan model, all cheekbones and legs, and Luke had replied, "Drag me."

Jeremy could second-guess the blue of the sky, but the evidence was pretty solid that Luke liked boys.

Jeremy snapped his eyes back to his empty plate, but Alexei's attention was hot enough to burn his cheeks. This was the treat, or the test: just say something. Luke also liked the kind of flashy action movies no one in Jeremy's family ever wanted to watch, so all Jeremy had to do was bring up *The Fast and the Furious*. "It sounds great on the new sound system at home..." Something like that. Something cool.

"We have a little business to discuss." Alexei nodded to Yuri and Helene. "And there is a task I would like our witch doctor's help with."

The Melnyks all straightened in their chairs, their attention sizzling as Jeremy grabbed his messenger bag from the floor and pulled out two burlap witch bags.

Luke winced, and Camille leaned forward. "Oooh."

"Quite," Alexei said. "A client found these in their home, luckily before they managed to hurt anybody. I'd like an inventory of the contents and a swift execution."

Luke nodded. "Yes, sir."

"Wonderful. Jeremy will stay with you until that's done — call me if there are any problems." He turned to Jeremy. "I won't need long, but take your time. Call me when you're done, and we'll come pick you up."

Sure he would. He'd want a debrief on everything Jeremy had said to Luke, and there would be nothing to tell him. "I'll take the subway."

Alexei arched one sly eyebrow but didn't answer. He followed Helene and Yuri downstairs and left Jeremy alone with the twins.

They wouldn't let him help clear the table—Luke did it while Camille spread a piece of newspaper and dumped out the first bag. "You *are* a sexy thing," she said to the pile of ash and sinister little objects.

Jeremy didn't see it. "How does this work?"

Camille turned back to the table and picked through the mess with her bare fingers. "I see what pieces they used and guess how they layered together. We're trying to rebuild the puzzle."

Jeremy nodded, and Camille gave him a canny look. "'Puzzle' is not just a metaphor for 'problem' here," she said precisely. "Whoever made this created it with a specific focus, just like drawing a picture. Then they broke it up and put it in this bag, and now we're rebuilding the picture so we can see what they were trying to do."

Jeremy sat up straighter to show he was paying attention. Alexei's magic was physical and instinctive, and so was his instruction. This was a real, tidy lesson—almost like getting to go to school. "I see. I didn't know it was such a science."

Camille grinned. A thrill of completion shimmered through him. Whenever he managed to say the right thing, it was like sliding a book into a neat gap on a shelf.

"That's exactly what it is." She brushed one of the objects clean, her smile turning wicked. "Ooh! That is not a chicken bone."

Jeremy blinked at the round piece of bone; his body

caught up before his brain, and he was already jumping back in his chair. It was a human knucklebone. Camille laughed.

"I was carrying that around!" he exclaimed.

She gave him an odd, appraising look. "Yes, you were. Do you know where they came from?"

Jeremy shook his head. "Alexei gave them to me this morning." In truth, he'd thought Alexei had made them himself, an excuse to give Jeremy more time with Luke. But this looked like a real attack. "I can text him and ask."

Camille's eyes widened. "We don't need to bother him."

"What's this, now?" Luke poked his head out of the kitchen. "Ah. Yeesh."

"Scaredy-cats." She dropped the bone on the newspaper. "The bone isn't even the worst part. I'm pretty sure this is belladonna *and* hemlock."

"Damn. Overkill?" Luke said.

"Very kill," she replied.

Luke walked back, heading deeper into the apartment. Camille kept picking apart the bag.

Jeremy recognized crinkled feathers and more slivers of bone, but a lot of it was ground to dust. "How can you tell the pieces apart? It all looks like dirt to me."

She tilted her head. "It smells different. And the vibes feel different."

She meant magic—nothing Jeremy would be able to perceive. He put his chin in his hand as she sifted through the dust.

When Luke returned, he'd changed his button-down and khakis for a white T-shirt and green basketball shorts. Jeremy looked down before he stared again—he hadn't been prepared for that, the shape of Luke's body different and clearer in the room.

"We'll have to burn those." Luke touched the chest of his T-shirt. "Just didn't want to get smoke on my clothes."

Camille was watching Jeremy expectantly—that had been directed at *him*. It stung, that Luke needed to justify something as simple as changing his clothes. Like Jeremy was going to get offended. "Oh," he said. "That's fine."

If he struck up a conversation and finally got the nerve to ask Luke to hang out, Luke would definitely say yes. Whether he wanted to or not. It made Jeremy's skin crawl. He needed a sign, even the tiniest clue—a too-long glance, any touch at all—that Luke might really be interested.

Luke had one earbud from his headphones in, the other bouncing against his stomach, and he put a box on the table. "Going to get some stuff together. Grab me if you need anything."

Camille waved him off. She worked in silence, sorting and taking notes, as he left down the stairs and returned with a tall saint candle and a lighter. After he put them in the box, he hiked the waistband of his baggy shorts up his hips.

Jeremy looked away quickly, but Camille hadn't caught him watching. She was glaring at Luke and asked, far too sly for the words, "What are you listening to?"

"This playlist Max sent. He's on his way over."

Camille's jaw dropped. "No."

"Sure." Luke shrugged. "He texted me. He likes rituals."

"Luke." Camille spoke with the significant weight of someone trying to be patient. "We have to respect Jeremy's time."

"Oh, I don't mind," Jeremy said. Camille made a fleeting exasperated face, and Jeremy understood too late that she didn't actually care about his time.

"He doesn't mind, see?" Luke nodded to Jeremy. "Max is all right; you'll like him."

Jeremy pressed his lips together and looked sort of near Luke's eyes, and nodded. Here was his sign—Luke was hanging out with another boy. Jeremy was interested to meet him like he'd be interested in picking a scab.

"Max is *not* all right. He is a trial sent to test me." Camille's accent stretched like pulled taffy on the words, and she sounded like her mother. Luke ignored her, walking toward the kitchen.

Jeremy studied her slumped posture. Was this actually weird, or was it one of those things other people knew how to handle and he could never figure out? He rallied a smile. "Do you need help with anything else?"

Camille bolted up. "I'm so sorry! Yes, I'll get back to this."

"That's okay." But she was back to work, and no matter what he said, she'd just apologize again, on and on… Instead of trying, he shut up, and tried to go back to being invisible.

Chapter Three

Luke's parents' voices, fast and sharp, carried from the front room as he went downstairs, but when he opened the door, they fell silent. They had the wide-eyed faces of two kids caught stealing treats. "What?" he said. "What did Alexei say?"

"We'll talk about it later," Yuri said. "How's it going up there?"

"Just getting some stuff. We're almost ready to burn everything."

"Take it out back, then," Helene said. They glanced at each other and back at Luke, examining him like he might have gotten a secret tattoo while they'd been gone.

"Will do," he said. "You two keep it weird."

Helene huffed a wry laugh, and he shut the door to gather supplies from the backroom shelves. Luke's mother had designed this room to make customers believe in and buy magic, covering the floors with secondhand rugs and putting pink and purple bulbs in the lamps. It was comforting, the dim light and familiar routine and the heft of a half-empty bottle of lighter fluid in his hands. He focused on the music in his earbuds, breathing with the beat. It was the last playlist Max had sent him, and he had half an hour to come up with an opinion on it.

The long morning's anxiety had sunk under his skin, and now he was worried about Max in that same borderless, unmanageable way. Music was the only thing Max would talk about sincerely, and if Luke could catch that thread and draw it out, maybe he could unravel the rest of Max's defenses. The problem was, Max liked the weirdest stuff. Luke listened to whatever was slick and fast on the radio, and he didn't have the language for this one topic Max cared about.

This song was some experimental hip-hop situation. Max had texted him the link with a message that said *this made me think of you,* and Luke had liked that so much he ought to have loved anything. But he couldn't understand what made the rap parts special, and the only thing that sounded unique was that it disappeared into long interludes of ambient noise that made him miss the beat. It got grating if he listened to it for too long.

He hated it.

He hated it so much he couldn't figure out why it made Max think of him, and the only explanation he could come up with was that it was hip-hop and he was brown. He wanted it to be something more specific than that, but if he asked Max to explain, then Max would know he hadn't understood it.

He threw a tub of table salt in the box so hard that both Jeremy and Camille jumped. Camille didn't say anything, but she pursed her lips to say, *Look, you are already upset.*

Luke took a deep breath.

Camille turned back to her notes, scribbling. "I'm almost done."

Jeremy reassembled the mojo bags for their destruction. All the handling had taken the edge off the spell that had made them, but Luke could still feel their vibe. These were almost metallic, the jaw-jangling cringe of biting down on aluminum foil.

Luke and his family had gotten a lot of mileage—money for jobs, favor from the Kovrovs—out of his skill, and they made it sound like a noble calling or remarkable gift. Often, Luke felt that way, too. But just as often, he was great at uncrossing because harmful spells were annoying, and he broke them for the same reason he'd smack a mosquito buzzing in his ear.

They set up next to the trash cans in the narrow alley behind the store. Jeremy took careful, picking steps. "This is glamorous."

Camille opened her mouth and closed it—guessing the risk of a joke misfiring before she spoke. "I bet Alexei only does magic at midnight, wearing a robe."

Jeremy paused, wide-eyed, and nudged her with his shoulder. "Robe optional."

Camille laughed out loud. "I get it, Rasputin."

Luke shook his head and got to business, dropping the mojo bags on the ground. He centered himself, standing tall over them. Pushing out a breath, he let it all go—the Kovrovs, his parents—because this was his part. He wasn't up on the politics or the clothes, but an uncrossing, he could always do.

He pulled a St. Michael's candle and a long lighter from the box. Lighting the candle for defense was a formality, but today it felt heavy in his hand. Meaningful. He focused and found himself thinking he should give them to Jeremy. He hadn't come up with that himself, so it must be something important. He didn't know what Jeremy's skills were, but he knew his own.

Jeremy took the objects with a small, knowing smile and spoke a few Russian words as he lit the candle. The flame caught and grew, its strength impressive and then impossible in the breezy alley. It stood still in front of Jeremy's chest like a glass sculpture of fire.

Jeremy held the candle in both hands, pushing its flame safely away from himself as it licked and crackled higher in the air. Only his whispering lips moved. The candlelight cut up the shadows, catching the bones and hollows of his face.

Luke had never seen Jeremy do magic—and had never seen any Kovrov do something so subtle. Searching, he uncovered another memory: Jeremy as a little boy, too shy in a roomful of attention to blow out the candles on his cake and hiding in a grown-up's lap as the light dazzled.

The flame settled, flickering on the wick, and everyone exhaled together. Jeremy lifted that distant, alien face as he pulled the candle closer. "Now."

Luke drew a circle of salt around the bag and dribbled a rough star of lighter fluid inside. "Get ready to jump back if it spits."

He touched the lighter's flame to the fluid and reeled back. The flame danced over the droplets before catching. The picking had taken the worst edge off the bags, but Luke hunted down that aluminum foil cringe.

The trick was to be stronger than the wicked thing. Luke could perceive the crossing in perfect detail—how it tasted, smelled, how it made his tongue curl in his mouth. Then, he could decide how the world should be instead, clear of that awful feeling. It worked because he was the only person who could do it; because he was the only person, it had to work. He felt the cringe, and imagined it clear, and held both of them in his head until only the one he chose was true. The cringe let go, and the flame over the bags soared up in a yellow pillar.

Behind him, Jeremy's gasp echoed its whoosh, and Camille said, "Show-off."

Luke grinned over his shoulder as he moved back. Jeremy stared, rapt, with the candle close to his chest. Camille nudged it forward. "Careful. Fire bad."

"Oh, right." Jeremy pushed it away.

"I think you can put it down now," Luke said, but Jeremy shook his head and kept the candle steady. He stared raptly at the fire except for quick glances toward Luke, like there was something he was watching for or studying.

A hot blue core bloomed at the center of the flame. Luke reached to pull Jeremy back as the fire sparked and popped, but Jeremy was already hopping forward, whispering over his candle with his face gone hard and sharp again. The salt held, and the flame settled.

Camille caught Luke's eye and tapped under her chin. His jaw had dropped. He snapped it closed and said, "That was slick."

Jeremy glanced up, smiling quickly, and hunched back over the candle. "It's… nothing, really."

Luke would have liked to know how that worked, but he could tell a brush-off when he got one. Instead, he turned back to the flame and let himself get entranced. It was easy to gaze at the still flame inside the salt, to be drawn into it. Its glow got brighter as the shadows in the alley grew deeper with the turning sun. Luke was so dazed he might have been asleep on his feet, until a lilting voice cracked the silence. "Look at you, hanging out with the trash!" Max called.

Chapter Four

Jeremy went from feeling underdressed to seriously grubby. Sweat stuck his hair to his nape and his T-shirt to the middle of his back, and this boy was fresh from an air-conditioned car. Max was shorter than Jeremy but built more like a grown-up, wider in the shoulders than the hips, and he had yellow-blond hair shaved close in the back and long over his eyes.

Jeremy knew him from Instagram, too, a ghost who flitted through Luke's pictures. The first time Jeremy had clicked through to Max's profile, he'd thought Max was famous—there were lots of pictures of him singing on stages, and other singers and concerts—but it seemed he was just more interesting than Jeremy.

Luke greeted Max with an open arm and his name. It took him a long time to get through three letters, *Mmmmax*. If anybody said Jeremy's name like that, he'd probably immolate. Max only dimpled and tucked himself under Luke's arm.

Camille scoffed quietly. "Sorry about them."

Jeremy's heart was loud in his ears, each beat ripping a

gap between his head and the alley. Parsing comments on social media was a whole different thing than seeing Luke put his hand on a boy's hip to squeeze him close.

"I can't stay. I have a thing," Max said brightly. "But I thought I'd come see the magic."

Luke's face did something terrible, melting with hurt and then turning rock-hard to cover it up. Camille made another little scoff.

Max, though, had his eyes on the pillar of strange fire.

Luke turned his attention there, too. "Jeremy brought us a couple of curse bags to burn."

"Ah, hey. I'm Max." The boy twisted under Luke's arm, a hand half-extended, but eyed the candle Jeremy held and pulled back. "Were you cursed, too?"

"No, no," Luke said before Jeremy could answer. "His family does magic." He caught Jeremy's eye. "Max is a normal. We met when I uncrossed his family."

"A normal!" Max shoved into Luke's side. "You are the *most* basic, you can't talk." There was a joking quality to his voice, but it didn't land. Ice radiated off Camille, and Luke's forehead crumpled.

Jeremy glanced down the alley, itching to flee. Luckily, the spell shattered, and the fire deflated, billowing more smoke than flame as the cloth caught.

"Careful." Luke stepped back, pulling Max. "You don't want burning cayenne in your eyes."

"Eww," Max said.

Jeremy licked his fingers and pinched out the candle. "I think that's it. Thank you for your help."

"No problem." Luke took the candle back.

"Can I walk you to the street?" Camille asked. Jeremy let her lead him down the alley, though he could get himself back to the sidewalk. Did he seem so helpless? He'd done powerful magic for them—he'd really helped that ritual.

Luke had barely even noticed, preoccupied with beautiful Max coming over to be mean to him.

As soon as they were away, Camille started whispering again. "I'm sorry about that. He's a little brat, but Luke is obsessed with him. We didn't mean to be rude."

Jeremy's chest felt tight, like he'd been running all afternoon instead of standing still. "It's okay. I'm not—I can talk to people, too."

That had come out weird. Camille leaned away, taken aback. "No, of course. Anyway, thank you."

Jeremy nodded. "You, too."

He burst onto the sidewalk like he'd escaped there. He was never going to understand it, so he turned his attention away, to the whole evening he had to himself. He inhaled the scent of tar from another neighborhood's street. Maybe he would get dinner somewhere on the way home. Maybe he'd stop at the comic shop. Maybe—

Maybe that sheet of warm, creamy white gleaming in the syrupy orange of the low sun was a Bentley Flying Spur, and maybe loads of people in Luke's neighborhood drove those. Or maybe not.

Katya stepped out of the driver's seat and around the front. She was professional in a pressed uniform and tight bun, but she threw an arm around Jeremy as she opened the door for him.

Alexei, waiting in the back seat, slipped his phone into his jacket and clapped his hands. "Your majesty! We've been awaiting your report."

"It was fine." Jeremy buckled in as Katya pulled the car into the road. "Camille made some notes for you about the bags, and Luke burned them. Oh, and I met his boyfriend."

"Bullshit." Alexei nudged Jeremy's arm, his face already lighting up in anticipation of a story. Teaching him Instagram had been the worst mistake of Jeremy's life.

"*Mmmmax.*" Jeremy shoved back. It was probably a lie—even he knew enough to know the quick, raw hurt on Luke's face wasn't how it was supposed to be—but maybe it would shut Alexei up.

Alexei twisted in his seat like he might be able to see through walls into the Melnyks' alley. "Well, that's great, then."

That sounded like a rabbit hole to some patented Alexei manipulation, so Jeremy ignored it. Because he'd said *boyfriend* out loud, he imagined it—the way Max's body had tucked into Luke's side—except in his secret mind, Jeremy imagined himself there. Luke was made of broad, sturdy squares, handsome in the effortless way of old movie stars, and there were few things in Jeremy's small life he liked better than looking at him.

The fantasy had gone sour—something was lost. It was fun to imagine Luke wanting him for real, not himself in someone else's place.

Though no one was asking, Alexei elaborated. "He's definitely queer, open to dating. You're practically in."

He was practically invisible. Jeremy didn't answer, so Katya said, "Get a life."

"*I* have a life," Alexei said, broadly suggesting other individuals in the car did not. Jeremy winced. As if he wouldn't love a life like Max's—concerts and parties and boys. Getting attention from someone as smart and talented as Luke Melnyk wasn't even the most interesting part of Max's day. Jeremy wasn't allowed to have all that, staying safe behind the part of himself that was too scared to try.

"Lay off," Katya said. "The Melnyk kid has a boyfriend."

"*Boyfriend.*" Disgust dripped off Alexei's words. "Who cares about that? Not some fifteen-year-old."

"Boundaries, Alexei," Katya said.

"Oh, that wasn't that bad."

"I'm seventeen," Jeremy said.

"Surely not." Alexei squinted like Jeremy might grow an extra limb.

Jeremy rolled his eyes.

"Well, the young prince wants him," Alexei said. "And a Kovrov gets what a Kovrov wants."

Katya's voice dropped an octave. "*Boundaries*, Alexei."

Alexei harrumphed. Jeremy slouched against the window. He'd stared too long once or twice, and Alexei was playing bored king, moving people around like chess pieces. Even Alexei and Katya talking about him like this made Jeremy want to melt into the car. If Luke figured it out, Jeremy would just expire. "I know you wanted a story, but I don't have one. We see them once every six months, and it's always awkward, and he doesn't like me. It's not going to happen, so just let it go."

Instead of answering, Alexei leaned forward and continued some conversation he'd been having with Katya. "You see? What else am I supposed to do with this?"

She slapped the turn signal. "It is on the record that I think this is a bad idea."

"Hush," Alexei said. "Your majesty, I have some news."

Chapter Five

Luke poured water over the embers of the bag and sucked it all up into the Shop-Vac as Camille walked Jeremy down the alley. As she returned, she and Max eyed each other like a pair of stray cats, hackles up.

She took the vacuum inside, though, and a breeze lifted the smoke away, leaving the dusty stone scents of brick and asphalt. For five perfect seconds, it just worked: Luke hooked his finger into a belt loop of Max's jeans and pulled him closer. Max's hips went pliant as he moved, and he lifted his face to nip Luke's lower lip in a kiss.

Max took a step back. "You're going to lose your headphones."

They trailed out of Luke's pocket. Max gathered them up and returned them, sliding his knuckles against Luke's leg through the fabric.

"I was listening to those songs you sent me." Luke tried to pull Max closer, but he stepped farther back and smiled—a real one, with deep dimples. He was too pretty. It was not right. Max Cooper had been created in a lab, test tubes bubbling and wires sizzling, by a scientist bent on destroying Luke's mind.

"Yeah?" Max asked. "What did you think?"

Luke swallowed. "It was cool. Different."

Max waited for more. Luke didn't have it. It didn't matter either way, because the door to the store swung open and Helene stuck her head out. "Luke, what are you—"

She saw Max and stopped, lips pressing together and nostrils flaring.

"I was just…" It was obvious what Luke was *just*. Way too late, he took his hand away from Max's hip.

Helene started, "Your father—" but Max said over her, "I have to go anyway. I was on my way to a thing."

Luke crossed his arms over his chest. "Right."

"Right," Max repeated. He looked nervously at Helene, but she stayed where she was in the doorway, so Max waved and skittered off down the alley instead of saying a real goodbye.

Luke waited until he was out of earshot, disappearing around the corner, and turned on his mother. "I can't have *one hour*—"

"We can't have one afternoon?" Her voice rose. "If you don't care about this life Mr. Kovrov provides for you, you could at least respect his time."

"I did what he asked me to." Luke waved over the damp spot on the ground, still smudgy with ash.

Helene clenched her jaw. "Your father and I need to talk to you."

Luke followed her, his anger spiraling slower so he was left with a hard pit of disappointment. He'd messed that up, with Max's songs. He could text, but he didn't know what to say.

Yuri was in the living room, sliding his armchair back into place now that the extra furniture had been put away.

Luke returned from his distracted thoughts to find the room heavy, something unspoken congealing between his parents. "Is something wrong?"

At once, Helene said, "Yes," and Yuri said, "No." Luke drew his spine up, bracing.

"Sit." Yuri gestured, and they settled around the table. "The Kovrovs have invited you to work for them." Yuri stopped at the end of the sentence with a grave look, like he'd said something profound.

Luke held his face still while his mind scrambled, sure he was savvy enough to understand if Yuri left it at that, but eventually he had to ask, "Don't we already work for the Kovrovs?"

Helene shut her eyes, pained, and Yuri smiled gently. "Of course," he said. "A new job. For you, this summer. Day to day with Sergei and Alexei."

"Wait—what?" Luke bolted upright in his chair. Working side by side with Alexei Kovrov? That was money and power and honor. His parents looked terrified.

"Grunt work, probably," Yuri said. "Lay magic. I did the same thing when I was your age—well, a little older than you." Luke was almost eighteen, but he was still in high school. "Alexei decided it was time to offer you the opportunity."

"Offer," Luke repeated. An offer from Alexei carried more weight than an offer from anyone else. He would have framed it as an invitation, graciously; maybe it would genuinely have not occurred to him that anyone might want to say no. Maybe he did it all the time, auditioning folks for bigger roles in the family business. Maybe it was rare, and Luke was something special.

Helene sighed. "Exactly. But I think—better you than Camille. If they try to put any spells on you, you'll be able to break them. And who knows what they could do with a power like hers."

There was nothing to say to that. They had somehow touched on every one of their family's sore spots at once: Camille's dangerous power, their debts to the Kovrovs—all this after Luke had been sneaking around with Max. The conversation was a pile of boxes stacked too high in Luke's arms, slipping from his grasp. "I don't understand. Why me?"

Yuri cupped his fingers and tapped them against the table, a gesture he made to collect his thoughts.

Helene stood up. She gave Yuri a heavy look: *you fix this.* "I'll be in the store."

Yuri waited for her to walk away before he spoke, and then winked at Luke. "It's all right, Lukonya. Take a breath."

Luke let his mind go still.

"All right. Did the Kovrov kid say anything to you?"

Luke shook his head. "Nope. He helped with the uncrossing."

"Helped? He did magic, too?"

"The protection. He put a charm on the candle."

Yuri frowned. "Weird. Was that weird?"

Luke's reflex was to say yes. Of course. Spending time with the Kovrovs was an obligation, a pain, always a little dangerous. Except, Jeremy hadn't been weird at all—nice enough, a little quiet. Luke and Camille hadn't spent so much time alone with him since they were too young to sit through lunch with grown-ups, five or six years now, and had never seen him do magic. Whatever he had done to amplify the candle had been spectacular. If Luke didn't know better— if he hadn't spent his whole life learning that the Kovrovs were, at best, an unavoidable nuisance like thunderstorms or taxes—he would have said he and Jeremy had made a good team.

"Not as bad as it could have been," he finally said.

"Good. Maybe that's how the whole thing will go."

"Dream big, Dad." Maybe Luke would be great at it.

Maybe he'd make a whole pile of Kovrov money and take Max to see some weird ambient noise band and they'd finally figure out how to talk to each other.

Yuri laughed. "Who was that kid who sassed his father and then fell out of the sky?"

"You mean Icarus?"

Yuri nodded with his chin. "Don't be like that."

Luke didn't think he was. "Mom is scared." Shorthand. Blaming it on Mom instead of asking, *Are you scared?* or *Should I be?*

"No," Yuri said, slow and reassuring. "I think she hoped we had more time. I admit, I did, too. I don't think anyone expected you and your sister to be so—" Yuri searched for his word.

Powerful.

"Talented. But that doesn't mean it's a bad thing."

"I can handle it," Luke said. "Tell me what it means."

"Ah, there you're getting past your old man. I never did go full-time, got shuffled out after the Malcolm war."

"The what?" Luke's voice rose on the question, and he swallowed hard. It felt like trying to remember a movie he'd only seen in bits and pieces.

Yuri tapped the table. Luke shuffled his memories like a deck of cards—cleaning the apartment to its bones for family lunches, putting on stiff suits for dinners, counting out 10 percent of every dollar he saw. The Kovrovs were such a small, surreal slice of Luke's life, it was tough to imagine what they might do when they escaped those narrow boundaries.

Yuri began. "I started working for Ivan Kovrov after school. That was Alexei and Sergei's father. Hard man. Mean like Sergei, smart like Alexei." Yuri sketched with his fingers on the table. "The Zhangs had most of Manhattan, all the businesses and the little magicians who worked for them in exchange for protection or clients or money, like we work for the Kovrovs. And the Kovrovs had all of Brooklyn, most of the boroughs, Jersey. The Damianis and the Malcolms, they were little guys, fighting for the scraps. Then one day, all the sudden, most of New Jersey stops paying. *No, we don't work for you anymore. The Malcolms have stolen them.*"

Yuri spread his hands wide. "The Malcolms do big magic. Old stuff. Changing the way energy moves through the world. They're not so powerful with the small business, but they can do some wild things. When I say they took New Jersey, I mean they *took New Jersey.* Ivan couldn't cross the state line without getting sick. We'd try to go into Jersey and get confused, forget why we were there.

"Ivan Kovrov, he loses it. Clamps down on his people. By this time, I've met your mother, so I let myself get pushed out of that close circle. Maybe there's not so much money in it for me, but there's a little more freedom, you know? So I don't know as much about what's happened since.

"Ivan's dead, and the old Malcolm doesn't go out much anymore, but his son Corey is head of the family now, and he hates the Kovrovs even more. I understand there are skirmishes sometimes—little fights, families changing loyalties."

"I wonder if that was what those bags today were about," Luke said. "Did Alexei tell you where they were from? Jeremy didn't know."

"No." Yuri gave Luke an assessing look. "The Kovrovs don't tell anybody anything they don't *need* to know. When they give you a job, you follow orders. You don't ask questions."

Luke nodded, eyes on the table.

"Lukonya," Yuri said firmly.

"I heard you."

"You have to be careful," Yuri said. "Don't ask questions, and never give them your blood."

Luke jolted, stung. "I'm not going to do blood magic. You don't have to tell me that."

"It's a powerful tool. When you see Alexei—"

"Come on, Dad. That's nasty."

Yuri thought for a long time, tapping the table in a slow, even rhythm, before he started again. "The thing about your mother was, I knew right away. She was perfect from the beginning. My parents, they hated it. Not only an American girl, but a black one?" He blew a long whistle and shook his head. "No way. I'd bring Helene to dinner, and they'd have single girls from the old country there to meet me. The last time we tried to talk to them was after you and your sister were born. My mother wouldn't even touch you. Her own grandchildren."

This story was their family's origin myth, its foundation. What came next, though, was new.

"Your mother's family is great, but they're across the country. Ivan Kovrov was always here. He gave us work and loans when we couldn't make rent. He adored your mother. Of course, he adored her power. And he'd tell me about how we were going to teach you kids our culture. He'd joke about how his sons spoke better Russian than he did, because there were more people here for them to talk to, and he'd tell me we'd make sure you kids could speak it, too."

That surprised Luke—he knew about six words of Russian or Ukrainian, all for food, and no one had ever tried to teach him more.

Yuri shook his head again. "When you're the Kovrovs' people, they make it feel like a family. Except, you miss a payment? You make a mistake? You'll find out real quick who their family is."

Luke patted one of Yuri's pale, mottled hands, resting on the table. "I'll be careful."

"I know you will. You're a good kid." Yuri squinted into

Luke's face. "That boy makes you happy?"

It felt like a hard left, though of course it wasn't at all. His dad didn't agree with most of his decisions, but neither of his parents was going to tell him who he could and couldn't be with.

He didn't want to give up the precarious thing he had with Max, but he probably wouldn't give anything up to keep it, either. Washed hollow, Luke answered honestly.

"Sometimes he does. Sometimes he makes me pretty miserable. I can't figure out if it's supposed to be like that or not."

Yuri laughed, breaking his flat face open. "If you find out, you let me know. All right, tell me what you learned today."

"No questions." Luke tapped the table like his father. "No blood."

Chapter Six

Luke was early the first morning he reported for work, so he rode an extra stop and took a looping walk through a corner of Prospect Park. He was overdressed, buzzing with his parents' warnings and admonitions, but it was a gorgeous day, and he got out of his head watching it. It was late in the morning, after commuter hours, and the park was full of nannies and children, athletic yuppies, and walkers with three or five dogs on webs of leashes.

Luke kept far to the right of the path, out of the way of the runners and cyclists, but one bumped his shoulder hard anyway. He turned, ready to be mad, and found Jeremy Kovrov's grinning face.

Luke gathered up his formal expression quickly, spine straightening, but Jeremy started bopping along next to him without seeming to notice, pulling the white bud of his headphones from one ear. "Hi, Luke."

"What up, Kovrov." Luke caught a nuclear blast of orange in his peripheral vision and looked down, afraid of falling in a manhole. Jeremy wore running shoes the neon orange of a road sign. They glowed from within. Probably an enchantment. "Those are some shoes."

"Orange makes you run faster." Jeremy matched strides with Luke and popped out his other earbud.

"That magic?"

"Science." All of Jeremy's running stuff was that garish—the leather and rubber armband, the grippy earbuds, the GPS watch, the shining red technical shirt, the slippery blue shorts. Luke's friend Short Wesley was a runner, but he didn't make it look nearly so expensive.

"You run every day?" Luke asked.

"Every day I can. I rest once a week, but I hate it." Jeremy wrinkled his nose.

Luke considered his bouncing steps, the wiry muscles in his calves. That sounded like more than working out to stay fit—a deeper, more intense drive. It was not something Luke would have guessed about him. He seemed much happier outside and running than he ever did during family meetings.

He took a turn Luke wouldn't have expected, then another, and Luke was lost, and they were in an alley. He followed Jeremy into Sergei Kovrov's backyard, another green space hidden inside the rectangle of the block's houses. Luke thought, *it's like a courtyard*, and reality tipped sideways. *I'm walking into a castle, and that kid in the goofy shoes is a prince, and here we are.* Inside waited a bright, spacious kitchen, shining copper pots and pale wood cabinets, and a raggedy trio of dark-haired little boys. "Jeremy!" said the middle-size one. "Who is that?"

"Who's in my house?" Sergei's body followed his .voice into the room. "Oh, Melnyk." His eyes flicked back and forth between Luke and Jeremy.

"Look what I found in the park," Jeremy said.

Alexei's younger brother, Sergei, was the family battle-ax. He was tall like Alexei but leaner, his muscle more practical than aesthetic. His nose was twisted from old breaks, and his brow jutted out in a shelf over his eyes. He wore a white muscle tank, and everything below his chin was covered in black tattoos.

"I knew all that running was bad for you," Sergei replied. "Melnyk, heel." He turned and walked away, and because Luke couldn't punch him, he figured the best play was to laugh as he followed.

"Don't be an asshole, Sergei," Jeremy called after them. Luke could have choked on his tongue—probably would have, before swearing at Sergei.

Downstairs waited a gray basement room. "These shelves store product," Sergei said. "These are new boxes of product. Is the assignment clear?"

"Yes, sir."

"Don't call me 'sir,'" Sergei said as he left.

It looked like any warehouse, raw metal shelving in creepy wells of light cast by bare bulbs. The damp, metallic smell of the air was so strong it was almost a taste. All that drama with his father about secrets and blood, and here Luke was alone, hauling boxes. Yuri should have warned him to wear work shoes.

Jars and boxes and bricks of herbs sat on the shelves, almost alphabetical and half-labeled. He wouldn't be able to keep much order, but nobody was going to care.

An old stereo hulked on one shelf, and Luke found something bass-heavy on the radio. He hesitated before opening the first box, thinking of Camille tossing around that knucklebone, but all it held were white candles and the narcotic floral scent of oleander.

Three boxes in, Jeremy appeared with a plate of chicken nuggets and carrot sticks and a glass of water. "For you. It's kind of kid food 'cause I made lunch for the babies, too."

"No problem. Thanks, Kovrov." Luke found a sturdy box

and sat himself there.

"Not that you can't take a real break, too. I know Sergei isn't a very helpful boss."

Luke shrugged.

"Okay," Jeremy said. "Do you mind if I put on my reading?"

That didn't make much sense, but Luke wasn't going to argue. "Sure."

Jeremy played with his phone and the stereo until a sonorous voice with a crisp British accent started to drone.

"*The Return of the Native.*" Jeremy wilted with apology. "It's in the middle, but like, you don't care what happened so far."

Luke nodded. He did not. "Summer reading?"

"Oh." Jeremy looked surprised. "No, I'm homeschooled. I use a syllabus online."

"Seems like you could skip it if you don't like it."

Jeremy shook his head. "I have to stay disciplined, or I'll never learn anything."

His tone was heavy, taking down the whole tone of the conversation, and Luke couldn't figure out how to answer. Instead of waiting, Jeremy ducked over to the open box Luke was working through and loaded jars into one arm, picking around in a brisk, practiced way. He took them to the same spot on a shelf and leaned all the way up on his toes as he unloaded again.

There was something about the way he moved, a combination of expansiveness and precision, that touched a nerve at the back of Luke's brain. When Jeremy's arms were empty, he whisked his bangs off his forehead and caught Luke's eye, and Luke thought, *I wonder if he's into guys.*

Not that it mattered. Luke took a gulp of water. "Here to supervise?"

"What?" Jeremy turned to him with a quick hop, mouth

falling open. "No. I'm not your boss."

Luke's jaw tensed, and he kept it closed—Jeremy might not be his actual boss, but it was a close enough thing he shouldn't talk back.

"I'm just working," Jeremy added. "The same thing you are."

The same? No. What was Jeremy trying to prove? Something must have shown on Luke's face, because Jeremy said tightly, "This is my job, too. If you weren't here, I'd be doing this by myself."

"I thought you were family."

Jeremy turned toward the shelves and away from Luke. "I am. My family works." He punched at his phone until the audiobook jumped back to the beginning of their conversation.

Boss or no, Luke took the hint and finished his chicken nuggets in silence.

After another round of jars, Jeremy paused and scowled up at a light bulb. He cupped his hands to his face and blew into them like they were cold—once, twice, three times, with big inhales between each.

He opened his hands in front of his chin and blew again. Small globes of light danced away from him, swirling in the current of his breath and finding their own smooth trajectories. They perched on the shelves and hovered in the air to fill the room with a cleaner, mellower gold light.

He kept avoiding Luke's eyes, pressing his lips together to suppress a smile at his own conjuring. Luke blinked, adjusting to the glow as if it were a glaring spotlight. He sipped his water and said, "Huh."

"Dark in here." Jeremy risked a quick glance Luke's way and broke out in a satisfied grin. "You going to help or just sit there?"

Luke got up and back to work. The light did no favors to

the storage up close, illuminating dirt, dead bugs, and some arcane bits floating in murky jars.

When a chapter of his book ended, Jeremy switched it to music—electronic alternative, bright and synthetic. The atmosphere lifted, and it started to feel natural to pass back and forth as they moved between the shelves and boxes. He didn't know anything about Jeremy Kovrov, but now that he thought about it, he had a scatter of old memories of the time they'd spent together as kids, playing games or doing little herb magic gigs in back rooms, just like this, while the grown-ups worked.

Luke took another stab at conversation. "What protection spell did you do on that candle?"

"Not a spell." Jeremy's voice was far away in the warehouse. "Just a prayer."

Luke crushed a stray twig of rosemary between his fingers. He'd allowed that magic into his ritual, with his sister and Max. It hadn't felt nasty enough to be worth lying about, but Jeremy must be. "Seemed real powerful."

"I pray like anybody else, and I light the candle like anybody else." Jeremy's voice followed the lilting rhythm of a well-worn argument. "I don't know why it looks different. Sergei says praying gives me a special focus, and Alexei says maybe I have a guardian angel."

Alone in the row, Luke grinned. That made more sense, and although it was definitely the focus one, it was also clear which explanation Jeremy preferred. "Sounds like somebody's looking out for you."

"That would be nice." Jeremy was closer now—his head popped around the end of Luke's row. "That uncrossing was the coolest thing I've ever seen."

He disappeared again.

That was a lie. Of all the people in the world, Jeremy Kovrov had seen some wild mojo. But another part of Luke, a smaller but truer place right inside his heart, thought, *Yes. I know.*

"This is cool." He gestured to one of the little globes of light, which quivered as his hand passed. "The light."

"Party trick," Jeremy's voice said, right behind him. He turned, startled, and Jeremy was grinning again. "I'm not trying to sneak up on you. You're too easy."

"Party trick?"

Jeremy didn't answer. A magician would have to be so powerful to blow off an unaided charm like that. Luke had forgotten that Jeremy was a Kovrov, what that meant. He walked back to the boxes and pulled out a fresh one. These jars were painted black and unlabeled, hiding something secret. He lifted one, testing—heavy, for its size. "What is this?"

Jeremy pulled his lower lip sideways. "I'll get those later." He took the jar out of Luke's hand to gingerly replace it before taking the box cutter and checking the labels on the remaining boxes. He sliced one open. "Last box," he said, although it wasn't.

They unpacked the box and listened to Jeremy's whiny-voiced singers. Jeremy lip-synced along silently and made a funny little sneer over every cuss word, curling his upper lip. Luke had known him for years and somehow learned more about him in one afternoon than all that time put together. It seemed he couldn't remember what they'd talked about during all those lunches and parties, and suddenly he was full of questions.

He came back from placing a last armful of spice-scented red candles to find Jeremy crouched over the jars, pulling his mouth back and forth through different grimaces as he turned one in his hand. "Ugh. I might just deal with these after dinner."

Luke nodded and stopped short. "Wait—you live here?"

Jeremy lifted his gaze halfway, still distracted by the jars. "Yeah."

Luke's mind spun, trying to catch hold of some memory of that. How could he possibly have not known that? "How are you related to the Kovrovs, anyway?"

Jeremy paused, eyes on the jar, then stood slowly, unfolding from his crouch. He looked slightly to the left of Luke's eyes. "I'm Sergei and Alexei's brother. I was adopted when they were teenagers."

"Huh," Luke said. "Why?"

The shatter of glass was muffled by a thick glop of congealed liquid. Jeremy gasped, jumping back, but he was splashed with red-black, and pieces of the jar he'd been holding littered the floor around a pool of blood.

"Whoa!" Luke stepped back, lifting his palms. "Oh no, I'm sorry, I—"

"It's animal blood," Jeremy said quickly. "It's fine." He wiped his hands down his hips and looked frantically back and forth. "I'll just get a mop, it's fine."

"Let me," Luke said.

Jeremy's voice was flat. "I think you should go home."

Luke swallowed hard. "I'm sorry," he said again. "That was the rudest question, I—"

"It's not that." Jeremy focused on that spot next to Luke's head again. "Nobody's ever asked me that before."

Luke's stomach dropped, like he'd stepped on something rotten instead of firm ground, but the squirmy sickness of it rose when it should have ended. It was wrong, a worse feeling than fear even as the two mixed together—it was magic.

He'd done magic.

No questions had been the first goddamn rule, and he'd done nothing all afternoon but ask question after question— about magic, about the Kovrov family—and his question must have broken a spell hiding one of their secrets. "Shit."

Jeremy's chin tilted, his whole face firm. "Just go, I'll—"

Before he could finish, the door opened, Sergei's body silhouetted in the brighter light of the hall. Though they hadn't been standing close, Jeremy started and jumped farther away.

"Jesus," Sergei said.

"I'm cleaning it up right now." Jeremy whirled and walked back into the warehouse, leaving Luke and Sergei alone.

Sergei regarded Luke quietly, his face hidden in shadow, and finally said, "That's enough for today."

Chapter Seven

Marta leaned so far over the kitchen counter her pale hair brushed the granite, running her fingers along the inside of Sergei's arm. Jeremy recognized his own pitiful attempts at flirting in her posture, but of course Marta was already in. She'd been with Sergei forever, and they had three kids. Honestly, it was pretty gross that she bothered flirting at all.

Sergei would not appreciate being made to wait, so Jeremy walked into the kitchen still covered in old blood. Marta looked up and lifted an eyebrow. "Looks like *someone* had a fun afternoon. How'd it go?"

Jeremy wiggled around them to the fridge for a glass of water, moving slowly and casually though his heart scurried. "We let the blood sit too long, so it thawed out. I threw it in the freezer anyway, but I don't know if it will work."

"We let it sit?" Sergei raised his heavy brow.

"*I* let it sit." Jeremy let his tone sink, sullen, because Sergei hated that. "I know."

Marta wrinkled her nose. "Eww. You know what I mean. With Luke." She said it like *Lu-uu-uke*.

Jeremy hovered next to the fridge, avoiding the walk past them again, and hooked a finger under one rubber bracelet, twisting it.

"Get a hobby," Sergei said.

"Katya told Alexei to get a life," Jeremy said.

Sergei grunted. "I hope she tells him that every day."

Marta looked hurt but recovered with a big pout. "We're just having fun."

"I'm not having fun." Sergei took a long drag off his beer, lifting his gaze to the ceiling. He would not like having to ask. He'd respect Jeremy for stepping up—for carrying himself like a Kovrov.

Jeremy cleared his throat. "He asked how I was related to you."

They looked at Jeremy with mirrored slow turns. "What did you tell him?" Marta asked.

"He said I'm his brother, of course," Sergei answered, fast and only half-attending to her. "Listen, I'll talk to Alexei—"

"No!" Jeremy was too loud, his ears full of his own pounding blood. He took a breath and started over. "Let me? I can tell him what happened or talk to him if he calls." He could, maybe, understate it a little. Not a big deal, the tiniest thing, Luke hadn't even noticed what he'd done. He'd figure out a way to say it so no one got hurt.

Sergei nodded. "That's your responsibility, then."

Marta sighed. "Why is this so complicated? Can't you just, like, grab him and smack one on him? I mean, what's the worst—" She sealed her mouth shut.

Jeremy's mind reeled away from the worst that could happen so hard that he took a physical step back. Quickly, he listed lesser horrors: "Total rejection? Crushing humiliation? Having to listen to you people have opinions about it?"

She laughed a little, more to glide past the awkwardness than out of any real humor, and that should have been the end, but Sergei just couldn't let it go. "No, see? The little princess—" he gestured to Jeremy with the neck of his beer— "has to let him come to her."

A freeze zipped down Jeremy's spine, but before he could say anything, Marta snapped, "Sergei!" She rubbed one finger between her eyebrows. "Don't you two start. J, cupcake, could you please go check on the boys? I thought I heard little feet."

Jeremy nodded stiffly and moved back around them. He paused in the living room, just out of sight, and listened to them hissing whispers at each other. Sergei's voice was low and short, and Marta spoke longer and higher with every sentence. Finally, Jeremy made out her words: "He'd be *safer* if you sealed him in bubble wrap! He'd also die of suffocation."

Jeremy's life was full of untranslatable concepts for which they used close-enough words, like *pochemuchka* or *schadenfreude*. Like *adopted* and *homeschooled*. Like *brother*.

When Jeremy was a baby, his nighttime cries had made their father angry and mean. Sergei, then fifteen, had not wasted time waiting for someone to help or wondering what to do—he'd dragged his mattress into Jeremy's room and kept it there for years, between Jeremy's little body and the door, until Ivan died.

It was only when Jeremy was older, when he and Sergei were fighting, that Alexei had told him about that. "I know he's hard to like," Alexei had said, "but he loves you."

There was nothing as simple as a *word* for that.

Marta and Sergei fell quiet, and Jeremy turned to get up the stairs before they caught him eavesdropping. He scurried up one level—the babies slept silently; Marta had invented those little feet—and trudged more slowly up two more, to his own room in the attic. He thought of words for Sergei the whole time. Brother. Keeper. Monster.

Chapter Eight

Luke spent a couple days sweating—every ding of the doorbell or beep of his phone could be Alexei Kovrov, coming to demand restitution for whatever Luke had broken.

Max, his favorite tormentor, must have used some drama-seeking sixth sense to discover that Luke was finally waiting for something besides one of his messages, and promptly texted.

What are you up to this weekend?

Luke, sitting behind the counter in the store with his coffee, said:

Working

At the store? Can I come bother you?

Store and Ks. Still working on schedule. Never a bother.

Cool. I have a thing in the city tonight. I could crash

with you after.

Luke put his phone down on the counter gingerly, the way Jeremy handled those rotten-smelling jars. He was tempted to pick it up and scroll back through Max's texts, counting the endless iterations of *thing in the city* and *crash with you*, Max's favorite words.

His phone buzzed, skittering on the counter, and Luke jumped. It wouldn't be like Max to send another text so fast—and it wasn't Max, but an unknown number.

This is Jeremy. Alexei asked me to ask you if we can pick you up around 1:30 for a job.

Instead of something normal, a thumbs-up or a "k," Luke wrote out a proper, enthusiastic answer.

Sounds great. I'll be ready. Excited to get to work today.

He was aiming for coolly professional and self-controlled, but all Jeremy texted back was *OK*.

Three hours later, a small horde of rockabilly girls took over the store, and it took Luke too long to notice one of them was lounging against the door, not shopping. She wore black leather pants, and her top hung over her hips in a way that might be hiding a gun. He noticed way too late that she looked familiar.

"Katya?" Luke asked tentatively. He was not on a first-name basis with Alexei's driver and had never been alone with her before.

The woman stood up straighter in surprise but smoothed her face and extended a hand. "Natalya. I work with Sergei. Katya's my sister."

"Gotcha. I see it," Luke said. "Let me go get Camille to cover this zoo."

When he returned from the back, Natalya was still standing by the door, examining her reflection in the glass. "Do you really think I look like my sister?"

"You have the same—" Luke opened the door for her and looked at her face as she walked past, but he'd lost the resemblance. She was not as pale as Katya, more golden, and—he was probably supposed to have noticed—much prettier. "Vibe," he finished.

That wasn't right, either. Little Katya could kill him with a well-timed flick, and Natalya's smile glowed.

"Sure we do," was all she said.

Sergei's black Escalade waited on the curb, basking in sunshine and stares. Natalya took the passenger seat and Luke got in the back. He found Jeremy, who threw him a "Hey" without looking away from his window.

"Hey!" Luke said, too enthusiastically, and brought his voice down. "How's it going?"

Jeremy turned toward him a little more. "Good. How are you?"

His smile was vague but encouraging, and an outsize relief washed Luke. "I'm always good."

Something about seeing Jeremy reminded him he'd never responded to Max. So, while no one told him where they were going or what they were doing, he pulled out his phone.

I could crash with you after

Luke wrote: *I'll let you know the schedule*

The first of Max's two virtues was that he never pretended he wasn't sitting by his phone. He wrote back fast: *You work too much, it's grim*

Luke smirked. He wrote: *Going to be grim with the Ks now*, and put his phone away. He laughed to himself, and Natalya twisted in her seat. "Jokes are for sharing, yeah?"

He laughed his nerves and searched for help, but Sergei

had his eyes on the road and Jeremy was looking mildly at Natalya.

"The joke is me, I think," Luke said.

Natalya reached back and slapped his knee. "Now you have to tell me. I give the best advice, ask anybody."

Luke turned to Jeremy, face bright, to lure him into the conversation. He would still have to apologize for what he'd asked about the Kovrovs, but half the work was getting Jeremy to act normal. "Is that right?"

He only shrugged. "Is this about that boy who was at the uncrossing?"

Luke couldn't figure out how to answer, which was an answer. Jeremy widened his eyes, which was another question, and Luke snorted, the answer.

"Everyone knows the story except me?" Natalya exclaimed.

"I don't know or care what any of you are talking about," Sergei said.

Jeremy knocked the back of Sergei's seat and kept his fist there, tapping as he glanced back and forth between Luke and the window. "To be honest, I didn't think he was very nice to you."

"That's just how Max is," Luke said. "He's all right."

Natalya laughed, a musical peal. "You don't need advice. You need balls."

Luke popped up his eyebrows and dropped them again. Before he had to drum up an answer, Natalya moved onto Jeremy, eyes narrowing with mischief. "And how's Raf?"

Jeremy groaned and covered his face. "He texted me on my birthday to let me know the age of consent in New York state is seventeen. How gross is that?" He pulled a face of absolute, hilarious horror, mouth drooping in a melted arch.

"It could be considered helpful," Natalya said brightly.

Sergei growled. "Eyes front. The age of consent in my

house is twenty-five."

"You had two kids and me when you were twenty-five," Jeremy said.

"Exactly," Sergei answered, in the same tone of voice Luke's mother would say, *Twins*.

At once, Luke said, "Who's Raf?" and Natalya said, "Did you write back?"

"I said, 'Stop texting me,' and he sent back a pizza emoji." Jeremy rolled his eyes as he turned to Luke. "Raf Damiani. You know, like, Damiani."

Luke nodded. Camille and Helene sometimes went shopping for supplies in the Damianis' place on Mulberry Street, and Luke was never invited, in case he accidentally broke a spell or binding and started a fight. Which, clearly, was a reasonable precaution.

Sergei hadn't said anything, though. Maybe he was fine — maybe Alexei hadn't noticed, or hadn't minded repairing the binding Luke had broken. Maybe — Luke was warmed by an unlikely hope — Jeremy had kept his mistake a secret.

"He thinks we're doing a Romeo and Juliet thing," Jeremy said. "You know, two houses both alike in *actually I'm just not attracted to you, leave me alone*." Natalya laughed, and Jeremy flipped a hand at her.

Luke stared at him, smiling and whisking his hair out of his eyes in the yellow afternoon light. So he was gay, or bi or something. Luke was oddly proud of him for joking about it so easily, even as Sergei grumbled and tightened his knuckles on the steering wheel.

"Would that not be allowed—" Luke clamped his mouth shut around the tail end of the question and then a frustrated impulse to cuss at himself. How hard was it to stop asking goddamn questions, to just shut up for a few hours? He didn't even care whether Kovrovs and Damianis could date, or who Jeremy might want.

Jeremy shifted in his seat. Sergei made a production out of a lane change. As Luke tried to map the mistake he'd made and figure out how to fix it, his attention snagged on Natalya. Something about her made his mouth run.

She wasn't just charming. She was wearing a glamour or seduction, some kind of sparkling mojo. It made sense as soon as Luke guessed it—a troll like Sergei would benefit from that balance as he worked—but he would have liked a warning before they'd let her grill him. Max was a vulnerable thing, a heartbreak Luke could see coming but couldn't let go; he wasn't small talk.

These people were the worst.

"No." Sergei threw the Escalade into park in front of a driveway. "No Romeo and Juliet bullshit in my house, either. No one cares about the Damianis. Time to work."

Sergei and Natalya unbuckled and climbed out of the car, but no one said anything to Luke, and Jeremy didn't move. Luke watched through the window as they walked into a convenience store up the block.

"Just like old times, huh?" Jeremy said.

Luke blinked. Old times? Something from when they were kids? He had no idea. "Sure. So what are—" Luke almost said *you and I* but changed his mind. "What am I doing here?"

"It's a little complicated. Sergei's going to call me when he needs you."

They sat quietly, staring out their separate sides. No one had yelled. Natalya hadn't used her interrogation skills to probe anything about uncrossing. It might all be fine. A great way to handle that would be to leave it alone, then, but something—an anxious itch to confirm it was truly all right, or a congenital inability to let anything settle at good enough—made Luke turn and say, "About the other day—" just as Jeremy started, "I just wanted to say—"

Jeremy pressed his lips together and nodded Luke on.

Luke gave it one more second to be sure and launched into the most uncomfortable apology he'd ever given. "I guess I broke some sort of magic down there, huh? A spell or something?"

Jeremy nodded slowly.

"I just wanted to say I didn't mean to," Luke said. "It was an accident. I wasn't prying."

The interest dropped away from Jeremy's face like a falling stone; the little prince was bored again. "Okay. It was probably one of Alexei's bindings. He has a bunch on all of us."

Luke's jaw dropped before he could control his face. Jeremy's eyebrow went up.

"I thought Alexei's bindings were a big deal," Luke said. He *knew* they were a big deal, the foundation on which the Kovrov family built their power, even though nobody understood how they worked and Alexei didn't explain. They kept you safe or they kept you trapped—he showed up to help just as something was going wrong. He made them with his own blood, a magic so old and arcane it made Luke queasy.

"They are a special power," Jeremy said. "But why wouldn't he use it to keep his family safe?"

Luke used a special power to keep his family safe, too, but he didn't trap them inside layers of blood magic to do it. All he said was, "Right."

Jeremy squinted at his face. "What?"

Luke shook his head tightly.

"Oh my god, *what*? Do you have a problem with Alexei?"

Luke's heart skidded in his chest. "What? No, no. I just—" He stopped and wiped a hand over his face, trying to rub off whatever too-honest expression was there.

Jeremy turned back to the window. "Whatever. It's fine."

He didn't sound fine. Luke gnawed on the pad of his

thumb, urges to *fix it* and *stop fucking talking* battling inside him. The air conditioning in the car was losing its battle against the sun, heat closing Luke's collar around his throat. He definitely should not sit in a stuffy car and argue theories of magic with this odd little prince. Luke got along fine with most everybody he met, but the one person he needed to work with all summer—whose family sent his parents most of their income—was the one person he kept insulting on accident. "I'm just not used to it. Bindings. Blood magic. I'll catch up."

"Blood magic isn't any different than using fingernails or hair," Jeremy said. "It makes the intention real."

"There are lots of ways to set an intention. What about your lights? That was intense, and you didn't bleed for it. It doesn't have to work like this—" Luke froze. He'd made his father's gesture to emphasize a point, tapping his cupped fingers against an imaginary table, as Jeremy turned to argue, and caught his fingers against Jeremy's palm. It wasn't a story about blood magic—it was a hand, warm and real. Luke snatched his own hand away, and Jeremy's head snapped up, brown eyes as wide as a startled animal's.

It was a lot like how he'd looked in the warehouse, when Luke was asking why Jeremy was a Kovrov at all.

"My bad." Luke gestured around the car, implying impossible closeness, although it was almost as big as his bedroom.

Jeremy ignored that. "Magic always has a cost."

"You're right. I don't even know why I'm arguing. I mean, I started this conversation in the first place to apologize." Luke laughed. It was essentially a fake laugh, but Luke's fake laugh was pretty good. He had a big mouth, so he opened it and people went along.

It worked—Jeremy smiled.

"If there's anything I should do to fix it, or anything I need to stay away from, let me know," Luke said. "And that's it, for real."

Jeremy shrugged. "I have to talk to Alexei. He can repair it if he wants to. I'll let you know if he says anything."

He was going to tell. Luke had no right to be disappointed. "Sorry again, for the mess."

Jeremy sighed, exasperated. "You don't have to keep apologizing to me. I'm not trying to get you in trouble or whatever. If that's all you're worried about, you don't have to be."

It was both what Luke wanted to hear and not how he wanted to hear it—Jeremy was speaking out the window again, arms tight across his chest and face flushed.

But before Luke could respond, Jeremy's phone beeped. "That's us."

He led the way into a little bodega. The lights were off, but more sunlight should have seeped into the room than did. Luke choked on a nauseating smell, like opening a bag of moldy bread—he glanced at Jeremy and found him calm and cheerful. The smell wasn't really there, but some nasty mojo was slinking through the room. He threw his arm in front of Jeremy's chest, stopping him from striding into the sludge— Jeremy stared down at his arm and back up at Luke with a mix of humor and horror, and Luke pulled it back.

This was a real job, no unloading boxes. Sergei, Alexei, and Natalya stood in the dark with a couple, a woman in her twenties and a slightly older man. Natalya gestured toward them. "Luke! Come meet Mr. and Mrs. Eyal."

Luke shook their hands. Mr. Eyal's grip was firm, too enthusiastic, and Mrs. Eyal hung on a second too long, like Luke's hand was lifting her from drowning.

"The finest herb farmers in the tristate," Alexei said. Growing herbs for magic was harder than growing herbs for food, with hundreds of arcane rules about moon and star cycles, watering and harvesting routines, precious soils, and grotesque fertilizers. It was difficult anywhere and almost impossible in the middle of New York City. "It appears someone is envious of our close relationship…"

"And crossed them," Luke finished. "Is that the moldy feeling?"

Impressed surprise scattered across their faces. "Mold." Mrs. Eyal's voice was choked. "On everything, all the plants, and…" She took a shuddering breath.

"Yeah, I can tell." Luke glared around the ceiling and corners. "I'll hunt it down for you." Mrs. Eyal took Luke's elbow. "Come. I'll show you."

She led him through one storeroom, filled with stacks of Coke and crackers, and into another with orderly rows of tables under heat lamps sitting cool and dark. Piles of empty containers reeked of bleach, but the moldy feeling still stuck in the roof of Luke's mouth.

A little girl, four or five, sat at a plastic Playskool table, coloring with her tongue between her teeth in concentration. She had thick, dark curls and black, smeary fractals of something like mold growing down her arms and up her neck. Luke took a reeling step back, and behind him, Natalya made a birdlike noise in her throat.

The girl's eyes filled with tears, and Mrs. Eyal sighed heavily. Luke froze in place, his chest heaving hard—he had not expected a hurt kid. They had time to talk about text flirting but not to warn him there was a kid? He turned to Sergei and Alexei, but Sergei was glaring at the floor, arms crossed, and Alexei just nodded at him. It was Jeremy, hanging at the back of their group, who stepped toward the little girl.

"Hey, Aviva. You remember me?" Jeremy crouched down next to her table, and she nearly leaped out of her seat, clapping her hands. Luke's chest eased, and he took a deep, calm breath.

Jeremy glanced up at Luke with an encouraging smile. They were working together again, like when he'd handled the protection spell so Luke could burn those mojo bags. He was like a trick painting that changed as you moved—the bored little prince from the car was gone, and he was the only one in the crowded room who would really help Luke get this job done.

Jeremy put his hands to his mouth and blew, opening a sphere of carnation-pink light. Aviva slapped it like a bubble, and it burst. He made her another, mint green. The light danced pastel over Aviva's round face and Jeremy's concentrating one, and it cut through the nauseating mold with a spear like a high, clear note of music.

Luke shook off and got to work, turning away from that light-sound vibe and toward the moldy one. The room was so thick with menace it was hard to find the source, like trying to untangle old Christmas lights, and Luke had an unusually crowded and attentive audience yanking at his attention.

The only ripples of anything different came from Jeremy's witchlights. They had a thread of protective magic in them, or just cut through the gloom. They were as calming as a cool hand.

"Kovrov," Luke said, and both Sergei and Alexei turned to him. "Ko—Hey, Jeremy."

Jeremy looked up.

"Could I have one of those?" Luke asked.

Jeremy nodded. His chest lifted with a big breath, and he made Luke a larger, bright white globe of light, waving it gently forward. It seared through the mold as it traveled and made a clean bell around Luke. "Perfect. Thanks."

Jeremy's lips quirked, and he turned back to the little girl as she tugged on his arm. Luke walked a circle around the room, the light tailing him. It cleared the air around a plume of the moldy smell, spilling out of the air conditioning vent.

Luke dragged over a step stool and pulled the grate off. He nudged the light in and revealed the burlap bag, curled small and innocent as a mouse. Luke smiled as he grabbed it and jumped down.

He closed his eyes and held the bag in front of his chest, bidding the moldy smell gone. It was easy to do with the light hovering next to him. The bag shriveled in his palm, crumpling like an animal whose bones had disappeared, and a soft chorus of *ah*s and gasps lifted from the adults by the door.

They were wrong. Luke kept his eyes closed, squeezing, as he walked—across the room, at the baseboards, just there. A second plume of the sick-sweet smell.

"Ha." Luke crouched to pull the board away from the wall with a *pop* and a puff of dust. Another bag had been tucked back there. "Got you," he said and brandished it toward Sergei and Alexei.

This bag was the true trick, hidden better so that the average magician might find the first one but fail to break the spell. Luke, though, was no average magician. He jumped up, tossing the bag and catching it again, grinning to the group.

Natalya and Alexei made matching tennis claps, ironic in a gentle way, like they just didn't know how to be sincere, but Mrs. Eyal pulled her hands together under her chin. The room was silent behind Luke—he checked and found Jeremy watching, eyes round, even as the girl tugged on his shirt for more bubbles.

Luke stood. "This is it, these two. I'll just burn some incense, and then I can destroy these at home?"

Alexei nodded, and Natalya went to find him supplies. Luke nudged the light back toward Jeremy and Aviva. "Thanks."

Jeremy nodded. He was so quiet in the group—he barely opened his mouth, not even to say *yes* or *thank you*.

Luke had done his job perfectly and even brought the fight in the car to a decent conclusion. If he could just figure out how to cure the hurt he'd caused, he'd have three straight wins.

Luke was staring. He looked away when Aviva clapped her hands through the ball of light, casting Jeremy's face back into shadow.

Chapter Nine

The thin, curling smoke of incense filled the room. Jeremy loved that smell—it reminded him of church, and maybe it was obvious, but cleansings always made him feel so *clean*. Sitting with Aviva, finally being able to do something he was good at, made the boiling discomfort and embarrassment Jeremy had been feeling since the car—since he'd dropped that jar and splashed himself with curdled blood—settle some. Aviva had more use for him than anyone else did, and she was more pleasant than most of them, too.

She dropped her head against Jeremy's shoulder and shut her eyes, sighing, as the black smudges covering her face and arms started to fade. "Sergei," he said, voice empty, and more clearly, "Look!"

Mrs. Eyal screamed and pulled Aviva up from Jeremy's arms. She pushed at the neck of her dress, checking her skin, and started to cry into Aviva's hair. Alexei went to her, and Sergei said something to Mr. Eyal. Jeremy got out of the way, sidling around the edge of the room, and came to Luke's side. Luke watched it all with his arms crossed and the barest smile on his face.

While Alexei repaired the binding, Luke went outside to call his sister. Jeremy meant to give him his privacy, but as soon as he walked away, Alexei caught Jeremy's eye and waved his hand *shoo*.

Jeremy stopped in the closed bodega. Luke stood outside, back to the window, and the dry smoke of Alexei's spell wafted from the other room. Alexei's bindings wove a web, and he, in the center, felt every twinge the way a spider feels her web catching flies. That was a bad metaphor, because it made it sound like an evil, stalking thing, and it wasn't— it only meant that he knew what was happening, when his people were in trouble or pain. It took a lot out of him, too. His mind stretched in a hundred directions all the time, and the people he'd bound to him haunted his dreams.

Alexei always said the Kovrovs worked hard for their people, and so they asked for very reasonable things in return: loyalty, compensation, occasional favors. He said the people they helped—he called it *helping*—were grateful. Jeremy had never questioned that, never had reason to believe otherwise.

Alexei didn't like people to know how vulnerable binding made him, how open to the world, so he kept it mysterious and swanned around in his Bentley. But even though Jeremy did know some of his brother's secrets, now that he could see things through Luke's eyes, there was a lot that looked awful. How even the sick little girl had been wearing a neat dress and hair bow, and Sergei hadn't even put on a real shirt.

And Luke seemed actually afraid of Jeremy. Every time a conversation turned real, he stopped himself and made a big show of deferential manners. He acted like Jeremy was a live grenade or—Jeremy gave in to a flash of self-indulgent bitterness—a spoiled prince who would throw a tantrum if he said one wrong word. Jeremy would never, but apparently the Kovrov name ran ahead of him and he was guilty until he could prove otherwise.

He *did* still have to talk to Alexei about the binding Luke had broken, whatever protection Alexei had built for him. He just had to figure out how to explain, that was all. Then Alexei would seal up whatever crack Luke had made by coming a little closer, and the wall would slam down between them again. Jeremy's chest hurt to think about it, but Alexei wouldn't have built the binding in the first place if it wasn't for the best.

Jeremy grabbed two purple Gatorades and left a ten on the register. When Luke pocketed his phone, Jeremy joined him outside. "Here."

Luke took a bottle slowly.

"I paid for it," Jeremy added.

"I know," Luke said, but he twisted the top off much faster and took a drink.

Jeremy couldn't figure out what to say next (*that was incredible—you are incredible*) so he kept quiet and watched a wine bar doing brisk business across the street. Luke tilted his Gatorade toward Jeremy. "Good job with the kid in there. Cheers."

"You, too." Shyness trapped Jeremy so tight he had to push his arm forward to tap his bottle against Luke's. One little compliment warmed him more deeply than all that fighting in the car had frozen him. He kept swinging like a boomerang, matching his mood to the last thing Luke had said, but knowing he was ridiculous only made him blush hotter.

Luke was probably just saying it because he'd been rude earlier, or to fill the quiet, not because Jeremy had done anything impressive. Occupying Aviva was a tiny help. For years, Alexei had been wooing the Eyals to exclusive Kovrov service. Freelancing among the different families was lucrative but dangerous—what Alexei offered, what made the Kovrov network unique, was protection. They'd said yes, taken a binding, turned down other buyers.

And then everything had gone wrong, peculiar molds growing like cancers over everything they owned. Alexei had promised to protect those people but had ruined their lives. Then again, Luke was only there to fix it because Alexei had called for him—oh, Jeremy was too confused. It was over. Luke was wearing a smile that might have encompassed Jeremy, and that was good enough.

"Are you going to burn those next?" Jeremy asked.

"Yeah. I was telling Camille. She'll want to take a look first."

"She builds curse bags, too?"

"What?" Luke said sharply. "No, of course not. She wouldn't do that."

"Oh. I thought, because she was so interested—"

"There's a big difference between being interested in how something works and going after somebody's kids."

Jeremy's whole body closed up, tight in his throat and chest and jaw. How was it even possible to be this bad at talking? If everybody else in the world was as bad at it as Jeremy, all of humanity would have been exploded off the planet centuries ago, and at least Jeremy wouldn't have to endure always, always ruining every conversation. Through his clenched jaw, he said, "Obviously, I know that. I was just *asking.*"

A wave of laughter from the wine bar washed across the street. When it faded, Luke said, "Right. My bad, I don't know why I keep—it was a mess in there. Couldn't you feel the, the—" Luke mimed something scraping down his neck. "Evil?"

Jeremy shook his head. "I believe you. But no, I couldn't feel it."

"Right. Well, it was bad."

"It wasn't our fault. We came here to *stop* it."

"I know," Luke said, as if he didn't think of it that way at all.

Jeremy closed his eyes, tight against his frustration. He had to decide which would hurt more: having these miserable, awkward conversations with Luke all summer, or asking Alexei to stop pushing them together. Alexei would be so disappointed. But Jeremy was hopeless it would get better— he always imagined that the next, or the next, or the next conversation he'd know what to say, and it never happened.

Luke cleared his throat. "I guess this is a bad time to ask you for a favor."

Jeremy started. "What?"

"I was going to see if you wouldn't mind helping us burn these again." Luke gave him another lopsided smile. "This is some bad mojo, and double, too. We could use your angel."

Jeremy's heart stopped beating. That was bad. You died if that happened.

"Aw, come on, man." Luke brought his smile closer and waved at his own face. "You can't stay mad. I'm doing the charm. Come help us."

Jeremy managed a nod as the lights clicked on in the store behind them.

Luke took out his phone again. "Cool. I'll give Camille a heads up. I bet Dad has more dumplings in the freezer."

"What?" Alexei said, as the crew spilled out onto the sidewalk. "Why do we get dumplings?"

"Just me!" Jeremy stuck out his tongue. "I'm going to help him burn the bags."

"Outstanding." Alexei took his giving-a-speech stance, squaring his enormous shoulders and lifting his nose. Most of the time it was hilarious, but Alexei took it seriously, and anticipation was a tight fist in Jeremy's chest. "Great work today. I'm very proud of both of you."

"Thank you, sir," Luke said, and averted his eyes politely as Alexei took out his wallet. Jeremy rubbed a fist over his giddy smile. They *had* done a good job—Luke had done a good job. A little binding paled in comparison to saving a whole family. They would keep him around, and Jeremy would show him what was past the name.

Chapter Ten

Luke got through the rest of the afternoon without any more fights, though Jeremy stayed weirdly quiet throughout Camille's investigation of the mojo bags, his prayers, and Luke's ritual. The best part of the afternoon was the wad of cash Alexei threw at Luke.

He used some of it to buy his family dinner, two whole chickens and a mess of sides from the grill up the street. Since the food was Luke's treat, Helene bought a bottle of wine. Yuri got out the building keys and took them up to the roof, spreading out a sheet next to the gently humming HVAC unit. Camille pulled some music up on her phone.

And dinner was a party. Their roof didn't have a spectacular view of the city or anything, but they got a lot of sky, painted in soft blues and buttery peaches by the setting sun. That was the light of the Kovrovs' favor: a little extra money, and a great story.

Luke told his broadly, with a lot of campfire-horror detail around the mold in the Eyals' store, how it had smelled and tasted and felt slimy against his skin. There was a lot to lie about, though: he wasn't going to tell his parents about fighting with Jeremy Kovrov, pestering him with questions he knew not to ask. He was ashamed of his reflexive disgust at the little girl's affliction, so he couldn't explain how remarkable Jeremy had been with her.

He was still trying to figure Jeremy out. Once he'd caught the vibe of the light Jeremy made, he had it, and he could study it at his leisure. It was distinct from what he thought of as the Kovrov vibe, a low, staticky hum that all the Kovrovs shared—both swirled around Jeremy, two notes that didn't harmonize. The higher tone rose when he did magic, and maybe when he got mad at Luke, but settled down when he was quiet. Something about it, the two separate pieces jangling for space on one person, wasn't right. It was an infernal problem and also not Luke's problem at all. He'd already asked about something that wasn't his business and was lucky he hadn't gotten fired or worse.

So he discarded all those details and told a story where he was a hero—the light rose as the air cleared, the little girl's skin washed clean—and Luke nodded as his family applauded.

"That sounds like the old days." Helene elbowed Yuri in the side.

He guffawed. "We didn't do much *un*crossing during the old days."

She smacked his chest lightly, and they leaned into each other, laughing together at nothing particularly funny. The wine bottle lay on its side, and behind them, Camille made wide, delighted eyes and mouthed, "They're trashed."

She leaned forward, propping her chin on her hand. "What did you do in the good old days?"

Helene shook her head. "Y'all don't know what it was like. Nowadays everyone has their territory. Everyone knows who they work for. Back in the day, it was a dogfight. You were playing defense every time you left the house. And you know, the best defense is a good offense," she added slyly, and dissolved into giggles again.

"You mean the best uncrossing is crossing the other guy first," Camille said, turning her nose up at Luke.

He ignored her. "What changed?"

Yuri waved toward the city. "After all the Malcolm business I told you about, things settled down. There's a shake-up every twenty, twenty-five years or so—the one before the Malcolm war was in the seventies, when the Zhangs took Manhattan from the Damianis. Find someone to tell you *that* story."

Camille sat up straighter. "Then aren't we about due? The Malcolm war was about twenty years ago."

"Why would you want a war?" Luke snapped.

Helene intervened, voice soothing. "Nobody wants a war. We're just telling old stories."

Luke nodded, but he hadn't been telling old stories. He'd been talking about today. The second attack in a couple weeks on Kovrov associates, if that's what those mojo bags from the family lunch had been. He should ask for more details about the Malcolm war—

He stopped his thoughts and wiped a hand down his face, exasperated. No, no more questions. He wasn't heading trouble off with this foolishness; he was causing it.

Distracted, Luke pulled out his phone and turned it over in his hands. He opened his text messages—he'd never written back either way about his schedule, and Max hadn't said anything else. Torn between wanting to reply that he was home and free, or that he was actually busy and no, he couldn't see Max, he never wrote back.

His phone vibrated on his chest a few minutes before one a.m. anyway. He was awake and waiting. He got up before he answered, moving quietly and crossing his fingers his parents were still sleeping off that bottle of wine.

"One second," he said into the phone.

Max mumbled something unintelligible. Luke's heart sank.

Max waited outside under the alley's single light, catching it like an old painting on his yellow hair and the two round spots of pink high on his cheeks.

"Don't you look like a picture?" Luke paused a beat. "On missing person posters all over Westchester." He waited out of Max's reach. The night alley still smelled like the day's heat, baking trash and asphalt.

Max made a weak noise and a lot of loopy movement. "You think you're so tough. Couple years, your family won't even afford to live here."

That was true. Sort of. It wouldn't take a couple of years, if it happened. Or it wouldn't happen, but only because now Luke was getting in deep with the Kovrovs. He stayed quiet for too long, and Max said, "That was mean, wasn't it?"

"How was your date?"

"Grim," Max drawled. "Maybe I should go out with you instead. Come here and let me be nice to you."

"How drunk are you?"

Max's hand tottered *so-so*. "Six out of ten." He reached over with the hand, but he slumped against the wall. "Don't be mad at me. I'm sorry."

"You are not," Luke said, but he lifted his hand and put it inside Max's anyway. Max started to prop himself off the wall, but Luke pushed him back, the littlest bit mean about it, and Max bit him on the chin, a little meaner.

The brick under Luke's hands remembered the sun, warmer than the air, but Max's skin was cool. His second virtue was beauty—he was a pleasure to look at, symmetrical and softly made. His eyes were a misty, mossy green you never saw in the city, where everything was gray or crayon-bright or dingy yellow.

Luke looked now. Once they went inside, he wasn't going to be able to turn any lights on. This was probably going to be his favorite part of the night.

Max wanted his kiss. He didn't lean up, but he parted his lips, wafting something rummy. When Luke ran his thumb over Max's lip, Max nodded heavily into his hand.

"Six, huh?" Luke said.

"Maybe you're too sober. Maybe that's been the problem the whole time." Max moved his arms around Luke's body and pulled.

"Maybe." Luke dropped his head and pressed his mouth over Max's slack one. Max's tension dropped at once, his body and his kiss melting into Luke's, and Luke rolled his shoulders down and let go, too. It was easy to let his scattered thoughts pitch higher and higher into static. If he closed his eyes, Max could be anyone.

The best place to make noise was the store, so that's where they went. The metal grates pulled over the windows let a few narrow stripes of the orange glare of streetlights into the dark.

Luke hoisted Max onto the counter instead of holding him up. He ran his hands up and down Max's back, which made Max drop his head and throw his arms around Luke's neck, sighing musically. It tore the armor off Luke's wanting.

"What do you want to do?" Luke was always careful to ask. Sometimes Max started without replying; sometimes he answered with alarming clarity; sometimes he said *surprise me*. Sometimes he fell asleep. Luke had started to think that was happening when Max sighed again and said, "Whatever."

Drunk, cranky Max was hard to handle, but later, when he fell asleep in Luke's arms, he was so sweet it ached. He usually snuck himself out early, so Luke was disoriented to wake up hot and crowded against his bedroom wall. "Hey."

He reached across Max's body for his phone. "Hey, it's after nine."

"No." Max turned into Luke's chest.

Luke gave himself ten seconds to feel it, Max's shoulders in his arm and breath falling on his chest. Then he noticed how terrible Max smelled, sweat and stale booze.

"Yes. Wake up. Nine. I have to get ready for work." He pinched down Max's arm until Max opened his eyes and groaned.

"How did I...?" Max trailed off into swearing and sighing. "I might as well sleep."

"No, hey." Luke slid a hand under the covers and kept pinching down Max's side and hip.

The door to Luke's room flew open, and Max squealed, huddling under the pillow. "Why hello," Camille sang. "Good morning! I thought I heard your beautiful voices." She gave Luke two cups of coffee and her prissiest glare. "Mom says to fix this or next time she will."

She slammed the door, but Max didn't move.

"Camille brought you coffee." Luke sipped one and waited.

Max sat up slowly, like he was still sleepy or too hungover or maybe like he was afraid of what came next. Luke handed over the coffee and used his free hand to bring some order to Max's hair.

He leaned into the touch like a little cat, inhaling the scent of his coffee without drinking. "That feels good."

"Do you ever want more?" Luke asked.

Max sighed. He leaned back against Luke's shoulder, and Luke's heart jumped, but Max lifted himself up quickly. "More of what?"

Luke couldn't say *of me* to prickly, hungover Max. "All of it. Anything. More than *whatever*." The words tasted bitter.

Max huffed. "No. And neither do you."

"I don't?"

"No. You just like having someone to impress with your magic."

Luke wasn't sure. "Sure I do."

Max got up and rummaged around the floor.

Luke touched the now-cool spot on his shoulder, where Max's head had been. "And I think you're"—*beautiful, gorgeous what's the*—"cute. You don't think that's enough to go on, magic and chemistry?"

Max pulled on his underwear, his jeans, and turned to Luke, face tight and expectant.

"You don't have to drink so much," Luke said.

Max lifted his eyebrows and nodded, like *yeah, there it is*, and took his shirt from the floor. He had bruised purple circles under his eyes and a red hickey under his jaw, and he was still beautiful. He was all sand and cream in the morning light, making elegant, limpid angles as he dug through his stuff. He twisted pouty shapes with his lips, like he was talking about how pathetic Luke was to an invisible person in the room.

"You don't," Luke said.

"You're right," Max snapped. "I don't. But I want to. I didn't come here for an intervention. That isn't what this is about, you and me."

"What's it about, then?"

"Fun. Convenience. You know that. It *is* fun."

"It isn't," Luke said, so vehemently Max took a step back. Luke's heart kicked his chest, running him hot all over. Out loud, those words sounded awfully true.

"You weren't complaining last—"

"You were a mess—"

"Not too—"

"I shouldn't even—"

"Don't, then."

"Maybe I won't."

Max snatched his coffee off the windowsill and hid his face in it. Luke pulled the sheet higher over himself. If Max was going to leave, he might as well go. Instead of telling him that, Luke took a deep breath and tried very hard to say something he wouldn't regret. "You're going to get hurt. I don't want that on my conscience."

"Yeah, it definitely sounds like you like me. That sounds like it would go great."

"Max. Come on."

He was right, though. When Luke thought of Max, he thought of looking at him, or touching him, or the way he acted when he was desperate. When Max was happy, he was shallow and vicious and always halfway out the door, and Luke sort of hated him. It was terrible to understand, and worse that Max had already known.

Max was quiet for a long time. "I think it's cool, how you save people. But I never asked you for anything else." He put his coffee back down on the windowsill with a sigh and tossed a wave to him. "Bye, Luke."

Chapter Eleven

Luke gave himself permission to cry in the shower, but nothing happened. He'd always figured he'd lose Max in a blowout fight or a bad night in a hospital, not a careful, almost kind talk on a bright Sunday morning. Good for them, those mature boys who'd broken up. It didn't feel like Luke was one of them.

Back in his room, his phone buzzed on the bed. *Max?*

He was losing it. Of course, it was only Jeremy, with a work schedule.

Can you do protection bags? I have to make eighty tomorrow and I could use the help.

Then Thursday Alexei needs his place cleansed and I told him you should do it.

So Thursday is definitely and tomorrow is only if you can.

Luke laughed to himself at Jeremy's texts, so detailed

and neatly punctuated, as he walked into the kitchen. He replied: *Free both days.*

"I swear to god, are you already texting him again?" Camille said.

She sat at the table with Yuri, who peered over his newspaper. In addition to working in the family store and supering the apartment building upstairs, Yuri sold magic on commission for the Kovrovs. He spent every morning looking for coincidences and connections that might lead to clients. He went online, too, but he started with the *New York Times* religiously.

Luke waved the phone. "Jeremy Kovrov. About work."

Camille pointed two fingers between her eyes and Luke's.

"Work!" he insisted.

"Lukonya," Yuri said, stone-faced. A knot slid down Luke's stomach. He had expected yelling, but this was so much worse. Camille slipped away down the stairs.

"I stopped it, all right?" Luke said. "He won't come around anymore."

Yuri tapped the table, and Luke sat down. "You deserve to be treated with respect."

Luke hid in his coffee. Yuri loved to talk about respect. It meant all kinds of things—kindness, integrity, worth, honor. He could have used any of those words, but he always said *respect.*

"I believe you'll earn that respect if you treat others with the respect they deserve," Yuri said.

Luke started to burn—his face, his spine. "Max didn't want anything serious. It doesn't always have to be a whole relationship."

"I won't hear that. What kind of man are you going to be, hmm?"

Luke sat and ached while his dad flipped through the paper. He was saved by his buzzing phone. Jeremy: *Great, 10 tomorrow at Sergei's.*

"Jeremy says I've got Kovrovs tomorrow at 10," Luke said.

Yuri frowned. "How is he related to the Kovrovs, anyway?"

Luke studied him before answering. The confusion, the dawning question. It was the broken binding, jostling the idea loose in Yuri's head.

"I asked Jeremy that the other day. He said he's their brother. Ivan adopted him when Sergei and Alexei were teenagers." He probably shouldn't have shared that. After Alexei got around to fixing the binding, Yuri would either know a secret or Alexei would go digging around in his brain to take it out.

"Really? How odd." Yuri's voice was distant. "Well, I missed a lot when you and Camille were little babies."

"Right," Luke said, though it wasn't that. It wasn't his business how Alexei monitored—or didn't—the bindings he made, but he did wonder if it might have been his own power making this one stay broken. Perhaps Alexei had tried to rebuild it, but Luke was stronger, or he had moved so subtly to unwind the binding that Alexei hadn't perceived it. "That's probably it. I'll go see if Mom needs help in the store."

He found her, and an unexpected crowd, in the back room. He stopped on the stairs. "You got the whole crew here."

Helene, Camille, and Luke's best friends, the Wesleys, sat around the big table. Helene worked busily over a group of poppets, pausing to cut a glance at Luke. Camille had a plastic cup of gold-white horchata and Short Wes draped his arm on the back of her chair.

At once, she said, "Short Wes brought me horchata!" and Straight Wesley said, "Wes wanted to flirt with the hurricane."

The   hurricane—that   was   Camille—shimmied

contentedly. Helene snapped a stalk of sage in half.

"Man, I don't get horchata?" Luke pulled out a chair and sat, realizing his mistake too late.

Short Wes gave him a look both gleeful and regretful, his face asking, *Why do you make me hurt you?* as he said, "I think Max is getting you one."

Helene snapped the sage again. Straight Wesley muffled a grin by rolling it into his lips, and Camille looked innocently at the ceiling, taking a noisy sip.

Luke drummed his fingers on the table and, twice as decisively as he felt, said, "Not anymore. It's over."

Short Wes made a skeptical sound.

"See? I knew you'd do the right thing. Even when you were a baby, give you some space and you'd make the right decision." Helene sounded happier and tucked the last scrap of abused sage inside a poppet.

Luke shut his eyes. *Space*, in this case, had meant six months and a pile of hurt, not an hour to choose his own bedtime. He knew why it was hard to talk shit with Max, not only because Max was needle-mean, a white boy from a nice suburb who didn't take anything seriously. It was because, even if Max had played by the rules, Luke wasn't looking for a game from someone he kissed. He loved playing conversation-roulette with his friends, and even his family, but the hope of intimacy was that maybe he'd get to put those weapons down. He'd never felt calm with Max. It was right to end it.

It was Max who had done the right thing.

No, it was Luke. Or, it was Luke, too. Upstairs, his father had asked a question, and downstairs, his mother had answered it. And now he had a job to do.

He pointed to the poppets. "What's that about?"

She waved a hand at the Wesleys. "These two. Look at them."

Luke looked at them. They seemed normal to him. He nodded to Straight Wesley. "Looking good."

Straight Wesley rubbed a hand over the back of his head, his fade a little tighter than usual. "Thanks, man."

Helene hmphed and dropped two poppets in front of Luke. "Seal those for your friends."

Luke brought one tiny doll to his forehead, hit with the cherry-pie-and-dirt smell of patchouli. He moved his lips but was too exposed, with the Wesleys sitting right there, to say the words out loud: *Defend Short Wesley. Defend Wes. Defend Wes.*

He sealed the second doll for Straight Wesley and handed them both over. "Keep track of those," Helene said. "Get Luke to burn them when they get ratty. Don't throw them out."

They *yes, ma'am*ed, and Helene dropped a third doll in front of Luke. "That one's for you."

It was a little too dense for its weight, but not heavy. The mojo had a warm vibe, like his mother's hand on the back of his head.

Camille finished her horchata with a slurp and dropped the cup in Short Wes's lap. "I'm going to open up."

Short Wes followed her out of the room, and Straight Wesley clapped Luke's hand and hugged Helene before he left. Luke sank in his chair, the poppet solid in his pocket. He traced its contours through the fabric with his thumb, Max's words spinning in his head. *I never asked you for anything else.*

Another thought cut the thread, his earlier question popping up with its own answer. Jeremy had said he needed to talk to Alexei, to explain what had happened so that Alexei could repair the binding. It had been days—he'd seen Alexei yesterday afternoon—but he hadn't done it yet.

Helene stopped on the stairs. "Honey? Are you going to

sit there all day?"

He sat up. "Sorry, Mom." It wasn't his problem. He could just leave it alone. "Hey, do you know how Jeremy is related to the Kovrovs?"

"He's a cousin or—no, wait." Her expression clouded. "That can't be right."

It played out on her face, too, the empty space where a secret had hidden filling up with confusion. Jeremy knew that secret was vulnerable and had chosen to leave it exposed. "He's their brother," Luke said. "Adopted. It seems like there's something weird about it."

Everything about it was weird. If there was a good reason to adopt a child and then go through a whole magical hassle to hide him, Luke couldn't think of it. Jeremy was always trotting around after Sergei and Alexei—he didn't even go to school. He prickled at the simplest questions and didn't talk in company.

"Those people." Helene shrugged and moved up the stairs. "Weird is the least of it."

Luke nodded in the empty room. He turned the memory of the fight in the car to a new angle: Jeremy's tightly crossed arms and flushed face. He hadn't been pissed—he'd been afraid. What had he said? *If that's all you're worried about...*

A strange way to say it, unless there was something else he wanted Luke to worry about. Something was wrong.

And he had left the clues for Luke to find them.

Chapter Twelve

Luke sat with Jeremy at a pale wood coffee table in Sergei and Marta Kovrov's living room to build protection bags. They made an assembly line, Luke filling bags with juniper and soap and Jeremy tying them off with his whispered prayers. It was sunny and cool, dotted with the kind of candles that didn't burn anything except money. Jeremy put some dark, confusing British show on a TV as big as a street mural, and laughed at it a lot, though Luke couldn't figure out the jokes.

Jeremy wore red track pants and a yellow T-shirt. It was possible that he would finish the outfit with something as horrible as shutter shades, or a vinyl children's backpack, if he had to leave the house. Sergei's sons ran in and out of the room, playing cops or soldiers, and Jeremy tackled them every time they got within arms' reach. Marta, a tall blonde in purple yoga pants, floated through with sodas and chips.

They were a happy family, and it seemed like Jeremy was a happy part of it. The shuttered, controlled boy from the car was gone. If he was in trouble, it was invisible.

But now that Luke wanted to ask, or tell him, or *help*, it

felt like a conspiracy that they weren't alone. As they were finishing their work, Sergei wandered in with a beer. "This shit again?"

Jeremy grinned up. "You don't have to watch it."

Sergei growled into his beer, and Jeremy laughed—giggled, even. The tattoo across Sergei's neck said *Marta*, which was a tribute to his lovely wife but also meant *war*.

"What's your problem, Melnyk?" Sergei asked.

Luke rearranged his scowl. "I don't get this show, either."

Jeremy gasped. "You could have *said*." He sounded genuinely pained. He tied off the last bag and whispered to it in Russian. "We're done anyway. Don't let me inflict *culture* on you anymore."

"This is just trash with accents," Sergei said.

Jeremy scoffed and handed him the remote. He packed up the finished bags, and Luke got up to help and took the dishes back into the kitchen.

Jeremy hovered behind, his voice small and unmistakably wistful. "I guess you're free to go."

"I could hang out." *Tell me, I can help.* "Do you have any big plans?"

Jeremy was looking at the floor. "Reading, maybe." He dragged his face up and grinned. "Maybe watch more TV that everyone *hates*. Come upstairs if you're staying, I can't anymore with these babies."

He led Luke through the living room, Sergei's eyes tracking them, and up three flights of stairs to the attic. Luke had to play off his short breath as Jeremy opened a door.

His room took up the whole front of the house, bright with sunshine from two deep bay windows and a skylight over the bed. There were clothes everywhere, and books and cords and half-full cups, the orange running shoes a glowing center in the mess. Luke caught a trace of the oniony, sweet smell that would have made his mom yell at him to clean his room.

Jeremy's unmade bed felt like getting away with something, though all it meant was Sergei kept different rules.

In the chaos, it took Luke a long second look to absorb what was on the shelves that lined the walls. Hundreds of the tiny lights Jeremy made in the warehouse paled in the full light of day. A dozen fish bowls made trickling sounds—an octopus the size of a tennis ball bobbed in the closest one. It sat next to a stack of slim Batman books, next to a tiny wooden marionette that stood without strings, next to a potted fern with pulsing purple veins.

"What is all this?"

"Party tricks," Jeremy said.

Luke turned, gaping. Jeremy sat on one of the windowsills, backlit, so he was all shadows and halo.

"You do this with your breath?"

Jeremy nodded. "Sometimes I make things out of clay or whatever and breathe them awake."

"This is incredible. This is some serious mojo." If Luke weren't seeing it all with his own eyes, he would have said it was the kind of thing people who didn't know anything about magic thought magicians could do.

"I guess. If you need anything totally useless, give me a call."

Luke shook his head.

Jeremy's shadowy shape shrugged. "You should see what Sergei can do."

Luke almost asked, but he changed his mind. Sergei could go straight to hell. Another shelf: a terrarium filled with neon pink and orange turtles the size of dimes, a boy-doll with a clockwork torso who swung his legs off the shelf like a child in a tall chair, a paperback book with a spine so worn with creases he couldn't read the title, a mason jar of glittering keys.

"I think the uncrossing thing is—" Jeremy cut himself

off. "I guess I already said that. It's cool, though."

Luke had rehearsed this, and he wasn't supposed to blurt out, "Let me help you," but that's what he did.

Jeremy froze. "Help me with what?"

"I know something's wrong." Luke sat on the corner of the bed. At an angle, he could see more of Jeremy's face, still and cautious. "And Alexei hasn't fixed that binding yet, because you haven't talked to him."

Jeremy winced. "I just haven't figured out how to tackle it. I keep expecting he'll bring it up and I won't have to."

"Is that all?"

Jeremy shrugged again and kept his shoulders up, curling in. "You said you weren't going to talk about it anymore."

"I know. My dad said not to go digging around in Kovrov secrets. If you tell me to drop it, I promise I will never ask you another nosy question again." Luke leaned closer and dropped his voice. "But if you're in trouble, and you want to tell me, I can help."

Jeremy blinked, his lips parting on an inhale, and blinked again, like he was trying to focus on a new distance. Luke made his face mild and patient, though his heart pounded, *Come on, come on.*

"It's not like that," Jeremy said. "I'm not in any danger." He pressed his arms across his stomach and avoided Luke's eyes. His sideways denial was a confirmation, and whatever was going on, he was terrified of it.

"What's it like?" Luke was already plotting his next move. Could he sneak something into the house? Or if he asked the right question, the way he broke that first binding, he could keep unwinding it. It was against the rules, but there were principles—like helping someone who had been hurt— that were more important than rules.

Jeremy started to laugh. Luke was so surprised it took him a double take to place the sound, to be sure Jeremy wasn't crying. "Oh, Luke. Look at you. It is not that big of a deal." Jeremy shook his head. "I'll tell you the truth if you promise that you'll believe me and keep it a secret and not do anything dramatic. Deal?"

"Deal." Luke was comfortably aware that he might be lying.

"Okay. It's a long story." Jeremy stood and walked to the center of the room, opening his arms like a narrator starting a play. "I am a firstborn."

Luke waited for details that didn't follow. "I'm sorry, I don't know what that means."

Jeremy deflated. "Way to ruin my reveal. You know, like, 'I'm so hungry, I'd give my firstborn child for a cheeseburger.' Then—" He opened a hand next to his face. "Nine months later, here I am."

Luke stared at him, smiling expectantly down as Luke unwrapped all his layers of understatement.

Had he—?

Then that meant—

Luke jumped up, shouting. "What? *What?* The Kovrovs do that?"

He hadn't been overreacting. It was worse than he'd thought, worse than he could have imagined. Jeremy lifted his palms, pushing the air in front of Luke's chest, and Luke sat back down, hunching into his arms and breathing hard through his nose. He could be of no help if Jeremy was scared of him, and he had to help.

"I told you," Jeremy said. "It's a long story."

Chapter Thirteen

Jeremy moved to the other side of his bed, shooting up a little prayer—*Please help me make him understand*—and sitting down against his pillow. Luke smoothed out the covers and stretched out on his belly to listen, his weight shifting the mattress under Jeremy's back. Oh, that was not what Jeremy had expected. Luke was so close, stretching out over Jeremy's bed—and he hardly seemed to notice. Like it, like Jeremy, was all just furniture.

Jeremy shut his eyes. This was a story to tell carefully. He thought, *Once upon a time*, and began.

"What you have to understand about the Kovrovs is that firstborns are a big deal. All the firstborn Kovrovs inherit this power, the binding. They can trade a little piece of themselves to hide things and protect them. You can imagine it like a spider's web—when Alexei put a binding on your place, he wove his web around it, and now he can feel that you're safe, or when someone is trying to threaten you. Depending on how he does it, he can make it more like a wall that keeps someone in or out, but that takes more out of him. Alexei says there was a magician like him in the court of Ivan the Terrible, but, you know, Alexei says a lot of things.

"They took this power everywhere. All over eastern Europe. All over the world. Every firstborn was another Kovrov who could follow a famine or a war or a lot of desperate people who wanted protecting. Are you following?"

"I'm following." Luke's face was iron. Jeremy hesitated. Most of the people in Jeremy's life already knew this story, had understood it before he did—and because of that, he'd never told anyone. Two poles stretched him between an untenable distance: how good it might feel to share this, to be finally known, and how horrible if Luke found it another reason to despise him and his family. This was a beginning, or it was the end.

He needed to reassure Luke or get some reassurance—he lifted one hand, like a touch might help, but it only twitched in the air before he pulled it back.

Luke's expression went softer. "You're fine. Take your time." He rolled his head onto one fist and lifted the other hand to nudge Jeremy's arm. That was close enough.

"My curse was laid on a girl named Maeve at the turn of the century," Jeremy said. "She was a first-generation Irish immigrant, and her family was hungry and sick. One of the Kovrov sons had made it here, too, following the wave of immigrants and building up another little kingdom in the empire. So Maeve made a contract with Ivan Kovrov's great-grandfather and offered her firstborn son in exchange for her family's health and safety.

"The contract says *son*, specifically. I don't know why, probably the old Kovrov thought boys were more important than girls. But it was lucky for her. She lived, and her parents and brothers, and she had three daughters, Moira, Siobhan, and Edna. We lose the family's trail there, but we assume they had daughters, and they had daughters. And so, it wasn't until about seventeen years ago that Maeve's descendants had their firstborn son."

"You," Luke said.

"Me. And I obviously do not remember, but apparently, Ivan was *pissed*. Because he didn't want that! What did he need with some stranger's baby? His wife had already left him, so it was just him and Alexei and Sergei. He tried to cancel it or get out of it but—the curse has consequences. We'll get to that part.

"Ivan died when I was four and passed the contract to Sergei in his will. I'm bound to him now." Jeremy lifted his bracelet-laden wrist. "This one?" He grabbed the fine metal chain and wiggled it up to show how it was smaller than his hand, stuck on his arm. "Sergei has the same one."

Luke took Jeremy's wrist, hand gripping firm, and pulled his arm over, frowning down at the bracelet. He brought it so close his breath heated the inside of Jeremy's arm.

Jeremy's own breath stopped. "What?"

Luke looked at his face again, eyes connecting, and let go. "Sometimes, with magicians, I can feel their vibes. There are two different ones that come off you. I couldn't figure it out, but it's that bracelet. It has its own vibe."

Jeremy scrambled to sit up straighter and move a little bit away from Luke, taking enough space to think more clearly. "Oh."

"What does it mean?"

Jeremy twisted it around his wrist. "It means I'm a Kovrov. Or belong with them, I guess. And every day at noon and midnight I have to be here, in Sergei's house."

Luke's eyes narrowed. "'Have to?' Or what?"

"Or I come back. Like—*pop!*—right back here. Once I'm inside I can't get out. The doors are like walls." Talking about it made him feel it, the house sealing closed around him. He pushed it away with a big sigh, and it caught all the junk he'd made and floated around the room with a metallic tinkling. Jeremy's face seared. Alexei said his tricks were a gift, balancing out his curse, but all they ever did was lay his feelings bare.

"So, that's my story." He clasped his hands in his lap. "I know it sounds bad. But Sergei is great. The best. I have a great life with him and Marta. He didn't ask for this, and he has tried everything you can think of to get us out of it, and he doesn't hurt me. Honestly, I want to live a normal life."

Luke had his chin in his hand, studying Jeremy's face like he could see through Jeremy's skin. "That's it?"

Jeremy's heart kicked up, slamming so hard it articulated each up and downbeat: *LI-ar, LI-ar.* He swallowed and wrapped an arm over his stomach. "Is that not enough?"

"No, I meant—you know, maybe Sergei hasn't tried everything I can think of." Luke smiled that loose, charming grin that was not any less effective because Jeremy could tell he did it on purpose. "You are talking to the hoodoo prince of the South Bronx right now. My mama says I'm touched by the hand of heaven."

Jeremy believed her. "I think everyone's mom tells them that."

Luke made his smile wider.

"Let me think about it," Jeremy said. "Don't go poking around."

"What would I poke around in?" Luke's voice was innocent, but his forehead knitted up and Jeremy could see him plotting.

"Luke! You promised."

Slowly, Luke nodded. "All right, I promised. Can I ask you a couple questions?"

Jeremy felt floaty around the shoulders, like he might drift up to the ceiling, from talking so much already. But there was still more to share, if Luke was interested. What he thought and how he coped and how he filled his lonely days. "Okay."

"Why didn't Ivan leave you to yourself? In his will?"

Oh. *Practical* questions. "They tried that when I was a toddler. Ivan signed my contract over to me, and I went catatonic. Sergei said it was really scary." Jeremy fidgeted at his bracelets, picking a loose thread. "It took them a couple of days to undo it, and they thought they weren't going to get me back."

Luke gawked, then whistled out slow. "Anything else like that ever happen?"

Jeremy nodded. "They tried all kinds of stuff when I was little. Different ways to burn the contract or break me and Sergei apart, and it—it never worked, and it always hurt."

Luke didn't whistle again, but he shook his head. His lips were full and smooth, and Jeremy wanted to touch them even when Luke wasn't lying in his bed pursing them. Jeremy shut his eyes. "It's fine. Honestly, it doesn't do that unless we mess with it. All I have to do is follow the rules."

"Noon and midnight?"

"Noon and midnight. During those hours I get sad sometimes, but that's just me." Jeremy blinked his eyes open—*who said that?*—and Luke was looking horrified again. "I don't know why I said that. Ask me something else."

Luke opened and closed his mouth before he found one: "How old is Sergei? Do the math for me."

"Sergei is almost thirty-one. He was fourteen when I was born, eighteen when Ivan died. Nineteen when he started dating Marta. They got serious fast."

"I bet. He found a girl who would look at his face, and he held on, right?"

"Marta picked him! She says it was love at first sight."

Luke made a wry face, like maybe that was less an endorsement of Sergei than a question about Marta. "Wait.

Why Sergei and not Alexei? Sergei was so young."

Jeremy didn't say, *I don't think Alexei wanted me.* He didn't remember what Alexei had gotten up to in his wild youth, and it was too much to explain now that he was more settled. Jeremy scratched his arm and thought of something else. "Ivan had a heart attack young. Honestly, I don't remember him, but I don't think he spent that much time thinking about anyone's well-being. It all worked out fine. I love Alexei, but can you imagine living with him?"

Luke didn't answer. His eyes lost focus, and he flipped over onto his back, bouncing the mattress again. It put more space between his body and Jeremy's, but he flopped his arms open, and one landed close to Jeremy's foot. Jeremy stared at the inches between them.

"That's so much energy," Luke said. "Where does it all come from?"

"What do you mean?"

"Energy. Magic is about channeling energy, the way we move electricity around through wires and water around through pipes. That's how my mom explains it. What does Alexei say?"

"Um." Alexei wasn't much for *how* or *why*, and it had never occurred to Jeremy to ask.

Luke barreled right on. "That would take so much energy. All this stuff you've made is practically nuclear. And—you said it moves you? Your whole body, through walls and everything?"

"I guess. It doesn't feel like moving through walls, more like disappearing and reappearing again."

"That is messed up," Luke said. "I don't know what to say. Is it all right if I say I'm sorry?"

A cold fist closed in Jeremy's stomach. Sergei always said apologies were meaningless, for weaklings and liars. "No."

"All right." Luke stopped talking and took his arm farther

away from Jeremy's leg, tapping his fingers thoughtfully against his other palm.

"It's a curse," Jeremy said. "You should know better than anybody. People have to live with stuff. I have to live with this."

Luke wiped a hand over his face. "Man, no. That's not what I do at all. And I've got to say this for my mom. You should say you're crossed, not cursed. *Curse* makes it sound hopeless."

Jeremy did feel crossed, like someone had taken him apart and put all his pieces back together at wrong angles. He liked Luke's different words and ways for magic, but it was all too much, too close. "Maybe in hoodoo you get crossed." He put on his heaviest, fakest Russian accent. "In Mother Russia, curse gets you."

Luke laughed more graciously than genuinely, but he hadn't called Jeremy a freak or a princess or drummed up a quick excuse to leave. And even if Jeremy was a liar, he'd also never told anyone so much truth at once. He couldn't figure out what came next, something secret or vulnerable or even more dangerous.

"I could show you," Jeremy said. "If you're interested."

"Show—?"

Jeremy wanted to curl up like a bug, but he was in now. "The disappearing. It's almost noon, we could go outside."

Luke rolled over to make eye contact, so close he dipped the mattress and tilted Jeremy's body. "You don't mind?"

Jeremy did mind. Or he should. He would have, under normal circumstances, but what had normal circumstances ever done for him? He rolled away from Luke and onto his feet. "Sure. Let's go."

Chapter Fourteen

Luke's brain skidded all frantic between questions and memories. Jeremy had been so shy as a kid—even now—hanging close to his brothers and too afraid to talk. But he'd been great with the Eyals' crossed little girl. Days later, Luke finally latched onto what had been so remarkable about that: he hadn't been afraid to touch her, had gotten right down on her level and hugged her mold-slicked shoulders. Jeremy lived in a horror Luke could barely get his brain around and had every right to be bitter or hateful. But it had made him good.

Something shadowy simmered in Luke's chest, and he checked himself after every breath to make sure that thing didn't become anger and point itself at Jeremy. Or at Sergei, who Jeremy checked for, stopping on the stairs, before he slipped them out the door like fugitives.

Jeremy peeked over his shoulder at the house's windows and pointed down the street. "Let's go... over here."

"Is Sergei going to get mad?"

"Oh, well. He'll be much happier if he doesn't have to

think about whether he's mad." Jeremy shot a little smile up at Luke. He had big eyes, a warm, reddish brown, more interesting on the second glance than the first. Luke looked away.

They stopped on the corner where the quiet side street met the busier avenue. Luke waved a hand at the bustle. "Won't people see?"

"Not really. They won't notice. You might get a little disoriented, but when you figure it out, come back to the house."

The not-quite-anger bubbled higher. "All right."

Luke checked the time on his phone: 11:56. He had time for another question, and an insistent conviction that all he needed was the right one, but he was getting too deep in his feelings to think. Before he could consider the wisdom of it, he asked, "Are you in touch with your birth family?"

Jeremy's body jumped like he'd been smacked. Lips tight, he shook his head. The *no* was bigger than the answer—he was rejecting the whole idea of the question. Quickly, Luke said, "So, homeschool, huh?"

Jeremy took a deep breath and nodded. "I went to kindergarten, and I've taken classes here and there. I can go to college, too, if I stay in the city, but, uh—" He slid his gaze up to the sky. "Honestly, I'm trying not to think about it yet. I have some time."

He kept saying *honestly*, the little liar. So he was talking around some secrets—fine, only it was hard to imagine what was worse than this. Luke nudged his arm. *Relax.* "My mom would trade us in a minute. They're all mad because I don't want to go to college, and they worked hard to save up."

Jeremy had the piercing look of a little bird, head tilting and elbows jutting out like wings as he put his hands on his hips. "Why don't you want to go to college?"

"I want to get EMT training, and do that or maybe be a

firefighter." Everyone was always fighting with Luke about this, and it brought out an old defensiveness. "It's a good job. I think I'd be good at it. If I got a job in the city, I could still do uncrossings for the store."

"That's perfect. You would be good at that." Jeremy's face went soft with a smile, and all the tension went out of Luke's body in response. His mind stopped whirring around in the background and stilled in the warmth of having this dream understood.

"The thing is, I wonder, when the paramedics get called, how often is it mojo? Something, like…"

Jeremy's smile didn't waver. "Something only you could help with?"

That was just it. Luke's whole body filled with light, but before he could say anything else, Jeremy's watch beeped.

"Here we go." Jeremy reached forward, hesitated for half a second, and took Luke's hand. Luke started, clenching tighter around his fingers and scanning for some threat. Instinctively, he turned his body to shield Jeremy's from the street.

Jeremy gave his fingers an encouraging squeeze, though his cheeks went pink. "Just so you get all the evidence."

"Ah. All right." Luke took a breath, pushed it out slow. They stood on the sidewalk holding hands, and he kept his eyes on Jeremy, solid and dressed like Play-Doh and apparently about to disappear. Jeremy looked up at the hazy sky, shifting from one foot to the other.

"Nervous?" Luke asked.

Jeremy giggled. "A little. It stings."

"What?" Luke's stomach dropped. "Wait, *what*? It hurts you?"

"Not really. This close to home, it'll hardly be a pinch."

"Why didn't you tell me that?" Luke took a firmer grip on Jeremy's hand and started pulling him back to the house.

"You don't have to do this, then."

"It's okay—"

"It's not. You're not supposed to—to just hurt." He should know that. Someone should have told him. The anger boiled over, and Luke was yanking hard on Jeremy's arm before he understood the resistance was Jeremy pulling back.

He was strong for a little guy. "Wait! Hold on, wait."

Luke stopped and turned.

"I know what I'm doing," Jeremy said. "I want someone else to—"

Luke stumbled forward. The empty sidewalk pitched like the deck of a ship, and he grabbed the low garden wall to steady himself.

Garden wall?

Where was he?

Luke studied his palms as his memories reassembled. He waved through the air where Jeremy's torso had been, and his anger erupted, molten and consuming. Maybe it was the magic, disorienting him, or maybe something about watching the laws of physics crack had messed with his head. Whatever it was, Luke marched back to the house in a hot rage at the Kovrovs, at the world, at anything that could trap a child like that and force him to claim that he was fine.

What if the house caught fire? What if he got hurt or sick and had to go to the hospital overnight? What if he wanted to go home with someone? Why wasn't Jeremy *furious*? Why weren't they trying to uncross him *right now*?

Luke threw open the front door. Jeremy stood in the entryway, his back and a slice of his profile framed in the living room's light, and physics bent again. This wasn't just mojo. This was—a small thought, and Luke pushed it away even as it came to him—way out of Luke's league.

"I had to tell him!" Jeremy was yelling. "He figured it out, but he thought it was something bad—"

Sergei, out of sight in the living room, bellowed so loudly he made Jeremy's shouts sound like a mouse. "What, it's not bad enough for you? You think this is a game, kid?"

"It's *my life*, and *I get to decide*—"

"Is that him?" Sergei shoved Jeremy aside as he pushed into the close hall. He was enormous, red-faced, louder than a train, and the veins in his neck stood out so far, they warped his ink into twisting shadows. "Go away. You hear me? I said get the hell out!"

Luke woke up from Sergei shouting in his dreams, and his phone told him it was midnight.

I get sad sometimes but that's just me.

He rolled over on his back, memories of the afternoon painting his dark ceiling like a movie scene. His skin itched. He'd wanted to check on Jeremy all afternoon—take a train right back and just look at his face one more time. To make sure Sergei hadn't hurt him. To make sure they understood that Luke hadn't meant to hurt him, either.

He thought about Jeremy's crossing, facts shifting around in his mind, and the look on Jeremy's face when he said, *You would be good at that.* Luke's insides were stretching out of his skin, reaching to explore Jeremy's story and his lies and— how did he deal? Something metallic crashed on the street.

I get sad sometimes but that's just me.

Luke picked up his phone.

He put it down again.

He picked up his phone. He wrote a text message:

There were two muffins baking in an oven. One said wow it's hot in here. The second one said oh my god! A talking muffin!

He sent the message to Jeremy Kovrov.

He put his head under his pillow and held it there in the heat. He didn't breathe again until the phone buzzed.

Jeremy: *Haha*

Chapter Fifteen

Six days a week, Jeremy took his anxious heart to Prospect Park and let it be wild. He ran until his lungs squeezed and pushed past that, until they opened up again. He ran through the burning in his legs and brought them all the way to jelly, ran until the sweat fell off his body in clean sheets, ran until his mind spun out as flat and endless as the road.

Or, he ran until 11:30 a.m., when his phone alarm beeped because he needed to head home to make it by noon.

On Wednesday morning, his mind outlasted his heart and lungs and legs, and he staggered into the house on weak quads at 11:54. Sergei stood in the kitchen—he would never have said he was waiting, and Jeremy would never have said he expected that, so he only returned Sergei's nod and got a glass of water.

Jeremy hauled himself up the three flights of stairs with his arms and the railings. He opened his bedroom door into a blind wall of panic—there was *someone in his room*—until Natalya locked eyes with him. The fear bled off like water as he clapped a hand over his chest. Natalya worked with Sergei nearly every day, making rounds of Kovrov associates, and it wasn't unusual for her to hang around the house. It was, though, weird to find her in his room. "Natalya! You scared me."

"Sorry, J. I wanted to say hi." Natalya flipped her hair over one shoulder and plopped onto Jeremy's bed. "See how Operation: Seduction is going."

Wouldn't he like to know? Maybe she should ask Luke, and tell Jeremy what he said. It had felt so close to real, reaching for Luke's hand. But Luke was always polite and conscientious, unless he was mad. Jeremy had little experience with the line where good manners crossed over into friendship, and couldn't tell if they were there.

He only rolled his eyes. "Katya said you all need to get a life."

"I know, we're so nosy." Natalya pouted. "But we care about you! We want to see you happy. You're so sweet to indulge us."

A complicated feeling, affectionate and guilty, tugged behind Jeremy's navel and pulled him across the room to her. She cared about him. He should indulge her. He pushed his sweaty hair back, sat on one of the windowsills, and confessed, heart thrilling. "Luke's been texting me."

Natalya leaned forward, elbow on her knee and chin on her fist. "What does he say?"

Jeremy shrugged. "Jokes and stuff."

"That is promising. So now it's your move."

"Alexei said I should play it cool."

"I have to tell you a secret." Natalya leaned closer, and Jeremy found himself tilting in, too. "You are cooler than Alexei thinks you are. You're like your brothers—you think you're these tormented romantics, and everyone can tell, but all anyone can see is that you're glaring at them."

It didn't make sense that he was like his brothers when

they were so different, but—well, it wasn't often that anyone called Jeremy cool. "He has a boyfriend."

Natalya snorted. "He has a problem that someone needs to solve."

Jeremy didn't answer that. He wanted to believe Luke was available way, way too much to think about it objectively, and he didn't know the rules well enough to break them. "Help him understand there are possibilities." Natalya said *possibilities* like it meant something dirty. "I'm not saying pin him to the wall. I'm saying, flirt a little. You know."

Jeremy shook his head.

"You *know*." She put her hand on Jeremy's forearm. Her fingers were cold on his hot, sweaty skin—why was he sitting here? "Touch him a little bit when you talk." She looked down and back up. "Give him the eyes."

Jeremy pulled his arm away and gave her his most skeptical frown.

"No, you can do it," Natalya said. "Look at the floor."

Jeremy looked at the floor.

"Now look at me."

He looked up.

"Don't smirk like that. And put your chin down more so your eyes get big. Here."

It was easier to give her what she wanted than protest. He let her push his chin back and practiced looking down and up again, which seemed more like a great plan for running into something than for getting a boy to fall in love with him.

Natalya left when Sergei hollered for her. Once Jeremy was alone and the attic room settled around him, he had only a second to think *that was so weird* before his phone beeped against his arm.

Jeremy glanced at one of his clocks (12:14) and wiggled his phone free of his armband. Luke had written: *Camille got mad at Dad for buying the wrong kind of bacon and he's yelling in Ukrainian*

A second text came while Jeremy watched: *No one else speaks Ukrainian*

Jeremy dropped face-down on his bed and screamed into the mattress. It took him a few minutes to think of what to write back. He went with: *Yikes be careful!* and waited, chilly with sweat.

Nice she's in trouble not me for once, Luke said.

It was hard to imagine Luke in trouble. For what? There was a joke there, something about bad boys, but Jeremy couldn't put it together. Another text came through: *Update she jinxed him and his shirt caught on fire, if I'm not here when you come over tomorrow it's because I'm still hiding in my room*

Heart in the palms of his hands, Jeremy wrote back, *OK if that happens, I'll come save you.*

Chapter Sixteen

The job: cleanse Alexei's apartment. No questions, no blood. Yuri hadn't said anything about *no fool texts*, though, had he?

The Flying Spur pulled up in front of Helene's Thrift and Sundry promptly at three the next afternoon, its stubborn snout gleaming above the dirty sidewalk. The horn honked, but Luke was already waiting.

Katya was a tiny woman in a neat uniform who still looked like a video game assassin, watchful and wiry, ready to fly off the ground in a bolley kick. When she opened the door for him, Luke stammered his thanks and hesitated on the sidewalk.

"Get in." She was so abrupt he could only obey.

Luke expected Alexei or maybe no one to be waiting in the back seat, but it was Jeremy again. He smiled an open, luminous smile Luke had never seen from him or imagined from anyone named Kovrov, and said, "Hi, Luke."

It was a tough call whether the smile was because of Luke's texting fixation, or if his attention was consumed as entirely as Luke's was by his cap.

Jeremy wore a New York Mets snapback the exact shade of a green highlighter backward on his head, hair sticking out underneath. As the car pulled into the street, Luke shook his head showily. "Kovrov, bad news. I think you're growing a brain tumor."

Katya snorted extravagantly. Jeremy laughed, pulling his hands together at his chest. "I love this hat. I'm never taking it off." It must have been new—a silver sticker shone on the bill.

"And the Mets? Not the Yankees?" Luke clucked his tongue.

Jeremy reached back to touch the decal, fingers playing over the stitching. "Oh. I don't care about sports, to be honest. This was the only one in the color I wanted."

"God. I bet it was."

Jeremy laughed again.

"For real, I don't care about the Yankees, either," Luke admitted. "But I have to say it, for the Bronx."

"Oh, yeah." Jeremy looked out the window and touched the Mets decal again with tripping fingers. "What are sports in Brooklyn?"

"What. Are. Sports," Katya repeated. "Honestly, J."

Jeremy laughed, whining, "You *know* what I *mean*," and since he seemed happy to laugh at himself, Luke joined, too.

"Oh! The Nets." Jeremy flipped the hat around so the offending snaps pointed directly at Luke. "I bet I could get a Nets hat."

Luke sucked his teeth. "Now that, I can't look at. It's got to be the Knicks."

"You should tell Alexei that," Katya said. "He's always trying to get rid of Knicks tickets."

"Knicks is cool. I could do that." Jeremy smiled again, right at Luke. He was flushed with laughter, very pink under his green hat, and kept biting at his lips but couldn't take his smile down.

Luke looked away, heart thudding hot. What a bad idea. A Kovrov. You might as well decide one of the half-mortal sons of Olympus was kind of cute.

The thought tugged at Luke. Because, actually—it was like one of those demigods was interested in you. Luke counted trusses on the bridge and tried to clamp a *no* down over all the *yes* rising in his chest.

"Listen," Jeremy said. "Have you ever worn a lime-green hat? I bet you haven't."

"I sure have not," Luke said to Manhattan, rising outside his window. He sounded short, meaner than he meant to be, as he tried to get ahold of himself.

"I can't tell you how happy it will make you in your heart. You want to try it on?"

"No. No way."

"Here, you have to try it," Jeremy said, and the hat started flapping around Luke's head. Luke squawked obligingly and wrestled him off—Jeremy's wrist in his hand, Jeremy's breathless laugh close to his face.

Katya waved a hand behind her seat. "Stop roughhousing in Alexei's car."

Jeremy flopped back, sighing, and settled the hat on his head so the brim cocked off at an angle. "Your loss."

Katya dropped them on the curb in front of Alexei's building. Alexei lived hard, or at least everything Luke had ever read about him suggested he did, and he was still young and so rich. Luke expected him to live somewhere that felt like his Bentley, luxurious and sleek. The red brick and glass building and the quiet block looked more like a horse-drawn carriage scene.

Eyes landed on the car with admiration and on him, as he climbed out, with expressions of surprise and confusion and something like horror. He felt hulking and shabby. An older woman's face turned ghastly as Jeremy popped out of his seat, twisting his cap sideways again, and maybe Luke didn't hate it so much, after all.

Jeremy ran up and threw his arms around the doorman's neck. "Luke, this is Eddie. Eddie, how are you?"

"I'm excellent, Jeremy, how are you?"

"Terrible. No one likes my hat."

Eddie chuckled and didn't say a word about Jeremy's hat, opening the door for them and hitting all the buttons in the elevator, too. Alexei's apartment was one huge room, a spiral staircase at the far end. A wall of windows showed neighboring high-rises and a peek of the East River. It wasn't carefully decorated the way Sergei's house was—the art on the walls didn't follow a pattern, and the gray L-shaped couch looked lavishly comfortable but not luxe. There was a sweatshirt draped over its back and a stack of dishes next to the sink. Alexei's bed, set into a nook but unhidden by any doors, was unmade, a nest of dark sheets.

"Has the witch doctor arrived?" Alexei trotted down the stairs. "And the young prince! Saints preserve us."

He had seen the hat.

Alexei wore sweatpants and a T-shirt. He stepped barefoot on a skateboard at the base of the stairs and rolled, wobbling, toward them. Luke tried to remember if he'd ever seen Alexei out of one of his suits before. He looked ten years younger, at least, and his face was less pretty, more chiseled and square.

Luke was coping with the idea that Jeremy was a real, regular person under all the money and power, but he would not—*could* not—entertain the same possibility about Alexei Kovrov.

Alexei hopped off the skateboard and pushed it noisily away, clasping Luke's neck and kissing his cheeks. "Cleansing! How thrilling. Someone has been doing wicked magic in my apartment."

"Someone?"

"Well, me," Alexei said. "How does this work? Should we be quiet? Do you need anything?"

"No, sir. You can do whatever you want, I don't mind." Luke walked to the center of the western wall and started a slow perimeter of the room, dusting lavender salt.

"Now," Alexei said to Jeremy. "What are we going to do with you?"

Jeremy yelped, and Luke checked over his shoulder. Alexei brushed his long hair back and pulled the green cap onto his head, snaps front. "Do I look like the Fresh Prince now?"

"No one knows what that means," Jeremy said.

Luke, who couldn't imagine anyone who didn't know what that meant, gaped, and Alexei winked.

Jeremy leaped up for his cap, but Alexei had several inches of height on him and held him back with a hand at his chest. "Gimme that back!" Jeremy shouted.

"Ah, our young prince. Who taught you manners?" With a quick flip, he got Jeremy into a firm headlock, standing placidly as Jeremy squirmed and battered him with useless fists. He grinned at Luke, as if they were in this together— haha, stolen children. He could have been any other big brother, though, and Jeremy was laughing as he howled.

Luke felt a weird, staticky vibe. It wasn't the place, but he scattered some salt anyway. The next time he looked over, Alexei licked a finger with a flourish and stuck it in Jeremy's ear.

"Mercy!" Jeremy cried. "You win!"

"Mercy denied." Alexei licked a clean finger and stuck it in Jeremy's other ear.

"No!" Jeremy wailed. "Stop stop stop!"

Alexei let go, folding his hands neatly behind his back. "Deal. If you make coffee, you can have your hat back."

"You're holding it hostage?" Jeremy asked, already walking toward the kitchen, carved out of the room by an island counter.

"Hostage-taking is a valuable tool and a fine tradition." Alexei sat on the couch and turned on the TV. "I personally have been taken hostage three times. The night I spent as Linh Zhang's prisoner remains one of my fondest memories."

"Oh, whatever," Jeremy said.

Luke took a break from sorting the stale, twisting vibes in the room from the now-familiar Kovrov static coming off Alexei, and watched Jeremy make the coffee.

It didn't have to mean anything if he just looked.

Jeremy's fingers skimmed over the buttons of Alexei's coffee machine, and a little sneer curled his upper lip as he parsed their meanings. He tilted his head, and his hair fell against his cheek, which made Luke's palms itch.

Luke moved on, salting evenly along the windows. He needed to bring some focus to this ritual if it was going to work, and perving on Jeremy and thinking about Alexei's creepiness were not helping. Instead of responsibly starting over, he finished his lap through the large room, fast between Alexei and the TV and even faster past the bed.

Jeremy stood at the counter while the coffee dripped, drumming his fingers on the countertop and wiggling unself-consciously to a song in his head. It wasn't the rhythm of Alexei's cable news, at least. Luke claimed a stool at the kitchen island and started setting up: His mother's porcelain dish. Incense, herbs. Candle. Lighter. Flame.

Jeremy's phone beeped, and he reached into the back pocket of his cargo shorts for it. Luke wasn't sure how long he'd been staring exactly there.

What was he conjuring into Alexei's apartment? Well. More shocking things had happened in this apartment than Luke's stares.

"Alexei, Sergei wants to know if you want to get dinner," Jeremy said.

"Fine," Alexei replied. "When and where?"

Jeremy texted, chatting with Alexei and pouring coffee. The incense filtered into Luke's head, and he was suffering for his shoddy focus now, thoughts spinning. *Focus. Cleansing.*

His head hurt, a spear like a brain freeze. There was too much smoke. The light burned.

He shut his eyes. Blood. He saw blood, gold hair, a blue eye. A blue room. A kiss.

Jeremy was in pain, hot in Luke's arms. His breath rattled in his chest. That was Jeremy, true as a memory.

Luke

Jeremy. A kiss. Falling.

"Luke!" A short, sharp blow popped on Luke's cheek, and he opened his eyes to Jeremy's face. He was upside down—or Luke was upside down—the room spun around him, stealing gravity.

"Are you real?" Luke asked. Jeremy's eyes bugged out. But of course he was—he had the cap back and was wearing it sideways, and only real life was ever that gruesome. The room stopped spinning, and Luke was on his back on the floor, a sharp ache in his left shoulder. He was ferociously thirsty.

"I'm real," Jeremy said. "You're back. What do you need?"

Luke swallowed. "Water?"

Jeremy went to get it while Alexei lifted Luke by the elbows and helped him to the couch.

"Alexei! What have you been doing?" Jeremy demanded.

"A little light scrying, maybe." Alexei eyed Luke suspiciously.

"Being a creep." Jeremy put the water in Luke's hand and guided it to his mouth. "Anything else? Are you sure you're okay?"

Luke closed his eyes and had to drag them open again, wrung out like a rag. "Coffee?"

Jeremy squeezed his shoulder before popping away.

"I saw something," Luke said. "Like—eyes?" Jeremy. And someone else.

He wasn't making sense, but Alexei lifted his head, alert. "Like a vision?"

Luke nodded. "Is that normal?"

"Normal?" Alexei repeated, sounding out the word. "It's not totally unprecedented. That is how I take others through the bindings. Although usually I can control—" He stopped, brow furrowing. "I'll be right back. Get me if he looks worse."

He left up the stairs, and Jeremy returned with Luke's coffee. There was a lot of sugar in it, more than Luke liked, but it helped to buoy him.

Jeremy's face was open and ragged, earnest under his neon cap. "That was scary. What was that?"

Luke shook his head. "I have no idea. Will you..." The room rocked again, swimming with Luke's vertigo. He'd only lost a moment, but it had left him sore and sick. He grabbed Jeremy's hand. Jeremy's mouth fell open but he didn't pull away. "Anchoring," Luke said, which may have been true. A fancy, magic-sounding word to ask for the comfort of a touch.

"Okay," Jeremy said.

Luke had seen a kiss, felt it. Jeremy. He was sure. The rest he couldn't place—a stranger's eyes and hair. It slipped away as he grasped for it, like a dream.

Jeremy frowned at their clasped hands. "I'm all right now," Luke said, but neither of them let go.

Jeremy turned Luke's hand over and touched the back, fingertips light. "I didn't know the cleansing would do that to you. I wouldn't have said you should do it."

"It doesn't. Not a simple cleansing. I think that was

something else." *I think it was you.* He'd seen Jeremy hurting, and the right thing to do was probably to warn him. But then what? *I was holding you. I saw a kiss.* That wire was too fine to walk.

With his free hand, Jeremy reached forward and touched the iron pendant at Luke's neck. "Is this supposed to protect you?"

Luke shrugged. "I don't think it's real mojo. It's a family thing. It was my grandfather's and then my mom's."

"Can I?" Jeremy asked, and even though Luke didn't know what that meant, he nodded.

Jeremy dipped his head forward and whispered in Russian. His eyes were on the amulet, ducked below Luke's face, and a red flush crept over his neck and ears. He said *Amen* and pressed his eyes shut, and then he leaned even closer and kissed the iron between his fingers.

It was over before Luke understood it—Jeremy's temple in front of his lips, Jeremy's lips close to his chest. Jeremy sat up again, hand light in Luke's. "Do you need to lie down? Or I can call Katya to take you home."

"No!" Alexei called, coming down the stairs. His gaze hit the couch, and Jeremy pulled his hand away. "Come to dinner, please, Luke. Sergei and I have some questions for you."

Chapter Seventeen

They went to a sports bar near Coney Island, a poster for generic Americana called Glory's. It was a single dark room with a square bar in the center and green-shaded lamps glowing wanly. The dozen TVs weren't playing anything interesting on a weekday in the summer—pre-shows for the evening's baseball games, talking heads on the sports nets and the news—and the only other patrons were a small group at the bar. The owner, Yaniv, came out to greet them, pumping Alexei's hand and speaking an enthusiastic mishmash of languages that Luke couldn't follow.

Yaniv led them to a raised corner booth. Alexei sprawled in the center like a king on his throne. Luke slid in and was intrigued, but not quite surprised, to find Jeremy following him, close on one side.

Alexei said, "Hmm," and fixed his gaze gorgeously into the middle distance, as if there were photographers in the room.

He kept asking questions—the store, Luke's uncrossings, and his vision during the cleansing. Luke left out everything he'd seen about Jeremy—a kiss, the only part of it that got more vivid, rather than fading, as time passed—but answered the rest. Jeremy, silent, fidgeted and flipped his cap back and forth on his head.

Yaniv brought pitchers of beer and water and poured glasses. Sergei and Natalya entered, in the middle of a conversation they stopped before they got to the table.

Instead of *hello*, Sergei said, "No hats at meals. Carry yourself like a Kovrov."

Jeremy huffed, but he took the cap off and ruffled his hair until it lay flat, a flurry in Luke's peripheral vision.

"Luke!" Natalya said, as if she'd been desperate to see him again. "How are you?" She caught the light, shining.

Luke deferred to Alexei, and he said, "We have had adventures today. Apparently I am so evil that performing a routine cleansing on my place caused our witch doctor to swoon." He sounded terribly pleased with himself, not as serious as he'd been when they were alone, and Natalya laughed.

"Swoon!" She flipped the gleaming waves of her hair over one shoulder. "Are you okay? What does that mean?"

Luke nodded. "I'm fine. I'm not sure what happened."

Sergei was quiet, peering from the shadows underneath the shelf of his brow. His glance flicked among Jeremy, Luke, and Alexei as if they were keeping secrets.

"All's well that ends well," Alexei said. "The young prince nursed him back to health. It's been a long time since my place has seen such a darling display of hand-holding."

Natalya smiled slyly, and Sergei's brow went up and then down. Jeremy flinched, making a pained sound so small only Luke would hear it, and iron-hard scorn filled Luke's chest. If they wanted to act like any assholes from school, Luke could treat them that way: stay absolutely calm, maybe faintly amused or bored, and never act like the secret they thought they'd discovered was truly important. "Sounds like you're missing out, then."

Luke kept his eyes on Alexei's twinkling ones as, next to him, Jeremy exhaled the tiniest laugh and squirmed in his seat.

Alexei smiled broadly, all delight. "Almost certainly."

Natalya leaned forward, chin on her hand and voice chipper. "How is your texting friend?"

Luke didn't place what she meant until Sergei scoffed. "Why is this all we talk about?"

"You mean Max," Luke said. "That's over."

Natalya arched an eyebrow. "That was quick."

"You caught me as it was swirling the drain. It was barely a thing." Luke sounded confident, even to himself, but the words were hollow. That had only been a few days ago. *I think it's cool, how you save people.*

Jeremy went still, hand close between them on the vinyl seat of the booth. Food began to come out even though no one had ordered, wings and fries and other bar food on big family-style platters. Alexei thanked the servers magnanimously, and Jeremy leaned up to Luke's ear to whisper, "No talking business while we eat. Not until Alexei brings it up again."

Luke didn't mind that—he wouldn't have minded dropping the subject completely—but Sergei tucked into his plate with a gloom that crept around him like smoke.

Jeremy kept reaching across Luke to get dishes, and it was hard to tell if it was bad table manners or an excuse to get his body close. The fries had marched across the table, so Jeremy helped himself to a few from Luke's plate. "Kid," Sergei said. "When are you going to grow out of that?"

Holding Sergei's gaze, Jeremy reached deliberately over and took another fry.

Sergei snorted. "This kid," he said to Natalya. "Every time I tried to teach him about sharing, he'd say, 'Yeah!

Sergei share!' and took whatever he wanted."

Natalya giggled. "You mean when he was a toddler?"

Sergei gestured in Jeremy's direction like *you deal with this*. "And right now."

Luke turned his plate around, fries on Jeremy's side, and nudged Jeremy's arm with his elbow. "No problem." Luke tilted his head closer and lowered his voice. "You can have whatever you want."

Luke started and checked Jeremy—aloud, that had sounded like a *line*. Jeremy was hiding a smile behind his napkin, neck glowing pink at the collar of his shirt. Maybe Luke had meant it as a line.

"You should definitely tell us more cute baby Jeremy stories." Natalya looked significantly at Sergei and swung her gaze to Luke.

Her glamour shimmered in the air around her, and Luke had a petulant urge to reach over and rip it off of her like a scarf. She glanced at him again, a different heat around her eyes, but Alexei was already talking. "Did we ever tell you how we found out about his gift?"

Jeremy laughed to himself and nodded, and Alexei leaned over the table. "I bought him one of those funny surprise eggs, with the toy inside. A little train. He was playing with that while I was eating his chocolate, and suddenly there is a full volume train whistle, I mean *screaming*. I thought I was being shot at, the prince made himself cry, and meanwhile this two-inch toy train is driving itself in circles on the coffee table."

As he finished, Jeremy blew a plum-size bird he'd folded out of straw wrappers off his palm, and it fluttered across the table to Alexei, the paper turning to crystal or glass. The delicate mechanics were so exquisite Luke's jaw dropped, but Alexei merely plucked it out of the air like a mosquito.

Natalya laughed. "What was his first word?"

Alexei blinked through a pause. "I'm afraid I don't know."

"Story," Sergei said gruffly. He didn't elaborate, and an uncomfortable vacuum opened up in the middle of the table.

Jeremy filled it. "Sergei read to me before bed. Every night, since before I can remember. We had Baba Yaga, and the brothers Grimm, and this huge Mother Goose book. It was like—" He drew a rectangle in the air, reaching around his head and chest. "This big."

Sergei snorted. "No, it wasn't, kid. You were just little."

"Aww." Natalya put a hand over her heart, and Sergei nudged her off. The conversation faded as if it had been pleasant. Luke couldn't figure these people out—were they so accustomed to all evil, or only the evil they'd done to Jeremy? Luke could imagine Sergei—fifteen or sixteen years old, with that dump-truck face but no tattoos or muscle—reading fairy tales to Jeremy with the same grim, relentless attention he turned to his food.

When Luke and Camille were little, Helene had made games of teaching them to control crossings and uncrossings: hide-and-seek with mojo bags, real herbs in their play kitchen. They would sit on a bench in a park, and Camille would capture a pigeon in an invisible cage and then Luke would set it free. They'd get ice cream if they managed so many in a row—three, five, twenty. He hadn't understood at the time, but Camille had progressed from trapping animals to hurting them with the same quick words. Helene stopped the game when they were eight, the first time Camille killed a bird. Luke had tried to bring it back to life and cried when he failed.

It's not your fault, honey, Helene had said. *Some things can't be undone.* Camille still used that jinx if she saw vermin at home.

Reading fairy tales to a baby like Jeremy would have

been a little bit like that game.

Jeremy took the last fry off Luke's plate, and Alexei slid the platter back their way. "Eat up. You'll have to keep your strength in case the witch doctor has another vision." He paused. "Is that likely? Does that happen to you often?"

That was the cue to take the conversation back to work. If Luke hadn't caught it, he would have felt it in the changing postures all around the table. Sergei perked up, Jeremy sat back, and Natalya flipped her hair again, finding a spear of light to glow in.

"No, sir," Luke said. "That's never happened before."

"My fault, then?" Alexei's voice was calm, giving no clues whether that question was genuine, or a trick.

Luke aimed for equal cool. "No idea. Anything I said would only be a guess."

Sergei glared. "I don't truck with visions."

"You don't think they're real?"

"I think they're real trouble, and only troublemakers have them."

Luke hesitated. He would have agreed—it hadn't made his day any better, and he never wanted anything like that to happen again—but the Kovrovs were coasting a current he didn't understand.

Jeremy sighed, and Alexei drummed his fingers on the table. "Seryozhka," Alexei said. "You're being unusually tedious."

Luke focused on the problem he could solve. "It could have been anything. Me, you, the tail end of an old spell. I wouldn't read anything into it unless something else happens, not unless you guys have something you want me to do."

"Brilliant," Alexei said. "That sounds very wise."

They fell back into silence over their food. The restaurant was picking up business, though a cushion of empty tables surrounded the booth. The door opened, letting in a wedge of yellow light, and along the light came a vibe Luke recognized. The chatter of the restaurant got distant and muffled, like someone had clapped a pillow over Luke's ears.

There was a lot of static—the scents of food, all kinds of vibes rolling off his companions—and it took him too long to place the harsh edge of the bad feeling on the air.

Cayenne.

The man who had entered the restaurant looked around, eyes catching places he shouldn't have bothered to notice— the corners, the rafters, the floor.

Luke flailed for Alexei's arm. "He's crossed. That man— something's wrong."

Jeremy said, "Huh?" Natalya gaped at Luke. But Sergei and Alexei both followed Luke's gaze to the door as the man drew his gun.

Chapter Eighteen

Whatever was festering between the Kovrov brothers evaporated in the heat of a threat. They were a finely calibrated machine, a bomb that had been waiting for its chance to detonate.

Alexei, trapped in the middle of the booth, leaped up and across the table, pulling a shining revolver from inside his jacket. His foot slipped on a plate, scattering the leftovers of their meal all over Luke's lap and the wall, but he didn't stumble. He vaulted over Sergei, who skidded underneath him, throwing his body between Jeremy and the gunman.

Sergei sprung open a knife, crouching so close that Jeremy had to jerk his chin away from the flicking blade, and dug it into the meat of his own palm.

His welling blood, the red shine of it and the sudden meaty smell, ripped Luke out of his shock, but he got no farther than, "Wha—" before Sergei slammed his bleeding hand on the table and everything went silent.

"Sergei!" Jeremy threw himself on an invisible barrier, beating his fists against thin air. His voice was too loud, echoing in the dome that had closed around them.

Alexei trained his gun on the man, who waved his aimlessly. Natalya was speaking, hands wide, but he wasn't looking at her. He kept scanning the rafters, the floor. This was a bad crossing, both malignant and poorly made.

Sergei stayed near the table, in front of Jeremy. It was impossible in an unbalancing way, making Luke's brain whirl, how Sergei stood close enough to touch and yet Jeremy couldn't, smacking his palm against a wall two inches from Sergei's back.

Luke tried to speak a few times before it worked. "What is this?"

Jeremy slumped back in the booth. "A binding. Just a physical one. That's all Sergei can do."

It seemed like plenty to Luke. He reached past Jeremy, jammed his fingers against cool marble in empty air, and snatched his hand back.

Jeremy twisted, trying to see around Sergei, but he was stuck between the binding, the table, and Luke. "I don't understand why they aren't all in here. We could all be safe."

That was backward—he should be out there. That man was crossed, and Luke should help. The man jolted into awareness, and his body twisted toward Luke. He lifted the gun deliberately, going still and sure as his eyes rolled wildly away from Luke and back again.

Sergei pressed his hand on the table again, and everything went black. Luke gasped. His pupils dilated as they searched for light, his eyes straining out of his head, but there was nothing but velvety black.

He reached for Jeremy on instinct, and Jeremy's hands scrambled back to him. He got a hand around Jeremy's wrist and déjà vu rushed him—laughing in the car. He wrapped his other arm around Jeremy's shoulders, pulling him away from that ominously solid wall. Jeremy felt familiar there, too, though that couldn't be right. He'd definitely never held Jeremy like that before.

He probably shouldn't be holding him now. Either Jeremy was feverishly hot, or Luke had gone cold. As he pulled his arm away, the vision came back, clear in the dark—Jeremy's warm body in Luke's arms. Maybe that was the déjà vu—he had seen this fight. Maybe he'd been given a warning, enough notice to keep Jeremy safe.

"Are you okay?" Jeremy's voice gave away a small crack, and that was all Luke needed to be brave.

"Yeah. Sorry. It's so dark."

Jeremy shifted and there was light, a thin glow from his phone in his hand. His lock screen was a little blue house from one of those nerd shows Short Wesley liked. Luke's brain scrambled to make the connection, grasping at every meaningless detail.

Jeremy lifted the phone closer to look into Luke's face. He caught his own, making his angles strange with the light shining up. His frown was a deep shadow between his eyebrows. "Sergei won't let anyone hurt us."

But what about all the people out there? The small light made the darkness heavier around their two faces. Because it was easier than arguing, Luke nodded.

The light went out. Jeremy shifted again, putting his phone away. They sat in the dark and the sound of their breath. Luke put his hand down on something slick and moving and lifted it in revulsion before he remembered the glass bird. He touched it again, more carefully, and closed it between his fingers. Its wings brushed his knuckles. Its smooth surface grounded him.

The darkness wavered. Sergei's voice: "Stay cool. Everyone's fine."

The binding shimmered gray and faded. Alexei still stood in the middle of the room. Natalya had the front door, Sergei the table, and though the restaurant was completely empty, they stayed in position.

Everyone's fine hadn't meant the crossed man. He lay on the floor, blood all over his face and a pulpy wound in his chest.

"Jesus!" Luke pushed out of the booth, past Jeremy. "Was he crossed? Did you find anything?"

Alexei's revolver shone in his hand. "Haven't checked."

The room tilted under Luke's feet. It smelled like cayenne and his own sweat and Jeremy's, acrid with fear, and the choking, metallic scent of blood. Everyone was looking at Luke, so he went to the man himself. *The body.*

The bag was easy to find, right in the man's front pocket. It wasn't made of the usual burlap or cotton, but blue plaid. The man's hand lay open next to his hip, and a wedding ring glinted through the blood on his palm.

"Look," Luke shouted, brandishing the bag. "He was crossed, and you killed him!"

"He drew a gun first," Alexei said mildly. "Can you dissect that and find out what he was doing?"

"We could *ask* if you hadn't shot him!" Luke put a hand on his chest, trying to keep his heart from clambering out of its cage, and smeared blood onto his shirt. The floor swerved again.

"Focus," Alexei said. "Can you dissect it? Or is that something your mother needs to do?"

Luke leaned over the bar and pressed his face into his arm to block out the smell of blood. Something caught his peripheral vision—Yaniv tucked under the bar, crouching.

Luke shut his eyes. "I can dissect it. But can we go somewhere else?"

Sergei's Escalade was parked out front. He had a first aid kit and a spare pack of gray muscle tanks, and Luke cleaned up and caught his breath.

In front of the restaurant, Natalya briefed Katya. Luke couldn't hear, but he watched their close heads. They looked more alike when Natalya wasn't focused on her glamour, two women of medium height and build with light-brown hair and kind of remarkable biceps. The glamour sanded all the uniqueness off Natalya—you might remember she was beautiful, but not how, specifically.

She gripped the back of Katya's head and kissed her forehead before she let her into the restaurant. Katya made an annoyed huff but didn't shove her off. When Natalya turned, she caught Luke looking. "Big sister privilege," she said as she approached. "I keep her away from the dangerous part, and she handles the mess."

Her grin had a brittle edge, so Luke didn't protest, but anger lit him up. The mess she was talking about was a person.

Luke took a spot in the middle row of the car, next to Jeremy, with Natalya in the back seat and the Kovrov brothers in the front. He made himself focus on the bag—this, at least, he could do. It was a deep, achy cold, like concrete in winter. "The plaid. That means Malcolm, right?"

Natalya nodded. "It's called tartan."

"These stones must be a Malcolm thing, I don't know. But the rest is standard nastiness. Bird bones? Mouse?" Luke pulled out a crumpled tarot card. "What's the seven of pentacles?"

Everyone turned to Natalya, who twisted a strand of hair around her finger. "Profit? That doesn't make any sense."

"Let me call Camille. She's better at cards." Luke called the counter at the store and sifted through the bag as he waited for the phone to ring.

"Helene's," Camille's voice said.

"Hey. I need—"

"Luke! Are you coming home?"

"I will soon, but real quick, what does the seven of

pentacles mean?"

Camille yelped. "Did you get a bag, too?"

"What?" Fingers fumbling, he put Camille on speakerphone. "There was a bag at home?"

"In a box of clothes. It almost got Dad, but he figured it out and threw it out back. Blue plaid, seven of pentacles. It means, uh, profit, investment, plans, harvest? I don't understand."

"Me neither," Luke said. The car was all blank eyes and shaking heads. The Kovrovs didn't mess with building spells by layering subtle meanings together—they bled on their problems, or threw money at them.

"There's used gum in this," Camille said. "So it's aimed at someone, but I can't tell who. Is there anything that shows a mark in yours?"

"I don't think so." Luke checked the bag more carefully, looking for hair or nail clippings. "Oh, wait—"

Luke pulled out six strands of hair, each three or four inches long and a fair, ashy blond color.

They all made pained, horrible sounds—a grunt from Sergei, a hiss from Alexei, a dramatic gasp from Natalya, and through the phone, Camille said, "What? What is it?"—except for Jeremy, whose voice was eerie with that resigned calm as he said, "That's mine."

Chapter Nineteen

Luke took them back home to dissect and burn the bags. Both were identical, except the one from the restaurant had Jeremy's hair inside, and the one from the store had a dry fossil of chewed gum. Camille caught Luke's eye, but she didn't say anything, and neither did he. Though there was no way to be sure, the little white scrap looked like the minty gum Short Wesley carried around. Luke bummed them off him at least twice a week.

The bags hissed and snapped as they burned. Jeremy stood patiently, candle in hand, and prayed, and Luke crouched next to him as the spell fought and died. He burned everything else in that donation box, too, even though he didn't catch any vibes off it. He couldn't stop; he wanted to burn everything he could find. A woman leaned out of one of the upstairs apartments and started yelling about the smoke.

Yuri made a whole batch of dumplings for Jeremy, though Luke ended up eating most of them. Helene made everyone protection poppets. They talked in useless circles for hours, sitting around the Melnyks' dining room table.

"Why do the Malcolms hate you so much?" Luke asked. He kept his eyes on Alexei, but his father's glance was sharp enough to cut his skin.

"They stole Jersey from us about, god, twenty years ago?" Alexei said. "It's been bitter ever since."

"That's it? Why Jeremy, then?" He hadn't even been thought of twenty years ago—unless it had something to do with his contract, sleeping in the Kovrovs' records. Luke filed that thought away.

Alexei shook his head slowly, face going tight. "It doesn't matter what happened in the past. They have no reason to try to hurt Jeremy now. I am going to take care of this. And listen, you little firebombs," he pointed at Camille, "no putting spells on the Malcolms." He swung his finger to Luke. "No breaking spells on the Malcolms. Not unless I tell you to. You two are strategic weapons, and I can't have you misfiring."

Luke chafed at that, though it was true. Spells fell away around him. His own investigation could leave a trail he didn't even know about. Still, when Alexei said, "I'll take care of Corey Malcolm. It will be a pleasure. Trust me," Luke wasn't comforted.

After the Kovrovs left, Luke stood under the stream of hot water in the shower until his skin ached. He tried to sleep, but blood ran behind his eyelids. At midnight, he was wide awake, pacing around the back room behind the store as the glass bird he'd kept darted from table to shelf.

He kept thinking, *Alexei didn't have to kill that man.*

But then he'd think, *That man might have killed Jeremy. If I wasn't there, that man would have hurt Jeremy. What am I going to do about Jeremy?*

The day spun around in his mind. He'd woken up wondering why he couldn't stop texting Jeremy, and now all he could think about was how he could get Jeremy away from the Kovrovs and hide him somewhere forever. He was in bad trouble. *You can have whatever you want*—who did he think he was?

The problem wasn't the flirting, though he kept thinking of Jeremy diving at him in the car. The problem was that he'd seen a kiss, and that vision felt like the future. It was an excuse—if it was going to happen anyway, he could make it happen, even though it was a bad idea, and pretend the fallout wasn't his fault.

Luke behaved. All the time, he behaved. He went to school and he worked with his parents and he didn't smoke up and he didn't get in fights. Even the Max thing was Max's mess.

Finally, feeling like a human tornado, he pulled out his phone and texted Jeremy: *What a day*

The reply took no time at all. *Tired of talking about it. Tell me another joke?*

He replied with the dumbest thing he could think of: *Where did the general put his armies?*

He waited, looking out the window at the piles of ash they'd left in the alley. The bird beat dumbly against the wall near Luke's arm—he couldn't control it, but it stayed close to him anyway.

The phone rang.

Luke thought, *Fuck*. He answered. "Are you sure you're ready for this?" He waited for Jeremy to say no. Just once, for someone else to show some sense.

"Where?" There was already laughter in Jeremy's voice.

Luke touched the window. In the room's weak air-conditioning, the glass was warm. "In his sleevies."

Jeremy laughed and groaned at once. "Oh, no."

Oh, no. "Oh, yes."

"Nope. No, no, nope."

Stop it right now. "Yes. Say it. Say, 'Oh, yes.'"

Jeremy was quiet for a long time. Luke opened his hand

against the glass. *Good*, he thought. *Hang up on me.*

"Oh." Jeremy paused. "Yes."

Luke squeezed his eyes shut. "I changed my mind. Don't ever say that to me again."

"Yes?"

"Stop it right now. You will hang up your phone if you know what's good for you, Kovrov."

Jeremy didn't hang up. "Can you not call me that?"

Luke put his forehead against the back of his hand on the window. There were lots of things he could have said, but the one he picked was, "Jeremy."

Jeremy's breath caught, a click through the phone. "You should hang up on me. I'm the one who, you know. All this. My family. Everything."

"I don't think I'm going to do that." It had been a long day, but Luke hadn't forgotten the beginning of it: that smile in the car. He'd known what he'd wanted before his vision and the attack, and he knew what he wanted now. "I think I'm going to kiss you."

Jeremy was quiet. Luke could see him: gaze sliding everywhere, stretching his fingers out to tap his palm against whatever was near. His bed. Luke rolled his face up, putting his lips on the back of his hand.

"Yes," Jeremy said.

Luke bit the back of his hand, and when he opened his teeth, he said, "Unless you make me faint again, with that."

Jeremy laughed, nervous or confused. "You're a little intense."

"That's true. In general. So now you've been warned."

"Okay, I can handle that."

Luke grinned against his hand.

Jeremy sighed. "Listen, the reason I called is about Sergei. What he said. That was uncalled for."

Luke had to think to remember: *trouble*. "Sergei's grown.

He can speak for himself." He turned away from the window to the dark, herb-sweet room. "I'm more interested in what you thought of Alexei killing that man."

As long as Jeremy had taken to answer every question before, he was quick and calm now. "I already said you should hang up on me."

"I don't want to hang up on you; I want to know what you thought."

"Do you really, or is there something specific you want to hear?" Jeremy spoke very clearly and sounded already disappointed.

Luke found a thick spot in a stack of carpet and sat on the floor, running his hand over the weave. "I want you to tell me you think it was wrong, too, but not because I'm trying to judge you. Nothing like that has ever happened to me before."

"Luke. That man had my hair in a bag with a bunch of dead bird parts. He pointed a gun at you. I know it's like, what if he was a stranger, an innocent person they pulled off the street? But what if he had killed one of us? I'm not sorry Alexei stopped him."

Luke found a loose thread and pulled. "It was the bag. It was in his pocket the whole time."

"All that time we were bound, they were trying to disarm him. It's hard to get to someone's pocket when they have a gun on you."

Luke didn't answer. He couldn't explain, but the horror of it—the danger of a firefight, the mystery behind those bags— wasn't as real as the memory of a corpse under his hands.

"For what it's worth, that doesn't happen hardly ever," Jeremy said. "Sergei's always making me turn off movies because he thinks it's dumb when people shoot each other too much. He says killing people is very complicated and expensive."

"Expensive, huh? Is that how he handles the cops?"

Jeremy's voice went even drier. "I doubt the police will get involved at all."

"Must be nice."

"Seriously? What do they even know about curse bags? They'd just end up hurt."

The weight of the late hour and the long day fell on Luke's spine, and he borrowed Jeremy's words. "You're a little intense."

Through the phone, the sound Jeremy made could have been a laugh or a scoff. "You've been warned."

I can't handle that. There's no way. The bird landed on Luke's knee. Its wings rose and fell, glinting in a smudge of white light. "I can handle that."

"No, you can't. That's all right. You're a good guy. You think I don't know we're the bad guys? I know." Jeremy paused, then all at once he said, "That's why I like you so much. God, you should have seen yourself today. I should have been scared but you were so brave, and I thought I could be brave, too, and I always have to come back here and I just want—" One inhale shuddered through the phone before the call went dead.

Chapter Twenty

Jeremy got up early and dressed to go out instead of run, in case his brothers needed him for work—that curse bag was about him—but Sergei was gone and neither one answered his calls. Marta was a pink dervish of *little favor* and *cupcake, would you mind.* Undoubtedly, she'd been told to distract him.

He was plenty distracted on his own, but he helped her to fill up his time. The little boys needed to be fed, cleaned, and dressed, and once that was done it was time to make lunch. She took Seryozhka—little Sergei, the second son given Sergei's name and the nickname Alexei still insisted on using for big Sergei—into the kitchen. He screamed and ran in circles around her as she tried to cook.

Jeremy sat at the coffee table with three-year-old Dmitri in his lap, and Vanya next to him, both coloring pictures from *Cars* in intent concentration. Dmitri could only scribble, but he was starting to get his swirls in the right colors and places.

Vanya was seven but colored ahead of his years, precisely inside the lines. Marta thought he was a genius. Jeremy wondered whether it was healthy that he cried when anyone made a picture "wrong," giving Elsa a red dress or Buzz Lightyear feathery wings.

None of the babies had shown magic yet, but Vanya would have the binding running through his veins, and the other boys probably had their own gifts. Vanya didn't seem suited to power, sensitive and persnickety, although he might grow into it. He would have to.

This was a conversation Jeremy's brothers must have had about him—whether he was cut out for power, a Kovrov man who could lead or a Kovrov vulnerability who needed protection. He went with them for congenial business lunches or to use his party tricks to dazzle clients, but they never had him help with anything serious.

He could help. He was sure he could. He might as well, because it wasn't like he could do anything else.

Jeremy dragged his thoughts away from all that and, like a butterfly, they alighted where they'd been waiting to go: *I think I'm going to kiss you.*

The buzz was like electrocution. It wasn't only that Jeremy craved kissing Luke Melnyk like chocolate. It was that he'd been so sure that this summer job thing was a story he already knew, a story about Alexei's big plans crashing to pieces against Jeremy's high walls. This twist changed the shape of the world. He'd lain awake for hours last night, smiling in the dark until his cheeks ached.

And what had Jeremy done with that? Picked a fight to defend a grisly scene and hung up on him.

It was probably his responsibility to text back or apologize somehow, but Jeremy had one social skill for when things went wrong—freeze like a bunny and let someone else handle it—so that's what he did. Noon's settling, the house sealing around him and the fog that might be his own bad mood and might be magic, didn't hit him as hard as usual. A new thread of anticipation swirled, shining gold through the gray.

Jeremy's phone beeped, lighting up with Luke's name. He'd snapped a video, his smile beaming through the screen. "Two peanuts were walking down the street. Suddenly, one was a salted!"

Jeremy huffed a small laugh. Dmitri twisted in his lap to try to see the screen.

"We have to take a picture, okay?" Jeremy told him.

"I want to be in the picture!" Vanya jumped up and ran behind Jeremy's shoulder.

Jeremy lifted the phone so it caught all three of them. "This is a serious one."

Both little boys frowned in unison, brows falling like their father's. Jeremy pressed his lips together and made his eyes large, and sent the solemn picture back to Luke.

Vanya settled back with his coloring book. Luke wrote back fast: *It's criminal how cute that is*

Do you want to come over tomorrow?

Jeremy wrote back *yes*—he felt it in his mouth, how the word sat on the front of his tongue, *yes*, and how Luke's breath had hissed through the phone—before he remembered everything going on. "Marta! Do you think it's okay if I go out tomorrow?"

In the kitchen, Marta squealed. "Only if you tell me *everything*."

Sergei growled about it, but he drummed up a car he deemed safe enough to take Jeremy to the Bronx. Luke was working behind the counter, and the street and store were busy, so Jeremy paused outside the window to settle his nerves. Luke had that big smile for everyone, and he always wore these plain T-shirts that made him all shoulders. Jeremy pulled his lower lip between his teeth to stop the impulse to touch his mouth.

Luke looked out the window and caught Jeremy's eye. His customer-smile changed, more flexible, and he gestured Jeremy inside.

Jeremy went to the counter, speaking brightly over the murmur of customers. "There's so many people here!" He spread his hands out over the enamel to stop them fidgeting.

Luke looked at Jeremy's hands, not his face. "Yeah, it's a good crowd." Luke dragged his gaze up so slowly Jeremy felt it on his arms and chest and neck. "Summer weekends. People want to be outside, exploring."

Jeremy leaned over the counter, dizzily close. "I miss the babies being in preschool, to be honest. So much baby TV. Seryozhka does the musical numbers? Not in a good way."

"Well, I have to work for a few more hours, but I can promise no musical numbers. You can come back here if you want."

Jeremy leaned farther over the counter to scope it out. There wasn't a lot of space. "Really?"

Luke's smile grew wider. "Sure. I have a chair and everything."

Jeremy crept around the counter like something would change when he crossed the line. Luke opened his arm over the pair of mismatched stools, torn edges of receipts, and blue and orange flakes of peeled-off nail polish. "Welcome to my castle. If you're good, maybe I'll show you how to work the register."

"Oh, *wow.*" Jeremy rolled his eyes, but he couldn't hide his smile.

The thread bracelets on Jeremy's arm had gotten dingy with smoke when Luke had burned his feelings after the restaurant, and Jeremy had cut them away, leaving a fuzzy tan line above his watch. Luke's eyes latched there, and he caught the underside of Jeremy's wrist with his fingers. He ran his thumb over the line, pushing the small hairs on Jeremy's arm against the grain in a way that made his whole body shiver.

Luke propped his other elbow on the counter, casual as if they did this every day. Jeremy had catalogued years of Luke's rare touches—he still remembered when Luke had switched from hugs to handshakes, at fourteen or so, his palm firm and dry. That memory felt more real than this touch— more reliable, the rule that this exception would prove. When a pair of girls with weighty armfuls of clothes approached, Luke jumped up and guided Jeremy away from the register with a hand on his waist.

Luke rang the girls up without talking to them, since they were deep in their own conversation. The next person in line was a young man with questions about where to get food in the neighborhood, and Luke opened right up, full of ideas. Last came an older lady, and Luke switched to Spanish. Even Jeremy could tell Luke's Spanish wasn't very fluent, just the necessary words for the store, but he slathered it with those wide grins and the woman was smiling, too, as she left.

Jeremy forgot to hide his fascination, and Luke turned and caught him. He bumped Jeremy's elbow. "What are you looking at?"

"It's cool how you can do that. Just know the right things to say to different people."

"Huh. I guess you learn, working like this." Luke cut Jeremy another glance, grinning. "I think it's cool how you're always just saying whatever you think."

What he meant was it *wasn't* cool. Jeremy had said something most people would have known to keep to themselves, and Luke was being nice about it. But it was hard to mind as Luke took Jeremy's wrist again, rubbing his thumb over that tan line like there was a ridge on Jeremy's skin.

Luke took a very deep breath.

"*Luuuuuuuuuuuke!*" The shout was a long, low syllable, like a booing crowd. Two boys walked into the store, one very tall with the stooped posture that came with being unsure about all that height, and a shorter one with tighter, hectic movements who led the way. He was the one who had spoken, and he locked onto Jeremy like a target.

Jeremy recognized them, though they'd never met—it was more intel from Instagram. It made him feel all pervy, and he opened his eyes innocently wide, as if he'd never seen these, or any other, people before in his life.

Into Jeremy's ear, Luke said, "Don't listen to a word they say." The tall boy reached across the counter to clap Luke's hand.

Before they could say anything, Luke did the introductions: "Jeremy, this is Straight Wesley and Short Wes. Wesleys, Jeremy." He touched Jeremy's sleeve, and Short Wes grinned.

He wasn't all that short—he was a hair taller than Jeremy—but he seemed so next to Straight Wesley, who was at least six-six. Even a recluse like Jeremy knew not to comment on people's bodies, and he wasn't going to say anything, but Luke nudged him. "You might as well ask. That's the whole point of their thing."

Jeremy took another glance around all their faces before he ventured a try. "Okay. How come you're not Tall Wesley and"—he hesitated—"LGBTQ Wesley?"

Straight Wesley snickered. "L."

Jeremy froze and scanned their faces again—he would have hated if someone made a girl joke about him and would have resented the person who laid the trap for it—but Short Wes only snickered back.

Luke was smiling proudly. "The first reason is when people say 'Gay Wesley,' he gets to give them his angry bisexual lecture."

Short Wes nodded and unrolled his hand, an elegant concession. "Congratulations, you passed the test. Anyway, you can't call a person Bi Wesley, that's offensive."

Jeremy rolled his eyes. "You grow up with Alexei, see if you can forget about bi people." He remembered too late that he'd resolved not to talk about his brothers, and as their faces started to show the connection—*Bi? Alexei? The famous one?*—he quickly added, "I think Short Jeremy would be way more offensive than Gay Jeremy."

Straight Wesley shook his head. "Blond Jeremy."

"What if the other Jeremy was blond, too?"

Luke made an urgent noise, but Short Wes got there first: "You're one of Luke's, though. Everybody knows about Luke and blonds."

Luke snorted, but Jeremy felt a giddy rush. He was *Luke's*? He leaned over the counter and kicked his feet up. "Is this why he told me not to listen to anything you say?"

Short Wes gasped, pretending to be wounded, and Straight Wesley nodded sagely.

"Absolutely." Luke opened his hand against Jeremy's waist and made the floor tilt, but he was only nudging Jeremy down the counter, shining his smile on more customers. "Keep not listening while I handle this."

Chapter Twenty-One

Jeremy's side kept heating Luke's palm as he rang a group of girls up. It took a long time, and he couldn't hear what Jeremy and the Wesleys were saying over the girls' talk. Short Wes pulled out his phone to show Jeremy something, probably on the Tumblr he tended like he was dating it. Jeremy and Short Wes both laughed, and Straight Wesley even cracked a smile.

Jeremy must have said something about Sergei or Alexei again, because when Luke finally sent the girls on their way, Jeremy was saying, "Yeah, he's my older brother."

Two Wesley jaws dropped. "Maybe not Blond Jeremy, then," Short Wesley said significantly. Jeremy flinched.

"Hey, are you done ruining my game?" Luke asked. "Don't you have anywhere better to be?"

Short Wes shot him some eyebrows, but they let Luke herd them out of the store. There was no way they weren't going to find Camille and start jawing, but that was tomorrow's problem. "See?" He returned to Jeremy. "Ignore them."

"I liked them," Jeremy said. "I shouldn't have mentioned my family."

"Why not? You can have whatever family you want. They shouldn't have been assholes about it."

Jeremy's lips quirked in a way that could have been a smile or a frown. Luke was pawing a lot and ought to stop, but he reached over again, closing his fingers around the line at Jeremy's wrist. He was ready to go in for a kiss right there, but it was too public and Jeremy seemed shy. He wondered what the Wesleys had said about him, what *everybody knew.*

Jeremy didn't seem bothered. He seemed, mostly, focused on the place Luke's hand held his arm, like something worth watching was happening there.

The floor tilted under Luke's feet, a slow, swimming shift, and he was smiling and stepping closer before he understood it was not because of Jeremy, that was *real*, something was moving—

The ground churned, throwing Luke sideways so his hip knocked the counter hard, and something around him, the building or the earth, moaned like a whale. Screams scattered from the customers, but as soon as that high pitch rose, everything calmed.

The door to the back room flew open, and Yuri and Helene spilled through. They were both staring at him –and at Jeremy in his arms. Luke caught up long after his instinct had made him do it—he had an arm around Jeremy's body, the other hand tucking Jeremy's head against his chest. He'd turned his own back to the shuddering glass in the windows.

Luke had to think about moving before he could step away, and Jeremy's fingers were slow to uncurl where he'd grabbed Luke's T-shirt.

"Does everyone want to leave through the back?" Helene called, and the customers hurried toward the door. Jeremy's phone rang, Alexei's face on the screen, and when Jeremy swiped the call open, Alexei's tinny voice said, "What's wrong?" before Jeremy could speak.

Yuri twitched his fingers to beckon Luke to the door. They went out into the sun and found the red insides of some unidentifiable animal strewn across the sidewalk.

They reeled back, hands over their faces against the stink, in the same motion. Yuri said a word that wasn't English.

"Fuck," Luke said.

Yuri pulled his collar over his nose. "Don't swear. What is that?"

Luke shook his head. It felt nasty—a rotten vibe enveloping the mundane horror of entrails on the pavement. Luke looked for plaid and didn't see any, but there was a scatter of stones, like the ones he'd pulled out of the curse bags. "Malcolms?" he asked. "Did they try to blow up the building?"

There were customers in the store, a dozen families in the apartments. People would have died.

"Tough to say." Yuri looked over his shoulder. "That might not have been the attack. It might have been Alexei's binding playing defense."

Luke followed his gaze. Inside, Jeremy and Helene were speaking together into the phone. "What is he doing here?" Yuri asked.

Luke crossed his arms. "He was hanging out."

He stayed steady—*I'm not doing anything wrong, I'm not doing anything wrong*—as Yuri studied his face.

Finding nothing there, Yuri turned, shaking his shoulders in exasperation. He stopped short and threw his arm in front of Luke, who searched the street for what he'd seen. Halfway up the block, two men were walking away.

They were on fire, the sun catching heads of red-gold hair. Luke didn't know the taller one, but Corey Malcolm was built like a ram, short and wide. The rumors about the Malcolms were a tempest: they did ancient, brutal Druid magic; Corey Malcolm had sacrificed his own sister to his gods; they kept a sacred fire that had burned, fueled by blood, since the fifth century.

Of course, their people probably said the same things about the Kovrovs. Rumors were only rumors. Maybe there were rumors about Jeremy, what he was to the Kovrov family.

They watched until Malcolm was gone. Yuri moved toward the door, but stopped Luke when he tried to follow, pointing to the mess on the sidewalk. "That's you."

"Me?" Luke gawked.

"With great power..." Yuri made a smug smile, but it faded fast. Dryly, he added, "Stay there. I'll bring out a bucket."

What do you call an Irishman who sits on your front lawn?

What?

Patty O'Furniture

OH NO!!!

Oh yes. Any news?

No. Was your dad OK? He seemed mad I was there.

He was okay and mad. Not your fault

Oh no.

It's fine I'm tough. I'm still going to kiss you

OK. See you Monday.

Camille wasn't there to lecture Luke along with their parents, so she hunted him down the next morning. At least she brought coffee with her lip, throwing Luke's door open after he tried to sneak to the bathroom and back to bed.

"What is this thing you have about blonds?" She gave him a mug and stood with her hand on her hip.

"It could be genetic. Mom liked blond boys, too."

That made Camille scream, even though it was true. Yuri shaved his balding head now, but when he and Helene fell in love, he was a tall, broad-shouldered rock-star type with blond hair to the middle of his back.

"Also, by 'this thing,' what do you mean, the two?" Luke said, bitter. If he had to live with a reputation, he wished he'd had more fun earning it.

"*What* a two, though." She sat down on the bed. "That brat and then the baby prince of the Kovrovs. You're going to break his sheltered heart and get a hit on yourself. And me. I'm too young and beautiful to die."

Luke closed his heavy eyelids, inhaling coffee steam. She was too young and beautiful to get killed by Corey Malcolm, too. And not every kiss ended in heartbreak. "It doesn't have to be that serious. No one's talking about true love."

"It's that serious if you're going to start messing around with a Kovrov!"

"*Messing around.* I've made it as far as his wrist. At this rate, I'll manage a kiss by New Year's."

Camille didn't scream again, but she made the shape with her mouth and smacked his arm with the back of her hand.

"Stop bugging me, and I'll take the store again today," Luke said.

It didn't work. "You can't possibly like him. You're having a rebound thing, or a—" She cut herself off, giggling. "I was going to say 'physical thing,' but it's too weird. Jeremy Kovrov!"

"What does—look." *I had a vision, so if you think about it, it's already happened.* Or, *Well, he's under a secret crossing.* Or, *It isn't about magic; it's about him.* Luke surprised himself with that one and turned the thought over carefully. He'd been flattered, and then intrigued. And what now? It was a cocktail of curiosity and protectiveness and hope. It was so easy to spend time with Jeremy. He'd laughed with Short Wes and hadn't been too cool to hold Luke's hand, and if there was anything more Luke wanted, he didn't know what it was. The idea of Jeremy was safe, even though he made the whole world more dangerous.

"Sure I like him. I never—he's shy and…he's really sweet."

She stared. "Sweet."

"Yeah."

"It's like we're talking about two different people."

She was right about that. "You just have to get to know him a little," Luke said.

Camille let a pause drag. "Truly. Be honest. Was that your gum in that mojo bag?"

Luke hid in his coffee again. He thought he'd escaped that question. "I don't know. There's no way to be sure. But maybe, yeah."

"Maybe." She didn't sound impressed.

"It could have been yours. You think I don't see you snapping your gum at Wes? Or his. Or anyone's."

"It could have been." She leaned in. "But was it?"

Luke's mouth twitched, and he sipped significantly at his coffee.

"Alexei Kovrov killed a man in front of you three days ago," Camille said.

"You think I don't know that?"

Camille opened her hands to the heavens like only they could help her. "Corey Malcolm's attacking us for no reason at all, and you're going with denial."

Luke shrank around his mug. "What do you want me to do? Fight Malcolm? I don't know anything about him, and Alexei told us to stay out of it. If I can't fix it, what's the point of worrying about it?"

She pointed at his nose. "That is a terrible way to think about your problems. That is why you always worry about your boy problems first."

She was not wrong. It made Luke jittery to think about his gum in the bag, but he could handle thinking about Jeremy, about Jeremy's crossing and how his hair had ended up in Malcolm's hands and what Luke needed to do to keep him safe. "You want to disobey a Kovrov's orders to go harass a Malcolm? Be my guest." Luke paused. "Don't actually do that."

Camille shook her head. "I'm not. That's not what I want you to do." She put a hand on his arm and made her eyes serious and liquid. "I want you to let Dad get you out, and find a boy to chase who isn't a Kovrov."

"Jeremy isn't—" Luke snapped his mouth closed too late. He'd promised to keep the crossing a secret. He wanted badly to say *Jeremy isn't a Kovrov*. Jeremy was a normal boy who'd gotten caught up in that nightmare family. He was stuck with Sergei, who didn't understand him at all. Luke was going to help him escape.

He took a deep breath and lifted one hand, fingers open and palm down. Camille's eyes popped wide, but she tucked the back of her own hand under his palm. Together, Luke clapped his other hand underneath, and she clapped hers on top.

They smiled together—they hadn't done that in years—but Camille sobered fast. Their handshake sealed secrets.

"He's not a Kovrov." A knot unwound in Luke's chest. "He's stolen. The Kovrovs took him to pay off a debt."

Camille's jaw dropped, and time slipped as Luke watched

his own reaction on her face. "What? The Kovrovs do that?"

Luke sat back, relaxing as she shouldered some of his burden. "It's an old contract—Sergei's as stuck in it as Jeremy is. They're crossed. I have to figure it out."

Camille didn't argue. She simply nodded. "What have you tried?"

"Not much." Luke had been so focused on the idea of that kiss, the past-future-vision one he remembered and anticipated at the same time. "He doesn't like to talk about it. But I'm working on it."

"Have you been able to feel out the mojo?"

"There's a symbol." Luke wrapped a hand around his own wrist. "One of the bracelets he wears. It's got that Kovrov vibe, but his is different."

"Well. That *is* interesting." Her eyes drifted toward the corners of the room, and she tapped her chin in thought. "What's the plan?"

Luke had spent the whole day before planning for a kiss. "I don't know. Try not to get shot, then make a plan."

She tilted her head to a scornful angle. He shouldn't tell her about the binding—but she saw his hesitation and pounced, catlike. "What else are you hiding?"

"I broke a binding," Luke said. "I just asked him a question. I didn't even know I was doing it, but the magic cracked right open. That's the plan—get to know him a little better and figure out how it works."

Camille tucked her chin so she could get that extra height from her skeptical eyebrows. "Get to *know* him, huh?"

He shoved her playfully. "I'm serious. You want to help? You could look into the stories."

"You mean fairy tales?"

Luke nodded. "This is some weird Rumpelstiltskin shit."

"Ah! Rumpelstiltskin has a Russian name, too, what is it?" She frowned in his face, as if he had any idea.

"I don't know. This is why I'm asking you."

She grinned. "All right. I'll look into it."

"Cool," Luke said. "Listen, you can't tell anyone. Not even Mom and Dad. I promised him. I shouldn't have told you."

"Sure." Camille studied him with a distant gaze, like he was a strange artifact. "You still have to be careful. *More* careful."

"I know."

She snapped out of her reverie and stood. "Just remember, if you can't take care of yourself for your own sake—you can't uncross anybody if you go and get yourself killed."

Chapter Twenty-Two

Luke worked alone in Sergei's warehouse all morning, radio fuzzy and light dim. He didn't lie to himself—he walked back and forth and waited for Jeremy.

He opened a box of black-painted jars, but he didn't know where they needed to go. A lap of the warehouse didn't reveal any clues. There was a lot of magic at play in the room; maybe more shelves were hidden from him.

Luke stopped and stood still, hands on his hips. He wondered what his family was doing that day, whether they were talking about him. If he let himself think about the dirty metallic scent of the basement air, it slipped into the way that restaurant had smelled after the attack—blood, fear, and magic. His conviction started to waver, but when the door opened, his attention turned like a light switch. Jeremy gave the boxes by the door a cursory glance. "Oh, look. You're already done."

He didn't sound surprised. He wasn't making eye contact, sliding his gaze around the room. His hands stretched open, fingers wide, palms tapping his own hips, and he turned shoulders-first to Luke. "You want to come upstairs and hang out for a while?"

"Sure," Luke said, mild as melting butter. "What would we find to do?"

Jeremy blushed heroically, but he drummed up a brave, "Keep making fun of me and you'll see."

With Luke following, Jeremy nearly jogged around the landing and up past the first floor. "Melnyk!" Sergei barked.

Luke stopped, turning slowly.

"All done?" Sergei asked.

"Everything but the black jars."

Sergei nodded once and raised his voice. "Kid, you got it?"

"Later!" Jeremy called, already gone.

Sergei drummed his fingers against his chest, and Luke could have sworn it was to show off the *KOV* tattooed on his knuckles. The silver bracelet gleamed on his other wrist.

"Go ahead, then." Sergei kept watching as Luke walked away.

Jeremy was right out of sight in the upstairs hallway. He clenched his fists and shadowboxed the air—*Kovrov*, he mouthed, right and left fist on each syllable. "Sergei is…" He shrugged and continued up the stairs.

The glittering chaos of Jeremy's room was a different world. It seemed like he'd cleaned up, in that most of the clothes on the floor were in one pile and there were no dishes.

"Did you really get yelled at because of me?" Jeremy asked.

"A little. Well, and then Camille yelled at me." Luke kept stepping, and Jeremy kept moving, like they were playing basketball and Jeremy was trying to box him out. He stopped and relaxed. Giving Jeremy some space, he wandered toward the shelves.

"Camille? You *are* in trouble."

"I know. I wouldn't say it was because of you. More about me, or our families. There's nothing wrong with you."

Jeremy had stopped moving, too, a pale smear in Luke's peripheral vision, but Luke looked at the wall instead of turning his head. An iridescent crystal cricket perched on a stack of hardback books: *Oliver Twist, Great Expectations, David Copperfield.*

"What happens next?" Jeremy said.

Luke turned. Jeremy leaned into the window seat, but he wasn't quite still—he kept lifting with his chest, like each breath filled him with fizzing soda bubbles. He looked like a person who was about to get his first kiss.

"Are you sure you want this?" Luke asked. "I didn't mean—"

"I'm sure."

"Then all you have to do is keep looking so cute," Luke said, which was a dumb line and would have made Max or anybody scoff at him, but made Jeremy smile and look at him, finally. He was two steps away, so Luke closed the distance easily and took his jaw to tilt his face up. Jeremy shut his eyes like he was bracing for a crash. Luke waited, giving Jeremy the time to relax or say stop and himself that second to linger, to look. This was his favorite part, the moment right before the kiss.

He fit his lips over Jeremy's as lightly as he could, and pressed forward once, twice, Jeremy's lips going softer each time. He nudged Jeremy's lower lip down with his own, easing his mouth open. Jeremy followed, but his fists clenched tight against Luke's chest, so tense he nearly vibrated. Luke pulled back, running his fingers between Jeremy's shoulder blades. "You're all right," he said quietly. "I've got you."

One second stretched to two—Jeremy's breath shuddered warm over Luke's neck—and his body let go all at once. He put his hands on Luke's face and jumped forward, lips already parting for another kiss.

That was the sign Luke needed. He shaped Jeremy's back with his hands, and Jeremy's body tilted in like he was sure. When Luke slid a hand up Jeremy's spine to cup and move his head, Jeremy made a surprised sound and a soft one.

When Luke closed his eyes, it was all sharper, more real. He could have gone anywhere, but he only wanted to be here. It was all right if this was Jeremy's first kiss, because Luke was pretty sure he was making it phenomenal for him.

He kissed himself dizzy, and it still wasn't enough. He let his nose slide along Jeremy's cheekbone and slipped a peck against his hair before he made himself lift away. When he opened his eyes, Jeremy was looking at his own hands on Luke's chest, face dazed, with a faint concentration line between his eyebrows. Jeremy closed his lower lip into his teeth, and Luke used his thumb to pull it free.

Jeremy blinked up, like coming awake.

"You good?" Luke asked.

"Yeah. I'm okay." He slid one hand behind Luke's neck, sending an incandescent tremor down his arms, and pulled him back.

Chapter Twenty-Three

It ruined the drama to have to wait until one a.m. to storm
out of the house, but Jeremy was committed. He waited at the
front door for the clock and the car, staring at the blue paint
instead of making eye contact with anyone. Sergei stomped
off to bed. Marta spent a few minutes running between them,
wheedling and pleading, but when Vanya crept to the top of
the stairs to ask what was wrong, she left with him.

The house breathed. Without Sergei there to piss him
off, Jeremy slipped from anger to ache. He traced the seams
in the door, the smoothness of unbroken wood under his
fingers. He touched the doorknob and, dreamlike, it melted
in his hand. He laid his forehead against the door, but even
that was too close—it burned, hurting until he stepped back.
A stone formed in his throat, but this was the only thing he
could control, and he refused to cry.

The clock in the hall ticked over to one. The driver texted
his arrival. There was no one awake to see Jeremy's exit, but
he flounced anyway.

He sat in the back seat of a stranger's car with his head

vibrating against the window. The traffic was clear, and Manhattan flew past, flashing lights reaching toward the sky. Out of the house, out in the big bright-dark night, the hurt lifted. He was tired but not sleepy, fizzing with a hundred different feelings that didn't know how to sit together. His insides were too big for his body.

Jeremy didn't know the night doorman as well as Eddie, but he'd called Alexei and Alexei must have called down. The man said, "Good evening, Mr. Kovrov," before Jeremy could speak. All he had to do was smile and nod.

Alexei wasn't asleep, either. All the lights were on, and the TV, and he was still wearing gray suit trousers and a black dress shirt. A squat glass of something amber sat on the kitchen island. "Are you okay?" Jeremy asked.

"Am I okay? I'm not the one running across town in the middle of the night." Alexei grabbed his drink, and Jeremy followed him to the couch.

"Sergei yelled at me."

"Why would he do that?"

Jeremy tapped his hand on his leg. "Luke kissed me."

Alexei took a sip, eyes evaluating Jeremy over his glass: the pile of bracelets on his arm, the silver one that waited there. By the time he lowered the glass, his face was polished like a new shoe. "How was it? Good?"

Jeremy nodded. His lips felt bare and tingly—he tamped down an urge to touch them. "He checked if I was okay a bunch of times. He would have stopped if I didn't like it."

"As he should."

"I know. I just meant...it was really nice."

Alexei smiled. "Good. *Good*. Am I forgiven my meddling, your highness?"

"Maybe." Now that he had a sympathetic ear, Jeremy wanted to protect the details for himself. How easy it had been, how his body melted and his thoughts blurred, how

Luke always smelled like church and magic. How Luke had pulled himself away like it was work, gotten halfway to the door, and turned around to come back, laughing as he took Jeremy's face in his hands again. Jeremy had thought, *This is it, this is what the stories are about.*

It hadn't made magic, but it had been as perfect as any movie scene. Jeremy said none of that, and instead asked, "Is it different, kissing boys and girls?"

Alexei squinted into his glass. "It's different with everyone, if you pay attention. But I'm an old man now. They all blend together." He knocked back his drink and stood. "Pip-pip. Off to bed."

Hours later, Jeremy woke in a too-big quiet, newly emptied of sound. A shadow twisted in the hall outside the guest room. "Alexei?"

The shadows and silence resolved into Alexei, peering around the door. "Go back to sleep."

"What's the matter?" A reedy note of anxiety sliced Jeremy's bleariness.

"Nothing, nothing." Alexei stepped into the room. "I was just checking on you. Everything's fine."

Alexei tugged at the corners of Jeremy's bed, hovering, as if that was supposed to help him drift off. "Sit down," Jeremy said. "Tell me what's wrong."

Alexei was good at this move, turning over card after card until suddenly you were demanding that he do whatever he already wanted to do. He sat down on the side of the bed. "If I asked you to be careful, would you listen?"

Jeremy yawned. "I'm always careful."

"More careful. Run-on-a-treadmill careful?"

Jeremy searched for Alexei's eyes in the blue shadows. "I have to leave the house sometimes. What's happening?"

Alexei rubbed his face, like Jeremy was making *him* sleepy. "I had a little nightmare about you."

Jeremy waited. "That's all?"

"Nightmare?" Alexei repeated, like he was asking. "Maybe just a nightmare?"

Jeremy shut his eyes and sleep snatched at him. "What was it about?"

Alexei didn't answer.

Jeremy tried again. "What does Corey Malcolm have against me?"

Alexei sighed heavily. "I don't know. It doesn't make any sense."

"Well, what does he have against Sergei? Or you?"

"It's me," Alexei said. "You remember our fathers fought, his and mine?"

"Jersey."

"Yes, for Jersey. I was too young to be involved then, but it was Corey's first big foray into leadership. And a successful one. We'd give them a good fight today, if we had to, but we were no match for them then. Papa was too angry to be smart, Sergei and I were still kids, guys were quitting or defecting every day. Corey was ready to take over New York, or the world. Malcolm guys were after us all the time. Sergei got roughed up after school one day when he was, what, twelve?"

Jeremy's heart twisted. "I didn't know that."

"Mmm. A bunch of monsters. And Corey and I fought over a girl. It was very personal, another big mess. He won that, too. But that was the last big battle. Malcolm went after the Zhangs, and they allied with the Damianis to push him back, if you can believe that. The whole thing was over before you were even born. I can't understand why he's after you."

Jeremy's eyes popped wide. "Oh! Binding!"

"Pardon?"

"Luke broke one of your bindings on me." Jeremy had forgotten to tell him in all the chaos, but it might have been part of the chaos. Jeremy's face burned in the dark. He'd been preoccupied with Luke and forgotten to follow through on his responsibility.

Alexei wasn't angry—he only scoffed. "He most certainly did not."

"He did. He asked how I was related to you and Sergei, and it snapped. We both felt it."

"No," Alexei said. "I assure you, I would have noticed. And I wouldn't have bound that in the first place—it's not a secret you're my brother."

Jeremy chewed his lip. "Something happened. Could someone else have a binding on me?"

Alexei was still for a long silence. "I didn't think so, but who knows? I'll look into it." He dropped his face into his hands. "What are we going to do with you?"

He sounded so genuinely forlorn, and it was four o'clock in the morning. Jeremy had handed over his one card and only made it worse. "I'm fine. The only thing that's hurting me is weirdo brothers who won't let me sleep."

Alexei's weight shifted. "Go back to sleep."

"You want me to pray for you?"

Alexei made a derisive noise, but he turned his wrist over next to Jeremy's shoulder.

Jeremy put his hand over Alexei's and said, "Dear God, bless this weirdo."

Alexei laughed out loud. Jeremy shut his eyes, and the next thing he knew was white morning light and a fading, half-remembered conversation. Careful—be careful. He tried to imagine how being more careful would look, but all he could think about was Luke and whether he could get more kisses. It was a fresh new day, and he was no better off than he'd been the morning before, but no worse, either. He smiled into the pillow, and he felt huge and wild and not careful at all.

Chapter Twenty-Four

Luke's mother and sister were in a screaming fight. He couldn't make out words—they were downstairs, and he was not going to leave his room for anything—but every bang of Camille stomping up the stairs and slamming the door to her room was clear.

He gave it three minutes, listening for aftershocks, and when they stayed quiet, he crept down the hall and knocked on Camille's door.

"What?" Her voice snapped like a whip.

"It's me." He opened the door slowly, careful of projectiles. "What happened?"

She sighed and made room for him to sit on the bed. "Dad went Malcolm-hunting."

Luke's jaw dropped. Someone should have woken him up.

Camille nodded sympathetically at his surprise. "Sergei came and got him this morning. I wanted to go, too, but Mom's mad he went at all."

"Did Sergei want you?"

"He said it was up to Mom and Dad." Camille wrinkled her nose. "He'd be safer if I was there."

"You'd be in more danger, though."

She shrugged. "I can take care of myself. Anyway, *you* don't get to talk."

Luke snorted agreeably and didn't argue, letting her rest her cranky head on his shoulder. From downstairs, Helene's frustrated scream rattled the silence. Luke jumped toward the door, but Camille nudged his arm and pointed out the window, where Alexei's car poured like heavy cream onto the curb.

Katya let Luke into the back, and this time, expecting to see Jeremy, he found Alexei, smiling mildly. "Good afternoon. I have a couple of clients who could use one of your remarkable cleansings. I thought perhaps we could pick up our prince first."

"Yes, sir," Luke said. Alexei's smile twitched, and he turned his face away to hide it. So Jeremy had told him? Jeremy had definitely told him. Luke had never met anyone who shared so much with authority figures—but maybe it was different when the adults in your life were brothers, not parents. Luke hadn't even gotten around to telling his friends.

As Katya pulled the car into the street, Alexei reached into the front of his jacket, taking out a deck of cards. "Pick a card, any *cahd*," he said, like a street magician.

Luke shuffled. They were soft with use but not tattered, except for brown stains along the short sides. Luke started— that would be dried blood. He stopped abruptly and flipped over the Jack of Clubs, noting it as fast as he could before tucking it back and returning the deck.

Alexei sat the deck in his open palm. Luke followed his gaze down and watched as—though Alexei didn't move—the deck disappeared.

Luke strangled down a horrified noise. It was like a

fake magician's trick, without any room for sleight of hand. And it was not delightful the way sleight of hand could be—it reminded Luke of Jeremy ripping away on the sidewalk, the untenable physics of his crossing. It was fairy-tale logic, unbendable rules warping around the whims of a witch or king, and nothing like the legible, chemical kitchen magic Luke had grown up with. That kind of story magic was supposed to be impossible. It would be better if it were impossible.

Alexei rolled his wrist again, the Jack of Clubs face-up on his palm.

"Cool," Luke said, though even to his own ears he didn't sound like he meant it. "Where do they go?"

"Hmm?" Alexei returned the card to his jacket pocket, a heft to the movement suggesting he'd retrieved the deck.

"The cards. When they disappear. Where do they go?"

"No idea." Alexei shrugged.

"You don't have a theory?"

"I don't believe in theories," Alexei said. Katya made a thick, mean noise, and Luke glanced up front. Her shoulders were set like cement.

Luke was missing something—the point of that demonstration, the reason for Katya's disgust. "Have you ever lost anything doing that?"

Alexei made a *humph* with a wry, grimacing smile. "No."

With all the irony, there was no telling what he meant: no, he hadn't, and the question was absurd, or no, sarcastically, because of course he had.

"Stop encouraging him," Katya said flatly.

Luke sat back. This was too weird, the kind of game you only won by refusing to play. It didn't escape him that Katya, who had more common sense than the rest of the Kovrov team put together, was annoyed with something about him.

"Just trying to lighten the mood," Alexei said. "Would

you rather I bluster about the young prince's virtue? Surely no one would respect that nonsense from me."

In spite of himself, Luke laughed—one quick snap, which he hid behind his hand. Katya groaned, but the fire had gone out of it. And shortly, they were double-parked outside Sergei's house as Jeremy hopped down the front steps, a shaft of light in a yellow shirt and orange plaid shorts. He looked so ridiculous all the ice melted in Luke's chest.

The work was fake. Alexei took them to an apartment building on Ocean Avenue, where Luke shook hands with a nice young couple and burned some incense. Alexei didn't even offer to take him home—he left Luke and Jeremy on the sidewalk. "You will call me," he said, "at the *first* sign of any Malcolm."

"Yep!" Jeremy said.

"I'm serious."

"You're full of shit," Jeremy said, so decisively Luke gaped at him. Jeremy grinned at Alexei. "We already know you have dudes on every block between here and the Bronx Zoo."

Luke hadn't known, but of course that was right. Left to his own devices, he would have made some plan to take Jeremy out and would not have been able to protect them from Malcolm spies or another attack. "My dad and Sergei went Malcolm-hunting this morning."

"Malcolm-hunting!" Jeremy repeated, like it was something delightful.

Luke shrugged. "That's what Camille called it."

"See?" Jeremy lifted his chin triumphantly to Alexei. "You can't keep secrets from us; we know everything."

"I may have taken some precautions." Alexei's smile mirrored Jeremy's, warm. "But I am respecting *boundaries*, so you don't have a tail. That means, if you catch sight of any gingers at all—"

"I'll call you." Jeremy cocked his head to one side. "No, I'll call Sergei."

Alexei laughed. "Perfect. And don't go to Jersey."

"Why would we go to New Jersey?" Luke asked.

"Millions of people go to New Jersey every day." Alexei slipped into the car, past the door Katya held for him. "I'm sure I don't know why."

As Katya returned to her seat, she cast a look over the pair of them. Luke had another uncomfortable feeling she was weighing him and unimpressed with the number.

"Is this weird?" Jeremy asked as the car pulled away. "Did Alexei make it weird?"

Luke huffed. "That's what's going on Alexei's tombstone. 'Here lies Alexei Kovrov. He made it weird.'"

Jeremy giggled and turned up the street.

"I think he might have threatened me," Luke added, following. "I mean, he made a deck of cards disappear and acted important about it. Was that a threat?"

"*I* don't know." Jeremy paused and must have realized that wasn't comforting. "Alexei barks more than he bites."

That was also not comforting. "Are you going somewhere?"

"Oh. I was heading home. Do you want to go to the park? We can get ice cream."

"Outstanding." Luke rocked his hand forward, brushing one finger along Jeremy's palm. It was the smallest touch, but it stopped Jeremy cold on the sidewalk. Luke rubbed his hand over his upper lip to hide a smile.

"You better be careful. My brother will disappear you."

Luke dropped his gaze. Quickly, Jeremy said, "Oh, *that* was weird, wasn't it?"

Luke shook his head. "When I saw that deck disappear, it made me think of when you—when you showed me your curse." He turned over his hand, thinking about Jeremy's dissolving inside it.

They stopped at a crosswalk, and Jeremy leaned in, nudging Luke's shoulder with his own.

"Is that what happened when you were born?" Luke asked. "Your family had a baby, and then—*pop*?"

Jeremy made a strange freezing-flailing motion, like he had to stop himself from running into traffic. "No."

"No?"

Jeremy scraped his hand over his head. "Maybe. I don't actually know."

"How can you *not know*?"

The light turned, and Jeremy hurtled into the crosswalk. This was why you were supposed to wait three days to text. No—it was why you weren't supposed to grill adopted people about their birth families. Luke's mother would have given him an earful.

He caught up at the curb and said, "I'm sorry," as Jeremy said, "It's complicated!"

Luke grabbed his elbow, and Jeremy jerked to a stop, huffing. Half the block turned to look. This was going great. "I'm sorry," Luke said again. "That was way out of line. I understand."

Jeremy twisted his lips. "I know I'm weird. I *know*."

"I didn't say that." Luke let him go, turned him back up the sidewalk to get him moving. "I don't think that."

Jeremy rolled his eyes. "Sure you don't."

"I don't," Luke said. "It's the mojo, everything your family can do. It's so different. I can't figure out how it…"

He stopped to think, and Jeremy looked up at him, eyes so raw and open it made Luke grave with the responsibility of getting this right. "My mom says magic is like language. People all over the world learn different languages, but they're using the same bodies to speak. They talk about the same things. Just the words are different."

"Okay," Jeremy said slowly.

"I feel like I'm trying to learn to speak Kovrov, but you guys are...ants who communicate by rubbing your antennas together."

Jeremy yelped in surprised laughter. "Oh my god!"

"Exactly."

Jeremy picked up Luke's hand and brought it to his face, blinking his tickling eyelashes against the back. Even as he did it he started blushing, but Luke caught his fingers and gave them a little squeeze before he let go.

"There are words in some languages that don't translate to others," Jeremy said.

They came to another crosswalk, and Luke stopped to consider. "That's true."

"And there are a bunch of sounds in other languages that are hard to make, like the German *R*, or sing-songs—"

"All right," Luke said. "It's just a metaphor."

"You called me an ant!"

Luke gave him a smile he hoped was reassuring. "I didn't mean it's weird. Just different, for me. Do you have anything that could help me understand, like books or papers or—" Luke stopped as Jeremy's face went sharp again. He didn't answer.

"Only if you're comfortable with that," Luke said. "Of course."

Jeremy shook his head and said, "I'm not," so quietly that Luke read it on his lips instead of hearing.

"That's fine," Luke said. The green edge of the park, dark with shadow, rose on the left. Luke took Jeremy's hand, good and grabbed it, and moved toward it. He stepped off the path and guided Jeremy under the trees. It wasn't as cool or quiet there as it looked from the outside, but it was more private than the street.

"Don't be upset. All I meant to say was hi." Luke put

his lips over Jeremy's and his hands around Jeremy's waist, waited through Jeremy's sudden tension and slower relaxing, and guided Jeremy's mouth open with his own to taste his little gasp.

It took Jeremy a long time to open his eyes. Finally, he said, "Hi."

Luke pitched his voice low. "I've been thinking about that since we stopped yesterday."

Jeremy made a strange half-laugh and dropped his head on Luke's shoulder. "I can't believe it was only yesterday."

"Long night?"

Jeremy sighed. "Let's go get ice cream." He tugged Luke back to the path, heading into the park, and after Luke had thought the conversation was over, he added, "In Sergei's house, it's always a long night."

Chapter Twenty-Five

By the time Luke walked into the kitchen the next morning, Camille was already on lunch. He'd been on the phone with Jeremy until after one, filled with warring delight at his goofy texts and horror at the slow-ticking seconds of his crossing's midnight rule, and it had taken a long time to settle and let him sleep.

"Yes, come to papa." Luke grabbed half her grilled cheese off her plate and took a big bite. Camille shot back a French word that would have stung anybody else, but her jinxes bounced right off Luke. He smiled as he chewed.

"Luke." Helene lay back on the sofa. "Don't devil your sister."

Around his bite, Luke said, "I have to go soon."

Helene grimaced, so Luke finished chewing and swallowed before he finished. "Alexei'll be here. I have—"

"I know. *Work*."

Luke turned one of the chairs around at the big table and sat facing her. "The Eyals again. That first family, with the little girl? He wants me to check up on them."

"That shouldn't take long," Helene said. Behind Luke, Camille made a wheezy scoff around a bite of sandwich.

"Yeah, we'll see what he wants me to do after."

Helene sat up, drawing her spine straight. "Luke Walker Melnyk."

"Oooooh," Camille said.

"If my only son is going to *lie to my face*—"

"I'll see what Alexei wants me to do after," Luke repeated, a band closing around his chest, "and then Jeremy wants to go to a baseball game." He held his voice calm. Luke had asked him, had made the plan, and if he didn't count hanging around the store or with Jeremy's brothers—and he didn't—it was their first real date. He held the idea of *first* close and tender and would rather not have discussed it with his mom.

Helene's face was doing something Luke's own must have done a lot: *Ha! I won. Wait—now what?* "Say it's a Yankees game at least."

Luke opened his palms. "I'm offended."

"Is he going to wear that hat?" Camille asked. "That hat offends me."

"If it's not the hat, it'll be something worse." Luke's voice gave him away. It was like warm syrup, slow and sweet. He sounded like all the trouble he wanted to cause.

Helene flinched back into the couch. "Luke. That family."

"Jeremy's not like the rest of them."

"Neither were they when they were kids."

Luke shook his head. She would understand if he could explain, if he hadn't promised. "I know what I'm doing."

"You don't know—"

Luke's phone buzzed in his pocket. It was nothing, a snap from Short Wes, but he jumped on it to tap out of the talk.

"I am *talking* to you. I'll take that phone away."

"Good luck. I'll go get a new one, since I pay for this myself."

Camille made a little *hmm* sound like he'd scored a hit, but Helene looked furious and stood up. "You live in my house, and you will participate in my family."

"I'm checking Snapchat. That's it. You are the ones who always make things about betraying the family."

"I'm not making anything about anything. I'm asking you to think—"

"I did think. You just don't like what I decided." Luke was surer every day, as Jeremy's kisses got braver and Luke started to rely on his calls. They were doing something right, something real—Luke wasn't ready to name it, but he'd never felt it before.

"You're seventeen; you can't make decisions."

"You weren't that much older than me when you met Dad! I was old enough to go to work for them, wasn't I? All I do is—" His parents were the strictest parents he knew, and he wanted a little credit for all the effort he put into following their rules and working hard and earning money, his constant unending trying. They talked about him like this reckless animal, and all he felt was the weight of responsibility. "You just hate him because he's a boy. You hated Max, too."

"Max was trouble! We have been nothing but supportive—"

"You're not being very supportive right now." Luke's voice dropped out of the last words, his bravado giving way.

Camille made a small, abrupt sound, like the secret he'd told might spill out of her and fill the gaps in this broken conversation. Luke turned and squinted, willing her silent; she gave him a sympathetic grimace.

Helene stood and crossed her arms. "What aren't you telling me?"

Luke swallowed hard, choking the secret down. "Nothing. I just don't know why you want to fight."

She waited. Camille got up, rinsed her plate, put it away,

and went downstairs, all before Luke or Helene moved.

"You'll tell me when you're ready," Helene said. "I'll be waiting."

Luke stood. He was so much taller, and looking down at her steadied his wavering. "I have to go."

She pursed her lips. "I thought Alexei was picking you up."

"No, I'm going to meet him." He swiveled past her, heading for the door. "I have to—I'll see you later."

"Luke!"

"I have to go."

Luke tripped down the steps, slamming into the humidity in the alley. He went a few buildings down, out of sight of the windows, and crouched against the wall. It was 12:07, and though Jeremy was fine, and even happy, Luke couldn't settle his clawing thoughts.

It didn't make Jeremy any safer to keep the secret—it protected Sergei, or the Kovrov family. The silence and denial only closed Jeremy's trap tighter. Luke would not be able to hang around working the edges of the crossing forever, wouldn't help anything that way. He had to try some real magic, organize the evidence, and build a ritual. He had to talk to Jeremy, or his mother, or someone, but first he would have to decide what to say.

Luke took slow breaths until he could speak steadily. He called Jeremy, who answered the phone with a *Hey* that took two lilting syllables.

"Hey yourself," Luke said. "Listen, I'll meet you at the Eyals'. Don't need to pick me up."

"Oh. If you're sure?"

"Yeah, I'm already on my way." Luke pushed himself up and started walking. He'd called instead of texting, to hear Jeremy's voice, just because he could. It was clingy, and it should have been the wrong play. But that wouldn't even occur to Jeremy, and if it did, he wouldn't mind. He had about as much chill as the Sahara.

"Oh my god! *Ohmygodohmygod.* Spider! Luke, *code spider.*"

"You don't have to say 'code' if there's actually a spider."

"It was in my hair!"

"All that running is bad for you."

"Okay, *Sergei.*" Jeremy gasped. "How long do you think it's been there? Oh my god, where did it go?"

"Well, *I* don't know." Luke crossed the street before he walked past the store. He wasn't going to think about it right now. He wasn't even going to look at it.

Jeremy gasped again. "I think it's *in my bed.*"

Luke grinned big enough to get it in his voice. "Do you need me to come over there and smush it?"

A huff crackled in the phone. "Here lies Jeremy, murdered to death by spider poison while Luke made sex jokes."

Luke laughed, though an alarm started wheeling through his head. Jeremy was in his room, in his *bed*, and talking about sex, while Luke was baking on a crowded sidewalk. All he said was, "I think you can handle it. I'm almost at the subway. I'll see you in a minute, all right?"

"I might have spider powers by then."

"Cool."

"If it webs me, you have to come cut me free, okay?"

"Maybe."

"Luke!"

He was smiling as he slid the call closed. The fight and his fit were fading already, and he let them go, turning his mind to the afternoon ahead and his work.

Chapter Twenty-Six

Jeremy had figured the most expensive baseball tickets would be the best ones, but Luke set him right on that. They sat at the very top of the stadium, the last row before the sky. So high up, the air was blue and breezy, more like a midwinter memory of summer than the reality of humid garbage and sweaty pits. Luke showed him how to watch the game from that view, not pitch by pitch but as a dance among all the men on the field.

Also, in the middle of the afternoon on a Tuesday, there weren't many people up top with them, and whatever conditions Luke was always checking to decide whether it was safe to touch in public were satisfied. He sat with his arm around Jeremy's shoulders, stealing kisses when the game was slow. The trick was, it seemed slower from a few stories away than it would down in the bowl.

Kissing scrambled Jeremy's wires more than it was probably meant to. Luke moved Jeremy's face with his hands, way more *up* than felt completely safe, and Jeremy hung there, vulnerable, before Luke dove in. Then something inside his chest rushed up, and his thoughts vanished in burning, buzzing white. After Luke pulled away, he would have to use his hands to put Jeremy's face back down again.

Between kisses, when Luke was talking about baseball or telling stories about his friends, Jeremy watched him out of the corner of his eye. Luke was high-strung in a sneaky, backward way, making a big performance of how casual he was being. Something was wrong, and he didn't want to talk about it, which was fine—Jeremy's life and his family and most of what he was doing here with Luke shivered on an unsteady foundation of not-talking-about-it—but there was no reason to make it such a production.

One thing Jeremy wasn't talking about was that he'd had a fight with Sergei. (He fought with Sergei all the time; once, after a particularly bad one, Sergei had sat down on the floor next to Jeremy's bed and said, "It's okay, kid. You yell if you need to. I can take it." The memory would sometimes make Jeremy ill with gratitude and other times, when he had good reason to be angry, even angrier.) Sergei had said nothing so kind the night before. What he'd said was, "You'll never find what you're looking for with someone like that."

Anger changed the shape of Jeremy's spine, made him taller—it honestly felt like his head popped off. "Someone like that! What does *someone like that* mean? Do you mean *a guy*? Do you want to talk about this?"

Sergei's face had gone flat—no, he did not want to talk about that. Jeremy'd had this terrible feeling that what Sergei meant was *black* or *Ukrainian* or *poor*, and he would either say something gruesome or say something to try to excuse his gruesomeness and Jeremy would have to know that about him forever, and so Jeremy said, "Don't ever talk to me again!" and made a run for it up the stairs.

And that was *that* problem well and solved, certainly not lying in wait to explode later. Pip-pip, as Alexei would say. In the yellow light of afternoon, with Luke's kisses unraveling all his defenses, thoughts kept arriving uninvited with other interpretations of what Sergei might have meant. Someone blithely, rashly confident, beyond all reason and evidence. Someone who thought he was better than Jeremy's family. Someone who kissed like he had to be so careful not to break anything in his sure hands; like Jeremy was hoarding all the oxygen in the world; no, like there was plenty of regular oxygen out there but Jeremy had some special, better kind; like he'd had a lot of practice.

Sergei had only been so mad because he was afraid.

Luke leaned forward with his elbows on his knees to watch a high pop-up, and Jeremy ran one finger down the arch of his back. He still thrilled that he was allowed—and, with each touch, lost a breath to anxiously wondering when this was going to get taken away. When Sergei was going to assert his authority, or Luke was going to change his mind.

Luke glanced over his shoulder for a beat, then twisted around. "This is nice, getting to chill for a minute. Just being with you."

Luke was quick with the lines, but something so simple threatened to undo Jeremy completely. "Don't talk to your nachos when I'm sitting right here."

"Ha." Luke sat back. "For real though, these are not good."

"I'll eat them."

Luke passed them over, and Jeremy tried one. It was sort of like eating cardboard dipped in plastic, but not in a bad way.

"Sergei does feed you, right?" Luke asked.

"I'm hungry! I ran eight miles this morning."

Luke's jaw dropped. "Why, were you lost?"

Jeremy laughed, and all the stupid feelings he was trying to play cool came bubbling over his lips in a spill of light. He clapped a hand over his mouth like he'd burped too loud.

Luke danced his fingers, making the light splash and melt into the sunshine. "Do that again."

Hand still clamped over his mouth, Jeremy shook his head.

"Please? I want to see."

It was hard to stay embarrassed when Luke was looking so entranced. Jeremy took a deep breath and blew a bubble for him.

Luke caught it with a pop. "You're doing this on purpose, you little monster. There are *people* around."

"You asked me to do that!"

"Not the light. Sitting there all pretty, when I—what?"

Jeremy went as rigid as a dead thing on the sidewalk, paws up. "Don't call me that."

"A monster? I was kidding."

Jeremy shook his head once, tightly.

Luke blinked. "Pretty?"

Jeremy crossed his arms over his chest.

"For real? But you—" He gestured up Jeremy's body, encompassing his pink T-shirt and long blond hair and the way he swooned when Luke kissed him and all the other princessy things about him.

"I like this shirt," Jeremy said.

"I like it, too. I think you look pretty in it."

Jeremy's body jerked like he'd been hit. "All right," Luke said. "My bad, I'm sorry. I just don't understand."

A roar rose from the crowd like a low wave, chasing a long fly ball. Jeremy turned his attention away, watching the ball land neatly in a fielder's glove as the sound drooped into a sad *ohhh*. Luke sat back in his seat, staring flatly out at the game.

When Jeremy was tiny, before Sergei had given his second son his name, people had called Jeremy "mini Sergei" or one of the Russian diminutives. He'd followed Sergei around like a puppy, and Sergei hadn't minded because he'd dealt best with his responsibility by keeping one eye on Jeremy all the time. Even Jeremy didn't know how or why he'd branched off, preferring books to martial arts and excited squeals to low growls, but Sergei had taken it like a betrayal. Somehow Jeremy's blossoming personality had been a choice: there were two ways to live, and he'd picked Alexei's.

Jeremy knew in theory that was wrong, but that didn't mean he could untangle all the roots of it. He figured out what he wanted to say and got it all out in one go. "I dress like this because I like it, but also because I want to get the girly thing out of the way *before* people say it. The point is *not* to make you say it."

Luke needed only a fraction of the time Jeremy did to collect his response. "First of all, I didn't say you were girly. Second, even if you were, that doesn't mean anything. My sister's a girl, and she can kill rats with her mind."

It meant something to Jeremy. They were skirting too close to things he couldn't talk about, to things he could barely think about without getting hot and sick. The curse that trapped him was undeniably princessy, and, too, he suspected the reason he couldn't get free was that he was missing some vital princessy virtue. He wasn't loving enough, or lovable, or whatever intersection made those the same thing, and if he couldn't figure out how to be good enough in that way, for Luke or for some other person, he was never going to move forward at all.

The heat pressed too close, and Jeremy took a wet, shaky breath. Luke narrowed his eyes, curious.

Jeremy couldn't take it, and he couldn't—just couldn't—tell Luke the truth. Instead of anything real at all, he said, "Can she really?"

Luke nodded. He gave Jeremy an appraising look and

launched into a rambling, slightly scary story about the magic games he and Camille played as kids. His blustery confidence rose as he spoke. After an inning, he draped his arm around the back of Jeremy's seat. A half-inning later, Jeremy dropped his head on Luke's shoulder. He spent too much time fighting—with Luke, with Sergei—and it wasn't their fault he was so studded with land mines.

After another half-inning, Luke picked up Jeremy's hand to play with his fingers, whispering, "I am sorry," one more time. Jeremy sighed and started to say it was okay, or something, when the precise shape of one horrible word, loudly and clearly pronounced, zinged their way from a couple of boys who were walking to their seats a few rows down. Jeremy wasn't so bothered—you can't spend your whole life climbing out of luxury cars wearing neons without getting used to some shouting—but Luke stiffened, hurt or afraid, and dropped Jeremy's hand like it burned.

Jeremy's overstretched temper snapped, and he yelled back, "May your actions bind you!" The golden rule turned into a curse.

He said it to be cranky—he couldn't even kill rats with rat traps and had no particular skill with jinxes—but the boy slipped and fell onto the armrest between two seats, and slipped again when he tried to get up.

"Defend him?" Luke said, tentative.

The boy popped up, and his friends scurried to their seats. "Huh," Jeremy said.

"You can't go around cursing people!" Luke said, though it would have been more convincing if he wasn't laughing.

Jeremy shrugged. "They were bothering you."

Luke laughed harder, tension bleeding away. "My hero."

"You're *welcome*." The scuffle had drawn some attention—curious gazes hit the boys down the row, and Jeremy. He caught a turning-away figure he recognized in the next section.

Jeremy sat up straight. "What?" Luke asked.

"Natalya, do you see?"

She was fleeing down the section stairs. Luke frowned. "What's that about?"

"She's watching us, is what. Alexei said he was handling it; he said no tail. He promised—" Jeremy stopped and swallowed hard. The world was a dangerous place—but that was always true. He was trying to do something real with Luke, and he couldn't have that with his brothers breathing down their necks. He texted Sergei: *Don't spy on me!*

Sergei wouldn't indulge a text fight, but Jeremy still sat and fumed. He wasn't enjoying the game, and Luke was worrying about him, and it was all a mess. He was surprised when Sergei did reply, and got his foolish hopes up that it would say—he didn't even know what. Sergei had only written, *The hell are you talking about?*

Jeremy replied, *We saw Natalya I. hate you so much,* before he remembered he'd meant to stop fighting.

Chapter Twenty-Seven

After another afternoon cleansing for Alexei, they took a long walk back to Jeremy's house. Luke would catch the subway from there. The extra time together, the paradox of privacy on a crowded street, was worth it. Jeremy noticed things in a funny way—seeking out color and glitter like a magpie, staring unabashedly at interesting folks they walked by—and shared his delight at each detail by tugging on the hem of Luke's T-shirt and pointing with his chin.

As they got close to the house, Jeremy made a low, disgusted noise and looked pointedly away from one corner of the street. "Uck! Paparazzi."

"Huh?" Luke had never imagined worrying about paparazzi—his first impulse was more flattered than annoyed. "Where?"

"Over—" Jeremy stopped.

Luke followed his gaze to a car rolling its darkly tinted back window up and sliding away from the curb. "The silver one?"

Jeremy nodded. "I thought that was paps, but they don't

usually stop when you notice them. Or drive S-Classes."

That must have meant *really nice car*, because that's what was pulling away. "What do you think?"

"Malcolms?" Jeremy twisted his lips in thought. "Why don't you come in for a while?"

"Is that all right?" Luke hadn't been back in the house since their first kiss in Jeremy's attic. He didn't know what was going on between Jeremy and Sergei, but it seemed tough.

"We should tell someone." Jeremy waved vaguely at the corner the car had disappeared from, but he flashed Luke a smile. "And we could hang out."

They took Jeremy's shortcut to the kitchen door. Marta leaned against the counter, looking unsurprised. "Luke, it's been a minute."

"Well, you know. Been working."

"Mm-hmm." She glanced at Jeremy.

"There was a weird car outside," Jeremy said. "Somebody was taking pictures of us, but it was too fancy to be paparazzi."

Marta grimaced. "Uck."

"That's what Jeremy said." Luke couldn't hide a grin.

"I bet so." She waved her hand at Jeremy like he was pestering. "I'll talk to Sergei."

Jeremy rolled his eyes and walked away. That felt like the wrong response, so Luke said, "Thanks."

Marta made precisely the same eye roll and giggled as she said, "Go on, then."

They made it to Jeremy's room without seeing anyone else. As soon as Luke shut the door, Jeremy was on him, pressing his hands against Luke's shoulders and leaning hard into a kiss.

Luke slowed it down, cupping his hands around Jeremy's hips to push him back, creating enough space for breath between them. He snuck his thumbs under the hem of Jeremy's shirt, tracing the waistband of his shorts. He had more body hair than Luke did, but it was different, invisibly fine. He was like a little peach.

Jeremy smoothed his hands across Luke's chest, slow, like he was enjoying the breadth of it, which made Luke feel broader. Jeremy ducked his head, but his voice was sure. "Can I take your shirt off?"

Luke took a big inhale and went with him, thinking cold, boring thoughts as he sat on the bed, pulled Jeremy over him, and let Jeremy kiss him and take off his shirt. He lay back and put his hands behind his head, where they couldn't cause any trouble. Jeremy's expression was shuttered, but his eyes and fingers moved over Luke's body curiously.

"I want." Jeremy stopped as if that were the whole sentence. Luke wanted to roll Jeremy over and devour him; he wanted to put Jeremy in a glass box where no one, least of all Luke himself, could touch him. He wanted to put his shirt back on; he wanted to take his pants off. He wanted to know why everyone was angry; he wanted to know why Alexei wasn't. He wanted and wanted.

"Come here," Luke said.

Jeremy leaned down slowly, still thoughtful. He touched Luke's mouth. "You have the nicest lips."

Luke knew that, but he said, "Nah," as if he were shy of it. He caught Jeremy's fingertips in his teeth, and Jeremy's eyes popped round.

A single hard knock slammed on the door before it flew wide. "Keep this door open," Sergei grunted, already walking away.

Luke froze. Jeremy's fingers fluttered away from his mouth. Jeremy's expression melted apart, then tightened until his eyes were angry slits.

"What the fuck, Sergei?" He scrambled off Luke and ran out of the room. He slammed the door behind him, but Luke still heard him holler, "You can't just make up rules!"

Luke found his shirt and pulled it back on. It smelled like incense and sweat. Sergei's voice was a muffled rumble but Jeremy's rose. "—not my father! You're no one! ... You don't know anything!"

It started to rain, the patter drowning out some of Jeremy's words. Luke looked over the shelves until something caught him—a bowl with a pair of fish. He stared at them until he understood. It was a pair of humpback whales the size of guppies.

"You're not my father!"

"He already said that," Luke told the whales. One broke the surface, flipping, and splashed a tiny drop of water on the shelf below. They were so beautiful it made him want to sweep his arm across the shelf and watch it all shatter on the floor. Something twisted in his chest. He picked up one of the orbs of light, and although he couldn't feel it, it burst in his fingers, trickling over his hand like lava and dissipating.

"Maybe you don't *want* it to work!"

Sergei's voice rang: "I would *love* to get rid of you!"

The house got quiet. When Jeremy came back to the room, shutting the door with a *snick*, Luke had to tell his body to turn a few times before he managed it. Jeremy leaned against the door, curled over on himself and flushed red.

"You don't have to tell me if you don't want to," Luke said.

Jeremy's head shot up. "Did you already figure it out?"

Luke's mind raced in two directions at once, fitting clues together and reeling away from anything that might make Jeremy look like that. He lifted his hands in surrender.

Jeremy got rid of a breath like it was hassling him. "Follow me."

He led Luke down one level and into an office. It wasn't as nice as the rest of the house, dull and practical, with rows of metal filing cabinets. Jeremy pointed to a chair at the battered desk and went to one of the cabinets as Luke sat down.

Jeremy slapped a thin file labeled *Jeremy - 1* on the desk. Luke waited before he opened it, but all Jeremy did was sit down next to him and wait, too.

He took Jeremy's hand. It stayed slack in his, but Jeremy didn't pull away.

Luke started flipping. Two photocopies—a page of typed text from Ivan's will and a page in fine, scrolling Cyrillic. The second showed shadowy margins where the edges of the original paper were ragged from attempts to burn it. There were two signatures at the bottom, one precise and one a weak X.

The last piece of paper was typed as well, titled *Jeremy's Contract—English*. Luke found the sentence he was looking for right away, as if his eyes already knew where it would be on the page.

This contract will be rendered void and the child freed from his obligations to the Kovrov family only by his true love's first kiss.

"If you make a princess joke, I *will* have you killed," Jeremy said.

Luke had never wanted to joke less in his whole life. He squeezed Jeremy's hand; Jeremy didn't squeeze back. "That's not real mojo," Luke said. "That's just in the movies."

It was not possible—it could not be real. The contract was too old, the magic too precious. But Jeremy made a disbelieving squeak and pointed at the paper with his free hand, and there was no arguing.

Luke's adrenaline rose: *love love love love love.*

That meant Jeremy had thought it might be love.

It meant, now, he was sure it wasn't.

Luke felt bereft, too hectic to think, and he wanted so

much to put his arms around Jeremy again he couldn't think of anything else.

He made himself focus on the other words on the page, and the chatter in his mind fell silent. "I didn't expect it to say 'first.'" They'd had a first—and a second and a third and a dozen more. It was already too late. "I don't understand why you're still kissing me at all."

Jeremy whipped his hand away and rocketed out of the chair so he could pace around the room. "Fine. You and Sergei can kiss each other for all I care."

"Wait, what?"

"That's what he keeps—" Jeremy's voice cracked, and he paused and started again. "I'm still kissing you because I *want* to. Is that not a good enough reason?"

"Of course it is." But out loud, it sounded false. The paper glowed—*true love's first kiss*.

His dissatisfaction must have been clear. "Why were you still kissing me?" Jeremy asked. "That reason."

Though it had only been a few minutes ago, Luke couldn't remember what combination of want and hope had brought him into the house and up all those flights of stairs to Jeremy's room. He couldn't remember what the world was like before this piece of paper—before this impossible thing that Jeremy needed, and the corresponding truth that Luke wasn't it.

The paper swelled and shrank as Luke's head drifted away from his body like a helium balloon. He blinked hard but couldn't get the room back in order. Jeremy snatched up the paper and returned it to its file and the file to its drawer. "Do you want to go?"

Luke blinked again. That stung hard, but he kept it together. "All right." He stood, patting his pockets to check for his things. He wanted to insist on staying and run away at the same time. "I guess, if you want to call, then..." He was going to say something ignorant. He stopped.

As soon as he turned away, Jeremy spat, "Really? Really."

Luke spun back, arms out. Jeremy's hands clenched into fists at his hips, and for once he was not blushing. His face was white and raw. "We were about to—" Jeremy spluttered and started over. "And now you're going to leave."

"You told me to leave."

"No, I didn't!"

It took everything in Luke's power not to press his hands against his forehead like Jeremy was giving him a migraine, because Jeremy was going to give him a migraine. He held his hands against his legs instead, so they wouldn't move. "Jeremy," he said clearly. "Come on. What would you like me to do?"

"Just shut up and keep standing there like an asshole, can you do that?"

He could, although it was not easy. He figured Jeremy's move was to kiss him, but Jeremy didn't. He stood and waited, watching Jeremy's color come back. He closed his eyes. When he opened them, Jeremy would be standing in front of him.

He counted to fifteen and listened to the rain.

When he opened his eyes, Jeremy was farther away, face turned to the window.

"Am I waiting for something?" Luke asked.

"I was going to do something cool," Jeremy told the window. "But I'm still trying to decide if I'm going to kiss you or storm out."

"Great." Luke waited, looking at the back of Jeremy's neck, long and too slender for the weight of his head. "I would vote for the kiss, if that's still on the table. I'm not that interested in Sergei."

Jeremy turned and rolled his eyes, but there was something yielding about him—his shoulders tilting, his face pulling back to Luke—that made Luke think he was ready to be soothed. Luke weighed his line and spoke carefully. "Let me stay. I'll fight for you. Tell me that's what you want, and that's what I'll do. But you better be ready for a soldier, because that's what you'll get."

It worked. Jeremy moved away from the window and closed the distance between them, wrapping his arms around Luke's waist. He was always taller in Luke's arms than Luke remembered. He dropped his head on Luke's chest, but he had to crook his neck at an odd angle to do it.

"We can figure this out," Luke said. "I know we can."

"I like you a lot. I wish I were normal, and we could. You know. Be normal."

"Whatever. I've had bad experiences with normal. I like you, too."

Jeremy sighed, heaving in Luke's arms. "We should go. Sergei's going to come back." But he didn't move, and Luke wasn't going first.

Chapter Twenty-Eight

Luke made it home, soaked through and miserable, and sneaked up the back stairs to his room so he wouldn't have to see anyone. Unfortunately, Camille waited on his bed, nose in an enormous, dusty library book with a crooked old crone on the cover. "I started looking for curses in the Russian lore," she said without preamble. "Have you ever read 'The Frog Princess'? There's different versions, but in some of them the curses are broken with feats of magic—"

That groaning sound was Luke. His knees hit the floor.

"Whoa!" Camille leaped up and touched his shoulder, her words silky-sweet. "Hey, it's all right. No one told you this was trouble, for sure."

He pushed her off, hauling out every cuss word he could think of. Sure, no one had told him. No one had told him anything. Jeremy had been stringing Luke, his non-true-love, along with half-answers, and—worse, to Luke—he hadn't even given Luke a chance to try uncrossing him another way.

Love, Luke thought. *Love love love*. "Can you get Mom?"

Thirty minutes later, Yuri set a plate of potato dumplings

on the table, and the Melnyk family had a summit on the subject of true love.

"Like eternal, preordained true love?" Camille asked. "That's not a real thing."

"What do you know about it?" Luke said. "But no, it didn't say eternal or preordained in the contract. 'True love's first kiss.'"

She rested her temple on her fist. "Maybe love can be true. But that's not real mojo. Disney made that up."

Luke still thought so, too. But denial wouldn't fix it. "There's real mojo there. He *for real* can't leave Sergei's house. He *for real* can't go to school, or, or be with whoever he wants."

"Honey," Helene said. "Are you saying you're in love? Last month you couldn't let go of the other little troublemaker."

Luke had never felt this way about Max. That slow derailment was nothing compared to how fast he'd crashed into Jeremy. This was something different, but he didn't know if that made it love.

A small voice whispered, *If it were, he'd be free right now, and maybe here, and safe, with you*, and he ignored it. He stuffed a dumpling in his mouth, but they waited for him to chew and swallow and reply.

"I don't think it's fair that I have to decide that now. And I don't think it's fair that he has to wait."

"No, it doesn't seem much like fair has anything to do with it," Helene said. "But that doesn't mean *you* have anything to do with it. I told you, Luke, that family—"

"Exactly. *Exactly*, 'that family.'" Luke wrestled his voice down. "They stole him from his real parents. You want me to walk away from that?"

Helene returned his gaze without flickering. "Honey, the more you try to convince me you have to stay in this because those people are so evil, the more I hear I need to get you out because they could hurt my baby boy."

"I believe in true love," Yuri said abruptly. Helene pulled a face, wry and affectionate.

"I think, even though our first kiss was at that show," he said, "true love's first kiss was the one on the bridge. Right? The bridge?"

Helene's face went soft.

"Nah," Camille said. "You two don't kiss."

Yuri raised his eyebrows and swung an arm around Helene's shoulders, and then he swooped over her. All Luke and Camille could see was the back of Yuri's head, but Camille screamed anyway.

Finally, Helene deployed an elbow to get Yuri away. "Listen, we've been together for twenty years. By now, I'd say it's love. That's different."

"Is it different?" Luke asked. "Or is it just later? How do you know?"

Camille scoffed. "Well, one difference is they didn't need their families to push them together with some fake job routine."

Luke wanted nothing to do with that line of thought. He shook it off like a fly. He had chosen. He and Jeremy had chosen, together. Some outside force had decided against them, and that was his enemy.

"Well," Yuri said, but rather than elaborating, he nudged Helene and gave her a significant look.

"What? Am I missing something?" She looked between Yuri's knowing face and Luke and Camille's blank ones.

Yuri grimaced and pointed at Luke. "Don't get a big head. But. That boy has been in love with you since he was a tiny little thing."

Luke ran hot and cold. *In love?*

"How do you know?" Helene exclaimed.

"It was obvious," Yuri said. "He hid behind Sergei a lot

but he was always gazing at our Luke."

"Gazing?" Helene looked at Luke with way too much confusion to be flattering.

Yuri nodded. "But then he'd look away if Luke ever looked at him. You probably didn't notice because you never look at Sergei."

"Well, that's true."

"Sergei stopped bringing him around for a while, when you"—Yuri pointed at Luke—"started noticing boys, too. I always figured Sergei was trying to stop it from happening. But here we are." It sounded like Yuri thought *here* was a pit of quicksand.

It checked out to Luke—Jeremy remembered more from when they were kids. His sweet shyness, his sliding eyes. He must have had some idea about Luke, some fantasy or hope, that Luke wasn't living up to. Luke tasted acid, sick—he was over here falling in love, and Jeremy was getting to know Luke better and falling out of it. "I can't handle this."

He knew right away it was wrong. Yuri's face turned thunderous. "You shouldn't have done it, then."

Camille sucked her teeth.

Luke said, "I didn't mean…I didn't mean it like that."

"I hope not. Who taught you to jump between your young men like this? I don't want to hear you failed to treat him with respect."

Luke wanted to protest—he wasn't jumping anywhere; he was being so respectful his body was driving him to distraction—but his jaw wouldn't work.

Yuri took a breath that heaved his shoulders. "What does the young man say?"

"Huh?"

"Your young man. He asked for this production? It makes him angry like this?"

"Of course he—" Luke stopped. Angry? Maybe sad. "He

lied to me."

"Lied to you, or kept his business to himself?" Yuri emphasized the last part.

"It would have been my business if some wild mojo happened!"

Camille snorted. "I bet not. You would have broken that curse with your fool mouth and said, 'Hmm, standard.'" She nudged Luke, and he pushed back. "Also, in case you forgot, some wild mojo *didn't* happen."

That sliced him so hard he had to pull away. They were all staring. "What he said was, it wasn't a big deal, and I shouldn't do anything dramatic."

Yuri put his elbows on the table and his head in his hands, and said, "Lukonya," like somebody was torturing him and that was the code word to start begging for death.

"Does he know you told us?" Helene asked.

Luke answered sideways. "I'm going to tell him."

Helene shut her eyes, too. Luke wasn't sure how everything had gone so wrong. "I don't understand. What am I supposed to *do*?"

Yuri tapped his points out on the table. "The right person is the person who brings out your best. It isn't, do you like him, is he good enough—it is, are you happy? Are you doing what's right? I think you are a young man of honor, and I think you need to decide how much compromise you can live with."

Camille started laughing. "Sure. Is that all?"

Luke's nerves spilled over in a laugh, too, she grabbed his arm, and they sat together and lost it as Helene shook her head and Yuri got up and walked away.

"You should probably tell him you told us all his business. And maybe you could mention"—Camille wiped tears of laughter off her face—"I'd love to see how a crossing that unbreakable works."

Chapter Twenty-Nine

Luke brought dumplings to the next summit, too.

"Yum!" Marta whisked the container away to warm them up.

Alexei was there, at Sergei's house. Jeremy lurked behind his elbow. He was barely dressed, still wearing his sleep clothes, including a Sergei-like white muscle tank that showed the sharp lines of his collarbone and shoulders. Luke almost forgot why they were there—but unless they figured this out, Jeremy wasn't his to look at that way.

Jeremy had dressed enough to pull on his green cap, angled and pulled low over his face, and the one eye it revealed was hidden behind Alexei.

Camille propped herself in front of Luke the same way, obscuring his view with her hair. She smelled soapy and herbal, like SheaMoisture and home, and cultivated her ferocity like a model, hand on her hip.

Alexei smiled with genuine, crinkling eyes. "Come in and look at our secrets."

Sergei's dining room held three of the biggest pieces

of furniture Luke had ever seen—a gleaming redwood table, a matching sideboard covered with plants and knick-knacks, and a looming cabinet full of enough plates to serve an army—under a high ceiling. Afternoon sunlight fell in warped squares through the window on one of the narrower walls, but it only made the rest of the room gloomier.

There were two folders on the table, *Jeremy - 1*, which Luke pushed to Camille so she could look at the contract, and another labeled *Jeremy - 3*. Luke started flipping through that. It was documentation of attempts to break or work around the crossing, and Luke had to admit it was thorough: fire, blood, water, herbs. All the notes ended with variations on the same nasty theme: *he screamed, he passed out, it hurt him. Nothing happened.*

Alexei sat down across from them, elbows on the table, and Jeremy slumped next to him.

"I have to ask," Luke said. "What's in *Jeremy - 2*?"

"Adoption papers and copies of my homeschool letters." Jeremy spoke through a clenched jaw. "Do you need to see my dental records, too?"

This was a new voice, flat and horrible. *Wait—*

Camille was already done. "You didn't tell me it said 'only.'" She looked up at Alexei. "This is all in the original, the 'only' and the 'first'?"

Alexei laughed mirthlessly and nodded. "The little witch is good."

"Sure," Camille replied. "Good enough to see it's impossible."

"What?" Luke asked. "Tell me."

"'The contract is void *only* when.' Don't you see? It's a, what do you call it, to get rid of the pressure?" Camille snatched her fingers in front of her face, taking the word out of the air. "A release valve. It's not meant to be a way out. It's just meant to close off any other way out." She paused. "I still don't think this true love thing is real mojo."

"How?" Luke asked. "It's in the contract, and the contract is real."

Camille waved that away. "I could make you sign a contract that said you'd do the dishes every day until you got me a micro-elephant. But you'd be doing the dishes for a long time."

Jeremy twisted his cap around and pulled it down so it covered his face completely. Luke weighed the two ideas, trying to figure out which he hated worse: Jeremy stuck in this house forever, or Jeremy breaking the curse on somebody else's mouth.

It didn't matter, because Luke wasn't going to allow either of those things to happen. He was going to find another way to fix this first. The attempts they'd already documented were more thorough than he'd expected, and it was a setback, but he'd find plan goddamn C.

Alexei put his hands on the table and spoke with the finality of a grown-up intervening. "We cannot prove a negative. The only way we'll ever know if true love is the answer is if one day, a kiss works. So there's no reason to discuss it as a hypothetical. All the young prince can do is follow his heart in these matters."

Muffled inside the cap, Jeremy said, "Can you not with the prince thing right now?" Red splotches colored his neck, and Luke would have thought this whole business had been a bad idea, except he started to think of a question. This question had some weight to it, a sense of dawning. A sense of *binding*. "What is up with all those generations of daughters?"

Alexei's head snapped up, and his eyes narrowed. He wasn't giving away much, but that face rarely gave away anything at all.

Marta returned with the dumplings on a platter. "Why does that matter?"

Jeremy lifted his cap long enough to cut a hard glance at Luke and eat a dumpling in one bite.

Even though Jeremy was hidden, Luke spoke to him. "You came after three, four generations of all girls. What are the odds of that? Especially if there were multiple sisters having multiple daughters? It has to mean something."

Camille got it. "That is mojo."

Luke tapped the table. "Tell me the spell."

"A protection? She signed the contract and wished she'd only have daughters, and there was enough energy to make it work for a few generations." Camille smiled. "Or, she turned it around. She lit a candle and promised she wouldn't have a son until he would weigh on this family like a curse. That's what I would do."

Luke nodded—that was definitely what Camille would do. "Whatever she did put a tripwire on the contract, and then before Jeremy was born, someone did something—"

Camille's eyes widened, and she pressed her lips tightly together. Luke stopped talking. That was a good theory, plausible and workable—but it was a delicate thing to sit in a room full of Kovrovs and ponder what they might have done to set that tripwire off.

"Jeremy isn't a curse," Marta said neatly.

Alexei stayed silent and thoughtful. Luke closed his eyes, feeling for new bindings around them, but Alexei was a blank page.

Jeremy pulled the cap off his face and dropped it on the table. "The Kovrovs seem fine to me."

"Did you talk about the gay thing?" Marta asked cheerfully, glancing at Alexei. His expression charred. Jeremy's body stayed where he was, but the rest of him left: his eyes lost focus and went blank.

"No," Alexei said. "We're not going to discuss it."

"You know we're not saying *we* have a problem with it,

but if the *contract*..." Marta trailed off.

Luke's body went cold so fast he felt dizzy. Camille put a hand over his. "Why do you think being gay matters?"

Marta smiled, like Camille had gotten on her side. "The contract is more than a century old. I'm just saying we should acknowledge the possibility it's not going to recognize a boy as Jeremy's true love. Or, you know, maybe a black person."

Camille's hand twitched once and pressed firmly over Luke's. "What, exactly—you're saying that Jeremy's really in love with a white girl and he slipped and fell on Luke?"

Something like a smile flickered around Alexei's eyes. "Long fall."

"Look, if that's what it is, we're not doing him any favors by being PC." Marta slumped back, her energy draining away.

They sat in awkward silence. Jeremy's face was terrible and dead, and Luke couldn't think of anything to say. Finally, Camille broke in again. "I was wondering if there are any other contracts like this. Old ones, or whatever, anything to compare it to."

Alexei shook his head. "If there were, they've been lost."

"Hm." Camille tapped the paper. "I'm working on this theory that maybe, since it isn't real magic, it's something she asked for. If she wasn't a witch, but she heard it in a story or something."

Alexei rolled his shoulders. "You're still trying to discredit it. I get the impulse, I do, but I don't see how that's productive. Assume we were to grant you that, hypothetically, there's no out for true love—what would you do then?"

Camille blinked at the paper. "Do you know if anyone in your birth family was a magician?"

"Camille—" Luke started, but Jeremy was already returning to himself, shaking off. "I don't want to talk about this anymore."

"Then we're done," Alexei said promptly, as if they

couldn't be trusted not to press, or maybe as if he was waiting to get the conversation over with. That was the key: Alexei was a liar, and he had a secret, but they'd lost it when Marta got them off track. There was no way to bring it up with Alexei there, though, and all Luke wanted to do was hide. He felt weak and sick for letting Camille defend him, but even as the conversation slipped away, he couldn't find a wall to put up. This was the idea he hated worst. He'd rather have heard Jeremy say, *You're not what I wanted*, than talk about whether some ancient piece of paper had a problem with brown boys.

Alexei gathered papers, and Marta took away the empty platter. Jeremy slid a glance across Luke.

"Do you want to talk before I go?" Luke asked.

Jeremy shrugged, but he led Luke up all those stairs and stood small in the center of his huge, wrecked room, frowning at the ceiling.

"I should have told her not to talk about your birth family," Luke said. "I'm sorry about that."

Jeremy tilted the tiniest bit closer. "It's okay. Marta knew she wasn't supposed to bring up…the stuff."

"Don't apologize for that. You didn't say it." Luke tried to brush it off, but it wouldn't budge. "She shouldn't be saying that to you, either. At least I get to leave."

Jeremy went stiff again, huffing and glaring back up at the ceiling. They were fighting again; Jeremy was angry again. Luke wanted to fix this crossing before Jeremy's true love swaggered up and ruined everything, before Jeremy's eighteenth birthday and college and the rest of his life were stolen by the Kovrovs. But if he kept pissing Jeremy off so much with the trying, he was going to ruin it himself. The end closed in on two fronts, like an army that had split its forces. Luke, caught in the middle, was not likely to win, but he would find a way or he would go down fighting.

"Jeremy, come on." Luke was begging, and he didn't care.

"What?"

"Why are you so mad? I'm trying to help."

"I don't want this help." He threw his hands out and pulled them back again, crossing his arms. "I thought I could deal with it, but I can't. I hate people acting like I'm a puzzle."

Luke drooped on the edge of the bed, elbows on his knees. "I don't think you're a puzzle. But I think we can solve this problem, which means making a theory and testing it, right?"

"No." The stone wall broke, Jeremy's expression melting in real fear. "No, I told you. Messing with the contract never works, and always hurts."

"You have to try something."

"I don't have to do anything," Jeremy said, his voice lowering. "Why would I torture myself like that?"

Luke bit back his first reply—*how could you not?* He couldn't imagine the complacency.

Jeremy opened pleading hands. "I told you not to make a huge deal out of this. I have a great life, I have a family who loves me, I'm safe and I can get anything I need—"

"All right," Luke snapped. "I get it. You have more nice stuff than anyone I know. I don't see how that's worth your freedom."

Jeremy stepped back, taking a sharp breath.

Luke rubbed his face in his hands. "Jesus, I'm—I'm sorry. I didn't mean that. No, I think I did mean that. This is terrible."

Jeremy threw his arms open. His face was a mask, rigid and blotchy. "Set me free, then."

Luke couldn't do anything except sit there. One easy answer: "I'm sorry. I *am* sorry."

Jeremy dropped his arms, but not his mask. Luke patted the bed next to him. "Come sit with me. Help me understand."

Jeremy sat, crossing his arms over his stomach. "This is

my life, Luke. It can't be a crisis every day."

"All right. But you only just explained it to me. I might need to have a crisis today."

"Oh." The room shimmered with light bouncing off turning gears and trickling water, and a hundred small bells chimed when Jeremy sighed. "So, you'd be happier if I was sad?"

"No, of course not. No one said anything about being sad." Luke was still sunk low over his knees, and he twisted until his face found the crook of Jeremy's elbow. He put a kiss there, another on the curve at the back of Jeremy's arm.

Goosebumps prickled over Jeremy's skin. "What are you doing?"

"Sneaking up on you." Luke slid a little higher. "See? You don't even know where I am. You're less angry at me, and you don't know why."

Jeremy exhaled a laugh. "I'm getting sleepy, very sleepy."

"No, stay awake." Luke sat up and pulled Jeremy closer to kiss that sharp spot on his shoulder that had been so tempting earlier. He whispered sugar into Jeremy's ear until he turned his face and gave Luke a real kiss.

"That's supposed to fix everything," Jeremy said, pulling away. "No more curse, and no one trying to hurt us, and they all lived happily ever after."

"I know." Luke kissed him again and thought, *happily ever after.* Jeremy fit so nicely against Luke's body, and even when they fought, they ended up making out, and Luke was happy with him, as long as they pretended there was no world outside. It wasn't the same, though. It wasn't enough.

Chapter Thirty

Jeremy didn't know what the old Kovrov had intended to do with Maeve's firstborn son, or whether there had been more people like him or what they had done with their lives, but Ivan Kovrov hadn't had any use for a stranger's infant. When the curse plopped into his lap in the form of a glowing baby boy, he did what he could to void the contract, break the spell, and free himself and the child. But there was only one way out—*true love's first kiss*, the rotten fairy tale of Jeremy's uncountable bedtimes—and that path was unsure and lengthy. Sometime during Jeremy's first year, his parents, whoever they were, asked Ivan for the one gift he could give them.

They asked to forget.

Ivan was a man of honor in his own way. Somehow—not through Alexei, who might have undone it later—he wiped them all clean. Sergei and Alexei had searched when they grew up, but there was a break in Jeremy's genealogy, and no way to trace back to his family and torment them with the fact of himself. His birth certificate said *Kovrov*, along with everything else in his life, and it said *Brooklyn* but that might have been a lie.

Luke's disgust was for Jeremy's strict boundaries and brothers, but what tortured Jeremy was the empty spaces, the losses so old he'd forgotten them. All the things he didn't know.

His birth parents had given him his first name, but he didn't know whether they meant to say he was exalted or he wept. He didn't know their last name or whether he had any brothers or sisters. He didn't know his family medical history, and sometimes he worried about it to agonize himself.

He hoarded a stack of college brochures under his bed, and Sergei and Marta never brought them up, but he didn't know if it was a secret. He liked the idea of going to school in California, but mostly because he liked the way the word *California* sounded in pop songs, and he didn't know if that was a good reason. Anyway, he didn't know if he would ever be able to leave home.

And when Luke and Camille left the house, he didn't know how he felt. A few minutes in Luke's arms had left his mind hectic and his body aching. He flopped face-down on his bed and let himself drift in the solid feeling of Luke's stomach against his own, the heat of Luke's breath against his neck, the springy-soft texture of Luke's hair. Everything about Luke's body made him aware of his own, made him want specific, impossible things.

It was probably best that before he could get too much momentum under that train of thought, the babies appeared in the attic. They had been taught to knock but didn't understand, or care about, the rules, so they tapped on the door even as they opened it and started to sneak in.

Vanya hung at the threshold but Seryozhka got down and crawled in, subtle as a hand grenade. Jeremy stayed still until Seryozhka got close, then flew up, roaring, and hurled him in the air.

Seryozhka screamed in panicked joy as Vanya ran in, shouting, too. Jeremy threw Seryozhka onto the bed. Vanya was getting too big, so Jeremy wrestled him up, dragging. Once he had a squirming, howling pile of nephews, he flopped himself on top of them.

Holding onto the side of his bed with one hand, he licked a finger of the other and stuck it in the nearest ear. The victim shrieked.

"Mercy!" cried Seryozhka.

"Anyone else?" Jeremy asked placidly.

"Mercy!" echoed Vanya.

He rolled off of them and waited while they attacked. Seryozhka threw himself across Jeremy's belly. Vanya tried to tickle him but ended up tickling Seryozhka instead, making him kick. Tenderly, Jeremy let his mind touch on the idea of one of these little boys growing up to take Sergei's place in his life.

Vanya sat up on his knees and caught Jeremy's eye. "Papa and Uncle 'exei are fighting about you."

Everything crumbled. "All right. Everyone off. Up, out, now." Jeremy nudged and cajoled them into the hall, following the small thunder of their feet on the stairs. He went after, padding lightly, until Sergei's low voice and Alexei's projecting one were clear from the living room. He sat on the landing above, wrapping his arms around his knees.

"Whatever he wants—" Sergei's voice dropped. "—these ideas in his head."

"I don't know why you think love and what he wants are these two different things," Alexei said. "Just because you're miserable—"

"I love my life," Sergei said. "That's the point."

"That he should end up like you?"

"Better than like you."

"You're not his father," Alexei said.

That wouldn't slow Sergei down. "You're not his friend."

The pause was dense. Alexei's voice was commanding when he spoke again. "We've all let this dating thing go to our heads. Me more than anyone, I admit it. We might as well let him have whatever freedom he can."

Jeremy's ears rang, blocking their conversation until Sergei started to roar. "*Enlighten* me. Tell me what it's like to be responsible for the kid, Alexei, tell me all about it."

This conversation wasn't going to go anywhere productive. Jeremy crept back to his room and checked the mirror behind his closet door.

His clothes were all wrong—he changed into his olive shorts, which always made Sergei frown and Alexei laugh because they were really too tight, and a lemon-yellow shirt that made him feel like nothing too bad could happen. It would also annoy Sergei, which was good. Jeremy was annoyed right back. He slipped on his bright blue Vans. He left his Mets cap on his dresser—even he could admit that the shoes and the shirt and the cap might be too much together— but he stuck a pair of white plastic wayfarers in his collar.

His hair was a mess, but after a shake it lay flat. He observed himself, this bright strange pixie he and nature had made. Did he look pretty? Was it bad if he did? If Luke thought he did? All he could see was how he'd stitched himself together.

Jeremy didn't know if he was going to fall in love with Luke, but he didn't think he was going to find true love dwelling on Luke all the time, either, if they called it off. He didn't know how his curse worked or what *love* meant, and neither did Alexei or Luke or anyone else, in spite of all the theories they loved to spew. He didn't know who it would be, or when or why or if. Most of the time, he thought he didn't know anything at all.

Before he left his room, Jeremy knelt by his window and prayed—a proper one, not the quick shots he usually relied on. He asked in English for wisdom, for guidance, for peace, and switched to his halting Russian to call, as he always did, on the intercession of Saint Sergius.

By the time Jeremy made it downstairs, Alexei was leaving. He stayed long enough to laugh at Jeremy's outfit and give him a hug. "Damn the torpedoes."

"Full speed ahead."

"Kid!" Sergei said, after Alexei was gone. "Let's go for a ride."

Jeremy's traitorous heart thrilled. When he'd been a kid, before Vanya was born, they would both get tetchy at noon, and Sergei had taken him for a drive every afternoon.

"I guess," Jeremy said.

"You want to put on some real pants first?"

"Sure." Jeremy pulled his sunglasses out of his collar and flicked them open. "As soon as you put on a shirt."

Sergei guffawed. He tossed Jeremy a protection bag as they walked to the car. Jeremy inspected it for clues—but it was just a bag, one of the ones he'd made with Luke. The magic worked either way, but there was something nice about knowing he and Luke had made it together.

They took Sergei's black '81 Corvette, such a convincing Batmobile that tourists took pictures of it and children ran up to touch it with smudgy hands. Sergei put on a classic-rock station, something they could agree on, and drove around Manhattan and toward New Jersey. This wasn't just a drive, but Jeremy didn't ask. Sergei would tell him if he needed to know.

Jeremy didn't bring up his own problems, either. The Corvette was loud, its engine and the radio giving them an excuse to not talk. He gazed out the window and sang along when he knew the songs. Though the day was brilliantly sunny, riotous with blue and gold, Jeremy's sunglasses and the Corvette's tinted windows kept it dark. This was Jeremy's New York, dim and fast-moving and distant behind a pane of glass. He knew that was a bad thing, but he didn't know how to change it.

They drove to a gas station not far past the bridge into Jersey and swapped the Corvette for a navy-blue Honda. Sergei untucked the keys from the wheel well like he knew where they would be, but he still didn't say anything. This car was quieter inside, all the unsaid things much louder.

As they continued down the highways, Jeremy's protection bag warmed in his hand. "You got that bag?" Sergei asked, scanning the sides of the road.

"Yep." Jeremy hugged it to his chest and thought about Luke's careful fingers sorting delicate flakes of soap.

As they crossed a river, it got worse—the bag pulsed hotly, like a heartbeat, and nausea rose in the back of Jeremy's throat. "You're okay," Sergei said quickly, though Jeremy hadn't said anything.

Sergei pulled over to the side of the road next to a stretch of scrubby grass and a line of trees. "You want to stay in here?"

A challenge. Jeremy got out of the car. Together, they walked toward the bad feeling. Under the tree line, shadows fell too thick to be natural, and Jeremy's nausea churned. He squeezed the bag and breathed through his nose.

Crouching, Sergei pulled a knife out of his back pocket and flipped the blade open. He touched it lightly under his thumb, and pressed the tiny drop of blood to the ground.

They waited. Cars on the highway roared at their backs, but there were no forest sounds from the trees. Sergei's face crumpled in effort, muscles standing out at the sides of his neck.

Jeremy's nausea sank as the ground rumbled, and a

suitcase-size rock burrowed up from the earth like a mole. It bounced oddly—the balloon of the binding Sergei had built around it. *Thunks* echoed deeper into the trees where more rocks popped up, the Malcolms' border crumbling as Sergei's power broke through.

Sergei stood, not quite suppressing a smile. "I'm no Alexei, but I've got a few tricks."

"That was awesome." Jeremy followed him back to the car, and they pulled back onto the highway unimpeded. They didn't go much farther—Sergei parked in the lot of a Spanish restaurant in Moonachie and stayed in the car, watching through the windshield.

"Being a Kovrov," Sergei said sonorously, and Jeremy thought, *Oh, no*, "is a privilege, but it is also a responsibility."

Jeremy said, "I know," but only because that was his line. He wasn't sure he was a Kovrov. Even if he was, it wasn't a privilege for him like it was for Sergei and Alexei and Sergei's babies, and it was a different responsibility.

"Do you know? Speak, kid."

"Am I a Kovrov?"

Sergei didn't miss a beat. "I've spent about seventeen years of blood and sweat to say so."

Jeremy glared at him, then remembered that he was wearing sunglasses and sighed.

"When I was your age, I was potty training you. Think about that."

Jeremy pulled down his sunglasses so Sergei could see his next glare. "You mean a nanny was."

Sergei grunted amiably, which was like a laugh, for Sergei. "I helped more than Alexei did."

They watched the parking lot, light, routine traffic. Jeremy wondered what they were looking for, but he didn't ask, so maybe he was a Kovrov after all.

Jeremy asked a bunch of other questions instead. "What

if it's my problem and doesn't have anything to do with him? What if my true love isn't him, but I have to learn something *from* him? What if you are the biggest asshole in the whole world? Have you considered any of that?"

"What if he's just some shitty kid who likes attention, and you're the only one talking about love?"

Behind his glasses, Jeremy shut his eyes. "Why do you say things like that?"

"Someone has to."

Jeremy was sure no one did. It wasn't like it hadn't occurred to him that Luke didn't love him the same way Jeremy did. But maybe with time—maybe with space. And maybe Jeremy was allowed to have something he wanted, even if it wasn't exactly the right, perfect thing, like anybody else. "Is it because he's a boy? Really."

"Guys and girls are different about sex." Sergei put his hands on opposite sides of the steering wheel as if he was showing where the teams were. "They just are. So if you decide you're chasing boys—"

"Because no guy in the history of the world has ever gotten his heart broken by a girl. It's actually impossible to like a girl more than she likes you." That wasn't right. There was so much wrong with what Sergei was saying, it was hard to pin down which part was bothering him. He tried again: "I bet my real family wouldn't care that I'm gay."

A chill came off Sergei like he'd opened a freezer. Jeremy stopped, too—that was too much. He'd taken it too far.

Sergei shook his head. "I'm letting it go. I will let it go. But I think your curse is exactly the opposite of an excuse to run around with anybody who catches your eye. I think you should hold out for the one. I'm going to tell my boys the same thing when they get as big as you, okay?" He scowled into Jeremy's face, expression unusual and strained.

"Alexei says I should fol—"

"Alexei knows fuck-all about love," Sergei said, too loud in the close space of the car. Jeremy shrank against the door. Lower, Sergei growled, "And not much more about magic, either. I can't have you end up like Alexei. You deserve to be loved, not to be somebody's whim. Really loved, kid. Is that clear?"

He said it like a Kovrov, imperious and practical, even though his words were tender. Something about it rubbed Jeremy wrong, but he couldn't grasp it, and then it was gone in a flood of thoughts about Luke. Jeremy couldn't stop wanting him just because one kiss had failed to break open the world. No one could live up to that.

"I said, is that clear?"

"*Yes, damn*," Jeremy said. "He didn't just catch my eye. I'm not stupid."

Sergei made a noncommittal *umph*. "Happened fast."

"No, it didn't." Even to himself, Jeremy sounded whiny.

"Oh yeah?"

Heat rose on Jeremy's face, but he needed Sergei to shut up, and he thought the truth would do it. "Since I was six."

Sergei was gratifyingly dumbstruck. Jeremy remembered the Melnyk twins playing knight and dragon, a game of pretend with real magic. Jeremy had consented to be the captured princess to Camille's dragon, because he hadn't yet understood, and hated, that princes and princesses were such different things. He didn't mind sitting and watching them toss and block little jinxes.

Camille had knocked Luke flat on his back and crowed, "I win!" She turned to Jeremy, shrugged, and moved on to the next game—none of them knew what you were supposed to do with a princess once you had one.

As Luke lay on the floor puffing, Jeremy's small heart had gone hectic with grown-up disappointment. With clarity he would never find again, he thought, *That's what I want*.

Jeremy still didn't know what happened to rescued princesses—or, mostly, what Luke would do with one. Maybe Luke was fascinated with Jeremy's puzzle, but when puzzles were finished, you dumped them back in the box.

"Huh," Sergei said, but before he could continue, his attention slung outside the car. Corey Malcolm strode through the parking lot, a slim redheaded man wary at his elbow.

"Oh," Jeremy said.

"Yeah," Sergei replied. "Take care of yourself, kid."

"Okay."

They waited, watching, until Sergei shouted a bad curse in English and a worse one in Russian, pounding the steering wheel. The sun gleamed on a wave of brown hair, lush as a mermaid's.

Natalya.

Chapter Thirty-One

"What does she know about you?" Sergei roared over the thunder of the Corvette as he brutalized the highway. "About the curse? Melnyk?"

"Everything," Jeremy said. He could hardly believe how much he'd told her, opening for her questions like a fish being filleted.

Sergei hurtled into slower traffic and slammed on the brakes. Jeremy's seat belt cut into his shoulder and brought him back to himself. "Why? Why would she betray us? What do I have to do with anything?"

Sergei raked a hand over his head. "She's been a Kovrov forever. Her dad worked for ours, and she ran with Alexei when they were kids. It did not even occur to me it could be her until you saw her."

"Me?"

"At the baseball game. I wasn't spying on you. If she was watching you, it was for Malcolm."

Jeremy was queasy with anxious, spinning thoughts and Sergei's driving. "My hair. In the curse bag."

"It had to be her."

"But *why?*"

"There's something." Sergei rubbed his head again. "I'm missing something. I can't remember. I bet Alexei's got another binding on it. Call him, will you? Put him on speaker."

Jeremy pulled out his phone and dialed. Alexei's voice was so bright it sounded strange, auto-tuned to plastic slickness. "Your highness! What is that noise?"

"Sergei's car. You're on speaker."

Sergei gunned the engine out of spite and had to slam the brakes again to keep from ramming the car in front of them. A horn bleated. "It's Natalya," Sergei said.

Alexei swore.

"What am I missing?" Sergei said. "You've got a binding on it. I know you do."

"It's not me," Alexei said. "Jeremy said Luke broke a binding, but it wasn't one of mine."

"Who else could it be?"

"Natalya? Corey?" Alexei said.

"The Malcolms don't get in your head. They mess with space."

"Well, it's not me. I would know if it was me."

Sergei sneered. "Hang up on him."

"Bye, Alexei," Jeremy said. "Let us know if you hear anything."

"Of course. Be safe, your highness."

Sergei commanded Jeremy to wait to talk to Luke until he called the Melnyks himself. Jeremy didn't eavesdrop but he didn't leave, either. He hovered in the hall outside the office, listening to Sergei's voice rumble and turn into a shout.

"And he didn't think to mention that? Let me talk to the little prick!"

Jeremy took a galvanizing breath and walked into the room. Sergei hunched over his desk, phone at his ear. Jeremy sat down across from him as if he were applying for a bank loan. "Jesus," Sergei said. "No, I didn't... Well, hell, what do you think I wanted you around for? No. Fine... Go ahead."

He dropped the phone on his desk with a disgusted noise. "Your boyfriend knew the whole time. Didn't think to mention anything."

"He's not—how did he know?"

"Well, he noticed she wore a glamour. He said he felt it when she asked questions." Sergei switched to a high, mincing voice that set Jeremy's teeth on edge. "'Mr. Kovrov, you didn't know?'" Sergei snorted.

"Luke doesn't talk like that." Jeremy sort of did, though. He heard it in his protesting voice and burned. "Two hours ago we were talking about you *not being an asshole* anymore. He's not the traitor here."

Sergei got his temper under control, wrestling it down. "Yes, okay." That was like apologizing, for Sergei. "Go on, then." He waved Jeremy out.

Jeremy stood and looked down at Sergei's head. He relished being taller. He knew he should take the rare, apology-shaped thing and go. Sergei focused on his phone, swiping with fake randomness.

Jeremy was so tired of having the same fights. Of course he was grateful for everything Sergei did for him, and had done since before Jeremy could remember. Of course he wanted to be badass and strong, too. He couldn't help that he never knew how to act or what to say.

Jeremy pushed his shoulders back, trying to think of something brave: something powerful, like Sergei, or moral, like Luke. "What are we going to do about Natalya?"

Sergei looked up from his phone like he was surprised to find Jeremy still there. "We'll take care of it, kid. I won't let anyone hurt you."

Jeremy was free to make the call, but too wretched with nerves. He had misplaced something important today, but he couldn't remember what it was or how to find it. He sat on his bed for hours, repeating episodes of his favorite shows that he'd watched so many times they were as worn-in as old shoes and swiping his phone open and closed, open and closed.

He couldn't believe he'd really thought Natalya was his friend. He thought of his hair in that blue tartan bag, of her creeping into his room and sweeping over his pillows and hats. He'd even caught her and been too worried about his little problems to see.

At dinner, his steak was all blood, and he left most of it on his plate. Luke didn't text or call, not even at midnight. Jeremy wandered downstairs and poked around the kitchen. He wanted macaroni and cheese, but he had a terror of using the stove during the midnight hour—what if he caught the house on fire, trapped inside?

He pulled a bag of bread out of the freezer and peered down at the toaster.

"Cupcake." Marta floated in. "Why are you still up?"

A lot of answers were true, so he went with the simplest one. "Too hungry to sleep."

She took the bread out of his hands. "Yeah, you didn't have much dinner." She put two slices in the toaster. "Sergei isn't going to let anyone hurt you."

"That's a little bit of the problem."

"Ah." Marta wiped the hair out of his eyes. "You need a haircut, cupcake."

Jeremy wrinkled his nose. "If I have my hair short, I look like a lizard."

She smiled and pushed his hair off his forehead. "Never."

He did. A gecko, with the skinny jaw and the wide-apart eyes. Also, Luke was always stroking Jeremy's hair when they kissed, or brushing it off his cheek as a little excuse to touch him. He twisted away, toward the fridge—cheddar, mustard, dill pickles, tomato—and asked, "When did you know you loved Sergei?"

She smiled, leaning against the counter with her hips. "Sergei was love at first sight. I saw him in the coffee shop at school one afternoon. He had this sweet little boy with him"—she reached over and knocked Jeremy's hair again—"sharing a piece of cake and reading a book. And you were bossing him around. I never expected someone like Sergei would have that side to him. I thought, I need to get to know this man."

"You loved him before you even knew him?"

"Yes." Marta was confident, but this all sounded off to Jeremy. He believed he had upped Sergei's cute quotient significantly—he still did—but he wasn't proof of Sergei's virtue.

Marta grinned. "And I hear you've been in love with Luke since you were six?"

Jeremy's ears caught fire, then his cheeks. Sergei told Marta everything—he'd guessed when Sergei shut up in the car that he was pocketing that baton to hand over to her—but it still killed him to hear it. He mumbled some sounds that weren't words.

"Tell me." She clapped her hands. "I won't make fun of you."

The toast popped up, and he busied himself making a sandwich. It was hard to talk to Marta sometimes, because if he said anything wasn't perfect, she'd get sad and he'd have to comfort her. He couldn't point out that there had been weeks on end when the Melnyk twins were the only kids his own age he saw, or that some families they knew wouldn't let their kids play with Jeremy at all.

And it wasn't only that, not anymore. Luke was always so confident and sure, always trying to do the good, right thing. Jeremy would pick Luke's cheesy lines and careful hands over anyone else in the world, even if he had to stay cursed forever. That, he definitely couldn't say to Marta. "I don't know. I just always liked him. How do you know what makes it love?"

Marta smiled. "He loves you if you can make him get your name tattooed on his neck."

Jeremy laughed, and Marta nodded at him, owl-eyed. She made a gesture like slitting her throat, to trace Sergei's tattoo. "Then, when he forgets how to act, you can say, dude, you are screwed if I leave you."

Jeremy sliced his sandwich into two triangles, and his stomach growled. He kissed her cheek and took the plate up to his room.

His phone might as well have been a brick.

It was almost one. He wasn't even a little bit tired. Finally, hands sweaty, he texted Luke: *I don't even know what to say about Sergei, and Natalya and everything. I didn't mean to put you in danger.*

Chapter Thirty-Two

Jeremy woke up overheated, with a constellation of bread crumbs stuck to his face. Three texts from Luke waited for him:

> *No way, you didn't do anything wrong*
>
> *& you send the cutest texts*
>
> *& hey, your court*

Jeremy stared at them. What kind of English was "& hey, your court"? It probably meant something like, *I'm exhausted by your cursed life and annoying personality. I noticed you look like a lizard person. Solve your own problems.* He put his plate on the floor and stretched out in bed, unwinding the bunched muscles in his neck.

His hips were sore, so he shouldn't go for a run. Sergei and Alexei would be chasing Natalya, and it might be dangerous. Jeremy wouldn't be able to help. There were things he could do, though: he could get up and stretch, play with the babies, eat something real. After one, he could borrow the neighbors' dog and walk to the coffee shop or the park.

He could read a novel or his physics textbook.

Or... Luke.

He closed his eyes, turning off the world. He opened them again, and the world was still distant and gray. He wondered what was wrong with his texts. He wondered if he could kiss his true love but then go back to Luke after.

Three hours later, Marta came in, knocking on his door as she opened it. "Cupcake? You want some lunch or anything?"

It was a gamble. If he asked her to bring him food here, she might. But she might also tell Sergei, and then Sergei would know Jeremy didn't want to get out of bed and that would make him mean.

Marta's eyes narrowed. Sergei was busy. Jeremy felt so gray inside. Charlotte, his octopus, glubbed in her bowl.

"Will you bring me some?"

He could see Marta running the same calculus he had, but in the end she brought him lunch and dinner, too. He stayed in bed as it got dark and light again.

One gray day every now and then was okay, but two in a row spelled trouble. Instead of breakfast, he got Sergei. "It's time to get up."

When he was thirteen and fourteen, and the babies were little, Jeremy had spent hundreds of gray days in his room or trying to stay there. He'd lost track of why it mattered to leave. If he could go no farther than a few hours from home, why did it matter if he went no farther than the attic bathroom? What was the point of going downstairs to eat lunch in the dining room at noon, rattling to another corner of his tiny cage? The distinction was so small, it was no distinction at all. And somehow, in losing the understanding, he'd lost the will.

Sometimes Sergei wouldn't let anyone bring him food.

Sometimes Sergei hauled him bodily into the car and left him somewhere, and he'd have to stay upright long enough to walk home or the curse would hurt him. Usually Sergei shouted, and sometimes Sergei cried.

Both Sergei and Alexei had apologized a lot, which he'd never understood. It wasn't their fault. He'd only wanted to stay in bed.

Jeremy was almost grown now. He knew why it made Sergei so afraid. He knew he ought to get out of bed.

Jeremy said, "I can't."

"You have chores," Sergei said.

"Go to hell."

Sergei didn't say anything—he turned around and left. That was new, and Jeremy sat in bed for a while and thought about how he'd messed everything up for good now. Sergei wouldn't talk to him. Sergei would let him stay here, locked in his tower forever.

Right before noon, there was a knock on his door. Alexei called, "It's me."

"Come in."

When Alexei peeked around the door, his face was different than Jeremy expected: less concerned, coyer. "Your highness. I brought you a gift."

Alexei opened the door all the way to reveal the sheepish and beautiful form of Luke Melnyk. He wore a black shirt and looked even hotter than usual. Jeremy did something suave and classic. Actually, he squeaked and pulled the covers over his head.

Alexei laughed like Jeremy had made a spectacular joke as he left, closing the door.

"I come bearing Hunan chicken." Luke paused. "Do you want me to go? I know this isn't leaving the ball in your court."

Why had he decided the ball ought to be in Jeremy's

court? Jeremy was clearly doing a shit job with it. He said something passionate and intense. No, he said, "You can't stay. I'm smelly."

Luke climbed onto the bed and burritoed Jeremy up inside the covers. "I don't care. To be honest, I like that."

Jeremy froze, and Luke snickered. His body settled around Jeremy's, solid through the layers of covers. "I hear you won't get out of bed."

It was hot inside Jeremy's burrito, but his face burned wilder. He said something intelligent and reassuring. Actually, he said, "I did some science work."

"Good job. I have all this summer homework, and I haven't touched any of it." One of Luke's hands moved under the covers. "Camille keeps finishing things out of spite. Here we go." A hand touched Jeremy's stomach, moving the fabric of his shirt against his skin.

Jeremy didn't understand the shiver that went through him until he'd already said, "Hey!"

Luke faded like a shadow, hand and arms and everything, though his weight still tilted the side of the bed. "My bad. I had an idea for something we could do. Not groping. But also, Sergei and Alexei wanted me to trick you into something."

Jeremy flipped the covers down and let lovely, crisp Luke see how rumpled and smelly he was. "Trick me?"

"Well. They said Sergei needs the house empty tomorrow at two and could I get you out of it. I think they don't want to tell you because it's about Natalya. That's just a guess."

It was a good guess. What a pair of lying manipulators. "Why are you telling me, then?"

"I'm not going to lie to you." Luke picked up his hand and moved his fingers over the scruff on Jeremy's cheeks. It came in patchy and wasn't cool at all. Jeremy was about to say, *Don't make fun of me*, when Luke continued, "Definitely not for your brothers."

Jeremy sighed and rolled into Luke. He had his face at Luke's hip, too aware of both of their bodies. He said, *I love you, take me away from these people. I want to try having sex, kiss me.* No, he said, "That's cool of you," and rolled away again.

"That's basic decency."

It was like being tortured. "Okay. I'm going to get a little less smelly, and then we can do your idea and then you can invite me out tomorrow."

"All right. Can I use your laptop?"

Luke clicked around while Jeremy found a new shirt. He took it to the bathroom to brush his teeth, shave, and put on some deodorant. He felt so much better right away that he couldn't remember why he'd spent so much time in bed. Maybe he didn't want to go back after all—maybe he'd take Luke to the diner again, or they could go for a walk.

But it was barely noon. The gray fell so hard again that he had to sit on the bathroom floor with his head between his knees.

When he walked back into his room, Luke was poking something on one of the shelves.

"These whales." Luke had that dark, intense look on his face, and he let his eyes travel down Jeremy's body. He could suspend Jeremy in midair doing that, but today Jeremy shrank away and sat back down on the bed. He pulled his knees into his chest.

"Sid and Cassie," he said.

"Huh?"

"The whales."

Luke glanced between the whales and Jeremy. He looked like he was about to offer to leave again.

"Don't mind me," Jeremy said. "I'm just a little gray today."

"Gray?"

That was an invitation to clarify, but Jeremy said only, "Yeah."

"All right. Do you want some lunch?" Luke sat down next to him with the takeout bag and handed over chicken and rice. It was Jeremy's favorite, and he was pretty sure he'd never said that to Luke, which he hoped meant that Alexei had bought it.

Luke pulled the computer over them and started up the video he'd found. He rapped along with the theme song, forkful of yellow lo mein like a microphone: *This is a story all about how my life got flipped...* Luke knew every word.

"You know the whole song?" Jeremy asked in delight.

"Everyone knows the whole song." Luke nudged Jeremy's shoulder. "Everyone in the world. But give it a couple episodes, you will, too."

Jeremy's laziness had left him too sludgy to eat much, but he picked at his food as they watched the first episode. He dropped his leftovers on the floor beside the bed and nudged Luke's arm. "Gimme a fortune cookie."

Luke gave him a funny look as he dug in the bag.

"I mean, um, please?" Jeremy added.

Luke laughed. "I like gimme better." He put the cookie near Jeremy's hand but pulled it away to lure Jeremy across his body. "Gimme a kiss first."

It was stupid to get shy after days and days of kisses, but something off-kilter inside Jeremy wouldn't settle, and he pressed his closed lips against Luke's with a scared feeling he couldn't name. Random shouts and rumbles kept cutting upstairs to remind him they weren't alone. Luke pressed the cookie into his hand. He curled away, trying not to think about how he burned all over, scalp prickling, and was probably bright red.

Luke had a big, goofy grin on his face. "I like how you blush so much, too. Let me know if there's anything else you need me to gimme you."

Jeremy was so hopelessly embarrassed he couldn't even open the fortune cookie. His fingers slipped over the plastic wrapper.

"Hey." Luke paused the show. "It's all right. Was that too much?"

Too much and not enough. Perfect, but only for someone else's life. "I keep thinking how Sergei wouldn't let us be alone in here, and then as soon as he needed something from you..." He felt inexplicably used. He risked a glance at Luke, who was rolling his eyes with his whole neck.

"Sergei is a racist, homophobic ass—" Something on Jeremy's face made Luke stop. More gently, he said, "All I mean is, don't let him get to you. But don't let me push you, either. I don't want to take anything you're trying to save."

"You're not." It wasn't what Luke did that frightened Jeremy; it was what he made Jeremy want. *Everything.* Even though all Luke would talk about was breaking up. "You're not doing anything wrong. You're—this is great. It's just—" One of Seryozhka's joyous shouts rang up from downstairs. Jeremy willed Luke to understand.

"Do you want to come over tomorrow afternoon? My parents have to see the building's owner. It will be—" Luke glanced at the door. "Quiet."

Jeremy could not make himself talk, but he nodded. Luke smiled a little with half his mouth and leaned forward, holding Jeremy's face and kissing him. His hands were firm, but his lips brushed lightly, almost teasing—he wanted Jeremy to do that chasing-forward thing again, and Jeremy's body followed instantly. He was going to get his everything, even if he had to hurry for it.

"All right," Luke said. "You're not going to learn anything like this. Pay attention." He turned back to the laptop, starting the show again.

"Is there going to be a quiz?" Jeremy had never taken a real quiz, but it was the sort of thing he might be good at if he had the chance.

"Life is a quiz."

When Jeremy opened his cookie, the fortune read, "You are dependable in business." Jeremy glared at it, looking for meaning, and when he decided there wasn't any, he twisted the paper into a thin rope and folded one end into a circle.

He cupped his hands around it, holding them to his lips and imagining the cool weight of metal as he breathed out. The paper changed against his skin, and he opened his palm to Luke. "Thank you for lunch."

Luke picked up the key, bright silver with an open bow. "What does this go to?"

"Vladimir Putin's secret dungeon in the Kremlin," Jeremy said. Luke blinked. "Nothing. It's just a shape."

"It's beautiful." Luke squinted close to the key. "You get all the details. I can see the lines on the metal like it got cut."

"It would be cooler if I could make locks to go with it."

"Cooler. Dangerous, though, right?" Luke grinned and dropped his voice. "I might end up stuck."

Jeremy didn't know what to say, so he tried to make his silence mysterious. He tucked himself under Luke's arm, dozy and gray and taken care of. Luke ran his hand up and down Jeremy's side, and Jeremy's body overruled his whirring mind and relaxed. This was one of Jeremy's favorite ways to be touched, though he hadn't known that about himself until Luke started touching him. It was thrilling and strange and almost unbearable to think there might be more secrets like that ticking away inside him, secrets only someone else could uncover.

He didn't get the song down, but he got the appeal. Luke laughed a lot more than he did, and at the end of the third episode, Luke asked, "Do you like it? You seem a little…"

"Gray." Jeremy didn't offer more, though Luke waited an extra beat.

"I see."

"Yeah. It's not your fault. This is fun." Jeremy ran his fingers along the seam at the outside of Luke's knee and felt Luke's breath change in his chest. Jeremy hesitated before he said the next part. "I don't like that there's a girly one and they make fun of him."

Luke twisted around so he could see Jeremy's face. His hand spread out over Jeremy's chest. "It's not—I mean—how you are is—"

"It's okay, though."

Luke took a break before he tried again. "There's nothing wrong with being the way you are. But you know I'm biased. I like that a lot." One of his hands pushed Jeremy's hair away from his temple and the other slid around Jeremy's side, over his back. "This whole thing."

Jeremy wasn't sure what that meant. Girly, smelly lizard boys with bad manners and facial mange? "You like weird stuff."

Luke snorted amiably and put his lips next to Jeremy's ear. "I'll like whatever I want," he whispered, which made Jeremy shivery again. Jeremy was embarrassed, so Luke probably liked that, too.

Jeremy stayed level, resting against his pillows as Luke kissed his neck. It felt nice, even through the gray, but there was something he wasn't doing right that made Luke stop.

"Carlton's the man sometimes." Luke reached around Jeremy for the laptop. "Let's find a good Carlton episode. And then I'm going to go, but I'll see you tomorrow?"

"Yeah."

"Let me know if you're still gray, and I'll come over here and take you out instead."

"I won't be." Jeremy flopped as Luke jostled him. "It's

harder than I thought it would be, hoping. But I can handle it."

Jeremy couldn't see Luke's face, but he felt Luke's surprise. That was all he wanted to say, and before Luke could ask any more questions, he said, "This is nice, though. Thank you for letting Alexei bully you."

"You're welcome. Anytime." Luke's hands moved with more purpose, rolling Jeremy's chin up. Jeremy closed his eyes. Luke stopped and hummed a little in a way that made Jeremy sway closer, almost there, and Luke pressed forward and kissed him. After, Jeremy dropped his forehead into Luke's neck without bothering to open his eyes, and Luke's thumb touched his lips. "You're too much," Luke said. "I can't take it. I really can't."

Chapter Thirty-Three

Sergei and Alexei sat in close conversation at the dining room as Luke was leaving, so absorbed that neither lifted a head. Marta and the little boys were playing a board game in the living room, painted in brighter colors, and she gave Luke a broad wink goodbye.

Luke stopped on the front stoop and shook himself out like a wet dog. It wasn't nothing to get all his systems firing in order, moving forward, left foot, right foot. On an instinctual level, it didn't add up: there was a warm, sleepy pile of Jeremy up there, and he was walking away.

Light dripped like honey from the trees. The whole afternoon had that golden quality, flaws filtered away. He'd lost hours in Jeremy's bed, letting their bodies adjust to one another, and the time had passed like a blink. It would have been perfect, if not for the layered horrors of Jeremy's family and crossing.

Luke couldn't shake the grimy feeling that he was acting someone else's part, an understudy in a play. Jeremy's true love crept over everything like a shadow. Luke didn't care about that guy, whoever he was, but if he cared about Jeremy, then maybe he should.

Turning the corner to the avenue, he shook himself again, catching some mystified eyes. He thought, *tomorrow*. He wasn't going to make it home like this, not without embarrassing himself, so he popped into a corner bodega for a break. He needed something cold—he thought maybe a popsicle, then that sounded too sexy, then everything sounded sexy, and he stuck his head in a fridge.

Tomorrow.

In search of a distraction, Luke latched onto that: what was happening tomorrow? Not at his house—that he knew. He was in control, he could take it slow and walk his boundaries, he could be so, so careful—but at Sergei's.

Something about Natalya. Something they didn't want to explain. Something they needed to clear the whole house for.

Did that mean they were going to kill her? The idea wouldn't settle, slippery like a fish, but it wouldn't go away. Alexei was a murderer—the blood had smeared Luke's own hands. He'd killed that man for drawing a gun on his family, more or less in self-defense—what would he do to the person who put Jeremy's hair in that man's pocket?

Luke knew it was real, but even the attack he'd been there for felt glossy and amplified, like a movie scene. If he tried to imagine interrogation, torture, cold-blooded murder—he kept seeing Jason Bourne.

Yuri had said, *You'll have to decide how much compromise you can live with.*

Luke was still standing in front of the open fridge, the attendant glaring balefully at him from behind the register, so he took a bottle of iced tea and shut the door. It was not difficult at all to turn the story so the Kovrovs were the villains.

Alexei had shown up unannounced at the store that

morning, leaning against the counter like they chatted all the time. "I could use a witch doctor."

"Yes, sir, what's up?" Luke guessed another little store or laundromat, a cleansing or mojo bag.

"Our prince won't get out of bed."

Luke's heart catapulted. "Did you call a doctor, is he—"

"No, nothing like that. I think he might enjoy some company."

Like Alexei knew, like he cared, as long as he didn't have to feel guilty about it. As Luke was leaving, Jeremy had said, "I'm taking a shower," but all he'd done was roll over around a pillow like he was going back to sleep.

Still, though, Luke had pulled Jeremy's hair out of a mojo bag that made a nightmare. Alexei had killed for him, might be planning to kill again. It wouldn't square up until Luke figured—and it was obvious once he had it—that nobody had to be the good guy. This story could be all villains.

He needed a sign.

Exiting the store, Luke held the door open for someone coming in. With her glamour down, it took him a long second to understand the little fawn-haired woman was Natalya.

She sparkled to life when she saw him, taller, darker, face breaking open in a bright smile. "Luke! No Jeremy today?"

This was the compromise Luke could live with: he mumbled in reply and reached for the door, ready to run and forget he'd seen her.

She grabbed his arm and pulled him into an aisle. "I wanted to talk to you about something."

Luke raised his eyebrows because he couldn't trust his voice. Natalya waited another awkward beat before continuing. "Listen, I know Sergei's being...like Sergei. If you and J need somewhere to go, you're welcome to my apartment. I'm rooting for you two."

Luke went cold. A few days ago, he would absolutely have

taken her up on that, and then what? Jeremy *trusted* him. A slow heat rose, became angry at her, at Jeremy's family and his own, at everything that wasn't the two of them. "So you can sell us out again? What does Malcolm pay you?"

Natalya jumped back, but no shield could stop the flash of horror on her face before she smoothed it. "Luke," she said, and the illusion she built wrapped around him like reaching fingers.

He brushed it away. "That doesn't work on me. If you're trying to hurt Jeremy, you're going to lose." He pushed past her and discovered how much compromise he could live with after all. He leaned close to her wide-eyed face. "You should get out of town. Just get away from us."

Chapter Thirty-Four

There was nothing Jeremy didn't love about the Melnyks', where everything was clean and practical and whispered of magic. It was too idyllic to imagine really living in.

He loved the store, which was filled with color and light and glittering bits of sequin and glass. Camille waited behind the counter with a knowing eyebrow. "Luke's upstairs."

"Oh, thanks." Jeremy's pulse started happening in unusual places—his throat, the palms of his hands. "Hey, I got you a present. To thank you for your help the other day."

This was mostly true. He pulled the plain brown box from his messenger bag and placed it on the counter. Camille eyed it, hands clutched under her chin. "For me? What is it?"

"Open it."

Luke walked through the back door, right on cue like a movie star and looking like one, too: white T-shirt, slouch in the doorframe, the bare skin of his long limbs. He made Jeremy dizzy, even before he gave Jeremy a once-over and a wide smile.

Luke turned to Camille and asked about the box, went through the whole thing again, but Jeremy didn't catch up until Camille screamed, and the kitten-size elephant he had made climbed onto the counter.

"No!" she said. "Yes! No! Is this a micro-elephant?"

Jeremy made a little bow. "Custom order."

Luke started to laugh. He looped an arm around Jeremy's neck and pressed a kiss against his hair. The elephant rose on its hind legs, trumpeting tinnily.

"What's its name?" Camille squealed. "Does it need to eat, or, or—"

Jeremy shook his head. "She's a toy, not an animal. You can name her whatever you want."

"I love it. I love her!" She picked up the little elephant, who wiggled in her hands. While Jeremy watched, Luke's hand skimmed down his back.

"You look good today," Luke whispered.

"Full color," Jeremy replied. It was even almost the truth.

"I think we'll leave you to it," Luke said, and Camille smiled up beatifically.

"This doesn't mean true love is real!" she chirped at their backs.

"Sure it does," Luke called as the door closed behind them. "It also means I never have to do the dishes again."

When they were alone, Luke whirled Jeremy around by his hips. His bag knocked against his back and pushed him into Luke.

The back room was dim, the lights low. The sun filtered purple through curtains, and Luke was extra devastating in it. All the shadows made his eyes brighter, so when he looked at Jeremy, it felt intent and hot. He started to say something and stopped himself. Jeremy filled it in—too much was wrong, he'd changed his mind—and Jeremy's nerves got the better of him. He dropped his gaze to his hands, pulling a yellow rubber bracelet until it stretched white.

In the end, all Luke said was, "Let's go upstairs."

Luke's room was tiny—maybe it had been half a room, once—just big enough for a twin bed and dresser. The windowsill served as his nightstand, with a lamp that curved down toward his pillow. That bed didn't seem like it would fit Luke by himself, much less… Jeremy cut the thought off.

The room was as scrupulously clean as the rest of the place, a dark green spread smooth over the bed. Jeremy gawked in the doorway, afraid to touch anything.

Luke sidled behind him and took the strap of his messenger bag, lifting it over his head. He spread his other hand over Jeremy's stomach, pulling him close. "Hi there. What would you like to do this afternoon?"

Jeremy tried to laugh, but the sound was a nervous exhale.

Luke moved his hands, rubbing Jeremy's shirt against his sides. "I want to—anything. With you. But, listen. You know I respect you, right?"

Jeremy tried and failed not to laugh at that. "Okay. Sure."

Luke turned him around to hold him eye to eye.

"You look so serious."

"I am serious." Luke smelled so good: there was the incense, and sage and juniper and lavender, and something warmer underneath. Jeremy was getting distracted by it, but Luke stayed steady and earnest.

"Okay. Yes. I know." Jeremy thought *now kiss me,* and Luke did.

He slid his hands under the hem of Jeremy's shirt. "Is this all right?"

Jeremy nodded, and Luke lifted Jeremy's shirt off in a tipsy *whoosh.* Luke was kissing him before he had his bearings back, rubbing up and down his back, while Jeremy hung on his shoulders to stay upright.

Luke pulled his mouth away, rolling his forehead against Jeremy's. "What do you want? For real."

"What do you want to do?" Jeremy asked slyly.

"Make it good for you."

Jeremy fake-glared, and Luke grinned for real. "It's not a trick question. It's just better to decide first. I don't want to go too far."

"You won't. I like this. I want more."

Somehow, that was the right thing to say. Luke's hands tightened on Jeremy's back. "I can do more." He swallowed so hard Jeremy felt his chest move. "We'll take it slow. One step at a time."

Without consulting his mind, Jeremy's body had gone all wriggly. "Maybe one step at a time, but, like, fast."

"You." Luke drooped so his face skimmed Jeremy's shoulder and chest. "Damn. Are you trying to kill me?"

"Um." Jeremy went pliant as Luke got them arranged, sitting on the bed and pulling Jeremy over his lap. Jeremy draped his arms around Luke's neck, and Luke hiked him closer. These kisses were new, more—Jeremy could tell right away that everything that came before had been beginner stuff. When they needed to breathe, Luke didn't pull away. He nuzzled pecks along Jeremy's collarbone or rolled his neck open for Jeremy to kiss him there.

It was almost everything Jeremy had ever wanted. The weight of bracelets dragged his wrist, and he couldn't have stayed the night; even if he could have, Luke's parents were afraid of his family and wouldn't want him to.

Luke had his hand on Jeremy's knee, and then his leg, and it was easy to stop worrying. He slid it higher, cupped Jeremy's hip, and it was hard to think about anything else.

Luke leaned back, pressing Jeremy's waist to hold him away, and breathed hard through his nose. His eyes squeezed shut so tight his forehead wrinkled. "One sec."

"Don't stop." Jeremy tried to tug him closer by the wrist, but when Luke opened his eyes, the look there, cool and hungry and awed, was so intense it stopped him. He sat back on Luke's knees and let his grip soften around Luke's hand. Watching, Luke pulled his lips between his teeth and shook his head, as if something impossible were happening.

Jeremy wondered what Luke saw. He felt tediously possible, hemmed in on all sides. He was constantly happening to himself, and didn't find it all that special. He thought he should say something sexy. He said, "What?"

Luke laughed.

"You laugh at me a lot."

"You're pretty funny." Luke sat up slowly, his hands hovering like he'd forgotten what to do with them.

"What's next?" Jeremy asked.

Luke looked up. "You tell me."

Jeremy huffed, but he could say it. "I want to have sex. Maybe not anything advanced, but we can just...be... together. Right?"

Jeremy caught some of Luke's smile before he hid it, ducking into Jeremy's neck. "You are so sweet. You could sell hot chocolate in hell."

"I'm not trying to sell anything," Jeremy said. "Do you not want to?"

"I want to," Luke said heavily. The heat of his breath, the vibrations of his voice in his ribs, pressed into Jeremy's skin. "But I don't want to mess this up."

Jeremy blinked at the wall. "Oh. I probably wouldn't even notice."

Luke snorted. "Not like that. God, you're—" He sat up and put his hands under Jeremy's jaw. "I wish it was me. But it's not, Jeremy, and if you meet your *true damn love*, aren't you going to wish you kept all this?"

It hit Jeremy like a slap or a splash of ice water. He twisted off Luke's lap and clambered gracelessly to his feet. "It's not a *joke*."

"I'm not joking," Luke said. "What if you end up stuck

because you gave your first to the wrong person?"

"What if I'm too careful, and that gets me stuck?" Jeremy crossed his arms over his stomach. "I haven't thought about all these what ifs, because it was supposed to be *you*. You're supposed to—"

He stopped himself in time, but he might as well have shouted *love me*. Luke's forehead crumpled. Jeremy's skin prickled; he turned, scanning for his shirt.

"I'm sorry," Luke said, soft in a way that reprimanded Jeremy's yelling. "We just—we have to be able to talk about stuff—"

"It's all you *ever* talk about." Jeremy turned again. He had to find his shirt. "I've heard enough."

"That's not fair." Luke's voice was so rough Jeremy stopped and turned slowly back to him. His face had gone hard. "You can't mess around with me while you wait for someone else, *and* get mad when I try to change your crossing, *and* get mad when I deal without changing it. There's nowhere left for me."

Jeremy stepped back, stunned, and pressed his arms over his stomach. Luke made him sound horrible. He wasn't waiting for anything, didn't *want* anyone else. But he also didn't know what the future held.

It wasn't supposed to be like this. Jeremy was supposed to be happily-ever-aftering right now. Jeremy squeezed himself harder, trying to press the thought out of himself—hope fit more comfortably than bitterness—but it tumbled him like a wave, stealing his air.

"I didn't mean—" Jeremy started, but he couldn't finish. He had meant it, every kiss and prayer, even the foolish, impossible ones. Like a plant that had grown sideways in poor light, he was too used to making do. Luke would want something real—deserved it. He was right. It wasn't fair for Jeremy to drag him down.

"Hey," Luke said, much more gently. He reached for Jeremy's elbow and pulled him closer. "Talk to me."

Jeremy's arms crawled up his chest, following their own instinct to cover him. Luke twisted to the side and got Jeremy's shirt out from underneath his leg to hand it over. Jeremy pulled it on and felt more naked, standing there avoiding eye contact. Neither one of them was moving, and he had some time. He thought about what he wanted to say, and it came out perfect, like his words never were. "I'm with you because I like you, not because of the curse. If it meant I was stuck, I'd still want to be with you."

Luke jolted like Jeremy had electrocuted him and took his own time answering. "I think I like you too much to let you do that."

Jeremy shook his head. He grabbed his bag from the floor and threw it on. "Sorry to *bother* you, then."

"Jeremy, no." Luke stood. "Come on."

The only thing Jeremy didn't like about Luke was how he always said *Come on* during fights, as if the only reason you could disagree with him was that you hadn't caught up yet. Tears burned behind Jeremy's eyes, and he squeezed them closed. Luke's hands on his waist made him jump.

"Don't touch me." Jeremy pushed away too hard and crashed into Luke's dresser. He yelped in surprise—it didn't hurt, just made a lot of embarrassing noise—but Luke shot his palms up, stricken, as if he'd shoved Jeremy himself. And that was even worse, Luke thinking it was *his* fault, when of course it was only Jeremy, flailing around and ruining everything.

Whatever they had made collapsed around them, messy and claustrophobic, and Jeremy couldn't imagine finding a way forward again. All he knew was that he had to get out of there before he cried, because he couldn't imagine anything more humiliating than that, and his whole life was already humiliation enough.

Chapter Thirty-Five

Jeremy stood in front of the candy in a convenience store down Luke's block until the treacherous heat behind his eyes started to calm. He waited for the roiling hurt and shame inside him to settle, but they didn't and they didn't and they never would. He was going to feel like this forever.

He stared at his phone's black screen, pretending he had a decision to make. But his options were limited, and even if Sergei was done with Natalya, Jeremy wasn't ready to face him.

Instead of *hello*, Alexei said, "Your highness! How may I serve?"

"Could you come pick me up?" His voice sounded pitiful, and he hated it. More firmly, he said, "Or send a car. Sergei said no cabs."

"Of course. Scots on the loose. Where are you?"

"A bodega on East 149th Street in the Bronx."

"Where? The Melnyks'?"

"No."

There was a long pause. "Ah," Alexei finally said. "Next

time, if it's easier, you can just say *rock bottom*."

After they hung up, Jeremy made some selections. Three candy bars. Four. He made a slow lap of the store, looking for something to soothe his mood.

He frittered away his attention at a stand of sunglasses until one pair caught his eye. They were huge aviators with hot pink plastic frames and iridescent mirrored lenses, and they were, if he was entirely honest with himself, the most important sunglasses he had ever seen. He put them on and used his phone's front-facing camera as a mirror. The boy on the screen had no cheekbones, and no eyebrows, and not a thought in his head. Jeremy had heard luxury goods described as aspirational before, but he'd never understood it until he put these sunglasses on his face.

They would be the best fourteen dollars he ever spent.

For so long, wanting Luke had been another on the long list of things that made him feel lonely and weird. How could it be that having Luke made him feel just the same way?

When the Flying Spur rolled up to the curb, Jeremy was waiting outside the store in his new sunglasses, steadier after a Snickers and two Twix. The front passenger window slid down, and Alexei leaned over from the driver's seat. "Your car, my prince?"

Jeremy checked the back as he climbed in. "Where's Katya?"

"Working."

Katya's job was driving Alexei around, so she obviously was not. Something rebellious caught Jeremy's tongue. "I know you were with Natalya. I'm not stupid. You can tell me."

Alexei glanced at him, weighing. "Someone tipped her off. She's gone. Left town, I believe."

"Oh." Jeremy was a terrible Kovrov; he felt a wave of pure, traitorous relief.

"You'll have to come back to mine for a while. Sergei is

quite colorful. Unless there's somewhere else you want to go?"

Jeremy shook his head. They turned a corner, and his breath hitched and stopped—*Luke.*

He stood under a basketball hoop with the Wesleys. Straight Wesley dribbled a ball back and forth and the other boys were talking, Short Wes laughing and Luke covering his face and shaking his head.

Jeremy twisted to keep watching as they drove. Short Wes slung an arm around Luke's shoulders, and Luke took his hands away from his face. As he looked up, his eyes landed on the gorgeous, glowing, far too distinctive car. Jeremy jerked away from the window. Alexei's attention was palpable. There was nothing Jeremy wouldn't give to have someone to talk to who wasn't bound to him by familial or financial obligation.

Alexei gripped the gearshift fiercely. "You will tell me if he hurt you."

Jeremy shook his head, gaze drifting back to the window.

"I will destroy him," Alexei said, not in a growl like Sergei would, but calm and casual.

"*No.* It wasn't like that. It's just—it was stupid." Jeremy's voice cracked, and he swallowed. "It was me."

Alexei stopped at a light and peered into his face, thoroughly blocked by the wonderful sunglasses, before nodding. He didn't speak again but rubbed Jeremy's head vigorously, scratching behind his ears, as if Jeremy were a small dog. It was a classic Alexei move, so familiar with years of repetition that it was comforting.

They drove into Manhattan. The Flying Spur's ride was fluid and quiet, sealing them in and muffling the shimmer and zoom outside, and Alexei kept talk radio murmuring low. The stores and crowds changed abruptly—they were in one world, and then they were in another. The same magic crackled under all of it, but that didn't make anything better.

Jeremy didn't feel like crying anymore, but he could have gone to sleep forever. Or for a few decades, at least. He wanted to sleep until someone simply and comprehensively defined *love*, however long that took.

He could sleep like that here. Nowhere he knew was further outside day-to-day reality than this car. He'd curl up in the corner while Alexei ran errands and entertained dates. "Don't mind him," Alexei would say. "He's taking a break."

No, Alexei would say something way cooler than that. He'd put his arm around some pretty man or woman and say, "The young prince is dreaming of love." Sergei had said, *I can't have you end up like Alexei*, but Jeremy could think of nothing better. Alexei had probably never cried in his life.

"Alexei?"

"Mmm?"

"Do you really believe in true love?"

"Yes." A beat. "I think it's a curse."

Jeremy thought about that for a while—the true love of Alexei Kovrov. He hadn't met very many of the people Alexei dated. Like most of New York, he followed it through the tabloids. Although... "Alexei?"

"Mmm?" It was a small syllable, but Jeremy heard the laugh in it.

"Did you and David break up because of me?"

Alexei was so surprised he let it show on his face, a twitch that traveled from his mouth to his eyes. "No," he said quickly. "David. Wow. I didn't even know you remembered him. I haven't thought about him in years."

Jeremy watched him contain his expression. He should get some pink sunglasses, too. "Was that a lie?"

Alexei's lips curled a little. "It wasn't because of you, not really. Tell me what you remember, and I'll fill in."

"I had my—we were outside." Jeremy touched the seat

next to him, the fine, smooth texture of the leather and the tiny hard seam of its stitching. He'd been six or so. It was not the first time he suffered his consequences, out of the house at noon, but it was the first one he remembered. "I just remember you were together for a long time, and I liked him, and I never saw him after that."

"You did like him," Alexei said. "We were together for three years, off and on. Not that long, really. Do you remember why you were outside?"

Jeremy shook his head. Alexei was self-contained again, eyes distant. "He was watching you. We told him not to leave the house, but I didn't tell him why. So he left anyway, for lunch, and he took you out. Obviously, he flipped when you disappeared and called the police, and we had to try to explain that." Alexei stopped.

"And?"

"And, well, I was furious. You were home alone for hours, and you didn't understand why it had hurt. I told him what he'd done, and he was angry with me, too. We did break up after that fight, but it wasn't you. I think something about you made him understand all the rest of it. He was always very good, and I was always a Kovrov. Better to let him go before he got hurt."

Jeremy chewed his lips. Luke was very good. Jeremy adored that about him. "That's not fair. It wasn't your fault."

Alexei's sigh was complicated. "It was too much to ask, for someone else to live with what our family does. What we did to you."

It was like a hot white light; Jeremy had to turn away. "You are my family."

"Of course," Alexei replied. Jeremy was still fidgeting his fingers against the seat, and Alexei patted his hand.

Alexei's guestroom was shipwreck-themed, the bed made of—according to Alexei, for as much as that was worth—

reclaimed wood from an actual shipwreck. It certainly had the drama of a wreck, jagged-edged planks joined together as fluidly as waves. It was also a huge, cozy bed, floating inside the room's pale blue walls.

Jeremy slept fitfully, zoning out more than resting. When he couldn't drift anymore, groggy and hollow, he checked his phone, and it told him two hours had passed.

He sat up and considered the other things his phone had to tell him: there was a new trailer for the next season of one of his favorite shows, everyone was angry about something the president had said, Sergei said he could come home anytime, Luke hadn't texted or called. Well, of course he hadn't. Jeremy had acted totally princessy. He wouldn't have called himself, either. He wasn't sure what he even wanted to hear, much less what he expected Luke might say.

Prints of old maps, the boundaries nonsense and the seas dotted with monsters, decorated the walls of the shipwreck room. Jeremy got out of bed and got steady on his feet, staring at one, the shapes of France, Spain, and Portugal dwarfed by the dragon-faced serpents and fish-faced crabs in the paper ocean. He let his eyes slide west and found the spot he thought might be New York in a flicking forked tongue.

Downstairs, Alexei sat at the island counter, drooping blank-faced and over his silver bowl. It wasn't milk or water in there—the dense, metallic scent could only be blood. Alexei's palms lay open on the counter, crisscrossed with tiny scars.

Jeremy thought of the Melnyks' dustless, herb-fragrant back room and pushed it away again. He was a Kovrov. He should have known, the whole time, how that would go. He had told Sergei he might need to be with Luke to learn some lesson for his real true love down the road, but he found he didn't like the learning much at all.

He checked Alexei's pulse, dripping like molasses but steady, and held his hand under Alexei's nose to feel the shallow flutter of his breath. He was not dead, though he was a fool to be doing whatever he was without someone keeping an eye on him.

Jeremy found a slice of leftover pizza in the fridge and turned on the TV, scrolling restlessly through the channels. He wasn't paying attention and didn't realize Alexei had woken up until he heard the effervescent hiss of a bottle opening. He twisted on the couch. "You're going to turn into a ghoul."

"I believe that would be a step forward, morally," Alexei replied mildly. "Beer?"

Though Sergei and Alexei didn't care, Jeremy didn't drink much. He was afraid if he started, he'd never want to stop. But this time, he said, "Yeah."

Alexei flopped on the couch, trading a beer for the remote and scanning as dully as Jeremy had. He had discarded his suit for sweats and a tank, and he looked more familiar that way—less like *Alexei Kovrov* and more like Jeremy's big brother—but there was a harsh, distant edge to his face.

"What were you doing?" Jeremy asked.

"Don't you worry about anything."

Jeremy twisted his lips. The room smelled like blood. "That's a little worrisome."

Alexei stopped on a shot of an alligator roaring and cocked his head thoughtfully to the side. "I'm looking for something Corey Malcolm stole from me. I think he's after it again."

"Something about my curse?"

Alexei kept his eyes on the TV. "No. It has nothing to do with you. I know it's hard, my prince, but there's no shortcut. We would have found it years ago." He put his hand on Jeremy's shoulder, rocking him lightly. "All you can do is follow your heart."

Jeremy sighed. His heart was about as good a leader as

Alexei's was. He shut his eyes and, for as long as he could stand it, really imagined himself never breaking the curse. He imagined being sixty, Alexei seventy-seven, sitting together on this couch. They'd talk about arthritis or whatever. He'd go home to Vanya, who'd have kids of his own. Maybe Jeremy could help with them. Tears ached behind his eyes again, and he pushed the thoughts away. "From now on I'm going to kiss everybody, right when I meet them. Get it out of the way."

"If that's what you want," Alexei said.

I want I want I want

"I'm going to go to Tulane," Jeremy said. "It's never cold in New Orleans." And Luke told the coolest stories about visiting. Jeremy didn't mention that part.

"Tulane's a good school," Alexei replied.

Jeremy huffed and scooted over, snuggling into Alexei's arm. He hadn't done that since he was a little boy, and it felt awkward now, but he hung on. "I'm trying to have a temper tantrum."

"Okay." Alexei patted the top of Jeremy's head, and Jeremy rubbed it away. "You are ferocious."

Alexei seemed ready to drink and channel-surf for gore all night, so Jeremy, warmly fuzzy at the end of his beer, took the opportunity to carry his improved mood home.

"Let me call Sergei," Alexei said.

"I can take the subway."

Alexei shook his head, so strained that Jeremy didn't argue, and pulled Jeremy into a tight hug. "If I'd put in a custom order for a baby brother, I couldn't have come up with one I liked better than you."

"Aww," Jeremy said meanly.

"I mean it." Alexei's hand closed around one of Jeremy's shoulders, holding him so close Jeremy couldn't see his face. "I'm glad you were born. I hope you are, too."

Jeremy squeezed. "Don't be weird."

Because he knew it would make Alexei laugh, Jeremy pulled out his new sunglasses and shook them open with one wrist, looking dramatically to his left as he slid them on like James Bond. It did make Alexei laugh, but his mood didn't stay up for long. He gave Jeremy another long, tight hug. "Be careful."

Chapter Thirty-Six

*Call me. We should talk or not talk if you want. I'm
sorry about my big mouth.*

Going to get a bagel solved a chunk of Luke's problems. It got
him away from his family's prying eyes and anywhere Short
Wes might make fun of him again. And if the best bagels
were in Brooklyn, if it only made sense for him to circle closer
to Jeremy's house so he could leap on that return text as soon
as it came... Well, he had cover.

He got himself an everything lox, orange juice, and a
small corner table, and sat down to glare at his phone. Jeremy
would write back—he would. He had to. Anticipation closed
Luke's throat so it was hard to eat. Every time a blink of light
moved over his phone, he jumped. But it stayed quiet, and
tiny licks of fear and anger flickered in. Luke had called three
times before he sent that text.

What if Jeremy didn't want to talk to him again?

There was nothing about that conversation Luke wouldn't
take back. He'd been processing out loud and had meant

little of what he'd said and none of what Jeremy had heard. But people did make mistakes. He had faltered once, for one second, asked for one tiny reassurance. He'd been doing too much magic and not enough resting, and he was running on empty. The more his problems multiplied, the fewer solutions he had.

He was so deep in his own mess that he didn't recognize the body that dropped into the chair across from him until a second, startled look.

"You're a hard man to get alone." Natalya wore a black Coney Island hoodie a size too big for her, hood up over a bun. She had turned that glamour off or flipped it somehow, making herself more unassuming. A gray lump of stone hung from a chain around her neck, and though Luke couldn't exactly feel a vibe from it, he could feel a hole it created, masking or tamping the energy around her.

She picked up his phone and put it in her pocket. Luke kept his gaze down, on the table, mapping the room out of the corner of his eye. He was close enough to run to Sergei's house, and he could probably beat her in a fair race—but a brown teenager running from a white lady through Sergei's neighborhood wasn't a fair race.

"You don't talk anymore?" Natalya asked. "That's okay. Listen."

She pushed back her hood and lowered her voice, drawing Luke closer to hear her. "Early this summer, I had a dream about a girl I used to be best friends with. When I woke up, I remembered her—which is when I realized I had forgotten her. Not, you know, grown apart, stopped thinking of her. It was like someone had gone into my mind and wiped her out."

Luke shifted forward in his seat, his hand moving to the little key Jeremy had made him, hanging on the chain around his neck. This was it, Alexei's secret—the key.

"Her name was Annabel Malcolm," Natalya said. "She

was Corey's sister. I got a call from him the next day—the same thing had happened to him. And I told him, I don't know what happened, but I know there's only one person who can get in your head like that."

"Alexei," Luke said.

Natalya nodded.

Luke glared. He shouldn't trust her. He couldn't trust any of them. He wanted her story so badly he could taste it, bittersweet under his tongue. He wanted it badly enough to swallow lies or reveal secrets of his own if he let himself get caught up. "You gave Malcolm Jeremy's hair. He could have been killed."

Natalya's face fell. "No. First, he told me he was just going to do a ritual. And, those bags, the seven of pentacles? A harvest? It was only meant to collect you two."

"*Collect* us? The fu—?"

Natalya shook her head once, tightly. "I know. But the only thing that was new was Alexei trying to get you and J together. I don't understand how it could have changed anything, but, Annabel disappeared at the end of one summer, and J was born the next spring—"

Luke gave himself away, gasping out loud.

Natalya's eyebrows lifted. "Ah-ha. What?"

Luke checked his words before he spoke them to make sure he was only linking pieces together, not telling secrets she didn't know. Natalya was the only person who might explain another side of the story. If she was wrong, he could take what he found out back to the Kovrovs, and if she wasn't, she could tell him what to do next. "I think there's a reason Jeremy was born when he was. It took a hundred years for this whole big family to have a boy? Nah. There's nothing in the contract, but maybe his ancestor put some kind of tripwire on it. If Alexei did something to that girl... it might be the reason Jeremy was born when he was. And why the contract won't break now."

Luke's orange juice went sour in his mouth. It was too bright in the deli, too loud. Too many people were getting their bagels like there was anything right in the world.

Natalya had disappeared inside herself, too—she yanked out her bun and pushed her hands back and forth across her scalp, tugging at big sections of hair with her fists. She kept a blank, distant gaze on the table for a long time; when she finally looked up at Luke, it was with a twisted, hateful face, like he had made this mess. "Let's go talk to Corey."

Luke froze, measuring again the distance to the door out of his eye. They threw the word *kill* around a lot, but when the Malcolms and Kovrovs fought, people actually died. "So he can cut off my head and put it in Alexei's bed?"

"No. You're not nearly as valuable as a racehorse." She paused, studying his face. "We're looking for the same answers you are, and Alexei's never going to tell you on his own. Either you think J's worth the risk or you don't."

Luke's breath left him and he dragged an inhale back hard. She was a master manipulator, vicious at it, even without her glamour, and Luke could see right through it. But he still followed her to her car.

Corey Malcolm was three inches shorter than Luke, but he was built like a machine and didn't try to hide the gun in his back pocket. He met them on the porch of a house built like an actual castle—it had round towers—somewhere in the twisting suburbs of New Jersey. They sat in white wrought-iron chairs around a matching table, delicate as a doily. Malcolm's shadow, the taller, younger man, stood a few feet away, keeping watch down the rolling lawn. At the corner of the property, a rough-hewn gray boulder punctuated the tidy border. The same emptiness Luke felt around Natalya dulled his senses here.

Luke didn't know where he was, didn't have a weapon or a car or his phone. He had nothing going but a smart mouth and the absolute conviction that he was the only person in this game who had his head in the right place.

Malcolm dropped a thick book on the table between them with a puff of dust. Luke thought it would be a spell book or some arcane text, but it was only a photo album, embossed with ivory flowers. "What have you heard about my sister?" Malcolm asked.

What Luke had heard was that Corey Malcolm had killed her, sacrificed her for power. His first thought was that it would be pretty reckless to say that to Malcolm's face; his second, that it was absurd. What kind of rumor was that? Where had it even come from? "Nothing I believe, sir."

Malcolm grunted, flipped the book over, and opened it from the back. A girl smiled up—it was a stiff, awkward portrait in front of a mottled gray background, but she was still beautiful, with round features like a doll and bright red-gold hair. Freckles spread over her nose and chest. Natalya made a pained noise.

"That's Annabel," Malcolm said.

They waited, like Luke ought to speak. "She's very pretty, sir."

"Look again."

Luke looked down and the photo was gone. He blinked—no, it was empty. He shook his head—there was some other girl there. "Jesus, what is that?"

"That's in my head." Malcolm turned pages. What should have been a boring family album was the nastiest mojo Luke had ever seen. Pictures slithered and flickered. The girl was there, she was gone, she was in one photo and fading from another. It hurt Luke to look at, and he couldn't resist the urge to pin her down like a butterfly, finding the photos where she was whole and focusing there. It was like any uncrossing: he focused on the images he saw, and imagined the images he wanted to see, shuffling back and forth between them until they were the same.

He didn't make the pictures stop slithering, but they slowed as he watched them, starting to feel more right.

"Shit." Malcolm stopped turning pages and looked up. "Is that you?"

Natalya knocked Luke's arm. "I told you, this one's doing something."

"This is in your head," Luke said. "You mean your memories?"

Malcolm nodded. "It's not that she just went missing, or might have died—it's that he took her out of the past, too. Out of reality."

"A family feud thing?" Luke asked.

Malcolm and Natalya looked at each other like they were trying to decide who ought to take a live ball.

Luke guessed again: "They loved each other?" That was a daunting thought, the true love of Alexei Kovrov. She must have been a whirlwind of a girl.

Malcolm stood. "I have something else to show you."

Luke followed him inside, through a sprawl of rooms set up like galleries—big, landscapey art, clusters of chairs no one had ever sat in, sculptures of pineapples and fishermen's knots. There was so much space, so much useless stuff, and the air conditioning was uncomfortably cold. It was luxurious in a way that even Sergei and Marta's house wasn't, more museum than home.

Malcolm led them up a huge staircase and down another hall, into a pale blue room with round walls and a canopied princess bed. It was the first place in the house that felt lived-in.

"This was my sister's room," Malcolm said. "It hasn't been here for years."

Luke snapped his head around to read Malcolm's drawn face. "Say that again?"

"The room. Either it hasn't been here or I haven't looked at it or—it's not clear now. It was hiding. My father says one night he came up to go to bed and it was here, like she'd never left."

Luke's stomach dropped like it had when he'd watched the cards disappear from Alexei's palm. "When?"

"The end of June, a Wednesday," Malcolm said. "Why?"

"Just wondering." Luke's voice was breathless with the lie. The last Wednesday in June, he'd been working in Sergei's basement and asked Jeremy, "How are you related to the Kovrovs, anyway?" The strange, shifting feeling of the ground rotting underneath him. He'd split a binding and cracked open the world, and it *was* about Jeremy, whatever had happened to this girl. He flexed his fingers, itching for a spell to throttle.

"It still smells like her perfume," Natalya said. "Eighteen years, and it still smells like her."

She made Luke notice the scent, a fresh, blue-toned sweetness. It reminded him of something Camille used, of bumping into her in the hall in the mornings, rock-paper-scissors for who got the shower first. It was a horror to imagine losing his sister in any way, but to lose her like this—having her sucked right out of reality, *forgetting* her... he wouldn't be able to bear it.

There was nothing he wouldn't do to fix it.

No, that wasn't true. There were boundaries.

"This isn't Jeremy's fault." Luke looked Corey Malcolm right in the eye. "You shouldn't have tried to hurt him."

"That's her life he's walking around in," Malcolm said.

"Wait, *what*?" Luke threw open his arms, and Malcolm

twitched at once toward his gun. Luke pulled his hands back to his sides and spoke calmly. "That's a big leap. It's got to be more complicated than that."

"More complicated than what? Alexei killed her, and now you're telling me that made some weird Kovrov shit create a kid."

"Right, *something* happened," Luke said. "But that doesn't mean we're talking about an even trade, her life for his. I don't think anybody was doing magic intentional enough to pull off something like that."

Malcolm shook his head. "That's just splitting hairs."

"If we're going to undo it, we have to know exactly what happened." Whatever Jeremy's ancestor had done to the contract was too old to find, much less fix, and Jeremy's out, *true love's first kiss*, didn't work. But Alexei was right in the middle, still squatting over his web of bindings like a fat spider, and those bindings were breakable. That was the hinge—break whatever Alexei had made.

Malcolm gaped like a fish. "Undo it? Could you—I mean, she's been dead for decades…"

"Has she?" Luke squinted around the room. It had been gone, but it had come back. Like the cards. "We're not sure he did kill her."

Malcolm's face slammed shut. "Splitting hairs. Dead, never existed—what's the difference?"

He turned away, pacing to the hall, and there was a meaty thud of fist on plaster. He was clearly too angry to be smart, but Luke filed the question away to work on later—there was a whole lot of difference.

Natalya changed the subject. "We went to high school together. A girls' school, not far from here. It's possible I introduced her to Alexei. My dad worked for his father. I don't remember that part." She trailed her hand over Annabel's desk, an artful clutter of stacked notebooks, pens, and piles of the stuff that Luke had on his phone—CDs, magazines, printed photos, three different calculators.

Natalya pulled a notebook forward. The cover was berry red, with *Pre-Calc* in bubble letters and *Annabel C. Malcolm* in a loopy cursive. She started flipping pages—the math notes were dwarfed by doodles and scribbles—until she came to a page that alternated text in black ink and sparkly teal. "This is me." Natalya pointed to the black. "And this is Annie." She touched the teal.

Teal: *Corey found out about A He told Dad*

Black: *!!!!!!*

Teal: *Ya C called me a whore then Dad did, so fun*

Black: *:(What are you going to do?*

Teal: *It's not worth a fight—told A it's over but he's being all clingy*

"They were together. But—Corey, earmuffs." Natalya waved at Malcolm, hovering in the doorway. "They were both with a lot of people. As far as we can tell, Annabel didn't think it was worth keeping up after their families found out."

"Two houses both alike in actually, I'm not that into you," Luke said.

"What?" Malcolm turned back to the conversation.

"It's something J said." Natalya's eyes lost focus as she replayed the memory. "And it made Sergei so mad. Do you remember?"

"I guess," Luke said. "I thought it was because Jeremy wasn't supposed to date a Damiani."

"But we all knew Jeremy didn't like him. There was nothing to be mad about." She pressed a hand to her forehead. "Oh my god. She dumped him, and Alexei...did whatever this is, and Sergei knows and—" she stopped and swallowed hard.

"And Jeremy is stuck with them," Luke finished.

"Can you really undo it?" Malcolm asked. "Could you bring her back?"

Luke traced the teal ink, bright and fresh as yesterday's notes, with one finger. The worse this story got, the surer he was that he had to fix it. "I can try."

It was a long drive back to the city, too hot in the toboggan Natalya called a car. "So, we need to figure out what J's ancestor did to his contract," Natalya said, for the third time in fifteen minutes. "And what exactly Alexei did to Annabel that brought back the contract, and whether we can undo that to free J or Annabel."

She'd gone too far off track. The secret to uncrossing—to any magic—was focus. "The question is what Alexei did to Annabel. It doesn't matter how the tripwire was placed if we know how it was sprung, and if we undo that, we uncross the whole thing."

She nodded. "Maybe I can talk to my sister."

"You haven't told her yet?"

"I'm keeping her out of trouble." Natalya paused. "And Katya…she has a hard time with gray areas."

Luke shut his eyes, pressing the heels of his hands over their tired ache. He hadn't eaten enough breakfast, and he was hungry, exhausted, and over these people and all their inside-out principles. "I need to talk to Jeremy." He sat up and glared. "Let me call him."

She shook her head. "If it's all the same, I'll keep the phone 'til I'm on my way out."

"It's not all the same, and I need to *talk* to him."

"J has been living with his brothers for seventeen years.

He can take it a little longer." She shot him a side-eye. "You don't want to go in there half-ready, making guesses. That's why I've been waiting. You get one shot to convince them. The Kovrovs are loyal to each other."

"Jeremy isn't a Kovrov."

"Does he see it that way?"

"He will when he understands."

Natalya made a skeptical face at the road. "Phone's yours when I drop you at the subway."

Luke stopped arguing and shut his eyes, waiting out the ride. It didn't matter either way if Jeremy wasn't answering his calls.

Natalya dropped him in an alley in lower Manhattan. "Go up and take a left; you can catch a train."

"What great service."

She handed over his phone. "I'll be in touch."

Luke checked it as he walked up the alley. No missed calls, no texts. He sorted through his notifications, making sure he hadn't missed anything else from Jeremy. He needed Jeremy talking to him, period, before he could talk about Alexei's past. He was closer to Brooklyn than home—he could go there instead. Turn on the charm. Bring flowers. No, not flowers, *shit*. Something chill, but fun, nothing that might insult Jeremy. Ice cream.

Luke wasn't paying attention—he was, as his mother always said, going to get lost in that damn phone.

Pain was a bomb on the back of his neck, sending red waves through his vision. He fought for his next inhale and by the time he had it, his hands were bound behind him. A gun pressed sharp in the middle of his back and his vision flashed brighter red.

"He trusted you!" The voice behind him belonged to someone short—it was under his shoulder, tight and furious. "I can't believe you'd betray him, you—"

"I wasn't." Luke's voice was hoarse. "Katya, is that—"

"Shut up, just shut up." Another blow hit Luke's lower back and stole his wind, and a third knocked him down. He tried to shout, but a solid kick in his stomach stole his breath.

Katya dragged him up and shoved him, stumbling, into the back seat of a car. It was something beige and nondescript, the upholstery cracked under Luke's cheek. "Katya, it's not what you think. Katya, *please*—"

"Shut up or I will shut you up." She slammed the door closed behind Luke's feet, walked around, and let herself in the driver's seat. "Save it for Alexei."

Chapter Thirty-Seven

Today was the perfect day for Jeremy to learn all about Henry VIII's wives and how they'd died. The stories were morbid and romantic and learning them didn't *not* involve lying in bed watching trashy historical adaptations on his laptop.

He didn't play with his phone or stare at Luke's message, but it buzzed in the back of his mind. He was still thinking about how to reply, if *thinking* was the best way to describe fretting in a static cloud embarrassment.

He was watching YouTube clips of different actresses performing Anne Boleyn's execution and deciding whether it would have been better or worse for Henry to have been there to witness it, when Sergei came into his room.

Jeremy sat up straighter. Sergei crouched by the side of his bed, the way he had when Jeremy was little and got sick or had a nightmare. It was cute then, and weird now.

"What's wrong?" Jeremy asked.

Sergei put his hand on Jeremy's bed—the *KOV* on his knuckles, a dragon's head on the back of his hand, his sons' names woven into the body that snaked up his forearm. "I have to talk to you about something, and I need you not to freak out."

A whole morning's anxiety wound itself into a single sharp spear and pointed at Sergei's clouded face. Thinly, Jeremy said, "Okay."

"I know I'm asking a lot," Sergei said. "Alexei and Katya are too angry to think. But we have a lot to figure out, so if you can keep using your head for me—"

"Please just tell me what it is." Jeremy pressed a hand to the pit of his stomach.

"We found Natalya. She came into the city to meet a contact and took that person out to the Malcolm house for a meeting with Corey. They were there for more than two hours." Sergei rolled his fingers into a loose fist, knocking it against Jeremy's bed. "Her contact was Luke Melnyk."

No. Jeremy's whole body pulsed in horror—he jerked away. But Sergei stayed still, and Jeremy took a deep breath. What would using his head look like? "I don't understand."

"Like I said, there's a lot to figure out." Sergei was so tense that a vein throbbed blue on his temple. "But there's some things about the timing that make sense. Nobody but me, Alexei, and Marta knew about the meeting Natalya missed, unless—you two figured it out?"

Jeremy nodded. They had. *Luke* had. Jeremy filled in the timeline—Luke had come over, snuggling in his bed; Natalya had missed her meeting, while Jeremy had been at his apartment, ready to—

Jeremy's brain shorted out and came back in on this morning, hovering over his phone while Luke was meeting with Corey Malcolm. "Oh my god." He put his hand over his mouth. "No. There has to be an explanation, there has to."

"That's possible," Sergei said, so gently that there was absolutely no way he believed it was true. Nothing was scarier than Sergei trying not to be scary. "Katya says if there was a good reason for this, Natalya wouldn't have kept it a secret from her. But Katya's angry. It'll be good to keep an open mind either way. We're going to talk to him now. I'd like you to come help us fill in the details, but Alexei and I can take care of it if you can't."

"I *can*," Jeremy said, by habit, and immediately thought, *Oh no, no I can't.*

Sergei was already standing, brushing his hands over his hips like he could dispose of the conversation. "Get changed and come on downstairs. He's in my office."

"He's *here*?" The floor—the ceiling over Luke's head in the room below—seemed to tilt under Jeremy's bed. Sergei only nodded and left the room.

Jeremy was still wearing pajamas. He switched his cotton pants for jeans from the floor and pulled his tank off. The whish of fabric over his hair reminded him of Luke peeling him out of his clothes, and he froze in the middle of his room, goosebumps crawling over his skin. *No no no*—he couldn't gather his scattered thoughts. Sergei's story had implanted an organ his body was rejecting.

He yanked open a drawer and got a clean T-shirt—red for power, though all the actually powerful people he knew were downstairs worrying about things much more important than their clothes.

His brothers stood together in the hall. As Jeremy walked up, Alexei smiled in an odd, plastic way. "Wonderful. Let's begin."

Luke was in a chair in Sergei's office, head in his hands. The back of his neck and the collar of his white shirt were dark with dried blood, and it was matted in his hair. Jeremy gasped.

Luke's head shot up, and when he saw Jeremy, he started to stand. There was another, cleaner cut on his upper arm, where someone had taken blood. His necklace hung out of the collar of his shirt, the iron of his amulet dark under the brighter silver of the little key Jeremy had made for him.

"Stay in that chair," Alexei growled, "or I will nail you to it."

Luke sat down hard, swaying.

Jeremy whirled on Alexei. "What is wrong with him?"

"Katya was enthusiastic in her duties." Alexei leaned against Sergei's desk, crossing his arms. "She was understandably upset by these particular traitors."

Luke glared balefully up at him. "I'm not—"

"You may speak when you are spoken to," Alexei said.

Jeremy put his hands out to balance—he was having trouble even standing still. "Stop. Everyone stop. What is going *on*?"

Alexei opened his mouth, but Sergei silenced him with a wave. Much more calmly, he said, "You've been working with Corey Malcolm and Natalya. It's time to come clean."

Luke shook his head. The motion was strange, a little like he was shaking water out of his ears, and when he spoke, his words slurred together. "Natalya found me *today* and dragged me to Malcolm's." He spat, pink with blood, on the floor. "Pretty much how this day's going."

Guilt churned in Jeremy's stomach, but Sergei said, "You were there for hours, and they let you walk. Did you cooperate?"

Luke paused before answering. "Mostly they talked to me. There was a girl—"

"What do you mean 'mostly'?" Jeremy's heart started to race. Sergei grabbed for him, but he shoved away and stepped forward. "Did you talk about me?"

Luke hesitated again. "I think we figured out something, about your crossing—"

"You talked to *Corey Malcolm* about my curse?" Jeremy pressed his exploding heart in, hand at his chest. On one level, he was afraid of the same things his brothers were afraid of, an enemy gathering information. Deeper, he imagined Luke presenting the details of their wonderful, useless kisses to a skeptical audience, and he felt sick. Maybe Luke hadn't set out to be a traitor, but that was betrayal.

"I was getting information," Luke said. "I was—"

"Giving *them* information?" Jeremy couldn't control his voice—he almost screeched.

"That's enough." Sergei clamped a hand on Jeremy's shoulder and mumbled, "Walk it off."

As Jeremy paced to the door and back, Sergei said, "So you're saying it started today. You're sure about that?"

Luke started to speak but snapped his mouth shut. Alexei scoffed, and Sergei cut a hand at him again without looking away from Luke. "Well?"

"I told her you'd found her out," Luke said, "but—" He stopped like he expected someone to interrupt him again, but no one did.

"But?" Sergei prompted again, voice dipping dangerously.

"I didn't know what you were going to do to her," he said. "I didn't tell her anything. I just said she should get out of town."

Jeremy could feel his pulse in his cheeks and clapped his hands over them.

Alexei made a show of checking a cuticle. "And while she ran our plans back to Malcolm, you figured, why not have Jeremy over? You're playing both sides, so you can fuck him anyway—"

"I said that's *enough*," Sergei shouted. Jeremy's vision swam, and he missed Alexei's reply—he didn't care anymore, he just had to *leave*.

"Listen." Luke's voice cut over the noise, hoarse but calm. Jeremy looked at him—really looked at him, his bright eyes in his bloody face. "Can I talk to just you?"

"No," Sergei and Alexei said at once.

Jeremy blinked at them. The room stayed quiet. He turned and found Luke still looking at him expectantly, waiting for him to answer. Like he had just as much say as his brothers did. A stream of light cut through all the grime building up inside him. "Yes."

"Absolutely not," Alexei said.

"Oh, you just stop." Jeremy looked at Sergei. "You can stay right outside."

The vein in Sergei's temple twitched.

"You said you wanted me to do this—"

"Okay." Sergei grabbed Jeremy's head and pulled it close, speaking into his ear. "Be smart. Get the facts." He dragged Alexei out.

Jeremy watched them until the door closed and dragged his eyes back to Luke. "Yeah?"

"I figured out something. What set off the tripwire on your contract." Luke slurred, *shometing*, but he was obviously trying hard to speak clearly. "I think it might be something we can change. The reason you were born when you were? It's because Alexei hurt a girl. Destroyed her memory."

"What? Like amnesia?"

Luke shook his head like he was scattering flies. "Destroyed the memory of her. Erased her from everyone's mind." Luke swallowed. "He killed her, Jeremy."

Chapter Thirty-Eight

Luke couldn't think or speak for more than a few seconds together before everything disappeared behind a blinding white wall. His head throbbed, and his back and chest ached. It all bled together, and he couldn't think past *it hurts it hurts it hurts.*

He'd finally gotten it all together and out, his hard-earned information, and Jeremy looked at him like he was speaking gibberish. "What?"

Deep breath. "Annabel Malcolm, Corey's sister." Deep breath. "They were together, but she dumped him when—"

Deep breath. "Their families found out. He did a binding, and she disappeared."

"Did Malcolm tell you this?" Jeremy's arms were crossed so tight his knuckles were white around his arms.

"Showed me pictures."

"Pictures? Of what? Alexei doesn't just *disappear* whole people."

Luke needed to explain why the pictures had been so horrifying, and convincing, but he couldn't think. "Pictures, but she was disappearing and moving." He pressed his hands to his forehead. "He took her out of reality. Like the cards. Her room was just like it was eighteen years ago."

"How do you know what Corey Malcolm's sister's room looked like eighteen years ago?"

Luke slumped over deeper in the chair, and Jeremy sighed.

"You're so hurt." He took one step closer, no more. "If you had *talked to me*, I could have told you not to do this."

Luke winced. It had been so real and added up so neatly, when he was talking to Malcolm and Natalya. He couldn't get the pieces in order again.

"You don't believe me."

Jeremy paused. "I believe that's what Malcolm told you. I believe you believe it."

"It's real," Luke said. "There's something going on with that girl. And the timing is right, from your birthday—"

Timing was the wrong word. The wall slammed down behind Jeremy's eyes. "Corey Malcolm tried to hurt us. Natalya was helping him. That's what's real, Luke." He moved to the door but stopped halfway and turned back. "I can't believe you would tell him about me. About—us."

Luke hoisted his throbbing head up and sat all the way back in the chair, taking the pressure off his chest, though it made his head swim. "I'm trying to help. You don't have to believe it to look into it." He stopped to catch his breath, and Jeremy waited for him to continue. "We could figure out how Alexei might disappear someone. Or if you don't want to talk to him, we could look into your ancestor, see if we could find your birth records—"

"Oh my god!" Jeremy shouted, throwing his arms open and snapping his hands to his hips. "*How many times* are you going to tell me you understand I don't want to talk about my birth family, and then bring it back up again? What is *wrong* with you?"

The door opened before Luke could answer, and Sergei and Alexei tumbled over each other to get in. Jeremy turned to them. "What do you know about Annabel Malcolm?"

Sergei Kovrov's brutal, unreadable hammer face was shocked. His jaw fell, but he didn't say anything. He clamped it all back down and deferred to Alexei.

"I saw Annabel for a while in high school. Is that what Corey told you?" He glanced derisively at Luke. "When her father and brother found out, they lost it, and Annabel ran away. They never found her. Horrible business."

Luke kept watching Sergei—his face was so tense that muscles jumped in his jaw and temple.

"Luke says you did magic on her," Jeremy said. "That you did something awful, and that made me get born. Because of the trip wire on my contract."

"Well, the first half of that sounds like something Corey Malcolm would say." Alexei sat back against the desk again. "And the rest is some bullshit Luke and Camille made up. You were there, you saw."

Sergei stayed quiet, glowering at Alexei. Luke willed him to speak up, say whatever he was thinking. It had been a mistake to tell the truth—they were just going to hurt him until he said what they wanted to hear. He needed support from someone to get out of this room.

Finally, Luke broke the quiet. "That's not the whole story."

Alexei rolled his eyes. Jeremy hesitated, shifting tiny movements back and forth as he decided who to turn to. Luke pressed his gaze into Jeremy's face, clenching his fists together. But Jeremy took a step toward Sergei.

That was it. Jeremy had chosen, and he hadn't chosen Luke. The Kovrovs switched to whispers, Alexei long and urgent, Sergei snapping back. Luke dropped his head and shut his eyes. A churning darkness swam toward him, and he tried to fall out of his soaring adrenaline and let it take him.

His father's voice: *You'll find out real quick who their family is.*

Luke made a quavering sound in spite of himself and slumped lower over his stomach. His head throbbed less but his chest hurt more. The door to the room swung slowly open, and Luke was hallucinating or dreaming or dead—he'd imagined Yuri's voice and conjured Yuri's image.

No—the Kovrovs fell silent and turned as one.

Yuri held his ground but put his hands up. "Mr. Kovrov. Just here to talk." He didn't even look at Luke.

"What are you—"

"Mrs. Kovrov was kind enough to call me."

Luke didn't even know who that was until Sergei pushed out of the room, shouting, "Marta!"

Alexei went red—almost purple. Before he could speak, Yuri lifted his empty hands higher and said, "Obviously, Luke has made some poor decisions. I'm sure he has learned his lesson. I think we'd all appreciate the opportunity to walk away."

"No," Alexei said.

Sergei came back, body filling the doorway.

Luke felt like a cockroach—like the splat that's left over after a cockroach. He'd been so careful with Jeremy, aware that he was bigger, and more experienced, that he had more power and the responsibility to be generous with it, but when it mattered, he had no power at all. His father was begging, and it was Luke's fault.

"As encouragement," Yuri said slowly, "consider that my daughter found some of Jeremy's hair. She is expecting Luke and me home in no more than two hours."

Luke tried harder to pass out, but he was whizzing into awareness. Every color—Jeremy's red shirt, Yuri's blue eyes—

was oversaturated.

"Are you threatening us, Yuri Melnyk?" Alexei asked coolly.

"I don't think so," Yuri answered, just as calmly. "I think we all know you would win in a real fight. I also think we all know we don't want a fight."

Jeremy put his hands on his neck, pressing the ends of his hair down, and everyone in the room glanced over as he moved. His face went white as Alexei said, "Luke for the doll, and he never contacts Jeremy again."

Luke's mouth fell open, but he didn't have words—only empty air. Jeremy looked at him once and then down to the floor, still as marble.

"Done," Yuri said.

It took another round of negotiating to organize moving, but Luke ended up alone in that nondescript car with Sergei. He slumped, eyes closed against the light. He saw Jeremy behind his lids—of course he did—but it wasn't any of the iterations of Jeremy's anger he'd seen over the past few days. It was Jeremy in his lap, smiling a little as he tugged on Luke's hand. Jeremy asking for one simple thing that Luke could have given him, instead of ruining everything with his damn fool mouth.

"I know I'm out," Luke said, eyes closed and head vibrating against the window. "You won't hear from me. But whatever loyalty you've got to Alexei, it isn't worth keeping Jeremy trapped."

Sergei was quiet for a long time, and Luke thought he was arranging an answer. But he just wasn't talking, not even to tell Luke to shut up, and pulled up behind the Melnyks' store without reply.

They met in the alley, trading Luke for a poppet in a wide no-man's-land between clusters of their two families. The Kovrovs kept the money, the power, and Jeremy, but Luke got to go home. Luke paused in the middle, pressing Jeremy's poppet into his hand. "Take it apart and burn the pieces."

It would have been better if Luke did it himself, but they were past that. Jeremy looked great in red, his skin bright and his eyes rich, which was a messed-up thing to notice, but Luke noticed it anyway. His whole body ached, so the sore press in his throat wasn't special. "If it has to end, might as well blow it up big."

Jeremy took the doll and left without saying goodbye.

Chapter Thirty-Nine

Jeremy listened on the steps as Alexei and Marta went to war. "Damn right I called a grown-up," she was yelling. "You needed one!"

"You had no right—"

"This is *my house*. My *children* are in this house."

Actually, currently, Marta's children were with her parents. Sergei walked up to the landing with a bottle of beer at his lips and the neck of another in his hand. He lifted it in Jeremy's direction, and Jeremy took the thought that he ought to say no, acknowledged it, and nodded as he accepted the beer.

"This might be the wrong call." Sergei sat down a step above Jeremy, who wiggled aside for his long legs. "Might need vodka for this one."

"We can get some later."

"Absolutely not. Start with beer, end up hungover. The only thing that goes with vodka is more vodka."

Jeremy rolled his eyes, but he couldn't keep the fire in it. Sergei wasn't who he wanted to scream at. How dare Luke, how could he talk to the Malcolms, lie to Jeremy's face? "I respect you," *sure*. Luke would believe anything anyone said about Jeremy's curse or his family, unless it was Jeremy telling him how he felt.

"They could have hurt Jeremy," Alexei bellowed. "That is on you!"

"You started all this! 'He's going to get old, it's going to get weird.'" Marta shouted back, lowering her voice when she mocked Alexei's. "*You* didn't think it through, and now *you* want to blame everybody else…"

Marta kept railing, and Sergei grinned with one corner of his mouth. When he caught Jeremy looking, he said, "That's my girl."

"Gross." Jeremy wrinkled his nose and didn't let his face show how his heart crashed. Oh, Luke. Jeremy had not stood up for him, either, and they—Jeremy thought, *we*—had hurt him so much. Luke was better off as far from Jeremy as he could get.

"Kid, you've got to get a haircut," Sergei said. "Start wearing it shorter. You have to stop leaving your hair all over."

He was probably right. "If I have my hair short, I look like a lizard."

"Better'n looking like a chick."

Jeremy glared. "One, that is offensive. Two, if you think I care what you think about my hair, I have *serious* problems today."

Sergei shrugged and took a long drag off his beer.

"You think Luke's onto something," Jeremy said. "Don't deny it, I saw you."

Sergei squinted at his bottle. "I don't know. I think there's more to the story than Alexei wants to admit, but I don't think your boyfriend filled in the gaps right."

"Will you stop it? He's obviously not my boyfriend." *It*

has to end. He wanted to keep snapping, but instead, sat up straighter and held his breath calm. "Why are you trying to pick a fight?"

Sergei glanced at him, and quickly away. He gestured to the racket downstairs. "Seems like the thing to do."

Jeremy huffed. "Cut it out."

Sergei nodded—ungraciously, but it was better than usual. "Katya lost her temper, too. Unprofessional. You mess somebody up like that, all it does is mess up the information."

Jeremy fought hard to keep hold of that calm. This was not a teachable moment, and he didn't feel like being taught. "I don't see why you're telling *me* that. I know."

Sergei cut him a side-eye, long and quiet.

"So they're both wrong?" Jeremy asked. "Luke and Alexei."

"Definitely. Kid, I have no idea what happened or what's going on, but I know for sure that both of them are wrong."

Jeremy snorted.

"Say he's right," Sergei continued. "Something we did broke something on your contract and called up the curse. I know it wasn't that Alexei hurt that girl in cold blood. Because if nothing else, plenty of Kovrovs killed plenty of people in cold blood in all those years before you were born."

"Do you think we could find out?"

Sergei twisted his mouth. "If Alexei bound it, Alexei should be able to unbind it. He *should* be able to remember without having to unbind it, and that is the trouble."

"I want to ask him. I want to try."

"Yeah?"

"Yeah. If there's a reason I'm here, maybe there's another reason I can't get free. Besides true love."

Sergei took another drag off his beer. Jeremy drank, too, slower sips that smoothed his sharp edges.

"So you love him?" Sergei asked. "Or—loved him?"

Jeremy saw Luke every time he blinked: Luke, smiling in his bed; Luke, slumped in a steel chair. "Oh, I don't know. I don't know what love is, and Marta and Alexei keep saying I'll *just know*, so that's a bad sign, but—" Jeremy swallowed, and mumbled out the rest. "That first one felt like magic. It should have been magic."

Something glass shattered downstairs, and Alexei roared like an animal. Sergei ran his hand back and forth over his close-cropped scalp, lost in thought. Jeremy looked away, straining to hear the conversation below. He jumped when Sergei grabbed the side of his head and put a dry kiss on his temple. "I love you, little brother."

Jeremy recoiled against the wall. "What are you doing?"

Sergei pointed with his beer. "I did that every day when you were little. I was so sure I'd break it. Kid, it might be unbreakable."

"Oh my god." Jeremy scrubbed his head. "Pull yourself together."

Sergei nudged Jeremy's arm with his bottle. "I'll take Alexei if you take Marta."

"What? No way."

"I can't talk to her. She's going to stay mad for at least twelve hours." Sergei rose and walked down the stairs.

Jeremy trailed after him. "*I* didn't marry her."

"Exactly."

Jeremy huffed and pushed past him. "Alexei! Alexei, I need to talk to you."

Chapter Forty

Luke stirred to a soft tap on his door, a sound so unlike anything his family would make that the senseless animal in his chest asked, *Jeremy?*

It was Camille, peeking in like he might be building a bomb in there. "Hey. You awake?"

Luke nodded, sitting up in bed. He had been floating half-in and half-out of sleep for...what day was it? Since his father had brought him home. Long enough that his head had stopped hurting, though his lower back ached and the cut on his bicep burned.

Camille wiggled in next to him, back on his pillows, and dropped a cornhusk poppet in his lap. It looked normal but felt awful—damp, heavy, and putrid with menace. When he picked it up, a beat tapped his hand that could almost be his own pulse, if it wasn't pounding so much faster than his own sluggish heart. "What is that?"

"I made a backup, obviously."

Luke dropped it, raw in shock. "That's Jeremy?"

"Don't be like that. They had you; I took him."

Luke's first wild impulse was to pick the doll up and put it to his lips. His second—hotter, lower—was to twist one of its little limbs. He plucked it off his lap and set it on hers. "No, I know. I get it."

She turned her head slowly. "You do?"

"Sure." Luke's jaw ached as he clenched it. "Alexei made Dad beg and still wouldn't give me up. I couldn't take it."

"That wasn't real. Dad had a backup plan."

Luke only shrugged again. Luke hadn't known, and he couldn't get past it, the crawling shame of it a sludge inside him that covered everything else.

A chill ran down Luke's neck, and he finally asked the questions that had been nagging him. "Did I mess everything up? Are we going broke?"

Camille studied him before answering. "It'll be all right. Dad said he'll figure out how to keep the apartment."

The cold feeling sank deeper, settling in like a conqueror.

"It's not your fault," she said. "It's them. The Kovrovs."

Luke pressed his shaky hands under his legs. Sure, it was all the Kovrovs' fault. But they weren't the ones who would suffer.

"What happened?" she asked. "Not the bad part. But before they got you? He said you found a secret."

It had felt so clear when Luke was talking to Natalya about it, but now, under the haze of pain and failure, he wasn't so sure. There was his theory about Maeve's tripwire on the contract, and then a big hole. A story about Annabel that he couldn't corroborate, and then a big hole. And then somehow Jeremy, disappearing right out of Luke's hands on a sunny sidewalk. That story was not worth what it had cost, and the impulse to keep trying to add it up wasn't as strong as his exhaustion. "I found—I don't know what I found. Something about why Jeremy is stuck. But how much am I supposed to care about helping him if he doesn't even want out?"

Camille tilted the poppet on her flat palm toward Luke. "Right. I get it. I thought you'd want to destroy this, is all."

"Maybe you should keep it. Alexei took some of my blood."

"But we're better than them, right?" Camille made the poppet dance. "Where's my lecture? I need all that, Camille you can't be a bad witch, Camille we're above that."

"I guess we're not."

Camille searched his eyes. "You're tired."

Luke nodded because it was easiest.

"Do you need anything? I can bring you some water."

"No." Luke tried to do something encouraging with his face. "I think I'll sleep it off."

Time slipped away. Luke thought he was only moping for a few days—*I'll get back to work tomorrow*, he kept thinking— but he found the moon a sliver in the sky one evening, and did the math. It must have been a couple weeks.

Luke had never lost time like that. It made him think of Jeremy's grayness, how outraged he'd been that his brothers didn't treat it like an emergency. Living it was more complicated than he'd expected.

He had lost his phone and hadn't gotten around to replacing it—didn't want to think about the cost. So he couldn't get a message from the Wesleys, just the Wesleys themselves.

He smelled them before they made it into his room. "Pew! What is that?"

Short Wes spread his arms. "Oud Gold! It makes me irresistible. What's yours, man?"

He nudged Straight Wesley, who made a much smaller version of the same motion. "Incense Silver."

Luke shook his head. No incense had sacrificed itself for the gasoliney fumes coming off either of them.

"Cool," Short Wes said, "I'm definitely taking grooming advice from somebody who smells like unshowered ass and misery."

"I *showered*." Luke sniffed under his arm. It wasn't nearly as bad as the pair of them, choking up his room.

"That's pathetic." Short Wes nudged Straight Wesley again.

"It's not great," Straight Wesley agreed.

"Also, you missed about nine horchata runs, so you owe us three rounds *at least*."

"That does not make sense," Luke said.

"What about horchata doesn't make sense?" Short Wes crossed his arms. "Come on. Put on a clean shirt and let's go."

They watched him. Straight Wesley stayed impassive — he was so good at that, it made him a little bad at anything else — but Short Wes started to heat around the eyes. It was obvious that they'd all been talking about him, that this was a ploy, and likely that if Luke couldn't get himself together for one horchata with his friends, the next ploy was going to be more serious.

He did not want to go out. He wanted to eat in bed, hogging the family laptop to monitor Jeremy's quiet Instagram and Max's buzzier one, and feel sorry for himself. But he could recognize both that he was being sick and self-indulgent and also that if he went now, he could buy himself a few more days of isolation in peace, so he got up and went to his dresser. "You going to watch?"

They cleared out while he changed and led him outside in a cloud of chatter and body spray that kept his family at bay. Short Wes kept detailed, dynamic horchata rankings, but he turned toward the place on Luke's block, another over-careful concession to Luke. "When last we met our hero,"

Short Wes said as soon as his feet hit the sidewalk, "he'd been ditched like an old sock in the middle of his game."

He looked expectant, like it was Luke's turn to talk. Luke was good at talking, usually. When he wasn't so tired. "That feels like it was months ago."

The Wesleys made similar vague noises, so in sync they practically harmonized, and left the quiet for Luke to fill.

"Camille didn't tell you?" he asked.

Short Wes shot him a glance. "It's all right. You don't have to talk about it." He jittered one hand across the air in front of him. "Ask the big guy about basketball."

"*Shit.*" Luke had totally forgotten about Straight Wesley's summer grassroots tournament, the years of college hopes he'd poured into it. "I'm sorry, man—how'd it go?"

Straight Wesley nodded. "All right."

Short Wes made a long *psssssh* noise as he opened the door of the restaurant. "Don't listen to him. Talked to all kinds of important people! He's going to be famous."

Luke got a round of horchatas as the Wesleys grabbed a table. Straight Wesley took two chairs, draping himself across both and making them look comically small. "I might not be tall enough."

"Stop." Short Wes blew the end of his straw wrapper at him.

"Big in high school isn't that big in college. When I play against guys who are all this tall…" He trailed off.

"You're used to it being easy," Short Wes said. "Just because you had to work a little harder doesn't mean you weren't good enough."

Straight Wesley shrugged. "We'll see."

Luke ducked his face over his horchata and took a long sip. It was heavy on his tongue—he'd been eating sweet, easy food for too many days in a row.

They were quiet, waiting for him. "That's what it was

like," he said. "Playing my usual game on a whole different court. I lost before I knew it was over. I was connecting the dots, I was so sure I had it all figured out, and now…" He glanced between them. "Did Camille explain it?"

"She said a lot of words," Short Wes said. "I didn't feel like they added up to an explanation."

"That's real." Luke's evidence had stopped fitting together. And even if it had, he didn't know how he'd go about uncrossing such a tangled old web. And even if he did, Jeremy had made his choice and it wasn't Luke. The only thing Luke was sure about was that somewhere, Corey Malcolm still believed the story they'd created, affirming his decision to target Jeremy. Luke had made nothing but mistakes. "It doesn't matter, anyway. He's not talking to me."

He gestured to Straight Wesley. "The court got too big."

"It's weird, though," Short Wes said, "because he's talking about basketball, and you're talking about a person."

"I'm talking about a crossing."

"A crossing on a *person*. Who you were *going out* with." Short Wes gestured with his horchata, scattering drops on Luke's face.

Luke scrubbed them away. "Watch out, man."

Short Wes put his drink down. "It isn't a game, is all. You think you know *everything* sometimes, because you know a lot about this *one* thing—"

"I know I messed up," Luke interrupted. "Thanks."

"That's not it." Wes shoved him. "Listen. You're beating yourself up so hard for messing up, your mom has to call me to babysit. You can't live like that."

Luke snorted, and it felt sort of good, so he let it open into a laugh. That was the perverse joy of being friends with the Wesleys: they never treated each other like they were fragile, so they could never be too broken. The proof was in the practice.

"There you go." Short Wes shoved him again, lighter. "That's what I'm saying. You lost one. That doesn't make you a loser."

Straight Wesley grimaced. "He's been a loser, though."

Short Wes made a sound halfway between a groan and cheer. "Merciless!"

Straight Wesley waved him off and leaned toward Luke. "Everybody knows girls, and whoever, hate it when you solve their problems. You have to just be supportive and shit while they suffer."

"Oh, yeah." Short Wes looked surprised. "I did know that."

"See?" Straight Wesley said. "Even the virgin knows."

Short Wes cheer-groaned again.

"Why?" Luke demanded. "For real, why do they want that?"

Short Wesley gestured with his horchata. "Because your solutions end up like this?"

At home, Luke did not get back in bed. He helped his mother make dinner and took a shift in the store. He got back to normal, more or less, as another week passed. He gave his dad most of his summer's earnings and spent the rest fixing his phone. He didn't say another word about the Kovrovs or Jeremy and didn't hear it from his family, either.

He pushed thoughts of Jeremy (stuck in that house, alone in the attic) down, down, away, below the surface of his consciousness, but they swamped him at night. He got in bed and remembered Jeremy there. Every midnight, he thought about texting. To say something angry. To say he was sorry. To say something dumb and get a laugh. Just to make sure Jeremy was safe. He wouldn't put his family in danger by trying, but whether he would if he could was a problem he could circle for hours.

He woke up over and over from obvious, exhausting

dreams: Jeremy was calling as Luke dropped the phone; Jeremy was drowning as Luke floated away. He dreamed that he failed to catch the crossed man in the restaurant, and Jeremy got shot, collapsing against Luke; he dreamed that it happened just like it did, except when he went to the body, it was Jeremy's, and he had Jeremy's wet blood all over his hands.

Luke was lying awake with his pillow on his face when his phone buzzed on the floor. *Jeremy?* He was a scramble of limbs trying to get to the phone and he flicked the call open without looking. "Hello?"

It was static crackling and a whoosh of air, nothing that made any sense. He pulled his phone away from his ear and checked the name on the screen three times before it broke through his fog. "Max?"

"I'm sorry." Max was slurring, but he sounded different— he wasn't drunk. He was crying. "I couldn't think of anywhere else to go."

Chapter Forty-One

Sergei and Alexei agreed that they would help Jeremy fill the holes in Luke's story, but they couldn't agree about how. They couldn't simply talk about what had happened so long ago, the story Luke had dug up—too many memories were hidden from them. Worse, they couldn't manage a conversation without fighting about it. They hated each other and always had. They grumbled over small things and battled over big ones. If one decided to try to be nicer, the other would act even more insufferable. They worked together fine, but the strain of the job pushed them even further apart.

Sergei believed that someone was trying to hurt Jeremy and was willing to find the information to stop it. He wanted to investigate from the world in—study the records or stalk the Malcolms. Alexei didn't say what he believed, but Jeremy suspected that hearing the girl's name, Annabel, had hurt him more than he could admit. He wanted to scour his bindings the way he always did, over a bowl of blood, but he wanted to build a full ritual around it with Sergei's blood, too.

As it usually went, Alexei didn't fight as hard, but he won

anyway.

Alexei was over every other day, consulting Ivan's records or measuring angles in the dining room. He bickered with Marta, glowered at Sergei, gave the babies nickels for saying cuss words. He made increasingly outrageous sexual comments to Jeremy, and Jeremy got sad and weird, and Sergei yelled at Alexei for being a pervert and Alexei called Sergei a prig and Sergei threw him out, and they did it all again a couple days later.

"What is with you two?" Jeremy asked after the door slammed the last time.

Sergei stomped away. "You want to dig around in our heads, you're going to find out."

As the hour of the ritual approached, all he and Sergei had to do was smoke a bowl of weed. Jeremy, strung out on anxiety, and Sergei, utterly earthbound, were both terrible at meditation. They needed help to melt into a ritual.

Alexei could slip off as quick as a blink, following the trails of his own blood to other places and times the way most people could recall a memory. He went almost too easily, drooping over his bowls of blood for hours. Every time he left, Jeremy worried that was the day he'd forget to wake up, soil himself and get sick with dehydration, and they'd have to put him away like Ivan had done for his older brother. Like one day Seryozhka or baby Dmitri would have to do for Vanya. Like younger Kovrovs had done in the courts of Ivan the Terrible and Peter the Great.

"Kid, I think you've had enough." Sergei took the bowl from Jeremy's hand and took one last puff before he wrapped it in foil. Weed made Jeremy feel large and porous, like he might float away. Like floating away would be fine.

It took the scraping edges off his worries—Alexei, Luke, Sergei, the contract, *Luke*—but it brought down the walls he'd built around all that, too. The part of his brain that had been writing messages to Luke all day every day for the past two weeks got bigger and truer. *I'm sorry*, these messages might say, or *How could you?*

"You made Alexei hide your phone." Sergei grabbed the hand Jeremy was patting against his pockets. "So you wouldn't do anything you'd regret."

"Oh." Jeremy studied his hands and found himself giggling. "I think I'm stoned."

Sergei laughed, too. "We should do this more often."

"No!" Marta stuck her head in the living room, glaring. "Come on, slackers. He's ready for you."

As the only one of them who had to get up at a regular hour, she was the most annoyed at having to stay up all night. Alexei was adamant about doing his rituals precisely at midnight, which Marta and Sergei dismissed as meaningless, another of his showman's flourishes. Jeremy had no way to know who was right, but he believed. Midnight meant real magic to him.

He trailed them down the hall as Sergei tried to pinch Marta's butt and she pretended to be mad at him. They usually kept that stuff hidden, for themselves, but it was late and everyone was jumpy, and the two of them were taking comfort from each other. Jeremy felt—in the detached, crystalline way of the weed—like he was being stabbed.

He stepped over a line of salt at the dining room doorway. Alexei sat at the end of the table in front of a candle and his metal bowl, arms crossed over his chest. He looked a lot like Sergei—his scowl made his brow sink over his eyes and his tank showed the eagle tattoo on his shoulder. There was something scary about it, all his shine worn off to reveal the Kovrov underneath.

He lifted his face and the impression faded. He looked like himself, but sadder. "Are you sure you want to see this?"

Jeremy blinked. "If you know what we're going to see,

you can just tell me."

Alexei raked a hand back through his hair and didn't answer. It was Sergei, sitting down on his other side, who said, "He means, neither of us is going to look good at the end of this."

Jeremy figured out their faces—they were scared. "I thought it was just memories. They can't hurt us."

Alexei sat up straighter. "It is just memories, and stay on your guard, because they absolutely *can* hurt you."

Marta took a chair at the other end of the table, put her feet up, and opened a blue paperback. "Make good choices."

Jeremy wrapped his right hand around Alexei's left wrist and found his hummingbird pulse. He extended his arm across the table for Sergei to hold. Alexei looked back and forth, making sure they were all ready, before he took Sergei's wrist, closing the circle and them into the dark.

Chapter Forty-Two

Alexei took his skateboard instead of one of the cars. It wasn't far to Coney Island from his family's house in Brighton Beach, and he liked keeping his destination secret.

The sidewalk vibrated in his bones. When he jumped over cracks, his joints clacked with a vicious thrill. There wasn't wind in Brooklyn in July, but he made some with his speed, clothes flapping against his sweaty skin.

Though most of Alexei's left forearm was scabbed over from his last fall, he wasn't afraid of hurting himself on the skateboard. Some of the things he was afraid of at sixteen years old included rejection, commitment, his desires for boys, his desires for girls, his desire for Annabel, his family, Annabel's family, his body, Annabel's body, wealth, power, shame, hope, all feelings, premature ejaculation, his own blood, and magic.

Annabel Malcolm wasn't afraid of anything at all.

She waited for him outside the line for the Spook-A-Rama with a Diet Mountain Dew in her hand and the sun fiery on her red-gold hair. A triangle of sweat soaked through her pale blue dress at the top of her stomach and one of the thin straps drooped off her shoulder, gliding across her freckles. She was perfect, and she was smiling at him.

He kicked up the board with a flourish right in front of her, flipping it into his hand, and she put a hand on her hip. "Do you think you're cute when you do that?" she asked.

"I know I am." Alexei grinned in a way he hoped was roguish. His heart pounded with exertion as the wind of his flight died, and sweat slithered down his back. He must look a wreck.

Annabel grinned back. "You are, actually. You dirtbag."

He zipped his skateboard into his backpack as they waited in line for their own little cup on the Spook-A-Rama's tracks. It rattled forward, and Annabel climbed into Alexei's lap, hotter than the boiling day.

"Jesus, we get it." That was Sergei, more the feeling of him talking than the sound of it, and he ripped Jeremy back into his own mind. He remembered where he was, at home, and what he was seeing. Alexei's hidden memories.

"You go, then," Alexei said.

Sergei was plodding through his pre-algebra homework as dutifully as a monk, so he was sure he wasn't doing anything wrong when the door flew open and his father roared in like a squall. "Liar," Ivan Kovrov said.

Jeremy felt Sergei's heart start to race, a ghost of his own slow pulse and the faint flutter of Alexei's against his fingers. At thirteen, Sergei was barely an adolescent, his lanky body and ill-made features still promising to grow into themselves. Ivan looked a lot like the Alexei they knew, but his body was thicker and his face hidden by doughy jowls.

Sergei had a twin bed and a messy desk and a small

mountain of hooded sweatshirts.

"Where is your brother?" Ivan asked.

"He went skateboarding," Sergei replied. His thoughts, hectic with fear, chanted *he's the liar not me he's the liar not me*, but they didn't settle on Coney Island or Annabel.

"You said he was with a boy," Ivan said. "I was barking up the wrong tree for two weeks."

"I just saw those videos. I don't know. I didn't—I don't know why you think he *talks* to me about this stuff, Papa!"

"You're hiding for him." Ivan's voice was calmer, and more frightening that way.

"No," Sergei said. "No, Papa, I don't know what he's doing. He's the liar. He has it all bound—"

Ivan closed the distance between them and took a fistful of Sergei's hair, twisting his face up. Jeremy felt it in his own scalp and neck.

"Gregori says he's with the Malcolm girl," Ivan said. "It's bound away from me. You find out what he's up to."

They were with Sergei, tapping his pencil against his homework, when Alexei came home. Sergei listened thoughtfully to the hollow roll as he coasted down the hall on his skateboard, the shower starting and stopping, and the muffled crash of grinding, feedback-heavy guitars in another room.

Sergei kept tapping. He didn't trust his father, and he didn't trust Alexei, and he hated the Malcolms. He didn't want anyone to get hurt, but mostly, he didn't want to get hurt himself.

If Alexei was messing around with a Malcolm, he must really love her. He wondered what that was like.

He growled aloud and shoved his homework onto the

floor, though the sound of the papers falling was muted and unsatisfying. Jeremy followed him down the hall.

"What were you doing?" Sergei asked.

Alexei scoffed. "Mind your own business, shrimp."

"Do you love her?"

Alexei's face was horrified, and then flat. "It's not like that. We're having fun."

Jeremy wouldn't have believed him even if they weren't in his mind, but young Sergei did. "Okay," he said, and left the room.

Alexei rolled off his bed and pulled open a drawer in his nightstand. He retrieved three candles, red, black, and white, and a pin he used to start scratching into their waxy sides. He was creating a binding spell, doubling down on an already-bound secret as his mind sizzled with panic.

"You were binding it while it was *happening*?" Jeremy asked. "Isn't that dangerous? What were you thinking?"

"By now you must know I wasn't thinking at all," Alexei replied.

They rifled through Alexei's memories: Annabel's bedroom, a cocoon of light blue; Alexei's feet in the sand and Annabel's gold hair whipping in the wind off the water; Alexei's finger tracing constellations in the freckles on her shoulder; Alexei whispering into the phone in the middle of the night, the sandpaper weight of his tired eyes.

Helene and Yuri Melnyk ran their business out of a small, meticulously clean apartment in the South Bronx. Helene, who carried a pregnancy like a planet orbited the sun, hugged Sergei.

"You're so big!" Sergei said.

Helene laughed. "I'll give you that one. But trust me, don't ever say that to a woman again."

Ivan growled at Sergei and turned a serene, professional face toward Helene. "Should you be up?"

Helene shrugged. "I'm hanging on as long as I can. We should have a few more months."

"There's two in there!" Yuri walked out of the galley kitchen. "Two at once! Mr. Kovrov, can I get you anything?"

"We can't stay. The product, if you would." Ivan handed Yuri a wad of cash, and he vanished into the other room.

"Ah!" Helene pressed a hand against the side of her belly.

"Is it okay?" Sergei's eyes went round with panic.

She smiled wanly. "Just one of the babies kicking. I think it's the boy, on this side. Do you want to feel?"

Sergei shrank back, shaking his head, and Helene and Ivan both laughed at him.

Yuri reappeared with a large cardboard box. Ivan waved, and Sergei took it.

The box was heavy in his arms. Candles, in red, black, and white. Sergei felt squeamish. "Papa?"

Ivan cut his hand quickly, *Not right now*, and kissed Helene's cheek. "Beautiful. I hope I won't have to ask you for any more before the babies come."

Helene patted her stomach where her son had kicked her. "They'll be all right. Maybe it will be lucky, having them stew in some heavy mojo in there."

Back in the car, Sergei didn't dare repeat his question, but Ivan put a heavy hand on his shoulder and answered it anyway. "I want you to get those to Alexei for me."

Sergei's mouth fell open, but protest and fear collided in his throat and nothing came out.

"He's got that binding on me, so I'll forget, but you remember." Ivan smiled, bringing his eyes down to Sergei's level. "He thinks he can win because he's got that power. But we're a team, you and me, right?"

Sergei's heart was *yes* and *no* and *please* and *help*, but there was only one right answer. "Yes, Papa."

A floodgate was open between Sergei and Alexei, memories pouring out and buffeting Jeremy like he was a little boat. He saw Annabel, Ivan, his brothers' smaller and softer faces, and in every image he could feel their fear. Alexei's tapping pulse against his fingers was his only connection to his own body, and he wasn't sure if he was breathing. *I want to wake up.*

The swirling stopped with a slam. His Alexei's voice whispered, "I've got it, I've got you," as the younger Alexei whispered into a cell phone so huge it was like a joke on a TV show. "It's okay, baby. I promise you're okay."

He sounded like Luke, which was to say, he was probably wrong.

Annabel cried into the phone, slurry with tears. "Corey told him, he knows. He took my keys and my wallet. He's going to freak if I see you again."

Alexei lay back on his bed. "So tell him you won't see me again."

"Alexei."

"We'll tell everyone we broke up. We'll make it big, start some rumors. In a year, we're free."

"And until then?"

"I can hide it, Annie." Alexei rolled sideways on his bed and pulled out the drawer of candles. There were only a few left. "You know I can."

"What are you doing with my stuff, shrimp?" Alexei shouted.

Sergei stood in the center of his room, thinking, *Wait.*

Alexei had the box of candles in the doorway, and Ivan was a thundercloud in the hall behind his shoulder.

Sergei's mouth opened and closed. Alexei said, "Are you *stealing*? You think *you* could do something like this?"

Wait wait—

One red, one black, and one white. A clock on the nightstand read 11:58.

Alexei scratched *Annabel* into the side of the red candle, *Alexei* into the white, and *Kovrov* and *Malcolm* into the black. Because he was alone in the room, he said, "I love you," out loud. He kissed the wax shape of Annabel's name, and he placed the candles in a triangle on the floor. He used the pin to prick his thumb and rolled a drop of blood over the white candle's wick, and rubbed the red candle's wick into a tiny Ziploc bag smeared with Annabel's russet blood.

He was afraid.

The lighter came to life, a punch in Jeremy's stomach. It took his breath. He was falling. Alexei's pulse stopped in his hand.

Alexei's voice: *Help.*

It was gray. Jeremy knew this gray: it was midnight, and he was being pulled inside, and he was falling and falling—

Gravity dragged him in two directions at once, stretching, spinning—he would be torn apart—

The grip around his wrist locked vice-tight, and Jeremy opened his eyes, gasping, in the rich red dimness of the dining room. Marta held Alexei's bowl over one of her plants, blood sloshing into the dirt, as she tore the ritual apart. "What is happening? What's wrong with you?"

If she was yanking them free, Alexei must have lost control. Jeremy's head hurt like a wound, and he dropped his forehead on the wood. One of his brothers was groaning.

"I said what's happening?" Marta's voice rose, shrill. "Where did you go?"

Alexei sounded like a ghost. "I think we went wherever I sent Annabel."

Chapter Forty-Three

"No. Luke, *enough*." Helene flipped on the living room light.

"I'm sorry!" Max said again. It was all he would say, over and over, though Luke kept promising him that he was fine. He twisted away from the light, face in Luke's chest. Something misfired in Luke's brain—first he wrapped his hands over Max's shoulders, then he pulled away to show his mother this wasn't his fault, then he felt awful and reached for Max again. Helene's face dropped.

Camille stuck her head out of her bedroom door. "What is—"

"Go back to bed," Helene said. "Shut the door."

Camille leaned back into her room like a rewind, and Helene touched Max's back. "Honey? Are you all right?" She looked to Luke. "What's going on?"

"I don't know. He said he didn't have anywhere else to go."

Her eyebrows popped up. "You can't go home?"

Max talked into Luke's shoulder. "My dad and—" He hiccupped. "Had a fight. I was staying with my friend but he—but I—I had to leave."

Helene pursed her lips and nodded once. She took Max's shoulders and pulled him back, saying to Luke, "Put some water on and go get some sweats. Give us a minute."

Luke didn't know if she'd guessed Max right, but she could play Luke like a tambourine. He felt a million times better with a task. When the water boiled, he poured it over Saint-John's-wort and chamomile. Helene crouched in front of Max on the sofa, speaking in a soothing melody. When Luke came back with clean sweats, she waved him off again. Max huddled over his mug, avoiding eye contact, so Luke left them alone. He snuck into his parents' room, where Yuri was snoring like an old bear, and sat on the bed to wait.

Yuri made a sleepy noise. "What did he do this time?"

"It's me, Dad."

"Huh. That bad?"

Helene came back to bed with her hand on her forehead. "He's more scared and embarrassed than hurt, I think. Lord, you gave me a fright."

"*You*," Luke said. "I almost had a heart attack."

"I'm going to bed. Go on and talk to him. Keep your hands to *yourself*."

Luke spread his arms. "How bad do you think I was raised, woman?"

"Shut up," Yuri groaned, half-asleep. "Go away."

Max was a face in a cave of blankets and hoodie on a corner of the couch. Luke sat on the floor next to him. "What's good?"

"Don't start."

"Just wanted to say hi."

Max raised his eyebrows. "Your mom said she's going to call my dad and give him a piece of her mind. Do you think that's real?"

Luke nodded. "You might get out of it if you call him

first."

"Grim." Max flopped back.

"Do you want to talk about it?"

Max shook his head.

"Do you want me to go?"

Max hesitated, and Luke almost stood up and left. "No," Max said. "Hang out for a minute."

"I can do that." Luke wanted to ask what had happened, demand that Max take better care of himself. Instead, with a sense of vague disbelief, he asked himself what a Wesley would say. "I can talk to my mom. We won't do anything you don't want. I'm here to support you." He opened his palm in an awkward lifting-type motion.

Max pressed a smile down. "Okay, thank you. A for sentiment, C for delivery. D minus overall."

"That doesn't sound fair."

"I'm factoring in all your previous Fs," Max said.

Luke nodded and reached forward to pat his knee.

Max pushed his hand away. "I said hang out. Don't you touch me while you're thinking about some other boy."

"I wasn't—"

"I can practically *hear* you."

"No, I mean, I wasn't touching you. Not like that. I was being comforting." He patted Max's knee again.

"You would be *shocked* how uncomforting that is." Max scowled, but it was pretty much a joke, and Luke gave him the full smile.

"Stop that," Max said. "You don't have to beg. Tell me what's the matter."

Luke kept his confusion off his face. "You don't want to hear all that."

"Sure I do. We're friends now, right?" Max kept his voice light, but something wobbled around his eyes and his hands clenched the mug.

Gently, Luke said, "Sure we are."

Max waved his hand like the queen. Luke was so tired he'd come back around to the fragile, shivery wakefulness of too much caffeine. "You remember Jeremy? You met him over here."

"Oh my god, and he was totally in love with you."

"What?" Luke woke right up. "How did everyone know that except me?"

"People on the *moon* could see. He was like—" Max put a fist under his chin, pointing it out and making wide eyes. He did look a little like Jeremy. "How did you manage to mess that up?"

Luke was stunned into a few seconds of silence—but once he started talking, he couldn't stop. He told Max everything. Max gasped at all the right bits and rolled his eyes at the gooey parts. Luke hadn't realized how much he'd needed someone to talk to who didn't have a bunch of opinions about the Kovrovs or Luke's business or the whole idea of kissing boys.

When Luke finished, Max said, "I knew there was a reason I came over here."

"Needed a story?"

"No. It's just, there's only one place in New York you can show up crying in the middle of the night and *not* be the most pathetic person in the room."

Luke covered his face. "Don't you try to hide!" Max said. "Luke, you are *the worst*. You're like a nightmare all the rest of us are trying to wake up from and we *can't*. Where did you even come from?"

Luke laughed into his hands. "Why are you like this?"

"*Life* is like this. You have to catch up, or people are going to keep trying to shoot you. How do you even sleep at night?"

"I don't." Luke put his chin on the couch and gazed pitifully up.

"Literally stop."

Luke sat back. Half-aware, he reached into his collar and rubbed the little key between his fingers. He kept thinking about taking it off, but he hadn't yet. He had half an idea he might need to try it in a lock—and even if Jeremy was over, it was proof that he had happened. "The stupid thing is, I'm still waiting for him to call. If he'd say sorry—"

"What? Why should he have to say sorry?"

Luke cast his arm open, as if the story had spooled out on the floor. He'd been in so much pain for that last awful confrontation that he remembered it as a nauseous blur, but there were images of Jeremy—staring flatly down at him, turning to Sergei instead of trusting him—as true as photographs.

Max shook his head. "Maybe you both lose points for the big fight, but you can't blame him for what his brother did."

Luke added that up and didn't like his number much at all. He hadn't let Jeremy apologize for his brothers when he'd been trying to make out; now he was holding Alexei against him as an excuse to stay mad.

"Is this why you're practicing being supportive?" Max asked. "He'd probably buy it if you could sound a little less like a robot."

Luke made a laugh-shaped sound. "I don't think I'm trying to sell him on anything anymore."

"That makes sense. You're probably better off without that drama." Max nodded. "Speaking from experience."

"Experience? With Jeremy?"

Max shrank away from Luke's eye contact. "No. You know. Speaking as some drama that people are better off without."

Luke blinked, letting that one sink in and making sure he hadn't heard it wrong. "Shut up. That's the dumbest thing I've ever heard."

Max fake-laughed, and Luke nudged his knee again. "I'm serious. Don't talk like that. There's nothing wrong with you. I won't have it."

"*You* won't have it."

"I won't!" Luke didn't imagine he looked very intimidating on the floor, but he puffed his chest up anyway. "You'll figure yourself out." He looked down at his palm, tracing its lines. "And Jeremy will figure himself out. And I guess I'll figure out how to let people suffer on their own."

"What?" Max's upper lip curled.

"That's what the Wesleys said I had to do. To be supportive. No trying to help. Just let 'em suffer."

"That's not—" Max paused, shrugging. "Well, that might be what the Wesleys said. But that's not what supportive means. Nobody's saying you should stop telling right from wrong. Just, you know. Believe other people can tell it, too."

Luke sat back on his hands, observing Max's face in his mountain of blankets. His eyes were still red, but the blotches in his skin had cleared, and he'd found a smile somewhere. "Max Cooper," Luke said, "how can you be wise about my problems and such a mess about yours?"

Max grinned, sticking his tongue between his teeth. "Luke Melnyk. Same question."

Chapter Forty-Four

Alexei showed up the next morning with bagels. Jeremy had a sweet blueberry with a thick layer of cream cheese; Sergei ate his dry with a stack of lox; Alexei opened a lox sandwich with tomatoes, capers, and onion that could have been the cover of a tourist magazine; and Marta ate whatever was left over after she got the little boys fed.

The plant Marta had poured the blood into had shriveled overnight, dry and charred black. Jeremy felt the same way— it was a hangover without the lumpishness, or a cold without the fuzziness. He couldn't drink enough water. Sergei dealt with his damage by stomping around with a scowl on his face, speaking in grunts. Alexei acted like he was on camera, sailing in with a story about buying the bagels and a kiss for Marta's cheek that definitely gave away he was faking it.

She waved at the dead plant. "What did you do to my goddamn fern?"

They rebuilt the story, using Marta's questions to make sure it all followed. They went back through what Luke had said, too, what Corey Malcolm and Natalya thought they remembered. Jeremy said, "Luke said she dumped you, and you killed her."

"Yes." Alexei faltered, tapping his fingers quickly across the table in a gesture Jeremy recognized as one he'd stolen. "Rather, she didn't, and I still killed her."

Marta made a little moue of horror. "Is she dead, then? It sounded...vague."

"After so many years?" Sergei spoke so low his words were one deep rumble. "She's not coming back."

"I don't know what those candles would have been," Alexei said, "but it wasn't anything subtle."

The candles had been driving Jeremy to distraction—Helene, younger, looked so much like Luke and Camille. It was all impossible: that the whole turning clockwork of the world could make one Luke; that Yuri's family, studying magic in Europe, and Helene's family, studying magic in America, could make exactly the two of them; that New York City could rise, glittering, out of the swamp to make a place for them to be together; that their son could be born so broad-shouldered and devoted and good at breaking curses; that Jeremy's curse could be built into the core of him; that Luke could have those perfect lips, even; and, most of all, that all those things could be true and Luke could still be *just some guy.*

"So can you fix it?" Marta asked.

Alexei looked doubtful, and Sergei scoffed.

"If you did it, you can undo it," she said.

Alexei shook his head. "It wasn't only me. And it was so long ago."

"Maybe that's why this one made me." Jeremy nodded at Sergei. "Like you said, there were people who were just killed before. But this one, this is something we could change."

Sergei's heavy brow sunk lower. "That's an awful big leap."

"If it is why you're here," Alexei added, "trying to change it is as likely to hurt you as set you free."

They went back and forth a few more times, convincing each other it was too dangerous and wouldn't change anything—which sounded like a contradiction to Jeremy. He wished Luke were there, so someone would say they should try because it was the right thing to do. Because problems were for solving and evil was for fighting, whatever the risk or reward.

Luke had fought this. He'd taken all those foolish risks for Jeremy's sake, and he'd been right every time. Jeremy didn't even know how badly they'd hurt him, or whether he hated Jeremy now or missed him a little, because they'd sent him away and forbidden him from even talking to Jeremy again. They'd cut him right out like a tumor, but he'd been the only one who wasn't sick.

And without him, Jeremy would have to do it himself. *Help me be brave.* He sat up straight. "I think we should do it. I think it's the right thing to do, and we should at least try."

His brothers blinked at him in unison, a shared surprise, and Sergei said to Alexei, "This is your fault."

"No." Jeremy pushed the whine out of his voice. "Don't talk about me like I'm not here. I'm serious. It's my curse, and I want to try."

"It's—" Alexei stopped abruptly.

Jeremy whirled on him. "It's what? You were going to say, it's my mistake, and I want to leave it forever. That's stupid. You think you can live like that, but you can't."

"Don't tell me what I can live with." Something sinister simmered under Alexei's words, but mostly he sounded tired.

"You asked for help," Jeremy said. "At the end, I heard you."

Alexei leveled him an unreadable gaze. "And you think fate sent me you?"

"I think *you* think that," Jeremy said. "That was the memory *you* found."

Alexei shook his head, but he was resigned, not arguing. "Even if that's true, I don't see what you could change."

Jeremy put his palms on the table and made his shoulders square. Luke had done all he could do; Sergei and Alexei had told him what they wanted to do. So it was time for Jeremy to decide what he was going to do.

"It's my curse, and it's my call. If you really believe I'm a part of this family, then you will not stop me from running my own mission here."

They froze like Jeremy had set a bomb on the table, *tick-tick-tick-tick-tick*. He leaned closer to Alexei. "We could *fix* it."

Alexei shut his eyes.

"Well, gosh," Marta said brightly. "If only you knew someone who was particularly good at undoing Alexei's bindings."

Jeremy froze.

Alexei raked his hair back, face relaxing. "You can go straight to hell, Marta."

"She's not wrong," Sergei said. "At least, we'd need to find out what Helene Melnyk did to those candles."

Marta clapped her hands and leaned toward Alexei. "Do you think Yuri's going to make you beg? If he does, can I watch?"

"*Straight* to hell," he said again.

"I'll get one of those big tins of popcorn, you know with the different flavors?" Marta drew a circle in the air and mimed tossing popcorn into her mouth.

Sergei caught Jeremy's eye and jerked his head toward the door. Jeremy followed him into the living room and grabbed him around the chest in a tight hug before he could say anything.

"Thank you," Jeremy whispered.

Sergei was quiet, but his heart kicked Jeremy's cheek. "Thank *you*, kid."

Jeremy shook his head. A little brother might have been Sergei's reason for growing past his father, but he'd done it on his own. "The thing is," Jeremy said, "I'm not a baby anymore."

"The thing is, I know you think that, but you are."

Jeremy stepped back and put his hands on his hips. "Do you know how tough I have to be to dress like this every day? Even just to deal with you?"

"I didn't say—"

"You do!" Jeremy said, voice rising. "All the time, you have something to say, about my clothes or my hair or my—" He stopped, with no way to finish the sentence. Luke wasn't *his* anything. "It doesn't make me weak to be different from you. It made me stronger."

Sergei crossed his arms, and the vein in his temple twitched once, twice. "You want to make a move on the Malcolms? We're short on soldiers, but we can get some intel out of Natalya if we can find her."

"No," Jeremy said. "I'm doing this one my way."

Chapter Forty-Five

Luke was still in bed when he found himself on the receiving end of a family meeting, all of them tromping into his room and staring down at him. This was going to be bad.

Helene sat on the edge of his bed. "Did I ever tell you about the worst night of my life?"

Luke shook his head slowly, unsure what was going to trigger the explosion.

"I was sixteen. My girls and I went to this terrible party out in the woods—you don't know about parties in the woods. That's why I raised you in the city, where it's safe. There was liquor in a bucket. That kind of party."

Camille looked as nervous as Luke felt, which was either a great or miserable sign.

"We drank too much, things got scary, this scumbag hit one of my friends," Helene said. "And we couldn't figure out how to get out of there, or where to go, or who to call who wouldn't make it worse."

She looked at Luke expectantly. He nodded.

"I thought, when I have kids, I'm going to be the person

they can go to. My house will be safe. This house." She put a cool hand on Luke's head. "I think I forgot that."

It was quiet—Luke's turn to talk. "Huh."

Helene threw her hands into the air.

"You can stop punishing yourself, is the point, I believe," Yuri said.

Camille smiled with all her teeth. "The point is, we talked about it, and we decided even though you're stupid, we like you, and we're going to keep you. Also—" She presented a little poppet that warped the air around it. "Are you sure you don't want to destroy this?"

"All right." Luke squirmed around Helene, still sitting on his bed, and got up. "Yeah, let's go light some shit on fire."

"*That's* my brother," Camille said.

In the living room, Max was on his phone. "Yeah, I'm coming home now."

"Is that your father?" Helene said. "Give me that phone. I have some things to say to him."

Max, wide-eyed, handed it over.

"*And you,*" Helene started. "What is wrong with you?"

Max looked at Luke, who nudged him toward the door. "Come on. You want to help us burn this?"

They headed downstairs with Camille. "What is that?" Max asked.

"Jeremy," she said.

"No way."

"They took my brother; I took him."

"Let me see." Max poked at the little doll's chest.

"Max!" Luke said. "Be careful."

"No way, he can feel that?" Max poked the doll again, and Luke closed it in a fist. It was as hot as skin, as Jeremy's wrist in Luke's hand. He wasn't sure, exactly, what Jeremy would feel, but he knew it was Camille's heaviest mojo, and that was not nothing.

Luke drew a circle of salt on the asphalt in the alley and took the poppet apart. "Is this a bird beak?" He pointed it at his sister. "Where did you get a beak?"

Camille leaned against the wall. "Don't ask questions you don't want to know the answers to."

"You are nasty."

"Dad got me flowers."

Max snickered.

Luke dumped the doll's contents—the mixed herbs, pepper, the beak, and a sliver of bone—into the circle. He rifled through and found two strands of blond hair. He did not think about Jeremy's hair in his bed, or Jeremy's hair, or Jeremy in his bed. He lit the strands of hair on fire and dropped them, and they burned away before they hit the ground.

Next came the mojo. He squirted lighter fluid over the pile of junk and touched it with the lighter. He half-assed the visualizations, because it was just too hard to think about Jeremy that closely, and when the flame caught, it spat so hard a lick of fire caught Luke's shorts.

Max gasped, Camille screamed, and Luke hopped in a circle, whacking it out with his hand. "Whoa!" Camille said. "Oops. Was that me?"

Once he was sure he wasn't on fire, Luke said, "You're all right. Wasn't paying attention." He had gotten used to doing this with Jeremy behind him, manning the protections. He'd forgotten he was flying solo.

And he'd missed this crossing letting go. The fire in the salt circle was just fire, a low, flickering flame curling the dry leaves. If any part of Jeremy had been there, he was gone.

Luke crouched against the wall and rubbed his face while he waited for the fire to die. Once it was down to embers, he dropped the husk of the poppet on top and—just in case—he thought, *Goodbye.*

Chapter Forty-Six

Katya drove Jeremy to the Melnyks' store in a Camry from who-knew-where. Forehead against the window, Jeremy tried to pray, but all he could think of was Luke glaring and spitting blood. Something petty inside him wanted to put every scrap of the blame on Katya, not because it was fair but because it was easier than blaming Alexei or Luke or himself.

Katya could tell, or guess. "I'm sorry I lost it on Luke."

Jeremy looked out the window. "I understand, if you thought he was hurting me. You don't have to apologize."

She clicked her tongue at the traffic. "No, I'm sorry. That didn't help anything. But when all you are is a hammer, everything looks like a nail."

"When all you *have*."

Katya shook her head.

Jeremy watched her profile. "Did you know the girl? Annabel?"

"No. Or if I did, I don't remember her specifically. All Natalya's friends were bad and glamorous. I was so intimidated."

Jeremy grinned. "You're so bad and glamorous now."

Katya snorted.

"Do you think—" Jeremy paused. "Do you think that's why Alexei turned out...the way he did?"

"Queer, you mean?"

"No!" Jeremy sighed. "I mean, like...sad. Alone."

"He's not alone. He has us."

"You work for him." Jeremy turned out the window. "And I'm his curse."

Katya was quiet. "Well. I don't know, J. But he has tried. Sometimes it just doesn't work out."

That gave Jeremy more than enough to chew on for the rest of the ride. She dropped him off a block away and stayed to wait out of sight. He was a mess of contradictions: Here to threaten, or to beg. Here to apologize, or to demand answers. He had worn a pink shirt to show he didn't care what anyone thought of him and because Luke might like it.

Luke was behind the counter, talking to his mother. Jeremy paused and watched them through the window. He was about to go in there and cause nothing but problems.

When he turned and saw Jeremy standing outside the window, Luke's whole face fell. Jeremy's cheeks burned, and he had to drag his hand toward the door—maybe Alexei *should* handle it, maybe it *would* be better to try the Malcolms first, maybe he could just run and figure out where he was going later—but he shook his shoulders out and went in.

Helene put herself between Jeremy and Luke, which didn't make sense because Jeremy obviously hadn't brought a weapon, and because if he had, she wouldn't be able to protect anyone like that.

"Can I talk to you?" said a tiny voice, not at all the one Jeremy was planning to use.

Helene stayed between them, but she looked at Luke, letting him answer. "Do I have a choice?"

"Sure you do." Jeremy felt a pinch—he was twisting a rubber bracelet against his arm. "It's important, though. It's about, um"—*your family and my family and me and murder and whether I can ever leave the house*—"magic."

Luke rolled his eyes. "Of course it is."

Jeremy threw his shoulders back again. "Okay, look. You can be a jerk about it if you want, but I'm here to say you were right and ask for your help. I'm sorry we didn't figure it out sooner and I'm sorry Katya hit you and I'm—I'm sorry I left, but that's how it is, all right? I don't know how it got so wrong and I'm sorry."

He sucked in air, all his gone hot around him. Anger danced just out of his reach, a pure, energizing fire, but all he'd done was say *sorry* fifteen times and drop his stupid heart on the floor between them. Luke stared at the ground like, *What is this? I never asked for this.*

Luke lifted his head and said, in a faint, mystified way, "All I wanted to do was help."

Helene shut her eyes with a wince.

"It's a long story," Jeremy said. "We might want to undo something Alexei did, so we could use your help, and also, your mom made a weapon, and we need to know what it was."

"Me?" Helene looked up sharply.

"It was some candles."

Helene rubbed the middle of her forehead with two fingers. "Flip that sign and lock the door."

Jeremy closed up the store and followed Helene back through the door Luke held open for both of them. He sat at the table and told the story they'd pieced together, heavy-handed with the details around the candles and Alexei's good intentions. Luke's attention was so focused and powerful it hit Jeremy's skin like sunlight, burning him pink.

After Jeremy finished, Luke turned that glare on his mother.

"Agrimony," she said. "I don't remember, but I'd bet on it. It turns the spell around on the caster."

"Agri—what?" Jeremy asked.

"Agrimony? It's an herb." She mimed turning with her hand. "It turns the spell around, like—"

Luke interrupted. "Giving someone candles with agrimony would be like giving them bullets you knew would make their gun backfire."

Jeremy nodded. "Alexei was doing messy work. Too much, too panicky. It was probably primed to backfire anyway."

Luke tipped his chair back and rubbed his hands over his face. "I hate agrimony. I should have *known* there was agrimony in here somewhere."

"Why?" Jeremy asked.

"The feel of it." Luke made the same hand motion Helene had, quick and angry, probably not aware that he was mimicking her. "It can keep turning around on you even as you try different things. Like whacking two magnets together the wrong way. Those notes Sergei made, about your crossing, how nothing worked. That's *agrimony*," he almost spat, and then turned to his mother again. "I can't believe you would sell that."

Helene gave him a flat, censorious look and didn't answer. Luke tried to stare her down, but he dropped his gaze first.

"Would you have done anything specific?" Jeremy asked. "Anything for Alexei? I know it's probably hard to remember—"

"Not that job, but I remember Ivan Kovrov," Helene said. "No, he wouldn't have told me who they were meant for or how they'd be used. He wouldn't have told me anything except what he needed."

A muscle twitched in Luke's jaw. Before he could say anything, Jeremy asked, "Exactly what he needed? All the details, or just the outline?"

"He'd just want it to work. He wouldn't care how." She paused. "I would not have guessed he'd give that to his own son. But I probably would have made it anyway. He was the boss. He made trouble with people who can take care of themselves."

Luke glared at the table. Tentatively, Jeremy said, "I understand. I've made things for my brothers just because they asked me to. We did jobs for Alexei this summer without making him explain first. I'm only now figuring out how to push back."

At that, Luke finally looked up. "For real?"

Jeremy shrugged.

"Well, you tell me how that works out." Luke glanced at his mother. "So you sold him the weapon, and you didn't know who it was for, but Ivan knew what he was doing with it. And when Alexei got a hold of them, he thought he was making a spell to hide them from their families. But he was doing way too much fool-ass magic, and when it backfired, he..." Luke looked expectantly.

"He disappeared her," Jeremy said.

"What does that actually mean?" Luke asked.

Jeremy opened his hands. "Well, that's where you come in."

"What are you going to do?" The space where Luke hadn't said *we* was enormous.

"We were thinking of doing a ritual." Jeremy's voice had gotten small again, and he cleared his throat. "To wind it back, and see if we can undo it or if it's connected to me. And if we did, we thought it would be good if you could help."

Luke didn't answer. He turned to Helene, and she tilted her head.

Hesitantly, Jeremy said, "If you want—obviously, we can pay."

That should have either solved the problem or made them mad, but they kept up that secret, silent conversation. Luke turned away first. "I think we can help, but we have to talk to my dad. I can let you know."

That was fair. No reason for it to hurt. Jeremy nodded and pushed his chair back, and Luke led him into the store alone. He turned on the lights as Jeremy flipped the sign and unlocked the door. He was going to let himself out, but Luke said, "Have you heard any more from Malcolm?"

Jeremy turned away from the door. "No. Sergei is still looking for Natalya."

Luke made a mean, twisty face.

"What?" Jeremy asked.

"Sergei couldn't tell she was wearing a disguise when he was working with her every day. He's not going to find anything."

Jeremy slumped over the counter. "I know. Luke, I already said you're right, you win. What do you want from me?"

"No, I wasn't—" Luke wiped a hand across his eyes again. "You know, with everybody else, I'm pretty good at talking. What is it with you?"

"The awkward is contagious." Jeremy spread his hands out like skittering bugs.

Luke grinned in a quicksilver flash before his face went serious again. "Nah. I think you talk about realer stuff. What I meant to say was, I'm glad you're fighting it." He tapped a line across the counter, hand closer to Jeremy. "When they showed me Annabel's stuff, all I could think about was what if someone hurt Camille like that. What I would do, if I were Corey Malcolm." His fingers walked another step closer. "And Alexei was the one who hurt her, who—" He stopped.

"I understand." Jeremy watched the counter sit quietly between his fingers and Luke's.

"But if I imagine losing you like that... If I was trying to protect you and it turned around on me..." Luke stopped and looked up, like he was surprised to find Jeremy still there. "Not that you were—or we..."

Not that they were anything or had found time to be. "I meant it when I said I was sorry." Jeremy searched Luke's eyes, but he couldn't read anything there. "I lied a lot and made this whole mess. But I'm trying really hard to do the right thing here, and I'm going to fix it."

He thought Luke would argue—that he had been trying to do that; that Jeremy should have helped earlier; maybe that Alexei and Corey, if not Jeremy himself, were beyond fixing—and he *saw* the argument on Luke's face. His lips pressed together, holding back words. All he did was nod.

Jeremy stepped back and put his hands on his hips so he wouldn't let them anywhere near Luke. He had his answers and his plan, and enough of Luke's silent, assessing gazes to weigh him down for weeks. "Let me know what your family decides."

And then he went back down the block toward Katya and home.

Chapter Forty-Seven

Luke showed up half an hour before midnight, a dream in a white T-shirt. The effect wasn't diminished by his mother standing at his shoulder, although Camille's glare was intimidating. She wore a thick layer of black lipstick like she wanted someone to ask her whether it was a metaphor.

Luke had texted the final *yes*, letter-true to his promise, but Yuri and Alexei had done the real negotiating. All Jeremy knew was that Alexei had been in the foulest mood all week. Marta was with the little boys at the Melnyk place, either because Yuri was generously helping babysit or as a demonstration of everyone's goodwill.

While they made small talk in the living room, Jeremy slipped away and got to work. He used a cake of white soap to draw runes on a piece of glass laid over the dining room table, copying from a tattered book of Alexei's. He focused on the smooth, powdered weight of the soap in his hand, the squeaks it made against the glass. As long as he kept the circle of his attention precisely small, he was fine. If he let himself think about the whole room—the other room—the plan unspooling ahead of him, his mood skidded underneath him like a derailing train.

Camille walked into the room and gasped. "Is that a grimoire?"

Jeremy nodded. "You can read it, if you want. Some of it's in Russian."

She made a soft *ooh* and plopped into a chair. The book was as big as an atlas and puffed dust as she moved it.

She was careful not to smear the runes. "What's this?"

He traced the circles. "Power and protection. I don't think they do anything, but Alexei likes them."

"I can hear you!" Alexei called from the living room.

"Are you sure?" Jeremy shouted back. "I said they don't do anything."

"Those runes were good enough for Ivan the Terrible," Alexei said, and Jeremy mouthed the rest along with him, "and they're good enough for a pipsqueak like you."

Luke appeared in the doorway and laughed as he saw. Jeremy looked up, primed to smile along, but Luke's glance slid away before he could make eye contact. Jeremy was back where he'd started—he wasn't sure if Luke even wanted to talk to him, too many layers of power and obligation between them, and couldn't ask without putting Luke in another terrible position—except that now he knew what he'd lost.

"Come look at this," Camille said. Luke walked around Jeremy to get to her. He smelled like incense, like maybe he'd burned some over his mother and sister before they left the house.

Camille pointed to the book. "It's like how Grandma Sophie lays out the bones."

"Yeah, it is." Luke caught Jeremy's eye. "You're sure that's not real?"

Jeremy shrugged.

"You might want to put some focus in it."

Jeremy looked up and caught Luke's eyes. He got focused, all right—just not on soap.

The next knock was Natalya and Corey Malcolm. Alexei's voice chilled the hall, even though Jeremy couldn't make out his words.

"Jeremy!" Natalya popped into the doorway, coming to Jeremy with her arms outstretched. He reeled back and would have fallen into one of Marta's plants if Luke hadn't grabbed his arm.

"He doesn't want to talk to you," Luke snapped.

Jeremy wrenched his arm away, though the shape of Luke's hand kept burning there. He *didn't* want to talk to Natalya, true, but he didn't want Luke to fight his battles, either. "I just have to finish this."

"Kid! I can't find the weed." Sergei's voice led his body down the hall.

"The what?" Luke squinted at Jeremy.

"Weed. Sergei and I use it to help get into the ritual."

Camille leaned around Luke with her eyebrows high on her forehead. "That seems dangerous."

"I think Marta finished it." Sergei leaned against the doorframe, squinting at the side of a red prescription bottle. "I have a couple Xanax or, this is some cough syrup from when Vanya had bronchitis. I can't tell if it's expired."

Camille's mouth fell open, and Luke looked a little desperate. Feeling exposed, Jeremy said, "I don't need anything."

"Your call." Sergei popped a brown pill bottle with one thumb.

The room felt too small, and when Alexei, Malcolm, and Helene came in, it could have burst. The plants rustled against too many bodies.

"Very well," Alexei said. "Let's begin. Miss Melnyk?"

Camille held a burlap bag under his nose. "One hair,

please."

Alexei dutifully plucked one free and dropped it in, but when she presented the bag to Malcolm, he grimaced.

"We should have an objective third party to do the truce," Malcolm said. "Are you going to enforce this?"

"Why do you care if I hate Alexei?" She sounded genuinely confused, and over her head, Alexei smiled.

Malcolm pushed a hand through his red hair and gave her a loose strand. She hopped up to perch on the edge of the hutch and whispered over the bag.

"So." Alexei surveyed the room. "I'll build the ritual to essentially create a meditative space that we will enter together. Everyone will contribute and should be able to have some degree of control once we go in. We'll explore our memories of the incidents in question. Be prepared to take action inside the ritual, but most likely we'll simply be watching, looking for an opportunity to unwind the spell in another, more structured ritual. Any questions?"

"Yeah." Malcolm looked around. "What the hell does that mean? What did he just say?"

"He's going to take some blood," Sergei said. "We'll go look at our memories. Pay attention."

"Why didn't he say that?"

Sergei shook his head like *don't ask me*.

"What did 'take action' mean?" Malcolm looked between Sergei and Alexei for an answer, but both looked vague.

"You know," Sergei said, "just feel it out."

Malcolm grunted in exasperation. Jeremy had to stifle a giggle, though he didn't know how he might answer more clearly. It was Luke who spoke: "It's fairy-tale rules. You guys do energy patterns, right? Rock and fire?"

Malcolm nodded.

"Cool. We do the same thing, but smaller. Herb magic. They don't do anything like that. Alexei just bleeds on shit and then he owns it. Fairy-tale rules. The witch, the king, whatever he is, he's in charge. My theory is—"

Jeremy felt oddly bare, cut open and analyzed like a cadaver. Alexei made a dry scoffing sound, but he didn't interrupt further, and Luke kept talking right over him.

"—the original ritual broke, because Alexei didn't have control of it. It was his father. Ivan's not here, but between you and my mom, you gave Ivan the power over that ritual, so you should be able to take it back. The goal is going to be to get the power back to Alexei, so he can repair the original break. Mom is going to figure out what she'll need to make to counteract the candles, if we have to do this again. Alexei is going to examine his spell so he knows how to change it. And I'll be watching for how I might uncross it, too."

Helene smiled tightly, just stretching her lips. Luke put his arm around her, and though she didn't look much reassured, envy ached in Jeremy's stomach.

"You're here to show us the other side of the story," Alexei said, sneering down his nose at Malcolm. "I can look at my memories, but I need to see what happened at your house. All you need to do is stay out of the way."

"While you root around in my head?" Malcolm crossed his arms and leaned back in his chair.

Alexei ignored him, putting his bowl in the center of the rune-covered table with a heavy *thunk*. He had a glass of milk and a loaf of bread, too, symbolic gifts for communing with spirits. Helene raised her eyebrows as he put them in place, but if she disagreed, she didn't say anything. "Most of you are here to complete the circle and fill out the memory. What I need you to do is focus on where you are, physically in this room, as well as what you're remembering. It's tricky to do both at the same time, but we almost got lost the last time we did this, and I was balancing fewer minds. Camille will be keeping an eye on us and can tear the ritual open if necessary, but it's much more comfortable for everyone if we can exit smoothly when we're done."

He paused and surveyed the faces. "Any more questions?"

Everyone looked around, catching eyes, giving each other sympathetic twists of their lips or brows. It felt impossible that there weren't, that they were just going to dive on in, but there seemed to be nothing else to say.

Alexei pulled a knife from inside his jacket—he was in a full suit for company—and sliced open a bag of blood. As it filled the bowl, its dense scent filled the air.

Camille pressed against the wall. "Is that human blood?"

"Cattle," Alexei said.

"Where do you get cattle blood?" she asked.

"Cows." Alexei winked, and Jeremy could see Camille remember she didn't like him and wasn't supposed to want to learn from him. She settled on the hutch, looking down at the truce bag as she turned it in her hands.

Alexei brought the knife to his own palm first, holding it over the bowl until a drop of his blood fell in.

"Mrs. Melnyk?" Helene gave him a hand—she turned her face away, grimacing, as he cut—and then Corey, who watched intently as his blood fell. Alexei took Jeremy's hand with an encouraging smile, and cut the pad of his thumb so lightly he felt only a tiny burst of heat. His drop of blood rippled thickly in the bowl, and he put his thumb to his mouth, tasting salt.

"And Luke." Alexei gestured him forward with the knife.

Luke shook his head. He wiggled a hand into his hair and presented a strand to Alexei. Alertness galvanized the room, Luke's curl bobbing genially over the center of the table.

Alexei paused for a beat and pushed a hard, frustrated breath out through his nostrils. His voice, as always, stayed cool. "Very well. You may be limited in the ritual."

Luke shrugged. Alexei took the hair and dropped it into the bowl, where it sank and left the red surface smooth.

The heat, the smell of blood, the little burn in his hand, and the claustrophobic press of the room all came together to make Jeremy queasy. "I have to go catch my breath," he whispered.

Alexei nodded. "I'll call you when we need you."

Jeremy stepped into the hall and out of sight of the room. He should have taken that Xanax. He should have known better than to try this at all.

Chapter Forty-Eight

Luke imagined a thread between himself and Jeremy, tangling when they got too close and yanking when they went too far. Jeremy left and the thread pulled. Luke had meant to stay and make sure he understood the spell, but as Alexei started murmuring over the bowl of blood, Luke sidled around the room and followed Jeremy down the hall.

He was in the peachy-pink downstairs bathroom with the faucet running and a damp hand on the back of his neck. His eyes were closed, lashes a thick gold fan against his cheek. Luke kept himself past the threshold. "Jeremy."

His eyes opened, and he turned off the faucet with a quick, stiff motion. "Oh, what?"

Luke put on a grin. "Why do matryoshka dolls make terrible friends?"

Jeremy tried to glare, but Luke had caught him by surprise, and there was a smile threatening around his lips.

"Say 'why.'" Luke stepped closer.

"You're ridiculous."

"'Why.'"

"Why?" Jeremy made the shape of the word, barely any sound in his voice.

"Because they're full of themselves."

Jeremy sighed, but he definitely smiled. "That's the worst one yet."

"No way. That one's almost legit."

"*Terrible.*"

"It's not as bad as the peanut joke."

Jeremy's face said, *Yeah, I guess so*, and his words said, "Did you want something?"

"Yes." Luke stepped into the room, close enough to touch the water droplets running down Jeremy's neck or the smooth skin inside his elbow, though he didn't. He caught Jeremy's eye and found him looking, though he glanced immediately away again. "I have to clear something up," Luke said. "When you came over, when we—when I was running my mouth instead of being with you, I wasn't saying I don't think I'm your true love. I was asking if you were mine."

Jeremy's eyes fluttered closed—like he was sick, like Luke had poisoned him. "You made it sound like I was cheating on you, or something. You made me sound *horrible.*"

"I know. Look, I was overwhelmed, and *I* wasn't ready, and I put it on you."

"I can't stop thinking about it." Jeremy hunched over the sink. "Whether I was using you. What I was even *doing* with you."

Luke couldn't have that, rewriting history—they had messed it up, but for a minute, it had been great. "I think you were with me because you wanted to be, and it was good. Other people's mistakes aren't your fault."

Jeremy threw his shoulders back to stand. "Then why didn't you ever ask me anything, instead of deciding how it ought to be?" He huffed. "You should have told me about Natalya. That you'd warned her."

"You should have listened when I did tell you."

Jeremy's jaw dropped. "You were right about the magic. I told you, I know. But you went about it *all wrong*."

Luke shut his eyes. "I know. And I'm sorry. Does it help if I was trying to protect you?"

"No." Jeremy's voice had gone soft, and Luke opened his eyes to find him staring at the ground, chewing on his lower lip. Luke's thumb wanted to pull it free, nudge it into a smile.

"I'm sorry," Luke said. "For real. Give me another chance, and I'll tell you every time."

Jeremy stared. Luke would have liked—something. A kiss, a confession. But he also wanted *this* boy, who was working so heartbreakingly hard to be brave and still definitely going to stand there getting redder until Luke made another move. He reached forward and took one of Jeremy's hands, moving his finger over the knuckles.

Jeremy didn't pull away. "You should get ready for this ritual. It's going to be heavy. Even just looking at Alexei's memories was almost more than we could take."

Luke nodded, but he was more scared that *nothing* would happen—they'd go watch some bitter old memories and find no way to change. What mattered was the difference Jeremy had already made. "I know you can take it. You've already done more than the rest of us ever managed. Kovrov and Malcolm in there, no guns, acting almost civil? That hasn't happened in decades, and that is all you."

Jeremy looked quickly at Luke, and again. "It's you," he said softly.

Luke ducked closer, stilling to be sure he'd heard right. "What?"

Jeremy went slowly red. "It's for you. I'm trying to—to meet you halfway. Fix all the messed-up stuff you were right about. Maybe we can have another first."

He stared out the door, and Luke ducked lower to catch

his gaze. Luke was warm all over, smiling irrepressibly. "I'd like that."

Jeremy shook his head, still looking too sad for his sweet words. "And then what? You'll come over and have family lunch with Alexei like everything's fine?"

Luke shrugged. "There was a lot about working with Alexei I liked. Some of what I didn't like is changing. I don't know. Do we have to plan a whole life just to get a new start?"

"My family's always going to be my family. I have to figure it out eventually."

Luke swallowed hard. "The world's going to stay complicated. You don't have to fix every piece of that." He paused, his jaw tight. "You just have to decide what you want to fight for."

With a crease between his brows, Jeremy moved his thumb over Luke's bicep, the fine, pale scar where Alexei had cut him. "I'm sorry I didn't believe you. I won't let them hurt you again." He stopped talking but kept his hand on Luke's arm, and Luke didn't answer, letting the touch speak for them.

Finally, Jeremy hit him with the big eyes. "What if we do all this and I kiss you again and it still doesn't work?"

Luke looked steadily back. "What if I kiss you again, and it does?"

"I know I should know." Jeremy shook his head. "Marta and Alexei keep saying I'll *just know*, but I never *just know* anything."

Luke touched Jeremy's shoulder, and when he didn't flinch, he pulled him closer. "I know. Let me be sure for both of us. My dad made this whole speech about what love is, but you know what? I just know. I've never felt like this before. This is something real."

Jeremy shook his head but didn't move away. "What was the speech?"

Luke rolled his eyes. "It was like, you're with the right person when you're doing the right things. The person who brings out your best. It sounded good, but it was another abstract thing to try to pin down."

Jeremy absorbed that slowly, teeth on his lip. Luke gave in, using his thumb to pull it gently free, and Jeremy's gaze popped up.

"Even if the ritual doesn't change anything," Luke said, "even if you're crossed, I want to be with you. I missed you like hell. Not the crossing, or the job. You."

Jeremy dropped his head forward, collapsing on Luke's chest, and Luke wrapped an arm around his back and hugged him in. He still spoke so quietly that Luke had to duck to hear him. "I don't think that sounded abstract, what your dad said. About love. That is what we're all doing here. That is exactly how I feel about you."

It was Luke's turn to blink all dumbstruck. Jeremy lifted his face close to Luke's ear. He whispered Luke's name, his voice breaking over the long vowel.

Luke put his hands on Jeremy's waist. "Yeah."

"What's the difference between a hippo and a Zippo?"

Luke jumped in surprise. A silent laugh shook Jeremy's ribs, and Luke was smiling before he told his face to move. "What?"

Jeremy leaned back to look in Luke's eyes. "One's really heavy and the other one's a little lighter."

A laugh punched out of Luke's mouth, and another. Jeremy gave him the smuggest little face he'd ever seen and slipped out of the bathroom. Luke stayed against the sink, dissolving into hysteria—the more he tried to stop laughing, the deeper it sank in. Alexei called his name, and he went back down the hall, gulping in air and wiping his eyes. He got himself together and pulled the door closed behind him, taking his seat next to Jeremy.

Alexei touched Jeremy's shoulder. "Would you do the candles?"

Jeremy breathed into his hands—one, two, three—and blew forward, sending light dancing around the room. A bubble touched each unlit wick, and the rest found perches on the plants and walls between. Camille brushed one away from her hair, frowning, and that seemed funny, too. Luke started laughing again, taking Jeremy's wrist. His mother squeezed his arm severely as she took hold of it, but it was too late. The vertigo of the ritual took him over and ripped away the last of his self-control.

"A little lighter," he repeated as the room faded around them. "Oh, man. I think I love you."

Chapter Forty-Nine

The room was darker than Jeremy, a city boy whose blackest nights were topaz and purple, had ever seen. He strained to see through candles that cast more smoke than light. They would have stung his eyes, if his eyes were really there.

He couldn't feel his body, nothing except the slow bump of Alexei's pulse under his fingertips. "Alexei?" he thought, looking for the easy reassurance of his presence, and when he didn't get it, a red surge of panic washed over him.

"Jeremy?" That was Luke. Jeremy focused there, keying into him. It was wrong that he couldn't find anyone else, but Alexei had built something complicated. Maybe they had scattered somehow.

Luke's voice in his heart said, "She looks like you."

Jeremy pushed his focus out of his own mind, to the vision: a stooped man with an even heavier hammer face than Sergei's; two younger men at his shoulders; the girl in the plain, drab dress. She had big, dark eyes in a gaunt face and strands of fine hair escaping from her cap. She seemed younger than Jeremy expected, maybe twelve years old, or maybe that was hunger.

"Maeve," Jeremy said. Her eyes stayed fixed on the Kovrov.

"I have come to beg your protection, sir," she said. If this were not inside his mind, Jeremy wasn't sure he'd understand her. Her brogue was different from the Irish accents in movies the way this smoky darkness was different from Hollywood's candlelit rooms, thick and impenetrable.

The Kovrov leaned back in his chair like a throne. "Magic always has a cost."

"You must know I do not have money, sir." She lifted her chin in pride just short of defiance, a gesture Jeremy recognized as his own. "But I am prepared to pay."

The vision skidded forward in dreamlike bounces, and Maeve said, "In the stories there are ways to end these spells. A secret to guess. Or a kiss."

"This is not a story," barked one of the sons, but the Kovrov waved a hand without looking.

"We are generous. Young lady, at what price your boy's freedom?" His face in the dim light was not generous.

"True love. If he meets his true love, he should be free to be with her."

The word *her* was a needle prick. The Kovrov smiled, all teeth like a wolf or Alexei, and brought the nib of his pen to the page. "Of course he should. True love." The Kovrov found that funny and repeated the words as he wrote: "True love. True. Love." He did not say *first* or *only* or *kiss*, though he must have written them down, laying a trap instead of an exit.

They watched the Kovrov cut his own thumb and Maeve's, dropping their blood into an inkwell. He signed his name, and Maeve, holding the pen in an awkward fist, drew her quivering X.

They followed the girl out into the street, which Jeremy

sensed as a stench, animal and rotten and revolting.

Maeve stopped on the street and pressed herself against a wall. She clutched her injured thumb inside a fist at her chest and with her other hand, she wiped at her face. Tears fell faster than she could stop them, sliding down her cheeks in sheets and soaking the high collar of her dress. She murmured Hail Marys through her tears.

"Let him be brave," she said against her hand. In the space of the ritual, something surrounded her that felt like magic. It was like a light Jeremy could hear or a note he could see—something high and clear. "Let my boy be happy with them. With the Kovrovs, ugh—" She stopped and shook her head. "Let him make them better. Stop this madness. Let him"—she choked on her tears—"matter."

There wasn't room for her to stay standing against the wall. She latched onto the words, repeating them like a mantra as she scurried home. *Let him matter, let him matter.*

The prayer could have wrapped itself around his contract, made a trigger like Luke said. But it wasn't a spell, or a plan, or a curse. She was just a desperate girl.

"Do you think that was real?" Jeremy thought.

"Yes." Luke sounded too sure to truly be sure, filling in a gap with swagger. Or maybe that was projecting. Jeremy wished he could see Luke's face.

"I was expecting a spell."

"No, it was just like one of your prayers. It even felt the same."

Jeremy tried to fit the pieces together the way Luke did—no Jeremy until there were Kovrovs he could be happy with, or Kovrovs he could make better, or a tide he could turn. "Alexei asked for help. Did I tell you that? At the end of the ritual he messed up."

"We have to find the rest of them," Luke said. "See if we can find Annabel next. Should we focus on Alexei?"

"Yeah," Jeremy said, but as soon as he thought, *Alexei, Alexei*, Alexei's pulse stopped against his fingers. Something was gone, either Alexei's pulse or his own hand.

"Luke, wait—" Jeremy's mind scattered, and he slipped off the focus he needed. "Luke? Luke, are you there?"

Chapter Fifty

Luke found the rest of them, the sense of an unsteady circle turning around him, over a scene he recognized from Jeremy's story. Alexei, around Luke's age, with shorter hair and a softer jaw, sat on the floor in front of a triangle of candles. "I love you," he said, kissing the side of a red candle.

Luke had gotten used to speaking inside this ritual, thinking words and making them heard, but he felt a wriggle of too much intimacy trying to reach out that way to someone besides Jeremy. "What's happening?"

Alexei's voice: "We undershot. Or overshot. Or she's gone."

"I love you," said the boy on the floor.

"This can't be it," Malcolm said. "She has to be somewhere." Images flickered too fast for Luke to keep up with—smears of red hair and giggles, a little girl across a dining room table, a grown girl whirling back on him in fury, tears in her eyes. They had to be Malcolm's memories, because Luke recognized the way he thought of his sister as someone he needed to take care of until he'd discovered this mysterious young woman sharing his house.

"I love you," said the boy on the floor.

"You see?" Alexei asked. "We're stuck in the loop."

The parade of images slipped faster than Luke could keep up with. "Have you tried not being stuck?"

He felt Alexei's disdain as if it were one of his own emotions, crowding out his own thoughts. But there had to be a way through. Jeremy had done this, taken charge and found what he was looking for. Someone had to do the same thing here. But what had Jeremy done?

This was all wrong—rushing and remote, like a movie, with none of the immediacy of Maeve's much older memory.

"This isn't it. Jeremy and I—Jeremy?" There was an absence next to Luke, and the steady tapping pulse under his fingers was gone.

Luke's own surprise and wonder were blurred in shades of everyone else's confusion and fear. He was tossed in the waves, no up or down, and he couldn't anchor himself without Jeremy, so steadiness kept slipping away. He couldn't even take a deep breath in this space, all mind.

But he could ask a question.

"Where are you?" he thought, looking for Jeremy. The question turned, slid into place. He'd been asking it for weeks. "Where is she?"

He saw the cards disappearing from Alexei's hand, but next, he thought of the card he'd drawn *reappearing*. Annabel's room had come back like it had never left—the paper in her notebooks fresh, the air still sweet with her perfume.

They'd been asking how and why and what they might do to fix it, but this question had been murmuring underneath. *Where?*

He centered the question in his mind, focusing. Gentle nudges of curiosity from around the circle settled it into place. The shape of the ritual spun out around him, a perfect silken web. This was something he could do—a new stage, but an old song.

He said, "Where is she?" and then, holding her yearbook photo in his mind, "Where are you?"

A gray mist bloomed over the bright candles of Alexei's memory. It cleared the vision like a movie screen, and Luke waited with a shuddering thrill for the next sight that would fill it.

The bottom fell out, and Luke felt the sick drop of a missed step—and another. One gasping silence stretched open, and gravity let go, dropping him into a flat gray that filled his eyes and mouth and nose. A vise clamped his chest.

He was alone—

There was nothing but gray—

His heart stopped—

He was falling—

He thudded back into his body, the web of the ritual pulling away from him. "I've got you," Alexei said. "It's okay. I've got everyone."

"I love you," said the boy on the floor.

Chapter Fifty-One

Jeremy woke up gasping, his lungs burning like they'd been empty for too long. The room was oppressively hot, the air gone thick as a clay, and he was so sweaty he'd slipped out of the circle, dropping Alexei's hand and sliding free of Luke's.

Everybody around the table was still asleep, chests rising and falling as one. He touched Luke's cheek and found it cool. "Luke?"

Nothing. He turned and pushed Alexei's shoulder. He moved with the pressure, elastic, but didn't wake.

He saw the pile slumped on the floor with an electric jolt. "Camille!"

Jeremy scrambled out of his chair. She was unconscious and had fallen off her perch on the hutch, landing with her limbs splayed. Her forehead was bleeding. Carefully, Jeremy turned her over. Her pulse was strong, and exhales tickled under her nose, but she didn't wake as he moved her. She still clutched the truce bag tight in one of her hands. He tried patting her cheeks and saying her name, but she was out as hard as the magicians around the table.

Jeremy straightened her skirt and pushed her hair away from the bruise on her forehead. She wasn't bleeding heavily, but she should have a bandage. He was caught in a decision, whether to run to the kitchen for a first aid kit or start ripping the ritual apart, when something in the room changed.

He followed the feeling, as if he'd finally caught one of the vibes Luke had tried to explain, but it was nothing so strange. It was only a noise—a new, jaggedly shaped breath.

Jeremy froze with his hand on Camille's forehead. She was flushed. She was real. She was a person, like Jeremy. It felt very important to notice that.

Skin squeaked on the wood table. Limbs and clothes rustled. His own pulse slammed in his ears.

Let him be brave. Jeremy stood up.

The girl on the table was as real as he was—as much as his heart wanted to protest, his eyes told his brain something else. Her shoulders were made of the wrong angles and her strawberry hair hung in lank strings, hiding her face. She crouched in the middle of the table, knees pushing up the hem of an old-fashioned white dress, and deliberately rubbed out bits of the soap runes around Alexei's bowl.

Her head swung slowly around, and she snatched Jeremy with round blue eyes. "I take it you weren't expecting me." She twisted her mouth around like a smile or a sneer or a scar. "This is the worst party I've ever been invited to."

Pinpricks of white light swam in Jeremy's vision. He fumbled for his phone, but it was dead. The clock on the wall said 12:49. Alexei and his midnights—every time Jeremy turned around, it was midnight, and he was a helpless prisoner.

He made his hand press forward, into Corey Malcolm's back, tugging his shirt, but Malcolm didn't move.

Jeremy managed to whisper, "Help."

She crawled a step closer over the table, moving a leg and

an arm and the other leg, but none of the sleeping magicians moved. "I'll do what I can, little man." She grimaced again and added heavily, "Because I think it's just you and me here."

Jeremy backed up until he hit the wall and then turned to the window, a single square. Katya's back was to the house, eyes on the street; Malcolm's man was out of sight, around back. Jeremy slammed his palm against the glass—"Katya! Katya, help!"

But the house was sealed closed around him, and she didn't move. His palm burned where he'd come too close to the outside. He pounded the glass with a fist, but it sent only a jangling ache up to his elbow.

Jeremy turned slowly. The girl was watching him, disdainful but amused.

He stepped closer, reaching for Alexei, and the girl tracked him, smearing the runes as she moved. He got Alexei's arm in his hand, squeezing, but Alexei didn't even twitch. Sweat stung Jeremy's eyes.

"What's your name?" the girl asked.

Jeremy's throat scratched with thirst, but he swallowed hard so that when he answered, his voice was sure. "Jeremy. And you're Annabel."

She made a sound like a laugh or a snarl or an ache. "Not for a long time."

She stood in the center of the table, looking down at the bowl of blood and the bread and milk. Standing, she was less wrong. Her angles were fine. Her strange dress was a plain nightgown. Her hair was only mussed, like she had been sleeping on it. She could have gone to bed a minute ago, not eighteen years in the past. She lifted her hand toward the chandelier, but her fingers couldn't connect with the brass. They drifted through, dreamlike.

"Are you a ghost?" Jeremy asked.

Annabel turned to him. The wrong thing wasn't her body, it was what was left inside it. Her eyes glittered, and her toes worked the runes.

She wasn't the enemy—they'd done this to find her, and here she was. But Jeremy hadn't expected it to be like this. His head ached with thirst and heat.

"I don't think so." She tried the chandelier again, head turning curiously as she watched her hand dissolve through metal.

Jeremy shook his head, and again, but the fuzzy, fevered feeling wouldn't clear. He pressed his hands to his temples, squeezing his brain back into place. "Something's wrong."

Annabel looked evenly into Jeremy's eyes, parted her lips, and took a big, deep breath. Her chest lifted, and Jeremy's burned, a fresh spear of pain slicing past his heart. He doubled over, clutching his chest, and tried to pant but couldn't find the breath.

When he could lift his head, Annabel was still staring at him. She stood with her arm over her head, fingers hooked firmly over one arm of the chandelier. She swung it slowly back and forth, plaster dust falling like snow.

"No." Jeremy's voice eked out of his throat in a harsh whisper, though he hadn't meant to hold it back. He was disappearing out from under himself as Annabel grew solid.

"Any port in a storm, baby," she said sweetly. "No hard feelings, I hope."

"I didn't—" Jeremy lurched forward, steadying himself on the back of Alexei's chair. "It wasn't my—"

"It wasn't my fault, either," Annabel said.

Jeremy walked around the table, hands on the chairs to hold himself up, until he got to Luke. He tugged on Luke's hair, *Wake up, help me, please wake up.* The candlelight hurt his eyes, and he pressed his face into Luke's neck. It was still cool.

"I can't believe you thought milk was a gift. You could have brought wine, you asshole." Annabel's voice had moved closer, and Jeremy opened his eyes as she upended the glass over Alexei, milk splattering down his face. Her head was cocked to the side, eyes flat and distant. "You didn't know anything about me at all."

"It was a mistake," Jeremy said. "He didn't—they didn't mean—"

"I don't care." She threw the glass against the wall, shattering it, and cut a sideways glance at Jeremy.

"Please." He turned it to a prayer when his voice gave out, *Please, please. I don't know what I did wrong.*

"No." She crouched down again, close. She smelled like candy perfume and rot, choking in the heavy air. Each of her exhales touched his face and burned in his chest.

Jeremy shook his head, but his voice was gone. A shudder racked deep through his body and the floor swerved again. No one was awake to hear if he said goodbye. He lifted his face, pressed Luke's jaw with his fingers to turn him, and put one more kiss on Luke's slack mouth.

Chapter Fifty-Two

Luke woke up with Jeremy's stuttering breath filling his chest. Vision bleary and limbs slow, he understood nothing about the room—the icy crackle in the air, the warmth slumping over his shoulder—but his bones knew first that Jeremy had fallen against him. Luke's body was moving before his mind, jumping up and gathering Jeremy into his arms. The temperature had dropped to a painful, bone-deep freeze while he was out, but Jeremy burned, sweaty like he'd been trudging through the desert. Adrenaline tasted acrid in Luke's mouth.

And there was another person in the room, hopping down from the soap-smeared table to investigate the lights dotted into the plants along the wall. A girl, with long red hair. *Is that Annabel Malcolm did we make her real did we bring her here how is that even—*

No one else was awake. Jeremy had been alone with her, and he was sick or hurt. Luke moved back, pulling Jeremy away without taking his eyes off the girl. She played her fingers between the light and the leaves, as casually as plucking a flower in a garden. Luke hooked his hands under Jeremy's arms to pull him back—he was hot as a stove to the touch, and his breath rattled high and shallow and way too slow in his chest.

Stepping back, Luke saw Camille's body on the floor and clenched his hands instinctively around Jeremy's ribs. A pounding like war drums rushed through Luke—this was the vision in Alexei's apartment. Jeremy's body, hot in the cold, his chest rattling. Fear and blood heavy in the cold air. The vision had been a chance to stop this, and Luke had missed it.

He let Jeremy rest against the wall and stood. Keeping his eyes on Annabel, he grabbed for the doorknob behind his back. He rattled it—locked, though Luke had been the last one in the room and hadn't locked the door. He rattled harder, turned a fist and banged it against the wood. He couldn't find his way out of the room and negotiate with the girl inside—he had to pick one and do it right.

Reaching deep, deep down for the first and truest lessons his mother had taught him, he put a courteous smile on his face. "Good evening, miss."

He spoke loudly, so someone outside might hear, too, but the girl—Annabel—ignored him. She cupped her hand around an orb of light and made it grow, sputtering into flame. Her eyes on it were hungry, and she licked her teeth.

Luke knew his way around that witchlight, how it burst in his hands or dissolved when he played his fingers in it. He focused, listening for the high note, and imagined the flame in her hand snuffing.

It went out.

Annabel clutched her fingers closed and eyed him, annoyed.

"Looks like we've had a disagreement here." Luke gestured to Jeremy and Camille with a calmness he didn't feel. His hand shook as he opened it in the air—he couldn't

334   THE UNCROSSING

lose *either* of them, *no wake up wake up.* "Maybe I can help."

She walked sideways around the table. Luke mirrored her.

"No, I don't think so. Everyone has been very accommodating." She glanced at Jeremy, who wasn't breathing he wasn't breathing *he wasn't*—he took another thin, rattling inhale. In the quiet, Luke caught Camille's exhale, slow and steady, only sleep.

Luke let go of the breath he'd been holding to listen and opened his hands, a helpless gesture that fell out before he could stop it. "I can make this right if you help me. Don't hurt him."

"Charming." Another orb of light, next to Annabel's shoulder, flickered into flame. Luke concentrated and put it out, but she'd gotten already a second and third.

"Stop," he said, hands wide, begging.

A flame lit next to his shoulder, catching the wallpaper, that Luke had to put out with his hands. His hectic pulse pounded black in the edges of his vision. He'd chosen wrong—she was faster than he was, and he could not claw his way out of this room with every sleeping body in it.

Her magic felt like ice crystals crawling across glass. Luke caught the icy thread guiding back to her, held it in his mind, and willed her frozen, still. He passed the ideas back and forth, the real freeze and the new one, and said it again, clearer. "Stop."

Annabel froze. Her shoulders jerked; her lip curled in an angry sneer; her shoulders jerked harder. He had her—she was pieced together from memories and old spells, more magic than human, and Luke could control that.

He snatched Alexei's jacket off the back of his chair and ran around the room, squeezing between chairs and furniture, to beat out two growing fires. The plants and wallpaper made more smoke than flame, choking Luke's throat. He threw his elbow over his mouth and breathed through it, beating out fires and thinking about holding her still, making her calm.

He dropped the remains of the jacket on the ground and hunched over, coughing until he could breathe. The hazy smoke smelled toxic. Annabel was close enough to reach out and touch, but Luke stepped back. "Just tell me how you got back, and we'll figure it out so everyone can stay."

"I don't need your *permission*," she snarled. Her torso and shoulders kept moving, twitching out of joint as she tried to writhe free. She fought back like a human, not a spell, and her panic raked nails down Luke's mind. "You let me *go*, you let—"

"I will, I just need you to not hurt anyone—" Luke glanced at Jeremy. His chest rose and his eyelids fluttered. Luke went dizzy with the relief of it and with holding his own breath to listen. It took too long, but Jeremy exhaled pure, the rattle fading in his chest.

"You only care about *that* one!" Annabel twisted. She had tears in her eyes, but her mouth kept sneering. "You only care about your*self*, all of you, living without me. He's been walking around in *my life*—"

"No." Luke's head shot up. Annabel heaved.

That was wrong—and it had been wrong when Corey Malcolm said it before, too. Luke ran around the table and shook Malcolm's arm, but he stayed gone, unconscious. "That's not what it is," Luke said. "Is that how you got here? That shouldn't…"

But if Malcolm had gone into the ritual focusing on that trade, taken back the power to tell his version of the story instead of handing it back to Alexei, it didn't matter what Luke thought the magic *should* do.

Jeremy, Camille, oh help help wake up Mom—
Mom—

"You turned the spell around." Luke glared at the bowl

on the table as if he'd be able to see where it had fallen under her control. Agrimony to turn the spell around on the caster, Annabel's blood on a candle. At least three different spells—the contract, the prayer, the candles—fit together like pieces of a mismatched puzzle, glued into place with fear and anger and the goddamn agrimony that always messed him up. They'd gone in to take charge of the whole disaster, and she had found a gap or caught a rope her brother had thrown, and wrested back control instead.

Luke had nothing to fix this. His mind whirred circles of *Jeremy* and *Camille* and *help* and Annabel's own riotous anger scrambling back up the connection between them. Luke's chest heaved, and his vision went black, and when he shook his head and focused again, she was free. She wrenched away and reeled back against the wall, panting—and smiling slowly at Luke. A fireball exploded by his head, extinguishing in one huge burst and leaving his face raw with stinging heat.

He tried again—focusing on the ice, imagining her frozen. "*Stop.*" But Annabel simply smirked, scrambling onto the table again and stretching to trace her hands around the chandelier, sending showers of sparks cascading down. She was getting stronger. She would drain Jeremy and come into this power, a broken thing laughing and lighting fires in a locked room.

Searching, searching, Luke's eyes landed on the bowl on the table. *Blood, every spell is in the blood—*

Annabel caught him. She crouched in front of the bowl, a wrestler ready to pounce.

Jeremy wasn't breathing, and Luke was twice Annabel's size. He sprung, diving between the chairs and over her body to get to the silver bowl. The attack was a gauntlet—his breath knocked out of his stomach, his knee against a chair as it fell, and Annabel's nails like claws down his cheek. He bellowed and she screamed and Luke was flying, a sick lurch. His back slammed so hard against the wall his vision went black. He blinked and shook his head, focused on Annabel, who was sneering so he could see her sharp white teeth.

The blood it's in the blood—

A flood of adrenaline washed away Luke's pain, and he jumped up. Annabel jerked close as he moved, but he didn't dive for her again. He went to Alexei, fingers scrabbling for the knife in his shirt pocket.

He flipped it open and dug the blade into his palm. It was painless, the creamy give of slicing through butter, until a burn raced up his arm. He opened his hand over one of the candles on the hutch and watched his blood fall on the wood, the wax, and the flame. "Defend Camille," he said out loud, "and defend Jeremy, and defend Annabel. Defend Jeremy, Camille, Annabel. Jeremy, Camille, Annabel. Defend us all."

He waited through the sharp burn of the knife, the truer burn of the fire, and the sting of dirty-penny smoke billowing into his eyes and lungs, until the magic started to shift in the room. Cold tentacles shriveled around him, the air growing warm and human again.

Twice more to seal: "Defend us all. Defend us all."

He shut his eyes and stood there and bled. Camille stirred and finally, finally, Jeremy coughed. Luke would turn, and Annabel would be sitting there, fresh as a new book, ready to get back to her interrupted life, or at least she would have had the grace to disappear again. He prayed, that was the only word for it, to every minor deity and faceless god he'd ever heard a story about: *let it be all right.* He mashed the heel of his hand along the back of his cheek and it came away wet with sooty tears.

Luke opened his eyes and turned around, pulling his hand away from the candle and cradling it to his chest. Jeremy and Camille sat on the floor, washed sickly green, and Annabel Malcolm was a waxy white corpse on the table.

Chapter Fifty-Three

Jeremy couldn't breathe, coughing, coughing, coughing so hard his lungs scraped up into his throat, the chaotic noise of the room crowding out all the places he was supposed to carry air or blood or his own brain.

"What the fuck?"

That was Alexei's voice, shouting—Alexei?

Jeremy coughed, and it hurt a little less. He found a smooth inhale and coughed it out more easily.

He breathed again.

He breathed.

Black spots scattered across his vision, and he blinked them down. When his eyes locked into focus, the first thing he saw was Natalya, with her elbows on the table and her face in her hands. She was crying.

A body moved past Jeremy's. Helene crouched on the floor next to Camille, who gripped her mother to stop swaying. "Mama?"

"Shh, shh." Helene turned to Jeremy and put a powder-cool hand on his cheek. "Honey, are you all right?"

Jeremy blinked at her and started to understand. "Am I alive?"

His voice was hoarse and tiny, but his words silenced the room. Alexei turned. Malcolm—he was the other person shouting, bellowing at Alexei—stopped and looked down, too.

Luke slumped against the hutch behind Alexei, blood on his face and smeared brown across his white shirt. He had his eyes shut against the noise. "She was going to kill you."

"I know. She said—" Jeremy stopped. He'd kissed Luke goodbye and woken up alive. "Did you save me?"

Luke shook his head. He was holding his hand against his chest like a wounded bird. Helene stood up and put her hands on his elbows, and he said, "I tried, Mom, I did try."

She made that soothing hush noise again. "Tried what, honey?"

Natalya wiped her hands harshly across her face. "Are we just going to *leave* her here?"

Malcolm and Alexei both moved and stilled, reaching for Annabel's body but afraid or unwilling to touch her.

"I can take her upstairs," Sergei said.

"I'll do it," Alexei replied instantly. He pushed his hair, sopping with sour-smelling milk, out of his face, and scooped her up, arms under her shoulders and knees. He was careful, as if she might crumble or shatter in his arms, but her body flopped solidly against him, hair falling in a tangle.

Jeremy flinched back, but he couldn't pull his eyes away. She was real, and she was *dead*. Had he killed her? Or as good as, fighting to keep her from tearing his life away? There were plenty of other people—some in this room—who seemed to deserve the punishment, but it was her body Alexei carried to the stairs.

Malcolm moved as if to follow, but Natalya put a gentle hand on his arm, and Sergei lumbered more roughly between him and the door. The spaces between them stretched, but eventually, Malcolm sat down hard in his chair.

Alexei was gone for a long time, and no one said anything. Camille clambered up from the floor and took a seat. Jeremy tried to follow, but his legs gave out, and Sergei had to help him. He felt scarily weak—it was hard to lift his arms, to keep his head up on his neck—and even the blood rushing back to his limbs seemed to come too fast. With too much to process, his fuzzy mind grasped at random thoughts—he was alive. Luke was hurt again. Something had changed, but maybe not for the better. He was alive. He could fight tomorrow, but oh, he wanted this night to be over. He was alive.

When Alexei returned, he filled the doorway. "What happened? Start from the beginning."

Luke was still leaning against the hutch, his hand against his chest. He shut his eyes and shook his head.

"We found my ancestor," Jeremy said. "It felt like talking to the saints."

"Fairy-tale rules," Luke said. "That was how I thought it would be. She set a condition on the contract, but it wasn't a spell or a curse or anything like that." He opened his eyes and found Jeremy's. "It was just a prayer."

Jeremy stared back, ready to believe. It hadn't felt like *reality*. But it had felt like *something*. "It was like—" he turned to Alexei. "It was like when you asked for help, when Annabel disappeared. You were just scared, reaching out the same way Maeve was all that time before, and…" He trailed off. Did he really mean, *And then you got me? Ta-da!* He felt so small, the tiniest cog in the turning world.

"And then Jeremy," Luke finished, like it made sense. "And all this."

Alexei's forehead crumpled briefly, his only acknowledgment. "And then?"

Jeremy shook his head. "I woke up, and Camille was on

the floor. When I went to check on her, I looked up, and—she was here."

"Here?" Malcolm's voice was hoarse. "Her body?"

Jeremy shook his head. "She was awake. But she was..."

He was too scared to finish it, but Luke did. "Wrong. Possessed or warped or something. I don't know."

"How can you not know?" Alexei asked tightly.

Luke waved his unhurt arm and hissed an explosive exhale. "How am I supposed to know? She was here, she was weird, Jeremy was fucking *dying*. I don't know how she did it. She wasn't exactly chatting. I did one incantation, the same candle, the same blood. I said all their names. I thought—" He stopped, swallowed. "I don't know what I thought. That it would work because it had to work."

"Fairy-tale rules?" Alexei repeated, sandpaper rough and dry.

Luke stared at him. "I did try."

Still croaky, Malcolm said, "I guess you didn't try hard enough, did you?"

Luke winced and didn't answer, but Helene turned and shot a look that ought to have burned Malcolm crispy. Jeremy wanted to go to Luke and—he wasn't sure. Kiss him or wipe the bloody sweat off his forehead or say no matter what, he was grateful to be sitting here. Luke was swaying against his mother, though, and Jeremy could only shift in his chair before he got dizzy again. Sergei moved behind him, putting a hand on his shoulder. He still hadn't said anything, but his brow hung low, face dark with thought.

"We have to get these kids to a hospital," Helene said.

"What about Annabel?" Malcolm looked back and forth, finally landing on Natalya. "What do we do?"

After a long quiet, Alexei said, "I know. We get a time machine, go all the way back, and when you find out your sister's got a boyfriend, you keep your fucking mouth shut."

Malcolm drew in an angry breath, but Alexei was still talking, low and subtle as poison, "You did this and you can live with it—"

"This is your binding. You made this—"

"I was protecting her from you!"

The shouting rammed Jeremy's aching head, and he ducked it into his hands. They had not fixed anything. Nothing was healed. Someone—Luke or Camille—made a deep, quiet moaning sound.

Jeremy missed Sergei's movement, but a falling wall of magic shook the room as Sergei slammed his hand onto the dining room table and bound Alexei and Malcolm into silence.

Jeremy lifted his head. Malcolm battered his walls like a moth at a window, but Alexei went still, arms crossed, looking at Sergei.

Sergei turned away, to Helene and the kids. "How do we walk out of here without anyone else getting hurt?"

Camille looked up at him like she'd remembered something obvious. "I can do that. The truce." She got to her feet, brushing out her skirt, and repeated the words pensively. "The truce."

Sergei opened his hand, *go on.*

"I can seal it," she said. "We walk away, and they can't hurt each other again without getting hurt themselves."

"You're sure you can put a lock on Alexei?" Sergei asked.

Something a little harder than a smile touched Camille's eyes and the corner of her mouth. "I can cross anybody."

Chapter Fifty-Four

Camille took a candle off the hutch and started to work. The spell stacked like bricks, a tower Luke could have pushed over, and she glared at him.

Luke got the hint and left the room. Sick with failure, he couldn't make himself look at Jeremy. He got as far as the hall right outside the door and sank to the floor, cradling his burned hand. Everything hurt, and his hand and arm were covered in blood. It was hard to believe that sticky red stuff was his own—when he looked down, his vision tunneled, as if he was trying to see something far away.

He was drained, attenuated—that blood magic had been a payment. Luke had made a sacrifice, had left something in that room. He twisted to peer through the door, Camille standing over the truce bag and Jeremy lying on the table, head on his arm.

Luke hadn't even hesitated. If he had the choice again, he'd do it every time.

He listened to the ritual instead of his own thoughts. There was more shouting and useless drama as Sergei undid the bindings. Every loud noise was a hot pop of white light in Luke's field of vision, sharp against the bruised, tender pain behind his eyes.

It wasn't long before Malcolm left the room, tramping past Luke without looking down at him. He went upstairs and came back with Annabel's body in his arms like a sleeping child.

Natalya and Alexei came next, pausing together at the door. She opened her mouth; he shook his head. She left without saying goodbye.

Alexei closed and locked the door behind them. He put his eye to the peephole and stayed there for a long time. Luke sat in the dark hall and watched Alexei's shoulders rise and fall too evenly.

Luke dragged himself up. Again, like this would be the time that made it clear, he said, "I tried to save them all. I said all their names, I—"

"It's okay." Alexei kept his face at the door.

"It's *not.*" Luke's voice rose, and he pushed it down to a whisper. "We killed her, you and me, I killed—I meant—I said all their names—"

"Okay." Alexei turned and put his hands on Luke's shoulders. "You're right. It's not okay. Come sit down."

Alexei unlocked the door and led Luke onto the stoop. The night air was cool and clean, and exhaustion hit Luke like a rock. He sat down hard on the step.

Alexei settled next to him more slowly. His hair and collar were wet, and he smelled like sweat and sour milk. "Tell me what you did. Slow down. *Breathe.*"

Luke got himself under enough control for one sentence. "I tried to get to the blood, to break up the ritual, but she stopped me."

"Is that what happened to your face?"

"What? What's wrong with my face?" As soon as he said it, Luke felt the pain in his cheek, a smaller fire than the one in his hand.

Alexei's jaw twitched. "Never mind. Carry on."

Luke slumped over his own lap. "I thought it had to be the blood. I gave some of mine, and I said defend them. I said their names, Camille, Jeremy, Annabel. But I think—I think I wasn't focused on Annabel right, because—she was hurting him, and I was scared, and—"

"Breathe," Alexei said again. "Jesus, breathe. So, you think if you were more, what, pure of heart, we'd be catching Annie up on everything she missed right now?"

"You're making it absurd on purpose." The night was darker than Luke was used to, the grand old trees on the block whispering as they blotted out the hazy glow of the night sky.

"No, it is absurd." Alexei scrubbed his hair away from his face. "That body hasn't had a glass of water or a meal in almost twenty years. You said yourself she was feral. Demonic. Maybe death is the best we could do for her."

"Maybe we killed her and you're talking shit in circles so it doesn't sound so bad." Luke meant to sound fierce, but his voice kept wavering.

"Maybe." Alexei squinted into the darkness so long Luke thought he wasn't going to reply, but he said, "There's nothing to repair. No reason to go back in. It's over."

"If you think so." Luke agreed but didn't want to—they were supposed to have fixed something, freed a loop that closed too tight around Jeremy. "I wanted to help. I wanted…"

Alexei nodded. "Listen, Annie was bad. We all were. But she wasn't evil. She wouldn't have wanted to become—" He paused. Uncertainly, he said, "Maybe that changed. Maybe she's free."

Luke's breath shuddered. If there was meant to be comfort in that, he couldn't find it. Alexei stopped talking, smearing his fingers across his lips.

"You loved her?" Luke asked.

Alexei made a low noise in his throat and let another pause stretch. "Maybe she never had a chance from the second her brother found out. I'm going to keep blaming him, if you don't mind."

If he had to guess, Luke would still have said it was Malcolm who had ruined the ritual—gone in with the off-kilter thought in his mind, the brick that had turned and brought the whole tower down. He didn't say it, though— because there was nothing Alexei, or anyone, could do right now, and it would only give Alexei another thing to hurt over. "I made all kinds of mistakes trying to protect Jeremy," he said instead. "And Camille crossed him with the doll trying to protect me. If she'd slipped even a little... It's just luck it worked out all right. It's just luck—"

"That it didn't work out for me?" Alexei shook his head and stood up abruptly. "Here is what I know, witch doctor. You are going to have a bad night. And tomorrow morning, you're going to wake up, and you're going to decide who you want to be."

Luke stood, too. Alexei's eyes were startlingly close to his level, as if Alexei had gotten shorter—though it must have been Luke who had gotten taller. "Is that how you deal with everything?"

"Me? Fuck no. I'm going to Vegas, first flight I can catch." Alexei reached for the door. "Now get inside and give Jeremy a goddamn kiss."

Kiss? Luke had created this night, convincing Jeremy they needed to unwind all this because it was wrapped around his crossing, and there was only one more step to see if he was right.

Luke noticed the key between his fingers—he'd reached under his collar and started rubbing it unconsciously. He'd thought because it was a key, there must be a lock—a room—a treasure. But Jeremy had already told him. It was just a shape.

Uncrossing, when it worked, was like finishing a puzzle or untangling Christmas lights, watching the disorder resolve into a single, understandable object. This was not a crossing—it was an avalanche, fearful desperation and misfired intentions collapsing together to trap Jeremy under the rocks.

Luke could not imagine walking in there, putting his mangled hand on Jeremy's sallow face, and making magic. They hadn't fixed anything—and, worse, they still hadn't had a conversation without arguing, hadn't looked at each other in pure daylight and chosen. It wouldn't be a kiss at all with both their families hovering outside the door, waiting to see if Luke would fail, yet again, to break Jeremy's crossing.

It didn't matter, anyway. Inside, Jeremy had fallen asleep, and Sergei was carrying him up to bed as Camille blew out the last candles in the dining room.

Helene took her children to the hospital, where Camille had a concussion test and Luke got eight stitches in the palm of his hand. They hurt so much more than the cut. He named each stitch for the Kovrovs and Malcolms, bitterly glad he'd have a scar so he would never forget what they'd lost.

He told the nurse he'd closed his hand over a knife. When the man pointed out that didn't explain the blisters on his palm or the human claw marks on his face, Luke only shook his head. He was too tired to lie, seeing a dead girl in the dark every time he blinked and blank emptiness when he tried to imagine a way back to Jeremy. But it was the wrong play—both Luke and his mother had to answer questions from multiple pinched faces about his family and how he hurt himself before they let him go home. He passed out in the cab and woke up shouting, reaching for Camille as she bled in his dreams. Alexei had not lied: it was a bad night. Four a.m. was witching when Luke finally reached the cold, narrow comfort of his bed.

Chapter Fifty-Five

Jeremy slept for most of the next day and through the night, but when his strength came back, it was like a shot of adrenaline to the heart. He woke up zipping with hectic energy. The whole house was quiet, so he went for a run, his feet drumming the pavement *a-live-a-live-a-live*.

When he walked back into the kitchen, Sergei's jaw dropped like a stone. "What the hell are you doing?"

Jeremy's pulse slammed in every part of his body. Did running always feel like this? "I almost died."

"I know," Sergei said. "I was fucking there. Shouldn't you be sleeping?"

Jeremy wasn't going to sleep—he was going to stay up every night and count the stars while he had them. He was going to call Luke and—well, definitely say something.

He checked his phone as he went back to his room. Short Wesley had posted a picture of himself delivering drinks (the caption said "potions"; Jeremy guessed horchatas) to Luke and Camille. They had matching stiff white bandages, Luke on his hand and Camille on her forehead, and sleepy bags under their eyes.

Also on his phone, he discovered Alexei had gone out. There were paparazzi photos of him acting like a toolbag—sloshing expensive champagne in a shiny suit, keeping a boy and a girl on each arm but not kissing anybody.

It took some convincing to get Sergei to find a safe car—he saw Malcolms in every shadow—but eventually, Jeremy went uptown. He found Alexei in front of the TV, slow-moving and faintly unwashed but mostly himself.

"TMZ posted the dumbest picture of any human that has ever been taken," Jeremy informed him, making coffee. "And it was of you."

"A Kovrov always delivers his best."

Jeremy brought him a cup of coffee on the couch. Alexei took a long, slow sip, his eyes drifting heavily closed.

"Have you even slept?" Jeremy asked.

"Nightmares," Alexei said, clipped.

Jeremy waited, but Alexei was quiet. He looked awful, cheeks sunken and skin gray, with heavy bags under his eyes. Jeremy's heart squeezed, for him and for Luke and Camille, injured in those pictures. Jeremy had not fixed himself, but he might have broken everybody else. "What do you think happened?"

"Well, once one photographer's got your tail—"

"Alexei."

He shut his eyes. "I don't know. Probably something I should have done years ago. Maybe it would have turned out differently."

"How? That's what I don't understand." Jeremy stood up, though he had nowhere to go, and paced to the wall of windows. It was drizzling, a cloud pressed against the glass. "What did we do wrong?"

"I don't know, my prince. I certainly should have had Katya outside the room, rather than the house. Maybe I should have had Helene or Malcolm build the ritual. Maybe I shouldn't have let Malcolm in at all. Maybe there was no way to change it without my father there. Maybe I made too many mistakes the first time around to fix this time." Alexei paused. "I keep thinking I should have made Luke give his blood in the first place. And then I think, if I had, and he'd been entirely out of weapons at the end…"

He looked at Jeremy's face in a thoughtful, disconnected way, like Jeremy was a painting instead of a person.

"Alexei—"

He snapped his head away. "There's a limit to my interest in discussing it."

"But what if—"

"I swear to god, Jeremy Kovrov."

Jeremy stepped away from the window but couldn't cross the room. "Maybe you could still fix it somehow. Get her back."

"We did get her back." Alexei put his coffee down so he could rake both of his hands through his hair, wiping away everything he didn't want to think about. "Corey Malcolm, my father, and I killed a girl, and the worst any of us will have to suffer for it is feeling bad. You don't need to try to make me feel better."

Jeremy came back to the couch and sat down, leaning against Alexei's shoulder.

"There is one piece I can't figure out," Alexei said, more gently. "Why did Luke wake up, when none of the rest of us did?"

Jeremy pressed his fingers to his lips. They burned, anticipation and something like guilt wound together inside him. "Because I kissed him."

"Ah." Alexei paused. "Fairy-tale rules. Just like he said."

Jeremy shook his head. Luke's fairy-tale rules had been about anointing someone king—about power and who would take it. But Jeremy hadn't been powerful. "I was just desperate. But so was Maeve, in the prayer we saw. And you, when Annabel disappeared."

"Mmm." Alexei dropped the subject like a too-small shoe. "Did you and the young man try again?"

Jeremy shook his head. He'd had the nerve when he thought he was dying, broken. But now he was full of hope again, and it was so much harder to bear. "I guess I should call him."

Alexei waited for more before he said, "I guess you should."

Jeremy twisted his fingers. "It's like all the pressure from the first one times a million. I need everything to be perfect first." The first time, he'd been terrified Luke might discover his secrets. Now, Luke knew it all—the curse and the weirdness and Jeremy's family and all their failures—and his choice would cut right to Jeremy's heart.

"Everything and perfect?" Alexei nodded. "It's good to set reasonable standards."

Jeremy whacked his arm around Alexei's chest, head-butting his shoulder in a cranky hug. "In stories, it always works all together. There's the kiss, or the big feat, or whatever, and it works and the curse is broken and the whole kingdom gets restored and there's, like, sunshine and violins—"

"I'd like to institute a ban on that talk in my home."

Jeremy huffed, but stopped.

Alexei scratched him behind the ears like a puppy, a gesture so familiar it hurt Jeremy's chest. "Call him. You don't have to fix my life and the family's whole history. You can have this."

"I have your permission?" Jeremy tried to laugh.

Alexei shook his head, still serious. "You don't need my permission."

Jeremy sighed. It was his decision—no one would take

the responsibility or the blame. "I'll call him. Should we order some food? You look really terrible."

Alexei gave him a censorious look, but he picked something from the Thai menu Jeremy pulled up and went to take a shower before the food came. Jeremy chewed his lip and glared at his phone.

He called Luke.

It rang for a long time, and Luke answered a touch breathlessly, like he'd run to another room. "Hey, you. How are you feeling?"

His voice was warm and rich and sent a tingle down Jeremy's spine. "I'm okay. How are you? I saw you were hurt."

"Nah, I'm all patched up. I'll be fine. I'm glad you called. I feel better already."

Jeremy smiled in spite of himself, at Luke and his lines. It was so sweet and so *normal*, suddenly Jeremy knew just what he wanted. He'd known all along. "Okay. I'll call you a lot. I like hearing your voice." He took a deep breath. "Luke, will you be my boyfriend?"

There was a long quiet on the other side. Jeremy's heart swelled so much he hugged his knees to his chest to hold it in, biting down on the fabric of his jeans.

"On one condition," Luke said.

Luke deserved a lot more than one condition, after all Jeremy had put him through. "What's that?"

"Let me take you out next week. Maybe…Tuesday?"

Jeremy grinned into his knee. He had no idea what day it was, but he said, "Of course."

Chapter Fifty-Six

The evening could not have been more beautiful, a breath of autumn cooling the summer sky. The sunset glowed a dusty pink, especially on Jeremy, rosy and ethereal wherever the light touched him. Most of Park Slope was out on such a pretty night, so Jeremy walked close. The back of his hand kept brushing Luke's, sending sparks up his arm.

Jeremy had a seasonal hot chocolate that wasn't supposed to be waffle-flavored but definitely smelled like it. The scent floated up every time he took a sip, making Luke look over and watch his lips touch the lid of the cup.

He wanted to kiss Jeremy so badly his teeth ached, but he had a plan and the kiss was still several blocks away. Real date—check. Leisurely walk home—check. Next: kiss him good-night at the door, gallant and sweet; send him inside for Marta to fuss over him; float home on the subway. He wanted to do this one right, savor it.

He still wanted Jeremy's crossing to fall away. He imagined a kiss on the stairs, a flash of light, that bracelet cracking and falling on the ground. The good-night and the floating. He could see just how it should be.

Luke smelled waffles. He watched Jeremy's lips on the cup and his Adam's apple working as he swallowed. He put the crossing in a box and put it on a shelf inside his head, and thought about all the other things he wanted that kiss to be, too. He was going to kiss Jeremy clear of the nervous way he kept hesitating before he touched Luke and, if he was lucky, he was going to make Jeremy do the thing where his knees gave out and he melted into Luke's arms.

Luke touched his own lips and looked away in time to catch another person squinting at them. "Have you noticed people keep glaring at us? I thought Park Slope was more evolved than that."

"Oh, yeah." Sadly, Jeremy said, "I think it's my hat."

Luke laughed. "We can always burn it."

"No!" Jeremy clapped a hand over his neon-green head. "I think...this is embarrassing. I got photographed with Alexei wearing this hat the other day. We were on some blogs. I think people are recognizing me."

Jeremy clearly didn't like it, so Luke stifled the part of him that did. "Yeah? Where were you with paparazzi?"

"He took me out to dinner." Jeremy paused, and his hand brushed Luke's with more purpose. "I made him take me out to dinner. He was brooding."

Luke nodded. He'd been doing his share of brooding.

Jeremy took Luke's hand and squeezed. "It's okay to be sad. Everyone was messed up. Sergei broke three plates."

"Camille's having the time of her life. She hasn't done a chore in days, keeps claiming head injury even though the doctor said she was fine."

"She earned it." Jeremy swung their hands together and let go as Luke was about to start wondering whether his palm was getting sweaty. "Alexei was so weird I had to come home and break a plate, too." His fingers brushed against Luke's wrist.

Luke's long gray days settled down in perspective. "You break plates when you're mad?"

"I thought I'd try it. It didn't help. Except then Marta kicked me and Sergei out of the house, and we went to the diner for a while. That helped a lot."

"There it is. I love that. Jeremy, the only thing keeping me up and moving right now is that I decided to be as brave as you."

That got Luke another *oh*—three on the night so far. He was collecting them like little trophies. Jeremy veered away to toss his empty cup and returned. Before he could reach for Luke's hand again, Luke moved closer, touching his lower back. They passed an older gay couple walking the other way and one of the men grinned at them. "*He* likes my hat," Jeremy said.

"I think he likes your boyfriend." Luke let the word hang there, and they both watched it float by.

"Probably. *And* my hat." Jeremy wiggled into Luke's arm, and the hand on Jeremy's back slid around to his hip. It slowed them down, and it took them a long time to walk the last block to Jeremy's house.

By the time they got there, Luke was stoned on Jeremy's warmth and closeness, the animated way he moved. Luke had to remind himself: the plan was kiss and leave. What, why was that the plan?

At the brick steps that led up to the door, Jeremy turned and pressed a hand against Luke's chest to hold him away. "It wasn't pretty, but it was real magic. We changed something important."

"He said he thought Annabel was free now," Luke said. "I can't decide if that's the most patronizing thing I've ever heard or the most hopeful. I want it to be true so bad."

Jeremy considered that quietly, taking his time, and Luke was already grateful that he'd get a real answer instead of some empty comfort. "Free is a really big word," Jeremy finally said. "But she's not trapped anymore. I think that matters."

"Yeah?"

"Yeah." Jeremy's voice lifted. "Everything I do now, I'm like, would my ancestor who crossed the ocean to get me here think this matters? Maeve didn't cross the ocean so you could sleep in! Maeve didn't cross the ocean so you could eat three cheese sandwiches in two days!"

Luke laughed. "I think she did."

Jeremy smiled up at him. "I helped Alexei as much as I could. You helped Annabel as much as you could. And I think it matters."

The high note of Jeremy's vibe was clear in the air, brighter than usual, or brighter compared to his bracelet cutting in and out like radio static. "Whatever happens," Luke said, "you matter to me."

"Do you practice all these lines?"

"Yeah, because you like them so much."

Jeremy muffled a laugh with his hand, and when he pulled it away, his face was different, with big, solemn eyes. "Either way, I want you."

Luke would show up at this house every day if he had to. He didn't care what destiny said—he had chosen, he would choose again. And that? That felt like true love. He put his lips close to Jeremy's ear and said, "I would choose you every time. That's what's true."

Jeremy answered with his fingers curling into Luke's shirt. Luke took Jeremy's hat off his head and held it against his back, bringing him close, and touched his cheek to tilt him up.

A smile stretched across Jeremy's face, so Luke gave him some space to relax. He waited there, paying attention, watching Jeremy's mouth go soft and his chest lift. This was his favorite part, the moment right before the kiss.

Acknowledgments

Thank you to the early readers whose feedback and encouragement kept me going through many five a.m. alarms. Thanks especially to: Casey, my first reader, for taking this story seriously in its awkward infancy and for its most vital editorial note ("I would like to take Jeremy home and just pet his angry little head"); Sasha, for your hours of editorial work and your dozens of supportive emails—I'm so grateful the internet brought us together; and Tini, for early professional insight when I needed it.

Rose, Becky, Jonathan, Melody—thank you for your reading, your advice, your questions, and your support.

Thanks to the welcoming family at Entangled Teen, especially Mark and Ashley for their enthusiasm and support. Kate, thank you for taking a chance on the early draft and helping me find Luke and Jeremy's spark.

Thank you to Pickle for keeping me company on many brainstorming walks and early morning writing sessions, and always, to Mel, my own true love.

About the Author

Melissa Eastlake lives in Athens, Georgia, with her partner and their dog. She's a 2017 Lambda Literary Fellow and *The Uncrossing* is her debut novel.

Discover more Entangled Teen books...

THE WISHING HEART
a novel by J.C. Welker

The bejeweled vase Rebel just tried to hawk now has every magical mobster in the city hot on her tail in a game of cat and mouse in a world she never knew existed. But freedom could unravel a love like Rebel has never known, or it could cost her her heart...

SUMMONER
a novel by S.D. Grimm

When Allie accepts a dare in a cemetery, she never expects what that might mean. She accidentally summons a soul who wants more than Allie is willing to give. And the boy next door could be the key to saving her. Except Cody has his own demons to slay that keep him closed off. But as the full moon approaches, so does their only chance to break the curse, and Cody will have to make the biggest sacrifice of all.

THE THIRD KISS
a *Love's Mortal Coil* novel by Kat Colmer

When master of the meaningless hookup Jonas and his longtime levelheaded friend Cora share an impulsive kiss, a love curse becomes dangerously real. Failure to break it guarantees Cora's death. But success may cost Jonas his own life...or worse—his heart.

Made in the USA
Middletown, DE
18 September 2017